21318

W9-BJE-615

OXFORD-ON-RIDEAU TOWNSHIP
PUBLIC LIBRARY
WITHDRAWN
BURRITT'S RAPIDS
P.O. BOX 119   ONT. K0G 1B0

MEMORY LANE

ALSO BY LAURENCE GOUGH

The Goldfish Bowl
Death on a No. 8 Hook
Hot Shots
Sandstorm
Serious Crimes
Accidental Deaths
Fall Down Easy
Killers
Heartbreaker

MEMORY LANE

LAURENCE GOUGH

M&S

Copyright © 1996 by Laurence Gough

All rights reserved. The use of any part of this publication reproduced, transmitted in any form or by any means, electronic, mechanical, photocopying, recording, or otherwise, or stored in a retrieval system, without the prior written consent of the publisher – or, in case of photocopying or other reprographic copying, a licence from the Canadian Copyright Licensing Agency – is an infringement of the copyright law.

Canadian Cataloguing in Publication Data

Gough, Laurence
    Memory lane

ISBN 0-7710-3437-7

I. Title

PS8563.08393M4   1996   C813'.54   C96-931012-9
PR9199.3.G68M4   1996

The publishers acknowledge the support of the Canada Council and the Ontario Arts Council for their publishing program.

Typesetting by M&S, Toronto
Printed and bound in Canada

McClelland & Stewart Inc.
The Canadian Publishers
481 University Avenue
Toronto, Ontario
M5G 2E9

1 2 3 4 5   00 99 98 97 96

The indications of a tracing are blunt starts and stops, tremor, hesitation and slow-drawn appearance.

Metro-Dade Police Department
document on forgery

Prologue

Block by block, rancid orange streetlights began to flicker on all across the city of Vancouver. By seven o'clock it was full dark. A hard rain fell heavy as lead. Churlish gusts of wind whipped up the outer harbour, tore small chunks of cloud from the greater mass and hurled them venomously across the bloated sky.

All over the city, the naked skeletons of murdered umbrellas rattled along the wind-swept pavement. Branches were violently pruned from the trees that lined the sidewalks and boulevards, and were flung heavily down upon passing cars and unwary pedestrians. Gutters and storm drains overflowed. Here and there, eighty-pound manhole covers stood on pedestals of frothy white water.

Downed power lines hissed lethally at nearly every corner. Busses were stranded and a stray dog was, in a moment, terrified and then overcooked.

Many square miles of jaundiced streetlights flickered and died. Tens of thousands of apartments were suddenly plunged into absolute darkness.

A few wise souls had working flashlights. Most lit candles. Soon the frenzied scream of fire engines tolled across the city.

The wind gained fury, as the night darkened. Huge trees were torn from the sodden, bubbling earth. Small houses were crushed.

Someone remarked that it was almost like living in California.

But this was the only smile in an otherwise grimly humourless day. The sky had been falling on the city and surrounding suburbs for nearly four weeks, twenty-seven days in all, pushing an entire month. People were getting rusty. You could drown simply by looking up.

It seemed as if it might go on raining forever.

1

Ross's last night in the slammer was not much different from the almost two thousand nights that had gone before.

No icing glistened on a goodbye cake.

No candles wavered in the semi-darkness.

No sparklers sparkled, nor were any *auld lang syne*-type songs briskly sung.

That night, the prison was about as quiet as a prison can get.

Somewhere a toilet dripped. Somewhere else a dreamer moaned, and a snorer snored. Ross lay on his bunk, listening to a peculiar clicking sound that he had heard before, from time to time, but had never identified.

It took him the better part of a slow-moving hour to work out that the peculiar clicking sound was a bored screw repeatedly loading and unloading the magazine of his semiauto.

The dreamer screeched in pain. Demonic laughter echoed down the ward.

Five years ago, his first night in the joint, two or three seconds after lights-out, his coked-up biker cellmate, a fat creep named Al Weiller, had come at him in a snuffly, loving mood. Ross had said, "I thought you'd never ask," then slipped in a thumb and popped out the biker's left eye.

Two weeks later, the same day Ross came blinking out of the hole, what the screws called IMU, the Intensive Management Unit, the biker came at him with all the finesse of a dump truck. He was armed with a knife. Not a cheapo sharpened spoon, either, but a genuine, made-in-China, stainless-steel buck knife with a blood groove and serrated upper edge. Ross took the blade deep into his arm, gritted his teeth, and reached up and popped out the eye again, slapped it hard as it swung against the biker's hairy cheek. Shrieking, the biker fell back in horror and disarray. Ross pulled the knife out of his arm. Blood spurted. He plunged the knife hilt-deep into the small bull's-eye that was the biker's heart. Then fainted dead away.

The prison shrink, a guy named Reynolds, *Doctor* J. L. Reynolds, had eased forward on his chair as he put the crucial question to him, asked him what he was thinking about when he'd killed the biker.

Ross was ready for that one. He said, "That it must be weird, looking in two completely different directions at the same time."

"With his eye dangling, you mean?" Reynolds chuckled. The shrink was about five foot six, maybe a hundred and eighty pounds. His fading red hair was shot through with streaks of grey. His moustache and full beard always looked as if they'd just been trimmed. He wore a brown tweed sports jacket, pants that didn't quite match, a white shirt that was carrying far too heavy a load. His head was a little too large for his body and his steel-rim glasses were a little too small for his face. His eyes were dark brown, not quite as lively as pancakes. He showed more gum than teeth whenever he smiled. The hair that spouted from his ears and nostrils had been clipped short, crewcut-style. His nails gleamed like the fenders of a showroom motorcycle. The tip of his nose was shaped like a miniature bum.

He put his silk-stockinged feet up on his desk and delicately scratched behind his ear with the soft end of an unsharpened pencil.

Finally Ross said, "Yeah, with his eye dangling. What is it . . . spiders? They can do that, can't they? Look in different directions at once. Up here, down there."

"Were you frightened?"

"Not at the time, in the heat of the moment."

"What about later?"

"Did I have a post-traumatic reaction?" Ross wore prison jeans, a plain white T-shirt, hold the logo. His arms were bare, the skin of his forearm raised up in a permanent welt where the knife had cut him. He leaned forward in his chair. "I wasn't frightened, Doc. I was terrified. Think what could've happened to me. That great big unimaginable thing called *Death*. Except I'd just killed somebody, and watched him die. So it was worse, in a way, 'cause death wasn't quite so unimaginable, any more."

"Did you, or rather, do you, feel any remorse?"

Ross put his hand to his jaw and mulled that one over for a few seconds. Not that he needed the time; it was just that he wanted the shrink to know for certain that he wasn't being spontaneously frivolous. Finally he said, "The guy was a couple of chromosomes short of human. I won't say he actually *deserved* to die . . . but at the same time, why should I have allowed him to live?"

Reynolds nodded. Demonstrating his mastery of body language, he showed Ross the palms of his hands. "Of course, it was a clear case of self-defence."

"That's what they said at the inquest, Doc."

"What do *you* say, Ross?"

"You've read my sheet. The only person I ever hurt was myself."

"And that poor fella in the bar." Reynolds nudged Ross's file folder with the heel of his shoe. Ross just sat there. Patience without limit. A con.

But though he was as immobile as a life-size bronze statue of himself, Ross's mind was hard at work, remembering everything in detail. The "poor" fella in the bar, Barry Flax. Barry was a stockbroker. Worse, he was extraordinarily talented, a genius of a stockbroker. The slick-faced prosecutor informed the gap-jawed jury that, in the twelve months leading up to the afternoon Ross had pounced on him, Barry Flax had grossed a cool five hundred and eighty grand. Think about it, ladies and gentlemen! More than half a million dollars! The fact that the hotshot broker had made his dough via insider trading and a trail of broken-hearted shareholders held no water. All that mattered was that he'd taken a licking and more or less completely stopped ticking. No longer was he a mover and a shaker, down there on the shady side of the street.

Fair enough, Ross had thought at the time. But now he was five years older, five years wiser. Nobody deserved what he'd given Barry. Five years was getting off light. Despite the circumstances, he was repentant. Genuinely repentant.

He'd hit Barry with a bar chair, whacked him into a kind of twilight zone between this life and the next. Barry had been in a coma six months, awakened to discover "Matlock" was his favourite television program. In his spare moments, he kept himself busy trying to remember how to brush his teeth. He had, in other words, lost his lust for life. Ross had rendered him, now and perhaps forever, pretty much unemployable. His savings had dwindled to zero. The bank had repo'd his Corvette and False Creek waterfront condo. His gorgeous blonde girlfriend had stepped into a taxi, and vanished. The broker had been forced to move in with his mother, who wasn't very goddamn happy about it.

The lawyer pointed out that Ross was flat broke. He instructed the jury in the self-evident truth that the only way Ross could hope to pay for his sins was with the tattered remains of his miserable life.

Ross forbade his lawyer to call as a defence witness the stripper and semi-pro hooker he'd believed himself to be defending from violent rape, and who was his beloved sister, Angela. She had visited him once, as he languished without bail in the city lockup, and made it clear to him that she couldn't offer up any evidence on his behalf because if their mother, who had a faulty valve, ever found out how her beloved daughter made a living, it would kill her. During the past several years, Angela had mailed their mom stacks of documents indicating that she, Angela, was a small-town kindergarten teacher happily married to a dentist named Walther, and that she and Walther had three darling children, all girls.

So Ross kept his mouth shut, and took the fall. He spent eleven months in jail, awaiting trial. He was given a ten-year term, but the time he'd already served was credited to his sentence, which left him with nine years and one month to go. Except for killing the biker, he was a model prisoner. His first parole hearing was a total flop but a great learning experience. The second time around, they green-lighted him for a cautious six months' worth of weekend day passes. At the end of that time he went before the board again, barked on cue, balanced a red-and-blue ball on his nose, and managed to keep a straight face as he gave numbingly detailed answers to an apparently endless series of well-intentioned, increasingly harebrained questions.

And now, finally, it was almost time to go. All he had to do was survive this last session with Reynolds.

The shrink said, "So tell me, what're you going to do, out there?"

"Get a job, I guess."

"Yes, of course. It's a condition of your parole, isn't it, that you make every reasonable effort to seek gainful employment. What kind of a job will you be looking for?"

Ross shrugged. Wishing to be polite, he tried to think of something that was at least borderline believable. But his mind had suddenly gone blank, as if God had taken a swipe at him with a giant eraser. "Heart transplants?" he lamely offered.

Reynolds vented a cynical chuckle. "You *are* still feeling guilty about Al. You have a strong need to be a healer, and that's so nice. But hardly plausible."

The shrink mimed climbing swiftly down a ladder. Ross's brow looked as if it had just been ploughed, as he struggled to understand what Reynolds meant. Finally he got it. The shrink believed he was aiming too high.

"Car wash?"

Reynolds beamed. He said, "It's worth a try. Hey, you never know." He gestured broadly. "After all, we're next-door neighbours to the land of opportunity. Some of that wonderfulness is bound to rub off. Osmosis by proximity!"

"Miracles *can* happen," said Ross.

"Now you're talking!" The shrink's face lit up, as if he'd just inhaled a double lungful of helium, touched a match. "By the way, there's something you ought to know, buddy."

"What might that be?"

"Your sister helped you with those assholes on the parole board. Went to work on me, too, though I blush to admit it."

Ross was astonished. "What'd she do?"

Reynolds smiled with teeth that had benefited greatly from the generous terms of the correctional system's dental plan. "The babe's a hooker. What d'you think she did?"

Ross had two options. Sit quietly or lunge headfirst into a canister of Mace. He had no doubt that a brace of screws lurked on the other side of the shrink's office door, truncheons in hand, cauliflower ears pressed against the polished mahogany. Those sadistic bastards. They'd rather kick his ass than chow down on pint bottles of Wild Turkey and platefuls of Sara Lee. He sat very still. The decision to suck wind might have been a real toughie, once upon a time. But Angela had betrayed him. The five years he'd survived in the joint, in tandem with the countless terrible things he'd been forced to do – to himself and others – in order to accomplish that insignificant task, had turned Ross into as tough a cookie as he needed to be.

He let his eyes go out of focus. His body went slack, as he assumed the posture of a man who was content to wait passively for someone else to tell him what to do.

Reynolds fumbled under his jacket for his fat gold pen. He ceremoniously unscrewed the cap, opened a spiral-bound notebook with a gold-embossed blue suede cover. He hunted for a blank page, scratched down two or three words in blood-red ink. Then he put his pen down on his desk and fished out another exactly like it. Ross sat quietly. Reynolds' breathing was laboured as he ponderously wrote two short paragraphs in green ink, blotted the page and shut the book. By way of bringing this segment of the interview to a conclusion, he tilted sideways in his chair and loosed a firecracker-sharp fart.

"Do you understand the significance of the green ink and the red ink?"

"Green is good, red is bad?"

Reynolds waggled the pen. A rainbow of gold flashed bright. "Green is *go*. Red is *stop*. Do you comprehend the difference?"

Ross nodded.

The shrink stroked his beard against the grain, and seemed to take small pleasure in the velocity with which the stiff hairs sprang back into place. "I hope you do. I wish it were so. But, off the record, I have serious doubts about your ability to reintegrate."

Ross felt as if someone had dropped a bowling ball into his unsuspecting crotch. He said, "Why is that, exactly?"

"Your cellmate. Gary. Garret. You and he were real tight, weren't you?"

Ross nodded. "We got along okay."

"Refresh my memory, Ross. What was he in for?"

"Armed robbery. Murder."

"The details, please."

"He and another guy, Billy, they robbed an armoured car. Shot a couple of guards . . ."

"How much of the money was never recovered?"

"Two hundred and twenty grand, if you can believe the cops."

"*Can* we believe the police, Ross?"

"Always, Doctor Reynolds."

"You must have been very upset, when your good friend Garret died."

"Not as upset as he was."

"He knew he was dying, Ross. There are rumours circulating within these sturdy walls that, shortly before he passed away, he told you what happened to the loot. Any truth to those rumours?"

Ross shook his head. For emphasis, he said, "Nope." Then he shook his head again.

"You're sure about that? Garret didn't have any relatives, not even a mother. Nobody had visited him except his girlfriend, for a while, and his lawyer, from time to time. You two guys were like brothers. He was dying, and you were up for parole. He left almost everything he owned to you. Doesn't it make sense that he'd tell you where he stashed the two hundred grand?"

"Yeah, I thought so."

Reynolds poked the blunt end of the pen into his hairy ear. "But he didn't agree?"

"There was his girlfriend. Shannon. If anybody got the cash, probably it was her. He really loved her. Showed me pictures, the letters she wrote . . ."

Reynolds waved all of that away. "We monitored the relationship, such as it was. And we've already talked to her. Many times. She has no idea what happened to the money. So, that leaves you."

"Garret didn't believe he was going to die," said Ross. "He was touched by the Lord, towards the end. He believed his bacon was going to be saved by no less an authority figure than God Himself."

Reynolds nodded thoughtfully. He removed the pen from his ear, wiped away an apparently sticky substance, slipped the pen into his pocket. "Didn't work out that way, did it?"

"Maybe the line was busy," said Ross. But Reynolds was looking out his office window. It was as if the shrink had given up on Ross, lost interest. Ross couldn't blame him. What were the chances that he'd successfully integrate into society, become one of a billion cheerful little cogs?

Not too good, really.

He leaned back in his chair. Reynolds' office was military-sparse. It was one of those places where there was a place for everything and everything had its place. Or was summarily executed, or got the hell out. Ross finally noticed that the ceiling was papered from wall to wall with thousands of large-denomination bills. A few bills came unstuck and drifted erratically down. Soon there was a blizzard. By the time Reynolds finally let him go he had to wade through drifts of cash that were crotch-deep, to get to the door.

Or maybe he was dreaming again, as his last night in the slammer drifted slowly by.

2

From the outside it looked like an ordinary, badly neglected, broken-down east-side house. The kind of place that, were it a self-respecting horse, would politely ask for a bullet between the eyes. Paint peeled away from the clapboard walls in drab and scabrous sheets, as if hoping to escape before the building came tumbling down. Detective Jack Willows was no carpenter, but to his eye all that was holding the house up was force of habit.

The front gate had fallen flat on its ass, but someone had taken pity on it, picked it up and leaned it against the faded picket fence. Willows stepped over the yellow crime-scene tape that twisted in the cold damp wind. A uniformed cop waved a four-battery MagLite in his face, mumbled a gruff apology, redirected the beam towards Detective Claire Parker's long and shapely legs.

Willows heard quick footsteps behind them. He turned. The MagLite's beam washed all the colour out of Bobby Dundas' handsome face.

Bobby said, "Get that fucking searchlight off me or I'll shove it so far up your baggy ass people will mistake you for a fucking X-ray." He smiled at Parker. "Evening, Claire."

Willows said, "What're you doing here, Bobby?"

"Detecting." Bobby wore a black fedora that went well with his cashmere overcoat, but he was quick to take advantage of Parker's umbrella. Willows hadn't even bothered to turn his collar up against the rain.

"Aren't you off-duty?"

"Yeah, sure. I was on my way home when the call came over the radio. Murder! How could I resist? Christ, I almost broke out in a sweat."

The flashlight had gone away. In the orange glare of the street-lights, Bobby's face had turned that same slick shade of yellowish green as the flesh of an unripe avocado. Bobby had come to homicide straight out of vice. He was the kind of guy who kept a flattering picture of himself – and nobody else – in his wallet. There wasn't a single cop in Serious Crimes who would admit to finding him likeable, and Willows was at the head of the list, partly because Bobby kept making moves on Claire. Bobby saw himself as an inevitable force, and didn't care who knew it. His first day on the job, he'd told Parker she was wasting her life, messing around with a married man. Especially an old dude like Willows, who'd done the father routine once and wasn't likely, at his age, to want to do it again. Willows and his wife, Sheila, had split up years ago, and Willows had recently initiated divorce proceedings. But none of this mattered to Bobby.

Willows and Parker made their way up the front-porch steps. Bobby kept his distance as he followed along behind. The porch light was on. Bobby posed beneath the naked bulb. The light cast shadows all over his face. His hands fluttered like the wings of a mortally wounded moth. Smiling, he said, "Okay, beat the truth out of me. I came over because I wanted to watch the master at work, see if I could pick up a few pointers."

As they made their way into the house, Bobby slipped his arm around Parker, pressed his hand against the small of her back. She turned on him, but before she could say anything he glided past, taking the lead. His cologne mingled with the stench of burnt food. A uniform leaned against the banister, rainwater puddling at his feet on the worn linoleum floor.

Parker glanced around. To her right, a narrow staircase rose steeply to the second floor. On the left an open doorway led to a living room cluttered with falling-apart furniture. A three-legged table reminded her of Jack's new cat, the accident victim he'd adopted, Tripod. Dead ahead, a cramped hall led to the dimly lit kitchen. Someone with a sturdy pair of boots and plenty of energy had kicked several holes in the lathe-and-plaster walls. A strip of green plastic sliced from a Glad bag made a brittle crackling sound as it flapped in the breeze coming in through a broken window.

Into her ear, Bobby Dundas said, "Can you imagine living in a dump like this? Not that it's a great place to die . . ." He touched her arm, his gloved hand trailing lightly across the fabric of her coat. Then, abruptly, he turned his back on her, seemed to forget about her. Parker felt a sudden surge of anger. Bobby was right – it was a dump. But she liked to think that nobody would live in circumstances like these unless they had to.

Too bad it wasn't true.

The living room ran straight through into the dining room. At one time it had been possible to separate the two rooms with a pair of sliding pocket doors, but the hardware had broken or the doors had come off their tracks, so they hung at an odd angle, broken and useless.

The victim sat in one of five mismatched chairs that surrounded the bright yellow oval of a fifties-era Formica table. He had fallen face forward on the table, and a pool of blood had gathered around him. The man was bald except for a horseshoe of dirty blond hair above his ears. He was in his mid-fifties, thin to the point of emaciation. He wore a sleeveless T-shirt and checkerboard pants, cheap running shoes. Blood had pooled in the crotch of the pants. There was more blood on a chrome-plated table leg, and on the shabby carpet between his stockinged feet. The dull black haft of a knife protruded from his throat. On the table in front of him lay a kitchen knife with a stubby, serrated blade. Parker moved in on him, as close as she could get. The man's eyes were pale brown, almost gold. He had died needing a shave.

Bobby winked at Parker. He said, "Looks like suicide to me, kids. Well thought out, too. He's even got a backup knife, in case the first one didn't work."

"Shut up, Bobby."

"'Scuse me?"

There were playing cards scattered on the table, but no chips or money. The victim's hand lay neatly before him, spread out like a fan. He'd died holding a full house – aces over kings. Sometimes, if a man wasn't careful, he could get a little too lucky.

A spill of fingerprint powder made her sneeze. The victim's skin was coarse and wrinkled. His pupils had shrunk to pinpoints, as if overwhelmed by the headlight of the big train that had overtaken him and crushed him flat. A feline howl of anguish and rage was followed by a sudden babble of voices from the kitchen.

Parker followed the noise to its source. Willows lingered for a moment, and then followed. A pudgy uniform leaned against a sink full of Salvador Dali plates and plastic glasses as he sipped at a can of Coke. Willows took a second look. The plates were made of cardboard; they were disposable. A woman who might've been the cop's not-so-sweet mother slouched in a corner, smoking a hand-rolled cigarette. The cop said, "This's Hilda. She's a player. There's another of 'em on the back porch, and two more upstairs."

"In separate rooms?"

The cop nodded smugly. He gave Parker the once-over, filed her physical description for future reference.

The woman was wearing baggy brown slacks and a pink angora sweater that Marilyn Monroe would've died for, if it hadn't already been too late. Her hair needed washing. So did the rest of her. She smelled of Bounty, a cheap fortified cooking wine, and many other, less easily identified liquids. Parker hunkered down next to her, made fleeting eye contact.

"Hilda?"

The woman nodded. She'd been crying. Her eyes were red, her cheeks swollen with grief.

Parker said, "You were at the table when your friend was stabbed?"

Hilda's fingers worked at her tangled hair. She muttered unintelligibly. Her loose body shuddered beneath the angora.

"Was he a friend of yours, Hilda?"

Hilda sniffed mightily. She peered at her reflection in the crusty oven door. What she saw must have pleased her. She smiled broadly, with a logjam of tobacco-stained teeth. "He was a good friend of mine. A *really* good friend. Share his last drop, know what I mean . . ."

"What was his name?"

"Richard Beinhart. But everybody called him Rick. Or Ricardo, or Richie Rich. But he didn't like those names all that much. So mostly we called him Rick."

"Were you sitting at the table when he was stabbed?"

"Yeah, sure." Concentration rumpled her forehead. She clawed a fistful of hair out of the way, tugged mightily at a surprisingly delicate ear. "Leastways, I *think* I was . . ."

"You don't remember?"

"Not really." Hilda leaned her head against the stove. She shut her eyes. Her mouth sagged open. She sighed.

Parker touched her knee. "Hilda?"

"Hmmmm?" One eye popped open; the other held its ground.

"Did somebody hurt him? Was there an argument, an argument over the cards? Is that what happened, Rick got into an argument?"

Hilda roused herself. She tried to stand up, lost her balance and began to topple sideways. Parker leaned into her, helped her find the wall. The pudgy cop made a gurgling sound as he drained his Coke. Hilda said, "I heard people shoutin'. Everybody was shoutin'. Yellin' at each other. Me too." She shrugged. "I got no idea what everybody was so mad about. It's fun sometimes, yellin' and screamin'." She jerked her cigarette at the cop. "Then Rick made a noise like he just did."

"Were you playing cards?"

"Yeah, sure."

"Poker?"

"Crib."

"Cribbage? Where's the board, the pegs?"

Hilda stared quizzically up at the naked bulb that dangled, cartoon-like, from the ceiling. "I sure hope I didn't do it," she whispered. "Rick was such a nice guy. I loved him like a brother, know what I mean?" She slid down the wall to the floor. Her head lolled on her shoulder. She began to snore.

Willows came in from the back porch. "Get anything?"

"The victim's name is Richard. She says they were playing crib. Fifteen-two, fifteen-four . . ."

"With the little pegs, right?"

"Her name's Hilda," said Parker. "Says she loved Rick like a brother. Said she hopes she didn't do it."

"You believe her?"

Parker nodded. "Absolutely. What'd you get?"

"Alvin Da Silva. The way he tells it, they were playing crib, matchstick a point. He remembers an argument, raised voices. There's blood all over his shirt but he has no idea how it got there, just can't remember. He told me Rick was a real nice guy and he hopes like hell that he wasn't the one who killed him. On the other hand, he doesn't know who could have done it. They were all the best of pals, bottom-of-the-bottle buddies . . ." Willows glanced over Parker's shoulder, into the living room. "Where's Bobby?"

"I thought he was with you."

Willows glanced down the shotgun hall to the wide-open front door. The wind had picked up, bellying the crime-scene tape. Two quick strides took him to the dining-room door.

Parker said, "Maybe he left."

"Or snuck upstairs to interview our suspects." Willows turned and strode briskly towards the stairs, leaving Parker to wonder why she'd said something so utterly stupid.

The pudgy cop rotated his empty Coke can, brought his hands together in a futile attempt to squash the can flat. Parker hurried down the hall after Willows, the slightly rounded heels of her plain-but-practical flats clicking like a steel ball on a slow-spinning wheel.

They found Bobby in the upstairs front bedroom, standing by the window, looking down at the street. He turned as Willows and Parker entered the room. There was blood on his knuckles. The room's window had no curtain. Lights from the emergency vehicles parked outside flashed anemically on the walls and ceiling. Bobby grinned, his teeth stained pink and blue. On the floor of the room's tiny walk-in closet, an elderly man had tucked himself into a ball, and wept silently.

Bobby said, "Good news, Jack. We got ourselves a perp."

Willows stared coldly at him. He'd never liked Bobby. The detective smelled too pretty to be handsome. He spent more on clothes than any other cop Willows knew, male or female. Bobby had been working homicide close to eight months. Jack still hadn't figured out how many pairs of shoes he owned.

Bobby slapped the blood-smeared wall. "I never laid a finger on him. Punched some plaster, that's all."

Willows crouched in the closet doorway. The man's face was unmarked, but when Willows rested a hand on his shoulder, he flinched mightily. Willows said, "I'm not going to hurt you. Did anybody hurt you?"

"Nope."

The man's eyes were a soft, evasive blue. His voice was hardly more than a whisper. His breath smelled of decay. He coughed, and Willows involuntarily drew back a little. "What's your name, pal?"

"Bill."

Willows jerked a thumb towards Bobby Dundas. "Did that man over there hit you, Bill?"

Bill thought about it. Finally he said, "Not so's I noticed." He gave Willows a crooked, uncertain grin. "I don't think so."

"Do you know what happened to Rick?"

"He's deader'n a doornail."

"Did you tell this officer that you stabbed him?"

"He *told me* I did it."

Bobby growled in disgust. Willows ignored him. Parker had positioned herself so she was standing between Bobby and the old man. Outside, the street was littered with police cars, media vans. An ambulance straddled the boulevard. Uniformed cops bantered with the crowd.

Willows said, "Bill, did you cut Rick?"

"No way. At least, I don't think so. Probably I was a little drunk. But Rick was a sweetheart. Why'd I want to stick a knife in him?"

"Somebody did. You were there. Didn't you see who it was?"

Bill tilted his head sideways, as if for a better view of the past. "Everybody was yellin' and screamin'. I saw the knife lyin' there on the table. It was spinnin' around, pointin' at everybody. I shut my eyes so it wouldn't be me." He clawed at his face. "Everything was kind of hazy . . ." He hugged himself and violently rocked to and fro. "Sometimes I drink too much and say stuff I shouldn't of said. Who doesn't, eh?" He wiped his hands on his shirt. "But I never tried to stick nobody in my whole life, so I kind of doubt it was me who did it."

Bobby said, "We got four suspects. They all tell the same story. Almost word for word. *Everybody loved Rick!* What is this, *Casablanca*? A bunch of falling-down drunks! There was an argument. They were all screaming at each other. We've got a victim, don't we? *Somebody's* got to be a murderer."

Bill said, "Maybe it *was* a suicide. That'd be my guess."

Downstairs, a violent crumpling sound was followed by a strangled shout of triumph. Parker's brain raced. What now?

Nothing much. The pudgy cop in the kitchen had dropped his Coke can on the floor, and stomped it flat.

3

Ross lay on his bunk, tossing and turning. It was scary, knowing that, come the dawn, he'd be on the other side of the wall. He hadn't become institutionalized during his five years in the slammer, but he'd made the necessary adjustments, and he felt at home in the yard, and in his cell. The world out there beyond those razor-wire-topped walls was no more real than the world he peered quizzically at through the eye of his television. All those impossibly pretty women, the shiny cars and big houses and apartments, all of it looking brand-new, unused, as if it had just come out of the box. Ross thought about brand-new women. He rolled over on his side. Now he was thinking about Garret again, the armoured-car robbery that had gone all wrong, the two hundred grand that had gone astray, a woman Garret's pal Billy had met and fallen in love with. Nancy Crown. The way Garret told it, Nancy was beautiful and rich, unfulfilled. Married.

Garret had ended up in William Head, doing a solid twenty-five years for murder in the first degree. But during his fourth year of incarceration Garret's stomach had started hurting, and they'd taken him to the infirmary. Six months later, he'd turned belly-up and died. A tumour . . .

But during their time together, Garret and Ross had gotten to be pretty good friends. Both of them about the same age, mid-twenties, and both of them in for a good long time. Both of them

20

killers and both of them with the same survivor's attitude – that life was a joke, so why not have a good laugh?

Garret had told Ross over and over again about the robbery, how Billy had run off with a bag stuffed with two hundred and twenty thousand dollars that had never been recovered. Garret wasn't worried about that, not at all. He claimed that he and Billy had worked out where to hide the money, in the event of a hot pursuit. Ross wanted to believe him, but never quite got there. He wondered if Garret had told his girlfriend the same unlikely tale. If so, it would go a long way towards explaining why she was such a faithful pen pal.

There was a rumbling in the walls. Somewhere not far off, someone had flushed a toilet.

Ross shifted on his narrow bed until his back was against the wall. He listened hard, but heard nothing.

Garret had told him about his whole life, those last six months. The abusive, alcoholic father who'd left home when Garret was fifteen. The mother who had adios'd a couple of years later. No drunker than usual, she'd tumbled down the back-porch stairs and snapped her neck. An instant winner in the quadriplegic sweepstakes. Congratulations, Mom. Ross didn't have much to brag about, either. His father, an accomplished lush, had considerately died of kidney failure shortly before Ross was old enough to miss him. His mom was okay, though. Straight as an arrow, a maid, gainfully employed at a downtown hotel. One of those special moms who was always there when you needed her, no matter what.

Without telling Ross what he'd done, Garret had written a will, and left him most of what little he owned.

His Timex watch. The eighteen dollars and fifty-three cents in his prison account. The clothes he'd bought for his trial: a pair of cheap shoes, a white shirt, a pair of black nylon socks and a funeral-black off-the-rack suit from the Bay. There was a faint but still-clear lipstick kiss on the shirt's button-down collar, and the suit was a little short in the cuffs, but Ross had nothing but his prison blues, so he was grateful for the gift.

Surprised, too. In his whole adult life no one had ever given him anything except a bad cheque or a headache.

But what Garret had left Ross that Ross valued the most was a whole head full of memories. Ross was a good listener, and Garret was the talkative type. He'd quit school when he was nabbed breaking into lockers for cash and drugs. He'd drifted from one low-paying job to another, with long stretches of unemployment in between. In time he'd hooked up with Billy, and they'd launched a career of breaking into cars for whatever scraps of wealth they might contain. He was still living at home when he and Billy, seduced by high ambition, tackled the armoured car.

It wasn't all bad, though. Garret had a girlfriend, Shannon, who worked a cash register at Zellers. He'd met her about a year before he was busted, and she wrote him a fat letter each and every week in the year, and for a long time had made the long, hard drive out to the prison once a month, rain or shine. Garret talked about her endlessly. Over and over again, in incredible detail, he told Ross how he and Shannon had met, where they'd gone on dates, what they'd done together. He'd describe a lunch they'd eaten at a certain restaurant, describe the restaurant right down to the style of the menu. He'd remember exactly what they ordered and how it tasted, what they said to each other, word for word.

Once, a highlight, Garret had let Ross take a split-second peek at a Polaroid Shannon had mailed him for Christmas. The girl had a terrific smile, lots of wavy, auburn-tinted-with-streaks-of-amber hair, the kind of improbably voluptuous, creamy-white body that Ross remembered from top-shelf magazines at the local drugstore. Garret said she'd mailed a dozen snapshots, but all but one had been confiscated, had vanished into the system. That night and for many nights that followed, Ross lay in his bunk and wondered what the other pictures had looked like, his fevered imagination taking him for a ride and then roughly bucking him off . . .

In the morning, Ross ate breakfast with the mob, then cleaned out his cell, packed his thesaurus and the rest of his meagre belongings in a cardboard box, changed into his new clothes and strapped on the Timex.

He signed some papers and was paid the few dollars he'd earned building fake antique pine furniture in the prison woodworking shop.

Outside, Ross waited for his mother in the shelter of a bus stop. The rain pounded down. He'd told her nine o'clock sharp. It was already quarter past. Where was she?

The road stretched away through low, tangled brush, scattered trees that chopped up the clay-coloured sky as it fell into the horizon. Ross divided his time into one-minute segments. For one minute, he stared down at his Timex, watching the second hand sweep around the dial. For the next minute he ticked off the seconds in his mind as he watched the road. At first he underestimated the time required for a minute to pass. But by the time a quarter of an hour had crawled past, he was accurate to within a few seconds, and judging how long it would take for exactly a minute to pass had become a game.

Finally he looked up and saw a tiny speck of light in the distance. His mother had never owned a car. Couldn't afford it. Until he'd taken his fall, she hadn't even had a driver's licence. Twice a month for the past five years, she'd borrowed the neighbour's car or used a hotel discount coupon to rent something tiny and underpowered from Hertz.

Today, she was driving a yellow Neon that looked like a stubby bolt of lightning. The car's brakes squealed. Ross opened the door and swung the seat forward, shoved the cardboard box into the back.

"Want me to drive, Mom?"

His mother gave him a look. She wore an over-large winter coat in frayed black wool, a dark blue cardigan, a paisley-pattern silk Hermes scarf, a black cloth mitten and a brown leather glove, knee-high patent-leather boots. She had the look of a woman whose lifestyle was a little haphazard, at best. But her mind was still sharp. Free was as cheap as you could get. The clothes, and probably her underwear as well, had been salvaged from the hotel's lost and found.

Ross climbed into the car and slammed the door shut. He slammed his mouth shut too, and kept it shut during the drive to the ferry terminal, the wait in the parking lot and the two-hour cruise across the Strait of Georgia to scenic Tsawwassen. The thought of spending the night in the bed he'd last slept in as a teenager made him feel depressed and sickly. When he said he was going to step out on deck for a breath of fresh air, his mother buttoned up her ridiculous coat and stuck with him, glued to his side like a ridiculously distorted shadow.

It seemed to him that everybody on board took one look at him and immediately knew him for who he was.

When he complained that all the noise and lights and strange people bothered him and that he'd like to go belowdecks to the car and maybe catch up on his sleep, she vetoed the idea.

What did she think he was going to do – see if he could find one of those pretty women sitting alone in her car, try to sweet-talk her into doing something to him? He might fantasize about stuff like that, but he'd never actually do it.

He was pretty sure he'd never do it.

His mother dropped him off at the house. She gave him a fresh-cut key to the front door, and then drove off to return the Neon to Hertz.

Ross entered the house and made straight for his bedroom. The small, excessively tidy room reminded him of his cell. He went into the kitchen. His mother still kept fifty bucks in the teapot, for emergencies. Well, if this wasn't a first-class emergency, he didn't know what was. He stuffed the bills in his suit pocket, went into the kitchen and got a garbage bag from under the sink. He felt eyes on him, and spun on his heel. A heavyweight ghost-coloured cat stared calmly up at him from behind a big glass bowl full of cat food.

He crouched down and rubbed his thumb and finger together. "Puss, puss, puss."

The cat used a massive paw to flick several pieces of cat food out of the bowl and onto the waxed linoleum floor. It lowered itself over its meal. A faraway look seeped into its eyes as its jaws crunched balefully. It batted more food out of the bowl and efficiently consumed it.

"Here puss, puss, puss . . ."

The cat gave Ross the once-over, and then strolled casually towards him, claws ticking on the lino. It bounded up on his thigh and then to his shoulder, where it stretched out across the back of his neck like a mini-puma. Its thick white tail lashed his cheek. A tongue like a rasp scoured his ear. He reached up, gently stroked the animal. It nuzzled him lovingly, and rumbled like summer thunder. Ross turned the cat's anodized-aluminum tag so he could read its name.

Kiddo.

He carried the bag into his bedroom and filled it with clothes, slung the bag over his shoulder. For a moment he thought about leaving a goodbye note. But when he glanced around he could see neither paper nor pen.

Down in the basement, the furnace clicked sharply. He heard the fan start up, as he walked into the living room on his way to the door.

It was still raining. The lawn twitched and shuddered. Fat drops fell from the electrical wires that drooped down the road. Across the street, an old man walked slowly past, hunched and miserable beneath a black umbrella.

Kiddo had followed him from room to room, as if on a leash. It butted its head against his leg, peered adoringly up at him.

Ross decided maybe he'd stay home for a day or two after all.

He went into the bathroom, turned on the shower and adjusted the flow of water. It took him a while to figure out that he had to turn the taps the wrong way. He stepped into the tub and pulled the curtain. It bothered him that he was in such a confined space, and that there was no one else around, no need to keep his back to the wall.

His mother had bought his favourite brand of soap and shampoo, a razor and shaving cream, roll-on deodorant, a tooth-brush and even his own tube of mint-flavoured Crest toothpaste. He should have been grateful, but all he felt was that she was trying to isolate him. As if he had a contagious disease, and she'd catch it, if she wasn't careful.

He lathered his body with the brand-new bar of soap, washed his hair, managed not to cut himself shaving with his new razor. When he was as clean as he was ever going to get, he turned off the water and stepped out of the tub and towelled himself dry, dressed in a black T-shirt and jeans. The jeans were a little loose around the waist. Medium-security as a weight-loss program. Now there was an idea whose time would never come. He wriggled into a pair of black cotton socks, white Nikes with a blue swoosh.

They had a late lunch of fried chicken and mashed potatoes, green peas. It had been five long years since Ross had sat down to a hearty meal of fried chicken, mashed potatoes and peas, but even so, it wasn't exactly a treat. A lifetime of the same meal could do that to a man. While they ate, his mother brought him up to date on the neighbourhood – who'd passed away, and who hadn't. She told him about the sweet young couple with the twin boys, who'd bought the house down at the end of the block. How they had dis-covered the first time it rained that the basement flooded and they needed a new roof. Stuff like that. He asked her where Kiddo had come from. The cat was a stray who'd wandered into the hotel one rainy night.

When she'd cleaned her plate, and wiped her mouth with a paper napkin, Ross's mother lifted her head and said, "What are you going to do with your life, Ross? Did you think about that, while you were away?"

"Yeah, sure. The first thing I got to do is pay a visit to my parole officer. A guy named George Hoffman. A real hard-ass." He noted the look on her face. Dismayed. He said, "Sorry, Mom. Wash my mouth. Anyway, Hoffman lined up a job for me, at a restaurant downtown."

Looking interested, maybe even a little relieved, she said, "Doing what?"

"Working in the kitchen." It was as close to the truth as he needed to be. He pushed away from the table, got a glass from the cupboard and a container of milk from the fridge. He emptied the last of the milk into the glass. Before he'd been sent away, she'd always bought milk in four-litre containers, big plastic jugs. How long had it taken her to get used to living alone, start buying smaller amounts of food and drink? Not long, probably. He drained his glass and put it in the sink.

After lunch, Ross carried Kiddo into his room and lay down on the bed. The cat soon purred himself to sleep. Ross stared up at the ceiling, the stained and rumpled plaster that was like a map of a country he'd visited a million times, and departed from with not a single memory.

He shut his eyes and thought about his life. His girlfriend had dumped him forever, the instant she learned that he'd busted up a broker. A couple of his buddies had written him from time to time, until they stopped.

Since then, nobody had loved him but his mother.

He conjured up an image of Cindy. His ex appeared on cue, but when he moved in on her the picture got kind of fuzzy. Who was she, anyway? Five years was a long time. He couldn't begin to imagine what she might look like. By now she might be married, a mother. He picked Kiddo up and deposited him on the bed. The cat grumbled, but stayed put.

Ross went into the bathroom. He turned on the overhead light, shut and locked the door, and peered into the mirror over the sink. The pale green eyes staring back at him were the same

eyes that had stared back at him in prison, but now he saw himself in a new light. He looked tough, and he looked bitter. He
looked like he'd spent most of his life getting his ass kicked, and
expected nothing but more of the same. He looked beaten. He
looked whipped.

He looked like nobody he'd want to know.

He went back into the kitchen. His mother stood at the sink,
listening to the radio as she washed the dishes. Ross picked up a
dishtowel and a plate. She glanced up at him, more quizzical than
pleased.

To his surprise, Ross remembered where everything went, the
stainless-steel cutlery and the dinner and side plates, the water
glasses. He was pleased to discover that nothing had changed.
When he'd put the last of the dishes away, he hung the towel on
the rack to dry, and then he took his mother in his arms and held
her tight and whispered in her ear that he was sorry for everything bad he'd done, and that he was going to try his hardest to be
a good boy from now on.

His mother cried tears of joy. Pretty soon Ross was crying too,
matching her tear for tear. Finally his mother dried her tears with
the dishtowel and laughed about nothing at all in a gargling kind
of way. She hugged him again.

Ross told her he loved her, and hugged her back.

Then he went into the bathroom, shut the door and locked it,
and studied himself in the mirror again.

Did he look a little friendlier? Not so's you'd notice. He was
going to have to keep working at it, chipping away, or look like an
ex-con forever.

When his mother had finished cleaning up the kitchen, she put-
tered aimlessly around the house for a little while and then told
him she was tired, that it was time for her afternoon nap. She left
her bedroom door open. He could hear her praying, the creak of
the bed as she lay down upon the covers, bone by bone. He turned
on the television and watched part of a quiz show. Kiddo leapt
silently into his lap. He crooked a finger and scratched the bridge

of the cat's stubby nose. Kiddo made a sound like a broken cement mixer; his ribcage swelled as he took a deep breath, and slowly let it out. The cat was a little overweight. Making up for lost meals, maybe. Ross shut his eyes. He was bone-weary but had no hope of dozing off. The unfamiliar sounds and smells of the house nagged at him, making sleep all but impossible.

As his mom cooked lunch, the chicken hissing and crackling in the pan, Ross had thought about the three different guys he'd met, none of whom had known each other until they landed in prison, who were guilty of assault with a frying pan. Three of them! And this was a prison for *men*! Would anyone who owned a frying pan soon be required to take a course in the safe handling of frying pans? Would the government eventually demand that all owners of frying pans register their frying pans, arrest and toss the book at anyone who'd neglected to store his frying pan in a safe place?

He dislodged Kiddo again, shrugged into his jacket and eased open the door and stepped onto the porch, shut the door behind him. Outside was big. Outside was huge. The size of it rocked him. He walked two blocks to the corner store and bought a pack of cigarettes, though he was astounded by the price. He asked for matches and they sold him a pack for a nickel.

He couldn't believe it. A nickel! For something they used to give away for free.

4

Willows' desk butted up against Parker's. If they were of a mind, and there was no one around to witness their shenanigans, they could shift forward in their swivel chairs and extend their legs and play an uncomfortable game of footsie.

But, at the moment, neither of them was in the mood.

Parker finished scribbling a note. She stabbed without malice at her blotter with the tip of her pen.

"Jack?"

Willows looked up. He leaned back in his chair.

Parker said, "We can't hold them forever. Even a legal-aid lawyer knows that much."

Hilda Stratten, Alvin Da Silva, William "Bill" Marks and their fourth suspect, Jennifer Wilde, were up on the Public Safety Building's top floor, ensconced in individual holding cells. They were being legally held as material witnesses, but Parker was right – time was running out fast.

She and Willows had split the quartet up and grilled them individually, following several lines of questioning. How could five people play a single game of cribbage? It transpired that the victim had been an onlooker rather than a participant. Willows had never encountered a case where none of the witnesses recalled the crime but all of them were full of remorse. Alvin Da Silva had told Parker that Richie was the nicest guy he'd ever known. Hilda had said he was a real sweetheart, generous to a fault. Bill Marks had told Willows that Richard had actually given him the shirt off his back, his last birthday. All four had claimed, individually and each in his own way, that he would jump at the chance to plead guilty, if the cops felt that was the right thing for them to do.

Grilled to a turn for hours on end, the four suspects had continued to weep and wail over the loss of their friend. Willows was convinced that their grief was the genuine article. Parker concurred. She said, "Maybe he did kill himself."

"Stabbed himself in the throat."

"Yeah, sure. Why not?" Willows' face was unreadable. She said, "The splash pattern on the victim's arm is consistent with a self-inflicted wound."

Willows remained unconvinced.

Parker said, "A bunch of down-at-the-heels, unemployable alcoholics. But I hope it was suicide. Living together in that falling-down house, getting along, day by day. They're always asking after each other. They really care about each other, Jack. And they all say the same thing: 'I hope I didn't do it, but if I did, go ahead and gas me.'" Parker tossed her pencil the way David Letterman did, making it spin. She snatched it out of the air. "Why don't we take another look at the crime scene."

By the time they arrived, they were into the small hours of the morning. Frank Sinatra time. The rain had stopped. The house looked to Willows like something in need of a match. They had learned from Alvin Da Silva that the house's owner was a dentist named Chris Bowers, who lived in Shaughnessy, one of the most expensive parts of the city. Bowers' home number was unlisted. For the next few hours, his office would be closed.

The house comprised a mini-slum in what was essentially a pretty decent middle-class neighbourhood. The east side was changing rapidly. Ten years ago it had been home to the blue-collar bunch. Now, a reasonably attractive east-side home was worth about twice as much as a similar west-side property had cost five years ago. Willows wondered when the upward spiral would end. Except for his pension, almost every penny of his net worth was wrapped up in his house – the home he had inherited from his mother. His wife, Sheila, was entitled to half of everything he owned. When she discovered he was divorcing her, she'd go after every penny she was entitled to, and more.

Willows toyed with the idea of making an offer on the murder house. One of the many negative consequences of violent death was a short-term drop in property values. Maybe he should jump in now. Wake up the dentist. Lowball him with a nothing-down offer and see what happened . . .

Parker had broken the police seal and was standing in the open doorway, waiting. He followed her inside.

The house had been shut up for several hours. Willows smelled dry rot, burnt food, the sickly sweet smell of congealed blood. He righted an overturned kitchen chair.

"Where do you want to start?"

"Upstairs." The way the people who lived here shared what they owned reminded Willows of his student days. In places like this, privacy was always at a premium. Any clues to the suspects' private lives would surely be found in the three upstairs bedrooms.

Willows took the stairs two at a time. Several dozen empty beer bottles were stacked against the wall on the cramped landing. Parker went into one of the bedrooms. Willows took another. A queen-size mattress lay on the bare wooden floor. The only other piece of furniture was a battered, fifties-era maple bureau. A raggedy waterfall of clothing overflowed from the open bureau drawers. This room was Hilda and Alvin's – their names had been scrawled on the door in black felt pen. Willows emptied and repacked the drawers one by one. The place was a mess, looked as if it had already been tossed. Willows gingerly sifted through the bedclothes and then grabbed the mattress and lifted it high enough to look underneath. Nothing. There was a tiny walk-in closet. He switched on his pocket-size MagLite. A dustball cowered in a corner. On a small shelf made of an unpainted board he found a back issue of *National Geographic*. He flipped through the magazine's glossy pages and there was Hilda, jauntily perched on the aft rail of a big sailboat. She wore a black one-piece bathing suit. Her hair was in short braids. Her smile was as wide as her face.

Willows studied the text. The picture had been taken onboard *My Girl*, a forty-two-foot gaff-rigged ketch leased by the Trident Corporation. Willows turned the page and discovered that the corporation was based in San Diego. Trident was a non-profit organization. The boat's volunteer crew were studying the causes of degradation in shallow-water coral reefs in the Bahamas. Willows checked the magazine's spine. The issue was ten years old, but Hilda looked at least twenty years younger. What had happened to her, in the interval, that had yanked her out of that life and into this?

He put the magazine back where he'd found it, and went into the front bedroom. This room, the victim's, was the smallest of the three. A narrow casement window overlooked the street. A black Trans-Am with tinted windows crawled past, radio blaring.

Parker leaned against the doorway. "How're you doing?"

"Not so good. Find anything in the other room?"

"An extensive collection of dustballs."

"Yeah, me too."

The bed had an iron frame, small iron wheels. Hospital surplus. But the mattress was firm and the plain white sheets had been recently changed. There was a clamp-lamp and a GE clock radio on the orange-crate night table, a full bottle of Smirnoff vodka inside the crate.

The six-drawer dresser was painted a glossy white. Willows was trying to steal secrets from a life. Like any educated thief, he started at the bottom and worked his way up, so he wouldn't need to shut one drawer before going on to the next. The first drawer held a pair of heavy, green corduroy pants and a pair of black rubber boots. Stuffed down in the bottom of one of the boots was a metal box secured with a sturdy padlock. Willows gave the box a shake. It sounded empty but weighed full. He turned both boots upside down. No key.

His splayed fingers swept across the bottom panels of the drawers as he yanked them open one by one.

Parker searched the night table. She checked the clamp-lamp and then the alarm clock's battery compartment. She upended the crate, gave the bed a thorough once-over, pushed the mattress back into place and sat down. "I'm getting all hot and sweaty, Jack. There's got to be a hammer or a screwdriver around here somewhere."

"Under the sink."

Parker trudged downstairs, returned a few minutes later with a rusty, wooden-handled hammer. She hit the lock three times, before the shackle finally snapped. Parker opened the box. A wad of fifties spilled into her lap. She did a quick count. Altogether, there was about eight hundred dollars.

Willows said, "Now we know why he didn't like being called Richie Rich. I wonder where he got the money?"

"Hilda mentioned that the rent was overdue."

Willows nodded. When a murder had been committed, the motive was almost always love, or money. Or the need for love, or the lack of money. He felt depressed, betrayed by the banal predictability of it all.

Parker drove them back to 312 Main. It was a complete surprise to all four suspects that their pal Rick had eight hundred and fifty dollars squirrelled away in a locked steel box. Willows and Parker discussed the case with Inspector Homer Bradley. Bradley was silver-haired, arthritic, pushing mandatory retirement. But he was one of the sharpest coppers on the force. Bradley green-lighted the quartet's release. Parker cautioned them not to leave town. Hilda made it clear they weren't going anywhere at all, unless someone lent them cab fare home. Parker dipped deep into her wallet. She offered Hilda a pair of tens. Alvin Da Silva offhandedly said he appreciated the gesture but that twenty might not quite cut the mustard. Willows added a rumpled five-dollar bill to the pot. He escorted the four of them to the Main Street exit, and then he and Parker took the elevator back to the third floor.

It was just a few minutes past seven, and the squadroom was deserted. Willows checked that his desk was locked. He yawned, and slung his overcoat over his shoulder.

Parker said, "Want to get something to eat, or go straight home?"

"Let's eat. Maybe if we have breakfast, we can trick ourselves into thinking we just got up." In a little less than two hours, Willows had an appointment with his lawyer, Peter Singer. But he'd neglected to mention the meeting to Parker, and he wasn't quite ready to tell her about it just yet. There were some things a woman was better off not knowing. No, that was a miserable lie. In truth, he was in no mood to answer the inevitable flurry of questions. Whenever the subject of divorce came up, Parker got kind of skittish. *Difficult* was another word that came to mind. Willows didn't blame her. Fate, or luck, had cast her in the role of the other woman.

Parker drove them to the Fresgo Inn, a twenty-four-hour more-than-burgers joint that was clean and cheap, served good food and plenty of it. She parked within an inch or two of a cream-coloured Harley Sportster, turned off the engine and dropped the keys in her purse. Willows got out of the car. Parker's dark blue skirt rose up on her thighs as she slid across the bench seat to get out on Willows' side. He gave her a frankly lecherous look. She tugged at her skirt and said, "You're the one who didn't want to drive straight home."

Willows smiled. He shut the car door and took her by the arm and led her across the parking lot towards the restaurant. "First the fuel, then the fire." He swung open the glass door and they went inside. The Fresgo is a self-serve restaurant. You order. You pay. You wait for your number to be called, you walk up to the counter and claim your food, and then you eat it. Willows poured himself a fat white mug of coffee. Parker helped herself to a teapot and hot water. She'd use her own brand of tea bag – she always kept a few in a plastic Baggie in her purse.

Willows ordered his usual up-all-night breakfast of sausages and hash browns, sunny-side-up eggs and whole-wheat toast. Parker ordered a fruit cup and brown toast, no butter. Willows paid. He collected a handful of cutlery, creamers from a chilled stainless-steel bin. Parker led him to a booth by the window. They sat down. Willows stirred cream into his coffee.

A bearded man in fringed black leather thumped down in the next booth, behind Willows. He smiled at Parker with those few teeth that were still in his possession. She sipped her tea, and ignored him.

Willows said, "What d'you want to do about Bobby?"

"Bobby who?"

"Dundas. Bobby Dundas." Willows hunched a little closer. His eyes were bright, his face looked as if it had been stretched a little too tight, and his skin had a faint yellow tinge. Maybe it was the fluorescent lights. Probably it was exhaustion.

"What d'you mean, what do I want to do about him? I don't want to do anything."

"He threatened our witness."

"You've done worse. And I've stood there and watched you do it, Jack."

Willows sat back. He blinked rapidly, as if his eyes hurt. He drank some more coffee.

Parker said, "Bobby might've been greased lightning when he was in vice, but he isn't going to cut it in homicide." She lightly touched the back of Willows' hand. "Leave him alone. Let him self-destruct."

Number fifty-seven was called. Willows glanced at the slip of paper the cashier had given him. Fifty-seven. He stood up.

"Want some help?"

"I'll get it."

"You'll need a tray."

Moving away from her, Willows waggled his fingers in acknowledgement. In lieu of a crash course in juggling, he would indeed require a tray. But it wasn't like Parker to point out the stunningly obvious. He was upset. She was upset. But they were upset about completely different issues, and only he knew it. It wasn't Bobby Dundas that was bothering him, it was his upcoming appointment with his lawyer. He plucked a dark green plastic tray from a stack of clean trays, picked up their meals and returned to the table, distributed the food. He sprinkled pepper on his hash browns and eggs, picked up his fork and began to eat.

Parker attacked her fruit cup with uncharacteristic fervour. She was a nibbler by habit, but it had been a long night, and she was ravenous. She ate a half-slice of toast, patted her mouth with a napkin. "You're tense because you've got an appointment with your lawyer in a couple of hours, aren't you? It doesn't have anything to do with Bobby. It's all about your divorce."

The biker's spoon clattered on the table. Staring hard at Parker, he scoured the bottom of his chili bowl with his tongue.

Willows said, "When did I tell you I had an appointment with my lawyer?"

"You didn't. Annie mentioned it."

Willows put down his fork. He leaned into Parker and kissed her gently. She smiled. "That was nice. What was it for?"

"Your patience, and understanding."

Parker kissed him back. "C'mon, let's get out of here."

Willows stood up. He took Parker's arm as she slid out of the booth. The biker stared at them as they left the restaurant. He was still staring at them as Parker started the car and backed cautiously into traffic. "You know that guy, Jack?"

"The biker? Yeah, I know him. Terry Sanow. Norm and I put him away." Norm Burroughs had been Willows' first partner. A good man, right to the end. He said, "Terry killed his wife. They were playing pool at some bar downtown, he lost his temper and bounced a cue-ball off her head. He caught twelve and did eight." Parker turned on the wipers. He fastened his seatbelt.

Parker said, "What'd she do, miss an easy shot?"

"Told him she wanted a divorce," said Willows. An ambulance shot over the crest of the bridge, on its way to St. Paul's. Willows saw the lights and then he heard the siren. If he were a dog, he'd bark. His window was down a crack. He rolled it up.

By the time they got home, Annie had left for school. Sean was flopped out on the sofa in the living room. A partially smoked filtertip cigarette was wedged behind his ear. He wore a black leather jacket, black jeans and a white T-shirt, ankle-high Doc Martens. His hair was in an abbreviated ponytail. He waggled his fingers. "Hi, Dad."

Willows said, "I thought you were working."

"I'm back on night shifts." Sean worked at a 7-Eleven over on Dunbar, a ten-minute bus ride from home. He grinned crookedly. "Yeah, I know. If some guy sticks a gun in my face, hand over the money."

Parker said, "I'm going to take a shower. You coming?"

A tread squeaked as Willows followed Parker up the stairs. Or maybe it was his heart.

Peter Singer was a little under six feet tall, twenty pounds over-weight. Most of his hair had migrated into his neatly trimmed beard. His nose was almost as small as Michael Jackson's. He had tired eyes, but his shirt was almost preternaturally white, and his dark blue pinstripe suit looked brand-new. His handshake was perfunctory. He waved his new client into a chair. "What can I do for you, Jack?"

"I want a divorce."

Singer snatched up a Bic pen that had been chewed to a nub. He flipped open a lined notepad. "What's your wife's name?"

"Sheila McKenzie Willows."

"She at home?"

Willows shook his head, no.

"How long she been gone?"

"A couple of years. Two years and three months. She was back about a year ago, to drop off the kids. I haven't seen her since."

"She in town?"

"Toronto." Willows hesitated. He said, "I haven't heard from her for close to three months."

Singer chewed another small fragment of plastic off his pen. "Is that unusual?"

Willows nodded. "She usually phones every five or six weeks."

"How many children are there, and how old are they?"

"Annie's fifteen. My son, Sean, is eighteen. They were living with Sheila in Toronto until a little over a year ago."

"She paying child support?"

"No."

"When she had the kids, were you paying child support?"

"Nine hundred a month. We made an arrangement with my bank so the money was automatically deducted from my account."

"The kids got any complaints about her?"

Willows shrugged. "Nothing serious. I don't want them dragged through court."

"The stick's for leverage, Jack. We won't hit her with it unless we absolutely have to. Tell me, do you love your children?"

Willows was taken by surprise. He said, "Yes, I do." He sat up a little straighter in his chair.

"Would you categorize yourself as a good father?"

Willows spent a little time thinking about that one. Finally he said, "When Sheila left me, I wasn't spending much time at home." He scratched his jaw. "I was a loving father, but I wasn't around as much as I should've been. Sheila and I weren't getting along. At the time, I wasn't aware of how unhappy she was. Maybe I should've been, but I wasn't."

"What's your current situation? Got a girlfriend?"

Willows nodded.

"She living with you, by any chance?"

"For the past few months."

"And before that?"

"We went back and forth."

"How do the kids feel about her?"

"They like her."

"They do, huh?" Singer smiled. Willows had never seen such crooked teeth.

"About your wife – if you haven't heard from her, how do you know she's still in Toronto?"

"Well, I don't. I just assumed she was still there, since she hadn't told me otherwise."

"You haven't tried to get in touch with her?"

"The last few times she phoned, she wanted money. I was relieved when she stopped calling."

Singer nodded. He bent over his notepad. Willows noticed that a gap in the surrounding highrises afforded Singer a partial view of the harbour, all the way to the grain elevators by the Iron-workers' Bridge. Singer pushed the pad across his desk, offered Willows the remains of his pen.

"I'll need Sheila's last known address, and her parents' address as well. Phone numbers, too."

Willows wrote it all down.

"She seeing anybody, that you know of?"

"Yes, she was. A man named Robert King."

"He a cop?"

Willows smiled. "No, something to do with the stock market. A promoter."

The lawyer stood up, came around from behind his desk and offered his hand. "That'll do for now, Jack. There's no point in setting up another appointment until we locate your wife. If you don't hear from me by the end of the week, give me a call, okay?"

Willows nodded. Singer had given him an odd look when he'd admitted that he hadn't heard from Sheila in three months. What had the lawyer been thinking?

Three months, and he'd hardly given Sheila a passing thought. Out of sight, out of mind. The job, the kids. Parker. He had a thousand excuses, but none of them were worth much.

He rode the elevator down to the main floor, made his way

across the crowded foyer and pushed through the building's revolving glass door. The moment he stepped outside he was slapped in the face by a cold, damp wind.

Only then did he realize how heavily he was sweating.

5

Ross loitered for fifteen or twenty minutes, until finally a bus came rumbling up the street. He queried a fellow would-be passenger about the fare. A dollar-thirty-five and he had no change. He ripped a two-dollar bill in half, folded one of the pieces into a tight square. The bus pulled up to the stop with a disappointed hiss of brakes. Ross climbed aboard, slipped his bogus money into the glass box, asked for and received a transfer from the pudgy, randomly scowling driver.

He got off at Fraser, directly across the street from Mountain View Cemetery. The rain had stopped, for now. He bought a couple of 6/49 lottery tickets at a corner store with sturdy metal bars on the windows and door. The city was changing fast, and not for the better.

He walked a couple of blocks down the street and entered what appeared to be an ordinary restaurant, but was something else entirely, though he wasn't sure what. There were pool tables in the back, people of all ages and sexes sitting around drinking coffee and smoking cigarettes, reading the paper. Ross covertly observed the scene. Not that there was anything wrong with sitting around drinking a cup of coffee. But there was a strange perfume in the smoky air, an overpowering scent of passive resignation. He was acutely aware of the seconds ticking past. As he stood there by the door, their lives and his life dribbled away continuously, in fragments of time that were tiny, yet easily measured by the cheapest clock. He felt as if he were looking at a waiting room full of people who had absolutely nowhere to go, and were beyond caring.

He bought two jelly donuts and a take-out Styrofoam cup of coffee from a dead-eyed kid wearing six tiny gold hoops in his ear. As the kid bagged the donuts, Ross told him he used to be a cop, had an addiction. The kid stared across the counter at him with caution and disdain. Outside, Ross spilled an inch of coffee into the gutter and began walking back the way he had come.

A woman in her mid-teens pushed a double stroller past him. She wore a wedding ring. You could see the flash of the diamond, if you looked close. She was a blonde. Ditto the kids. She wore a hip-length rain jacket in a glossy black fabric, tight jeans. He watched her hips move as she shoved the stroller through that part of her life, the one grid in a billion that the two of them happened to share. She was a good-looking girl, but how long would that last? Man, he'd put in five hard years, but she was looking at eighteen to twenty.

He came upon an entrance to the graveyard, stone pillars flanking an iron gate. He leaned against a damp column of stone, eating and drinking. Nipping and sipping.

When he was a kid, twelve or thirteen years old, he'd been in the kitchen one day after school, talking to his mother while she prepared dinner. She was at the counter, slicing carrots, and he was standing by the fridge. The gas stove was about midway between them. Suddenly the lid rose off a stainless-steel pot full of mashed potatoes, shot a foot into the air and crashed down on the stove. A split-second later, a double handful of mashed potatoes curved up out of the pot and flew six feet across the kitchen, landing at his astonished mother's feet. They could find no explanation for this phenomenon. Nothing like it had happened before and nothing like it ever happened again.

Did Ross believe in spirits? Yeah, kind of.

He swallowed the last of the second jelly donut, wiped his mouth and hands with a paper napkin, stuffed the napkin into the empty Styrofoam cup and shoved the cup deep into the hedge that surrounded the graveyard.

He stepped through the gate. Now that he was here, where was he? A middle-aged guy who was pruning shrubbery set aside his shears long enough to explain to Ross that he needed to find a man named Mr. Oswald, that it was Oswald's responsibility to show visitors how to get where they wanted to go, find whoever they were looking for. The guy pointed out a small stone building that stood at the crest of a miniature hill, far off in the distance.

Mr. Oswald was in his mid-sixties. He wore round wire-rim glasses that were a little too small for his face. His eyes were the colour of pre-washed jeans. His mousy brown hair sat on his head as if it would rather be almost anywhere else. His drab grey cardigan was home to a wide variety of buttons. His shirt collar had curled in on itself. His pants looked like Tweedledum's hand-me-downs. Mr. Oswald smacked his plump lips when he spoke, made a sound like someone tramping aggressively through a bog. But the habit so remarkably suited his character that Ross found it inoffensive.

There was a large-scale map of the cemetery on the wall, numbered grave sites, an alphabetical list of the tenants.

Ross told Oswald he wanted to view the gravesite of his brother, Garret Mosby.

"Oh yes, Garret. A new arrival. We have a few murderers staying here, but not many." Oswald gave Ross a sharp look. "I was unaware the boy had a brother."

Ross held his ground. "Well, he does. And it's me." Oswald came out from behind his desk with all the grace of a bumper car. He took Ross's hand, led him outside and pointed at the tangled branches of an oak tree about a hundred yards' distant.

"Do you see that tree? The oak tree?"

Ross nodded.

"In your opinion, is that a well-tended tree?"

"It looks dead, from here."

Oswald's smile was dotted with sesame seeds, tiny chunks of all-beef patty, a sliver of lettuce. He said, "No, the tree's doing fine. There's buds on it. A couple of months from now it'll be buried in shiny green leaves. What I'm talking about, I'm referring to the branches. Look closely. Notice how some of the branches point inwards? That is not an introspective tree. Charles pruned that tree, and he did it all wrong." Unsubtle pressure on Ross's arm turned him about eighty degrees. "Do you see that fellow over there, by the boxwood hedge?"

Ross nodded. It was the guy who'd given him directions.

"That's Charles. My son, my only child. The fruit of my loins. I *told* him what he'd done wrong. I *asked* him to try again. He flatly refused. Now I've got to do it myself, and fall off a ladder and break a leg. That or hire someone else to do the job, and pay for it out of my own pocket." Oswald gave Ross's arm a friendly squeeze. "Is that fair?"

"Not really."

Oswald stared bitterly at his son across the gently rolling lawn. After a moment he said, "There's only the two of us. Everybody else is dead."

Ross trudged down a narrow asphalt path. Garret had come to rest just past the mighty oak. His grave was marked by a homely slab of stone just large enough to fit in his full name and birthdate and the day he'd died. Garret had lived fast and died young. Or maybe a better word was immature. *He lived fast and died immature.* Somehow the reworked phrase didn't have nearly the same weight.

Ross lit a cigarette, dropped the match on the damp grass. He tried to imagine what might be left of Garret, in a year or so. Bones. Scraps of cloth. The plastic buttons on his shirt would last a thousand years. In a thousand years people would excavate the site and scratch their heads as they tried to make sense of all those headstones, all those buttons.

When Ross died, he wanted to be cremated. Shoved feet-first

into a blast furnace and reduced to a tidy pile of ashes. Better a quick burn than slow decay. But imagine the soul waking up at the moment he burst into flames, the soul assuming it had gone straight to hell. Ross stood there, the toe of his shoe resting on the slab, smoke leaking from the corner of his mouth. He imagined the flames racing through his coffin, that fragile shell collapsing soundlessly. Poof! went his gelled hair. His big green eyes disappeared in a puff of steam. His clothes were swallowed by the fire. *Ya gimme fever.* The marrow boiled in his bones. At what temperature would his skull spontaneously ignite? Bright beads of steel dripped into his thighs as the zipper of his black suit melted.

Ross sat down to avoid falling over. He felt the gathered coldness of the headstone suck the heat from his body, and he wondered, for the first time, what fate had befallen the biker he'd stabbed back there on the wrong side of the wall. The guy had been a loner, lucky for Ross. No friends, no family.

He glanced around. Distance had reduced Oswald's truculent son to the size of a bug.

Maybe the place got busy on weekends, when people had a little leisure time to dispose of. He shifted his hips, making himself as comfortable as the unforgiving stone allowed. He mashed the smoking butt of his cigarette into the grass, and lit another. Garret had died because his body had failed him. Something had gone wrong, and he'd died. What a devastatingly simple equation.

A sudden hunger for easy money turned Ross's gut into a tight knot. Two hundred and twenty grand. Did Shannon have it? He took a deep breath, held it for a moment and let it out in a rush. Sometimes it was better to turn your back on things, but all too often it was impossible to do what was best.

He walked as far as Main Street, caught a bus that took him to Broadway and then sprinted across the street against the light and flashed his transfer as he brushed past the driver of another bus. He sat at the back, in a window seat, and was carried west on Broadway for mile upon mile, to the intersection of Broadway and

Maple. There was an IGA next to the liquor store where the assault on the armoured car had taken place.

Garret had told him the store was a Safeway. The IGA must've been a Safeway, back then. The main thing was that the liquor store was right where it was supposed to be, and so was the 7-Eleven. Ross remembered what Garret had told him about the shootout. He smiled, as he pictured the fat guy who'd tried to hide behind a case of beer. But it wasn't all that funny, was it?

Ross saw the bright muzzle-flashes, heard the volley of shots, the shouts and screams. A stray bullet smacked into the liquor store's plate-glass window, spewed fragments of glass across a radius of thirty feet. Clerks hit the deck. A .357 Magnum hollow-point had silenced the fat guy who'd taken cover behind his beer. Ross's finger twitched as Billy pulled his shotgun's trigger. Garret shot from the hip. Loads of steel double-ought buckshot slammed into the two uniformed guards and knocked the life out of them, murdered them where they stood. He watched them collapse, saw their bodies sprawl across the snow.

Ross walked unsteadily to the curb. He reached out and pushed the pedestrian crosswalk button. Traffic slipped past, and then the light changed to yellow and then red. Four lanes of traffic ground to a halt. An orange hand, palm out, metamorphosed into a pure white dancer. Ross stepped off the curb, down memory lane.

The armoured-car guard was resurrected, shot dead a second time, slid nose-first across the bloody slush. Garret reloaded the shotgun, scrambled into the stolen Caddy. Billy hung onto a canvas bag stuffed full of money. He knelt by the open door, and chucked his biscuits. Sirens. Man, they were running out of time. Garret reached out and grabbed a handful of Billy's jacket, yanked him into the Caddy and punched it. They fishtailed across the parking lot, all of Garret's weight on the gas pedal. They shot past the armoured car, the flank of the vehicle almost close enough to touch. A red light flashed. The driver's-side door suddenly flew open, the protruding muzzle of a shotgun swung towards him.

His night vision was shredded by explosions of fire. He was deafened by the shriek of metal, as the Caddy absorbed multiple
fistfuls of buckshot. Both side windows and then the rear window
blew out. He was staggered by a heavy punch on the shoulder.
Razor-wire flailed at the wound. Blood splashed across his cheek.
The Caddy deflected off a parked car and across Maple, accelerated into the cinderblock wall of the 7-Eleven.

A horn blared. Ross discovered himself standing in the middle
of the intersection. The light had changed. A silver-haired woman
in a matching BMW had him in her sights. He jogged over to the
sidewalk. A skinny girl with starved eyes stared at him as she
walked past.

Man, oh man, he'd been right there, and barely made it back.

He crossed Maple, strolled across the strip of asphalt in front
of the 7-Eleven. He studied the cinderblock wall. No way you
could tell a stolen Coupe De Ville had punched right through
there, put its shiny grill up against the Slurpee machine.

Ross went around to the front, walked inside. He bought cigarettes from the girl behind the counter. As he accepted his change
he asked her if this was the place where the gas pumps blew up, a
few years ago.

She gave him a puzzled look, as if she hoped he was kidding,
but wasn't about to bet the farm on it. But then, the crime had
gone down more than five years ago. What front-liner in the
7-Eleven organization ever hung in there for that kind of seniority?

Man, he'd rather spend a year in jail than ten minutes wearing
one of those ugly corporate jackets. He went outside, stripped
the cellophane wrapper off the cigarettes, let the wrapper and
inner foil drop to the oil-stained asphalt. A guy going inside gave
him a black-hearted look. Littering. Was there a more heinous
crime? Ross gave the guy that same look right back, in spades.
He lit up, drew the smoke deep into his lungs. He was scheduled
to start his new life as a dishwasher at five and he'd been told
to show up at least an hour early, his first day at work. He was

hungry. By the time he'd found a restaurant and had something to eat, it'd be time to go to work.

Brillo's – Ross's new home away from home – was located in the newly hip neighbourhood of Yaletown. Located just south of the downtown core, Yaletown had originally been a warehouse district. The area had languished for decades, until the adjacent waterfront acreage on the north side of False Creek was sold at a criminally low price to a canny Hong Kong developer. Decades of industrial pollution had made the waterfront lethally toxic. Following the land's sale, many thousands of tons of contaminated soil had been trucked to the suburbs. Fresh soil was trucked in. In jig time the waterfront was declared safe for development. A dozen pricey highrise condominium towers emerged mushroom-sudden on the site, and were nearly toppled by a tsunami of eager buyers. Predictably, the development's success fuelled neighbouring Yaletown's revitalization. *Aletown*, some of the locals called it.

By the time Ross found the place, it was closing in on five. He loitered outside the double-glazed plate-glass windows. Though it was early, the wining and dining had already begun. The people inside were for the most part about his age, or younger, expensively dressed, smiling hard enough to bruise their faces. A happy couple brushed past Ross and hurried inside. The scent of expensive perfume made him twitch. A sudden burst of laughter rolled like mock-thunder across the gleaming, sharp-edged landscape.

A guy about twenty years old materialized out of the shadows. His face was shiny and hard. He wore a tuxedo. The way his pointy shoes reflected the light made them look as if they were made of water. A plastic nametag identified him as *Robert at your service*. Ross figured him for a car-shuffler. He showed no teeth as he asked Ross if he could help him.

Ross said, "Maybe. Go ahead, see what you can do."

Robert's face clouded over. "No, what I mean is, may I ask you what you're doing here?" He shifted his feet, getting himself squared away for imminent conflict. "What I'm saying, maybe you should beat it."

In the slammer, back there on the high side of the wall, Ross wouldn't have had much choice. The rule was: Do to, or be done to. But out here, it was different. Wasn't it? He took a deep, shuddery breath, shoved his hands in his pockets and said, "I'm the new guy. I got a job in the kitchen."

"Doing what?"

"Scrubbing pots."

Robert was an inch or two shorter than Ross but still found a way to smile down at him. Grinning, the car jockey pointed towards an open door that lit up a rectangle of alley, a battered dumpster. Ross gritted his teeth. He told himself he was a damn lucky felon, that scouring muck out of king-size pots was a fine way to earn a dollar. Fate in the guise of the parole board had blessed him in ways he could scarcely comprehend.

He walked himself into the square of light and took the three wooden steps one at a time, all the way to the doorway. Inside, the lights were bright and people were moving fast.

Ross's immediate superior was emaciated, unshaven, foul-mouthed and cavern-chested. His name was Orville, and it quickly became apparent that he cared nothing for any part of the world that wasn't a pot or pan. Ross was issued with knee-high rubber boots, a thick rubber apron and rubber-duck-yellow gloves that covered his arms to his elbows. He was led to a sink the size of a small bathtub, full to the brim with foul-smelling, steamy-hot water. A variety of primitive cleaning instruments hung from nails sunk into the wall above the sink. On the counter, several tons of metal and muck awaited his pleasure.

Orville lit a home-rolled cigarette. "What'd you do?"

"About what?"

Orville blew smoke in his face, sneered.

Ross said, "I punched a guy in a bar."

"Yeah?" Orville flicked ash into the sink. "You start anything around here, we ain't gonna phone the cops. We'll take care of you our own selves, get what I mean?"

"Sure," said Ross.

"Beat the piss out of you and toss you in the dumpster," said Orville with a threatening leer. Ross lowered his fists into the water and swam carefully around, made quacking sounds too soft for Orville to hear.

At a few minutes past ten, Orville grudgingly told him he was entitled to take half an hour for lunch. Ross hadn't thought to bring anything to eat, not that he had an appetite. The stench of grease and the sour knowledge that he was the lowest grunt on the totem pole had kept his stomach in knots all night long. Man, even the busboy had snubbed him.

He stepped outside. It was raining again, surprise, surprise. He leaned against the cold flank of the dumpster, shucked his gloves and thrust them in the back pocket of his jeans. His hands were ghostly white. His skin felt soft and pulpy. He wiggled his aching fingers and lit his first smoke since he'd started work. He flinched as he heard a fresh load of pots clatter down on the counter by the sink. There was a monstrous iron frying pan with a notch-shaped chunk missing from the handle that he'd already washed seven times. He didn't know what the frying pan was used for, but it always came back containing unidentifiable lumps of food burned black and crispy, clinging like glue.

Ross knew that when he finally went home and tumbled into bed he was going to see that frying pan in his dreams. The tip of his cigarette glowed bright as he sucked smoke deep into his lungs. Close behind him, someone coughed delicately, as if to gain his attention. He turned and looked.

A vertical bar of white materialized out of the darkness. A pale oval gradually took the shape of Robert's grinning face. He had somebody with him – another kid in a cheap rental tux. They walked slowly toward him until, all too soon, they were a little too close for comfort.

The other guy's nose had been broken over and mended at an angle. Ross read his name tag. *Ted at your service.*

"Got a smoke?"

Ross kept his eyes wide open as he fished the pack out of his shirt pocket. Robert snatched the pack away and skimmed it into the dumpster. Five bucks, gone.

Ted grinned crookedly. "Wrong brand, asshole."

Ross stepped back a pace. He jumped, clawed his way up on top of the dumpster. The bin was pretty full. No bottles, because the restaurant recycled its glass. But there was plenty of other stuff to choose from. Ross retrieved his cigarettes, shoved them into his shirt pocket. He wriggled intó his gloves and grabbed a double handful of vegetable sludge, and let fire. The gooey muck hit *Robert at your service* smack in the cummerbund. A complicated process of emotional osmosis wiped the grin right off his face. Ross dipped his hand into the garbage, reared back and fired. His face splattered with a kilo or more of something evil-smelling and viscous, *Ted at your service* backed away, stumbled and fell. Ross bailed out on the far side of the dumpster. In his apron and rubber boots, he clumsily hotfooted it down the alley.

He put three blocks between himself and the restaurant, sagged against a wall. When his breathing had steadied he crossed the street to a payphone, got the restaurant's number from the operator-computer, dropped a quarter. The phone rang once, and was picked up by a woman with a Québécois accent.

Ross identified himself. He asked the woman to tell Orville that he was a quitter.

She said there was somebody who wanted to talk to him, and asked him to please hold a minute.

Ross said *merci* but no thanks. He slammed the receiver into its cradle almost hard enough to break it, because a guy he'd met in the joint had advised him the vibrations would shake loose his quarter.

No such luck.

6

Annie was furious. She'd handed in the wrong French assignment and her teacher had insisted that she and a dozen of her classmates come in after school to catch up. How could so many of them have misunderstood the situation? Who lacked the necessary communication skills, the students or the teacher? Her anger flared to rage when her finished work was rejected because it had been written on lined rather than unlined paper.

Claire said, "I know it isn't much consolation, Annie, but you have to remember that teachers are just like everybody else – some are good and some are better than good, and some aren't much good at all."

But Annie wouldn't be mollified. "She's a horrible old *bitch*!" she hissed, slamming her textbooks down on the dining-room table so hard that the salt and pepper shakers jumped.

Claire turned away to hide her smile. As a rule, gritty language wasn't countenanced in the Willows household. But Jack was on the phone in his den, and Annie had a point. At the beginning of the year, that same French teacher's first assignment had been to have the students make protective paper jackets for their textbooks. Annie's had been functional but apparently not sufficiently snug-fitting. She'd lost ten marks right off the bat, and, unfortunately, the battle lines had been drawn. Parker gave Annie a quick hug. She said, "I'm making tea. Would you like a cup?"

"Yeah, sure." Annie brightened. Coffee was still forbidden, but as a result of intense and unrelenting lobbying she was allowed the odd cup of tea. They went into the kitchen. Parker wasn't exactly an *aficionado*. Her idea of a good cuppa "char" was a Red Rose teabag dunked in her favourite mug. Annie, on the other hand, had embraced the culture with typical no-holds-barred enthusiasm. She'd organized a trip to a health-food store on Fourth Avenue, and bought a bewildering variety of exotic mini-packs. Today's choice was relatively conservative: blackberry. Claire added a few grains of sugar. She and Annie sat across from each other at the kitchen table.

Claire said, "So tell me, how's your love life?"

Annie blushed prettily. The previous weekend she and David had dated for the first time. They'd gone to a movie, and then on to a White Spot for a burger. David had driven Annie home on the stroke of her midnight deadline, but declined her invitation to come in to meet her father. Parker didn't blame the kid. When David's car had pulled up in front of the house, Willows had been standing at the window. Squinting into the night, hands on his hips, he'd been the very picture of parental wrath.

Annie said, "David's okay. Too much of a jock, maybe . . ."

"How do you mean?"

"I dunno." Annie shrugged. She turned her mug in a half-circle, and back again. "He spends a lot of time with the guys. Shooting baskets in the gym, chugging around the track . . ."

"Chugging?" Claire smiled.

Annie said, "Well, that wasn't fair. I guess what I'm saying is that he spends a lot of time doing physical stuff, but he isn't interested at all in . . ." Annie trailed off, frowning.

"The academic side of things?"

Annie laughed. "Not exactly. But it's kind of boring, talking about sports all the time."

"How are his grades?"

"Okay, I guess. Kind of average."

"He's in grade eleven, isn't he? So he's only got another year of school. What's he going to do after he graduates?"

"He has no idea."

Claire sipped her tea. "Well, there's nothing wrong with that, I suppose. Kids are under so much pressure these days. Anyway, it's not as if he asked you to marry him."

Annie's eyes sparkled.

Claire said, "I hope."

A hinge creaked as the front door swung open. Claire leaned back in her chair to look down the hall. Sean waved negligently as he shut the door. The new cat, Tripod, hurried towards the kitchen. From the end of the hall Sean yelled, "Didn't you hear him meowing?"

Annie said, "I just let him out ten minutes ago."

Sean gave her an accusatory, disbelieving look. He shucked his black leather jacket and slung it across the banister, stomped down the hall towards her and then veered abruptly into his bedroom. His door slammed shut.

Annie said, "The thing is, David's really cute, but I hardly ever get to see him alone. He's always got a bunch of his dumb jock friends with him."

"Maybe you should dump him."

"Are you serious?"

"No, I'm kidding." Claire reached out and lightly ruffled Annie's hair. "*You're* the serious one, my dear."

Because of the nature of their work, and the fact that they were often away from home for long hours at a stretch, both Willows and Parker were in the habit of preparing meals in advance, and freezing them for future reference. While Annie did her homework, Parker used the microwave to thaw a pre-cooked Irish stew. She put the stew in a stainless-steel pot and set the pot on the stove to simmer. Technically, there might not be any difference between microwave and gas-generated heat, but somehow food heated on the stove always tasted better than if it had been heated by invisible rays in a plastic box.

While the stew warmed up, she made a salad of iceberg lettuce, red onion, radishes and a hothouse tomato, mushrooms and grated carrot. Barney mewed at the back door, and she took a minute to let him in. He and Tripod touched noses. Barney went over to his dish and began to eat. Tripod crouched on the floor behind him and batted at his tail. Barney was missing most of his left ear, and Tripod had only three legs, but the two cats were so similar in colour and size that they might have come from the same litter. But Barney was noted for his sulks, and was a slow and careful eater, while Tripod, who was younger and led a more active life despite his disability, was known for his sharp appetite. Shortly after Tripod had joined the family, Parker tried putting his food in a steep-sided bowl identical to Barney's. The cat had cried piteously, until finally Parker caved in and gave him a bowl of his own – a larger one.

She fetched down bottles of oil and vinegar from the shelf, pulped several cloves of garlic.

Jack walked into the kitchen, looking tense. He checked out the stew on his way to the fridge. "Want a beer?"

"I'll split one with you."

He got a glass out of the dishwasher, poured a short half into the glass and put the glass down on the counter next to the salad bowl.

Claire said, "Did I hear the phone ring, about half an hour ago?"

He nodded, nibbled at his beer.

Claire added a pinch of chives and twist of pepper to the salad dressing. She wiped her hands on a dishtowel, picked up her glass and clicked it against Jack's beer bottle. "Should I drive down to the phone booth by the IGA, drop a quarter and give you call?"

He frowned. "You mean, would I be more communicative if it wasn't so easy to communicate?" He drank some more beer. "That was my lawyer, Peter Singer."

"Really?" Claire leaned against the kitchen counter. "What did he want?"

"In his office this morning, I told him I hadn't spoken to Sheila in several months, and had no idea where she was. He was just confirming that I hadn't made any attempt to get in touch with her." Jack hesitated, and then said, "He gave me the impression he thought there might be something I wasn't telling him."

"Is there?"

"No, of course not!" The question had caught Jack by surprise. He said, "What the hell is that supposed to mean?"

"Nothing. I was just asking. Maybe she sent you a change of address and you chucked it in the garbage, instead of passing it on to the kids. I don't know." Claire gave the jar of homemade salad dressing a vigorous shake. "Let's not argue, okay? Dinner's just about ready. Would you mind setting the table?"

Sean ate in his room. Annie's mind was on her homework. Jack kept his eyes on his plate. Claire wasn't hungry, but forced herself to eat. As she picked at her food, her anger faded. It wasn't like Jack to flare up, go all emotional on her just because she asked him an innocent question. He had to be very worried about his wife. Three months was a long time, for someone who made a point of keeping in touch. Why hadn't Sheila's parents kicked up a fuss? She wondered if Jack was afraid he'd alienate her by expressing his concern about Sheila's uncharacteristic silence.

She glanced up, and caught him staring at her. He lowered his eyes. Her stomach twisted into a knot. She carried her dirty dishes into the kitchen and stuffed them in the dishwasher. Sean had cranked his damn stereo up so loud that the thump of the bass rumbled through the walls. She slammed the dishwasher door. Dishes clattered.

From the dining room, Annie yelled, "*Qu'est-que c'est le bruit?*"

Claire punched buttons, turned away from the machine and there was Jack, looking embarrassed and apologetic.

She said, "I'm feeling claustrophobic. Why don't we go out for a drink a little later?"

"Two drinks." He smiled faintly. "Maybe three."

"Three for you and one for me," she amended. "I'll be the designated driver."

"You drive me crazy," he said, and leaned into her and kissed her lightly on the mouth.

Willows had introduced Parker to Freddy's the night they'd wrapped up their first murder, eight years earlier. Willows drank at Freddy's because it was the only bar he knew where he could drink for free. Or, if Freddy was feeling the pinch, at a greatly discounted rate. Freddy had slowed down during the past few years. When Willows had first met him he'd been a musician, a piano player who toured the bars and had a richly deserved rep as a guy who liked to mingle. It was Freddy's fondness for women – especially other men's women – that had resulted in him being chained by a cuckolded gangster to a radiator in a cheap hotel, where the three middle fingers of his left hand had been reduced to bloody mush in a high-speed blender. Freddy was tough, but not that tough. Even Liberace played with all ten digits.

Freddy had fainted, been slapped around until he revived. Willows and Norm Burroughs had kicked in the door just as Freddy was about to lose an appendage that was, in a non-geographical sense, much closer to his heart than his fingers. Freddy's gratitude had been all but boundless. He'd promised the two detectives free drinks for as long as they lived. Burroughs had died of cancer two years later; Willows was still collecting interest on Freddy's self-induced debt.

Freddy expertly hooked a bottle of Cutty down from the shelf as Willows and Parker came in through the door. His wedding ring glittered on his thumb. He nodded in acknowledgement as Willows pointed at a rear booth, then pursed his lips and blew Parker a furtive, mildly comical kiss. "Want something to eat, kids? I got a special on hot wings . . ."

Parker frowned as she breezed past the glitter of the bar. "Something to eat, a special on hot wings . . . What's the connection, Freddy?"

Freddy was still chuckling over Parker's little joke when he served their drinks: a double Cutty on the rocks for Willows and a single, straight up, water on the side, for Parker.

"Thanks, Freddy." Willows dropped a twenty on the table. It was an important part of the ritual. Neither Freddy nor Willows were the kind of people who liked to take things for granted – nor cared much for people who did.

Freddy ignored the money, but lingered. The scar tissue on his maimed hand gleamed like old ivory in the bar's subdued light. He had the look of a man who had something to say, but didn't know how to spit it out.

Parker said, "Something on your mind, Freddy?"

Encouraged, Freddy slid into the booth beside her. Parker shifted, giving herself as much room as was available. Freddy fiddled with the wide-splayed collar of his tight-fitting, custom-made red-triangles-on-a-field-of-black silk shirt. He adjusted a gold-plated cuff link to enhance it's light-reflecting qualities.

Ice rattled against Willows' teeth.

Freddy spread his arms wide, in a gesture of abject helplessness and supplication. He scratched his nose.

Parker and Willows exchanged a glance.

Freddy sighed wearily.

Parker studied her glass. She raised the glass to her lips, sipped, held the alcohol in her mouth, swirled it around and swallowed, felt it burn as it went down. Yummy.

Freddy cleared his throat. "There was a guy in here this afternoon, no more'n three or four hours ago. Askin' about you." His eyes darted around like fish in an aquarium.

"Asking what?" said Willows.

Freddy shrugged. "I dunno. Various questions. This guy, he waltzes in, takes a seat at the bar, all friendly and relaxed. Said he was looking for you, heard this's where you liked to do your drinking." Freddy risked a furtive smile. "He didn't ask *why* you drank here. I don't know what I would've told him, if he did . . ."

"What did he want to know, Freddy?"

"Let's see now." Freddy rubbed the stumps of his fingers. "He asked me, Jack spend much time in here? Come in every night? That sort of thing . . ."

"How much I drink, in other words."

"Yeah, could be. And what kind of people you drink with, or are you the type of guy prefers to drink alone."

"What'd you tell him?"

"I told him the truth, Jack." Freddy's attitude had turned belligerently righteous, and it wasn't a very good fit. He added, "All I can say, I hope you ain't got something to hide."

Parker said, "Why'd you bother to give this guy the time of day, Freddy? What did he look like? Did you get his name?"

"Yeah, sure, of course I got his name!" Agitated, Freddy lifted a hip, plucked his wallet out of his pants pocket, withdrew an off-white business card embossed with blue and gold lettering. He grunted softly as he leaned across the table. He propped the card against Willows' glass. Bobby Dundas. "Know him, Jack?" asked Freddy.

"Yeah, I know him." Bobby's character, or lack of character, had been shaped by the years he'd spent in vice. Jack had never really liked Bobby; now he liked him even less. Willows emptied his glass. He turned the card towards Parker, then dropped it in his glass and handed the glass to Freddy.

"Want another?"

Willows nodded.

"Me too," said Parker. She waited until Freddy was out of earshot and then said, "What's he up to, Jack?"

"Beats me. Nothing I'd approve of, I bet." Willows stood up. "Back in a minute." He strolled over to the bar. Freddy was industriously wiping a shot glass, and had his back to him. He knuckled the polished mahogany. Freddy glanced up, registered him in the mirror. Willows said, "You've got *my* card too, Freddy." Freddy nodded. Willows said, "Next time my inquisitive friend walks through that door, pick up the phone and call me. Understand?"

Freddy turned so he was facing Willows. He said, "Yeah, I

understand." He thumped a matched pair of lowball glasses down on the bar, wiped sweat from his hands with a small white towel.

Willows stared hard at Freddy until finally Freddy looked at him, and then he said, "The guy's bad news, Freddy. Don't talk to him."

"Got it, Jack."

By way of apology, Freddy poured four fingers of whisky into both glasses. *Quadruples.* Willows was slightly cheered.

Parker watched him closely as he walked towards her, glasses in hand. He sat down, pushed a glass towards her. Parker said, "If I drink all that, it's going to carry me into the land of maudlin."

Willows smiled.

She said, "Is there any way Bobby might've got wind of the fact that you've got a problem with Sheila?"

"No way."

Willows knocked back about a quarter of his drink. He felt flushed, short of breath. Was he angry, or merely getting drunk? Three months. He said, "I should give her parents a call . . ."

He looked miserable. Guilty and angry. Parker reached across the table. She squeezed his arm. "It's a two-way street, Jack. You didn't phone her, but she didn't phone you, either."

Willows checked his watch. It was pushing ten o'clock. There was a three-hour time difference between Vancouver and Toronto. Sheila's parents would have gone to bed a couple of hours ago. He imagined the population of the country strictly in terms of time. In the West, people were drinking in bars, having a good time. Move across the prairies and they were yawning. A little further east they were in their pyjamas, brushing their teeth. And in Ontario and *la belle province* the citizens were dreaming sweetly, counting sheep.

He said, "Sheila's parents must know where she is. If they were worried about her, they'd have called by now."

"Good point," said Parker.

"You agree?"

"Certainly." Parker realized that she was choosing her words

with a view to their slurrability quotient. Was she drunk? She
didn't really care. Which was irrefutable truth that she was
definitely extremely drunk. The knowledge sobered her. She
turned in her seat so she could look directly behind her.

Willows said, "Something wrong?"

Parker gingerly shook her head, no.

It was a lie, and she rarely lied to him. But how could she satis-
factorily explain that she'd expected to find Bobby Dundas standing right behind her, close enough to touch?

7

That night, Ross got home late. The next morning, he slept in even later. When he finally did drag himself out of bed and into the kitchen, he found a box of Cap'n Crunch, a clean bowl with a spoon in it, a plastic tumbler and the sugar bowl neatly laid out at his usual place at the red Formica table. All that was missing was a map showing him the way to the refrigerator.

Ross sagged into a chair. Was he still a kid? In his sweet mother's time-addled mind, yes. And he doubted he had the slightest hope of growing a single day older.

He ripped open the box and spilled cereal into the bowl. His stomach growled. He went over to the fridge. Two-per-cent milk. Was that an oxymoron? He'd have to look it up. He poured milk over the cereal, filled the unbreakable plastic tumbler, grabbed the sugar bowl and tilted it over the cereal, gave the bowl a gentle shake. As he sat hunched over his breakfast he saw that his mother had, on his behalf, dropped two slices of white bread into the toaster.

Ross pushed the bowl of Cap'n Crunch as far away from him as his arms could manage. He tossed his spoon into the sink and got busy scouting the house for loose change.

Outside, it was raining again. Ross, standing in the scant shelter of the porch, turned up the collar of his black leather jacket. He lit a cigarette. Blue smoke tiptoed gingerly into the rain, and was cut to shreds.

Nothing moved but the rain. He smoked his cigarette to the filter and trotted down the porch steps, jumped the front-yard gate and sprinted down the street towards the bus stop. The bus stop offered no shelter; it was nothing but a post with the words BUS STOP painted on it. But there was a beige station wagon parked on the street only a few steps away. Happy day, the car was unlocked.

Ross climbed into the back seat. He sat quietly, smoking. From time to time he wiped condensation from the window. Finally the bus materialized in the rearview mirror. He dumped a handful of pennies and nickels into the hopper, demanded and received a transfer.

That bus and another just like it took him downtown. En route, he picked up a black umbrella with a wooden handle that was left behind by a man who'd almost missed his stop. Cruising along Georgia, his new umbrella protecting him from the downpour, he remembered a restaurant he used to patronize, all those years ago. The place was still there, pretty much as he remembered it, though the name had changed. He sat in a window booth. The restaurant was sunk below street level. A woman hurried by on the sidewalk, and he found himself sneaking a peek up her skirt. A waitress arrived with a menu. Ross ordered coffee, scrambled eggs, hash browns and sausages, toast. The girl was a little on the thin side, but cute. His age or maybe a year or two younger. Her spiky pink hair went well with her complexion. If her plastic nametag could be believed, her name was Puffy. She blessed Ross with a heart-breaker of a smile, oyster-perfect teeth. She asked him if he'd like to start with a glass of orange juice.

"Yeah, sure."

"What size you want?"

"Large," said Ross magnanimously. Another short skirt hurried past. The ladies were keeping close to the building, to avoid the rain. This time, he was careful not to exploit the view.

He kept an eye on the waitress as she made her way back to the kitchen to place his order. She wore a silk shirt that almost matched her hair, tight black jeans, heavy black boots. She turned and glanced back at him. He gave her a big smile, and she quickly looked away. So much for irresistible charm.

Another waitress arrived with his orange juice and coffee. She told him his breakfast would be along in a few minutes. Ross was subdued. It wasn't even noon, and he'd looked up a strange woman's skirt and terrified an innocent waitress. He drank most of his orange juice, and then the rest of it. He drank some coffee. His food arrived. He picked up his knife and fork, remembered the napkin, and what was expected of him. He put the cutlery back down on the table, shook out the napkin to its full expanse and laid it across his thigh.

Puffy blind-sided him as he pushed the blade of his knife into a sausage. She said, "You like k.d. lang?"

Ross had been caught by surprise. He chewed and swallowed. "Who're you talking about?"

Puffy threw back her head and laughed a little too loudly, for someone who was supposed to be working. "k.d. lang. The singer."

"Uh, right."

"You like her? I mean, d'you like her singing?"

"Yeah, sure." Ross sounded a little limp, even to himself. He added, "She's great."

"I like her too," said Puffy, smiling and laughing.

"Good."

"*I like her an awful lot,*" said Puffy, and got up and walked away, her hips hardly moving at all.

What was that supposed to mean? Ross made a mental note to look it up somewhere. He stabbed his fork into his eggs.

When the bill arrived he was astounded to discover that the orange juice alone was two-twenty-five. For a glass of orange juice! Add a dollar-ten for the coffee, five-ninety-five for the eggs and sausages. Ross dropped a ten on the table and walked swiftly towards the door. He was going broke fast. He needed a job.

Or some other, easier way of making money.

Digesting, Ross walked briskly east on Georgia for two or three blocks and then veered towards the new downtown library, which to his untutored eye looked like a really big sand castle artfully crossbred with a fragment of a Roman coliseum. Sort of like a left-over *Star Trek* set. One of those not-quite-parallel-universe situations. He strolled across a forecourt of interlocking concrete paving blocks, subtly guided by the architecture towards a wall of plate-glass doors. The joint was locked up tight. Ross lit a cigarette. The first thing you learned in the slammer was to keep your back to a wall. The second thing was how to wait. At 9:59 a security guard wearing scuffed black boots unlocked the first of the two sets of double glass doors. The library was open for business, and Ross was first in line. He'd decided to research the armoured-car robbery. He wanted to learn how much of what Garret had told him was truth, and how much was lies.

Entering, he discovered that the building was indeed huge. More paving blocks curved gently away into the distance. To his left there was a row of small shops, including a coffee bar, pizza joint, a Duthie Books store. To his right, a wall of glass opened on the main floor of the library.

He pushed open another glass door, and walked into the library proper. The place was maybe a bit too brightly lit. At the information desk he asked an elderly man wearing shiny bronze pants and a gold shirt and gold-rim glasses where he could find back issues of newspapers, microfiche machines. The old man leaned towards him. Was he hard of hearing, or about to fall over? His belly sagged into the protruding edge of the counter.

The man's brow cleared. "Third floor. Turn right as you exit the elevator. There's an information desk. You'll see the sign." He said something else, that Ross couldn't quite hear.

Ross said, "What?"

The old man's glasses slipped down his nose. In the act of pushing them back where they belonged, he seemed to lose track of Ross's existence.

Ross took an elevator to the third floor, asked a woman talking furtively into the telephone for directions. She pointed without bothering to look at him. He followed the line of her finger. The machines were not far off. They looked like primitive televisions.

He found another librarian, a middle-aged woman wearing a heavy gold bracelet and glasses far too large for her face. He explained that he needed back issues of the *Sun* and *Province* newspapers from January of five years ago. She smiled and led him to a shelf containing hardbound green copies of the *Canadian News Index*. She selected the volume for the year he was looking for, explained that searching for a particular subject was the easiest way to go, and pointed out the beige file cabinets where the spools of microfilm were stored. Ross opened the book. He looked up Crime, then Murder, and finally Homicide. The articles were arranged by province and date.

He borrowed a pen from another librarian and wrote down promising headlines, then went over to the cabinets. The microfilm was stored in individual boxes about twice the size of a cigarette package. He found the six he needed without any trouble.

He shucked his jacket and sat down in front of a machine. A well-dressed, grandmotherly type sat motionless at the adjoining machine, peering at a picture of a long-ago wedding. He turned to his own screen. His blurry image was reflected in the blue-tinted frosted glass. He stared blankly at himself. After a little while another librarian noticed him, and asked if he needed any help.

Ross said, "No, I'm fine."

The librarian hesitated. She was in her fifties, tall and slim. Her hair was short and glossy; chestnut streaked through with darker strands. Ross couldn't fault her for giving him a visual rousting. He had not slept well the previous night, and looked it. He wondered if she dyed her hair. Probably. But did she do it herself at home or go to a salon? He knew from bitter experience that he wasn't all that good at judging character, but believed she was the type who'd prefer to have things done for her, as long as she could afford it. He was considering whether it was a good idea to ask her about this when she walked briskly away.

Ross leaned back in his chair and shut his eyes. When next he took a peek at the world, the elderly woman was gone. Directions for operating the machine, complete with easy-to-follow diagrams, were taped to its flank. It took him about ten minutes to find what he was after. He shifted his chair so he was a little closer to the screen, and began to read the first article.

As he read article after article, he was relieved to discover that Garret's description of the robbery had been remarkably accurate, right down to the smallest detail.

Billy, as he'd made his desperate, blood-soaked run from the scene of the armoured-car robbery to Nancy Crown's opulent waterfront home, could have abandoned the missing two hundred and twenty thousand dollars at any point on the route. Or he might've left it in his getaway car, which had been parked nearby, a down-at-the-heels rustbucket Ford Pinto.

Ross examined a photograph of the car, counted the eleven stylized white arrows pointing at the police bullet holes in the vehicle. Ross kept reading. There were more than twenty articles of varying length, and he read all of them twice, and several of them three or four times.

Travelling west on Point Grey Road, Billy had run into a one-car, one-cop roadblock. Shots had been fired. Billy had crashed the Pinto shortly afterwards, the cop in hot pursuit. There was a picture of the cop. Donald E. Mooney. In his early twenties, a good-looking, clean-cut guy with short black hair, a straight-ahead look. Mooney had been first at the scene of the car crash, but his role from that point on was uncertain. The inference was that he had chased Billy on foot for a block or two, then lost him.

It was surely possible that Mooney had grabbed the bagful of money out of the Pinto and kept his mouth shut about it.

But anyone who had known poor dead Billy, or had taken the time to find out what he had been like, would figure that the kid had held on to his hard-earned loot right up until the moment he died. He'd gone to ground at Nancy Crown's house. It didn't make any sense that he'd head in that direction unless he intended to round up Nancy and head off into the sunset with her. From his point of view, wasn't it likely that a bundle of cash would seem the most plausible reason Nancy might go along with his hare-brained plan? The newspapers had portrayed her as an innocent victim, but Ross had his doubts.

He squinted once again at the lines of type that described Billy's end. That doomed boy had come to grief in the Crowns' swimming pool. Ran through a plate-glass door, bounced his head off the tiles and slid unconscious into the water. There was the merest hint of a suggestion that Nancy's husband, Tyler, might have saved Billy's life if he'd been willing to get his feet wet.

Ross studied Tyler Crown's grainy black-and-white photograph. Tyler was in the money business, but he looked like a pretty tough dude, with those beefy shoulders and that prematurely not-quite-bald, bowling-ball head, barbed-wire eyebrows and the cool, from-the-high-side-of-the-desk look in his eyes. Ross, staring at the photo, considered the possibilities.

Billy had probably dropped the sealed canvas bag full of cash somewhere en route between the armoured car and Nancy Crown's house. The most likely scenario was that he and the money parted ways some time after he abandoned the shot-up Pinto. An incredibly lucky passerby had stumbled across the bag and taken it home to see what was inside. Windfall. Since the money had never been turned in to the authorities, it was safe to assume that the passerby had kept every penny.

Or, the cop, Donald E. Mooney, had stuffed the money in the trunk of his patrol car and was planning early retirement.

Or, Billy still had the cash when he showed up at Nancy's. After he'd taken his header into the pool, the Crowns had taken a few minutes to hide the money somewhere in the house. When the cops asked the traumatized couple about the cash, they lied like snakes.

Ross liked that last plot best, because it explained why Tyler didn't fish Billy out of the swimming pool; if Billy was dead, it drastically reduced the chances of him spilling the beans to the cops.

Ross slipped another roll of microfilm into the machine. He struggled to divine Nancy's nature from the dot-matrix puzzle that was her photograph. What were her strengths, her weaknesses? What gave her pleasure, what might cause her unendurable pain? He leaned back in his chair. What was all this about *recovering* the money? For a minute there, he'd been acting as if he were the original owner. But that was what this exercise was all about, wasn't it – seeing the situation from somebody else's point of view? Slumped in front of the faintly humming microfiche machine, Ross considered the film that had unwound in his brain as he'd approached the 7-Eleven on Broadway.

Rage of gunfire. Screams of the wounded. The shotgun blast shredding the meat and muscle of Garret's shoulder. He'd *felt* the pain. It was as if he'd actually been there at the time, had come back for another look.

Spooky.

He left the library, walked back up Georgia to Granville under a drab, ill-tempered sky. Three busses and a little less than an hour later he disembarked by the Oakridge Shopping Centre. He cut across a parking lot, made his way into the mall. A security guard gave him directions to Zellers. Ross hadn't known what to expect, but felt kind of let down anyway. The store was one of those new-wave, aggressively no-frills places that seemed to be popping up all over. The display shelves were made of grey-painted metal. The linoleum floors obviously hadn't been waxed in years. The merchandise seemed of low quality. He wandered through the sporting-goods and toy departments.

Garret's sweetie looked a lot like her Polaroid. She was working one of six cash registers. She wore a shapeless, dark blue Zellers smock, no makeup that he could detect, no jewellery other than a watch. Ross covertly studied her. She apparently took her job seriously, for none of her customers raised a smile. She turned and looked his way, catching him by surprise. Thinking fast, he scooped up a twelve-inch-tall plastic Batman from a red cardboard bin full of the creatures.

Batman was hollow, a lightweight of only a few ounces. He had a raised seam right down the middle of him, head to toe, where his two halves had been heat-welded at the factory. His features were vaguely Taiwanese. He did not even faintly resemble Michael Keaton or Val Kilmer. His spray-painted eyes were dull and out of focus. His plastic body had no warmth, no flex. The head and his four limbs were locked in position. He was, literally, a stiff. Ross tried to imagine playing with him. It would be like playing with a miniature cadaver. He tossed the Batman back into a bin of identical Batmen.

Shannon glanced up, gave him a sharp look. Was that a cloud that had passed across her pretty eyes? He wandered over, grabbed a plastic container of breath mints from a rack. He put the mints down on the counter. She ran them over an infrared scanner. Eighty-nine cents popped up on the cash register. Ross handed her five dollars; the last of his bankroll. She made change, asked him without looking at him if he wanted a bag.

"No, but you could do something else for me."

She gave him a look she might have been practising all her life, she had it down so perfect.

Ross said, "The thing is, I'm broke, and I need a place to stay."

She reached for the phone by the cash register.

He said, "Don't you recognize me, Shannon?"

She hesitated.

He said, "It's me. Your pen pal. Ross."

Shannon suddenly looked as if she'd been dipped in a great big bucket of bleach. Her face crumpled.

Ross said, "Maybe I should've waited until you got off work . . ."

"No, it's okay." She glanced furtively around. No one was paying them any mind. She said, "You were supposed to call me. I'd almost given up. I thought you'd decided you didn't want to see me . . ."

Ross smiled. "No, that's not it at all. I had some things that I had to take care of . . ."

She stared appraisingly at him, as if trying to figure out if he was as dangerous as she had every right to think he might be. He tried without much hope of success to look honest and dependable, straightforward and true.

She said, "You don't look like the kind of person who would stab someone with a knife."

"I was defending myself. I had no choice. It was him or me, Shannon."

She smiled brightly, fetched her purse from beneath the counter, reached inside, brought out a small black wallet with silver trim. She unzipped the wallet and pulled out a crisp new twenty. "I'm off at seven. There's a dark blue Saab in the parking lot, to your left as you go out." She handed him the twenty. "In the meantime, maybe you'd like something to eat."

A middle-aged couple approached the cash register, wanting to buy a pair of gum boots and a child's comforter decorated with one of the more obscure Walt Disney characters.

"Seven o'clock, blue Saab." He stuffed the twenty into his jeans. His throat was dry. They had written to each other a lot, after Garret had died. The letters had become increasingly friendly. Eventually they'd shared their most intimate secrets, the way people do when they never expect to meet. But this was different. He said, "Okay, fine. I'll see you then."

But Shannon had segued into her Zellers salesperson mode, forgotten all about him in the blink of an eye.

8

The water as it rushed out of the tap looked like nothing anyone in his right mind would consider drinking. Willows half-filled a glass and held it up to the drab early-morning light that filtered in through the kitchen window. Was that silt, or sediment? He lifted the glass to his nose, sniffed gingerly. Annie came skipping into the kitchen. She said, "It's okay to drink. I heard it on the radio just a few minutes ago. It's . . . drinkable."

Drinkable. Now there was a word that utterly failed to whip up the least little bit of enthusiasm. Willows bent and opened a bottom cupboard door. He'd thought there was still some bottled water left, but the plastic jug was empty.

"It's because of all the rain we've had the past few days," said Annie on her way to the fridge. She swung open the door and critically evaluated the contents. "There've been some mudslides." She gave Willows a perky, sardonic, slightly goofy grin. "It's nothing to worry about. *Turbidity* is the proper terminology. They've dumped a bunch more chlorine into the system, so there shouldn't be a problem." She thumped a four-litre jug of milk down on the kitchen table, organized cereal, a bowl and spoon and sat down.

Willows poured water into the coffee machine. He turned the machine on. Hopefully the paper filter would screen out most of the larger chunks of debris.

Annie said, "Where's Claire?"

73

"Upstairs, in the shower." One by one, Willows dropped four slices of sourdough bread into the toaster.

Cereal crackled into the bowl. Annie sloshed in some milk. She picked up her spoon and began to eat.

Willows studied the flow of coffee into the pot. He checked the toaster to make sure the little levers hadn't been knocked into *burn*. All his life, he'd had a tendency to start the toast prematurely, but this morning he was going to try very hard to get it right. He watched the thin stream of coffee fall into the pot.

The telephone rang. He got the toast started and then crossed to the far end of the counter and picked up.

Inspector Homer Bradley said, "Jack?"

"Morning, Inspector."

"You had breakfast?"

"Not yet."

Bradley said, "Eleven-twenty Bute. Apartment one-one-seven. I'll send out for coffee and Danish, so nobody starves to death."

Willows sensed movement at the far end of the hallway. He turned, and looked behind him. Parker was in the front hall, sitting on the bottom step, lacing up her sensible black shoes.

Bradley said, "Use the siren, Jack. No dawdling, hear?"

Three slices of toast popped. Willows had cut the fourth slice too thick, and it had jammed. The toaster buzzed harshly. A plume of black smoke rose towards the ceiling.

Bradley said, "What the hell is *that*?"

"Me," said Willows. He winked at Annie. "It's the sound I make when I'm hungry."

Eleven-twenty Bute was a concrete seventies-era highrise with ungainly clam-shaped balconies. Apartment 117 was a ground-level bachelor situated on the east side of the building.

Willows parked in the alley. He and Parker got out of the car and started across a narrow strip of grass. A yellow crime-scene ribbon fluttered in the wind. Willows stepped over it, but Parker had to take the low road, because of her skirt. Willows stepped onto the apartment's patio, a scalloped half-circle of concrete. A potted plant stood off to one side, beside a cheap white plastic chair. A mauve glass ashtray had been placed in the exact centre of a matching plastic table. The apartment's sliding glass door was wide open. The apartment was stuffed full of uniformed and plainclothes cops. Willows bulled his way inside with Parker right behind.

Mel Dutton, the police photographer, sat on a black leather couch, beneath a poster-size black-and-white photograph of a nude black male riding a dazzling white stallion along a sandy shoreline.

Dutton was inserting a fresh roll of film into one of his Nikons. He seemed oblivious to the drama above his gleaming bald head. Parker eyed the photograph. Dutton said, "Somebody you know?"

"Could be," said Parker offhandedly.

Willows gave Dutton a friendly wave. "How's it going, Mel?"

"Couldn't be better," said Dutton, uncharacteristically. He snapped the back of the camera shut, wound the film counterclockwise until it was tight, and then shot two quick frames to advance the film. "I ever tell you about that coffee-table book I was working on, *Dead Bodies*?"

"Yeah, I think you might've mentioned it."

"About a million times," added Parker. Where was the body? Not in the living room or kitchen.

Dutton said, "Well, I finally got an agent. Just last week. A woman in New York. Emily Heneghan. Is the name familiar?"

"Why? Did she murder somebody?"

"No, but she claims she was Norman Mailer's agent, back in the days before he was famous."

"How could anyone possibly be that old?" said Parker.

Dutton wasn't smiling. "She phoned last night. Thinks she might have a publisher lined up."

"That's great, Mel." Parker looked up from Dutton's cherubic face as Willows brushed past her. Bradley was standing in the doorway to the right of the kitchen. He waved Parker towards him, then turned and vanished down the hall.

There were dozens of photographs hung on the walls on both sides of the hallway. There was a nude male perched on a big Harley-Davidson motorcycle. There was a cold, shrivelled, skiing nude on a chairlift. Another on a snowboard. There were nude males on water skis and in powerboats, standing on a diving board at an indoor pool. There were three solemn nudes in an elevator, two more waiting at a downtown bus stop. There was an action photograph of a nude leaping for a slam dunk.

Every single photograph had been autographed, more often than not with a few bawdy words as well as the signatures. The second common denominator was a complete lack of modesty.

There was an open doorway on Willows' left. The bedroom. Mirrored tiles had been fastened to the ceiling over the king-size waterbed. There were lots more photographs, but no change in theme.

Willows continued down the hall to the bathroom. Bradley waited by the open door. He wore a three-piece pinstripe suit in dove grey. His shirt was a dazzling white, and both collars had been buttoned. The knot on his silk tie was exactly right. His black lace-ups gleamed. His thinning hair had been neatly arranged. Up close, he smelled of Old Spice cologne, and Willows noticed that the cigar in his mouth had hardly been chewed at all.

"Morning, Jack. Claire."

Willows glanced around the glossy little room.

Parker said, "Who is he?"

Bradley shrugged. "Donald E. Mooney. The name ring a bell?"

Willows said, "He's a cop, was involved in that armoured-car robbery, about five years ago. The shootout. Those two killer kids, Billy and Garret . . ."

Parker said, "Who called it in?"

"Mr. Anonymous. The switchboard logged the call at three minutes to eight this morning. It was made from a downtown payphone."

Mooney was in his late twenties. He was clean-shaven, and his black hair was clipped short. He lay curled up in the bathtub, naked. His right ankle had been manacled to his left wrist. His right hand cupped his genitals and was securely held in place by many overlapping layers of silvery duct-tape. More tape had been repeatedly wound around his neck and mouth. His nostrils had been shut with a heavy metal spring clip. The shower head had been removed. A clear plastic tube about an inch in diameter ran from the water pipe down into Mooney's mouth, and was held in place by more tape. Willows moved closer. A slow trickle of water leaked from Mooney's nostril, tinkled softly as it ran down the drain.

A hand fell heavily on Willows' shoulder. He turned. Bobby Dundas' cheerful face was so close he could hardly get it in focus. Behind Dundas, Eddy Orwell, weightlifter, health-food junkie, and fellow homicide cop, loitered by the door.

Bobby said, "Morning, Claire. How's it hangin', Jack?"

"What're you doing here, Bobby?"

"Investigating a murder. All that shiny tape, guy looks like the leftovers from a Coors commercial. Mr. Silver Bullet." Bobby's fingers tightened on Willows' shoulder. Willows tensed. Bobby relaxed his grip. His hand slipped away.

Bradley chewed complacently on the cud of his cigar.

Parker knelt by the corpse. Mooney's eyes were pale green flecked with tiny nuggets of gold. His skin was cold. The way the blood had pooled in his legs, it looked almost as if he were wearing burgundy-coloured socks. There was blood in his close-cropped hair, a dark smear of dried blood on the tiles.

Two cardboard cylinders – empty duct-tape roles – lay on the bottom of the tub. The remains of a third roll hung from the body.

Parker shone her penlight down the drain. A drop of water sparkled bright as a diamond. Bobby crouched beside her. He was a smorgasbord of masculine odours – mouthwash, deodorant, aftershave, mousse. He rested his forearm on her thigh. "Find any *clues*, Claire?"

Parker stood up. Shone the flashlight into Bobby's eye. His pupil contracted. He shrank away.

From the doorway, Orwell said, "Yeah, in there."

Popeye Rowland pushed into the room. The M.E. nodded to the assembled cops, let his monocle drop from his eye into the palm of his hand. He glanced at the trio of black-and-white nude studies hanging from the wall behind the toilet. "So many lovely pictures, and they're all so nicely hung." He smiled at Parker. "Morning, Claire. If you need a suspect, give Mel Dutton a shake."

"Got a motive?" said Orwell.

"Professional jealousy, Eddy." Rowland peered at the corpse. "The perp sure knew how to handle duct-tape. It isn't easy to wind it around like that and get so few wrinkles. Remember that old James Bond movie *Goldfinger*? Maybe he's got a kid brother. *Silverfinger*." He touched the cold flesh not an inch from where Parker's fingers had grazed. "Brrrr!" He tugged lightly at a stiff index finger, then knelt and opened his ancient Gladstone bag, withdrew a digital thermometer in a plastic sheath. He slipped on a pair of latex gloves, lubricated the thermometer and eased it into place.

Bobby said, "That's *always* my favourite part."

Bradley gave him a mildly reproving look. Bobby said, "I bet it's Popeye's favourite part too. Isn't it, Popeye?"

Rowland glanced at his watch. He studied the freckles on the backs of his hands for what might have been an eternity, then withdrew the thermometer and wiped it clean.

Bradley said, "How long, Popeye?"

"Hard to say, exactly. Quite a while, though. Since somewhere between eleven o'clock last night and two o'clock this morning. I'll be able to fine-tune it after the autopsy. Midnight's probably pretty close. Why? Does Mel need an alibi?"

"Not yet," said Bradley. "But he might, if somebody tells him what you've been saying about him."

Rowland sheathed his thermometer and put it away.

"He drown?" said Bobby.

"How should I know?" Rowland waved at the tubing, the duct-tape. "It sure as hell looks as if the poor bastard drowned. But I won't know for sure until he's been autopsied." He glanced incuriously around, at the splashes of fingerprint powder on the bathroom walls and the glass shower door. Slips of paper from Dutton's Polaroids littered the floor. He stripped off his gloves and tossed them in a corner. "You going to cut him down now?"

Bobby said, "Be my guest. I got everything I need."

Willows turned to Bradley. "I missed my breakfast, Homer. Why'd you call me, if Bobby's on the case?" Was he whining? He hoped not.

"I'm putting two teams on it, Jack. You and Claire, Bobby and Orwell. You'll work independently, and report to me. I'll monitor the investigation and make the assignments. Written reports daily, from both teams. To start, Bobby and Eddy will canvass the neighbours, find out what they can about Mooney's lifestyle, friends and acquaintances. Jack, you and Claire can conduct your own investigation as you see fit, for now. *Nobody* talks to the media. Questions?"

Nobody had any questions. Willows said something about getting a cup of coffee, and turned and left the room.

Bradley spat a shred of tobacco accurately into the toilet, wiped his mouth with the back of his hand. "Got around to Mooney's closet, Claire?"

"Not yet."

"He was heavily into leather, rubber goods. He's got a stack of photo albums that'd make your pretty little head spin."

Parker bridled. *Pretty little head?* She said, "I doubt that, Inspector."

Bradley waved off her protest, using his cigar to advantage. He pointed the cigar towards the corpse's tape-wrapped testicles. "What d'you think. Does this look like a sex crime to you?"

"Well, yes. That's certainly what it looks like. But it's too early in the investigation to jump to that kind of conclusion, Inspector." Parker hesitated, and then added, "As I'm sure you know."

Bradley tilted his head in acknowledgement of the rebuke. He spat a little more tobacco into the toilet. "The dead crib player, Beinhart. You follow up on the dentist?"

"He's on holiday. Costa Rica, with the wife and kids," said Willows. "They left a couple of hours ago."

"They have reservations?"

Willows said, "No, it was apparently one of those spur-of-the-moment decisions."

"Stay on it, Jack." Bradley turned and left the room.

Parker examined the way the hollow plastic line had been fitted into the shower head's metal pipe. She sat on the edge of the tub and took a good long look at the corpse, then began a hands-on examination. Mooney's scalp above his right ear was swollen, the skin split and bloody. It was a superficial wound, but the blow had probably been sufficient to briefly stun him. Had his killer struck him or had he lost his footing in the tub, and banged his head against the tiles? Parker looked deep into Mooney's beautiful green, gold-flecked eyes. The pupils were no longer symmetrical, and differed in size. She checked his throat for bruising or other signs of strangulation. His skin was smooth. He had a small mole on his left shoulder. There was a thick mat of hair on his chest. His nipples were chocolatey brown, his stomach muscles well defined. Parker made a note. Did he belong to a health club?

The way the layers of tape bound his right hand to his testicles seemed like a hideously perverted display of modesty. Parker noted a hint of gold, peeled away a bit of tape. Mooney was wearing a watch, an expensive gold Tissot.

Even so, she still wasn't quite ready to eliminate robbery as a motive. She continued to examine the corpse. There were several small cuts and contusions on Mooney's knees. Had he been over-powered somewhere else in the apartment, and then dragged into the bathroom?

She touched the cold stainless steel of the police-issue handcuffs that encircled Mooney's left wrist and right leg.

She looked into his beautiful, ruined eyes. He was somebody's child, somebody's friend, somebody's lover. The life he had led, his sexual preferences and comic perversions, was of no consequence to Parker other than as it related to the investigation.

She hadn't known him then. She only knew him now.

Time slipped past. She became aware that there was someone else in the room with her.

Willows said, "The coffee's all gone. There's no tea. But I saved you a strawberry Danish . . ."

9

A hamburger joint. A muffin joint. A fried-chicken joint. There was even a made-fresh-while-you-watch submarine-sandwich joint. But there were lineups everywhere, and as the day slowly wore on the crowds thickened, became even worse. Noise. People. Time. There was far too much of everything. Ross was overloaded, distraught, getting a headache.

He decided to take a walk. It had stopped raining, but the sky was the colour of ashes, and the air was cold and damp. He walked for fifteen minutes or so and came across a park. He walked into the park, down a winding road that led him past small ponds, stands of trees, open grassy areas. A man sitting on a bench by a pond asked him for spare change. Ross gave him two quarters and a dime. The man took the coins into his mouth, gnawed at them and then spat them into his hand and tossed them over his shoulder, into the water. A brace of ducks paddled over and milled hopefully around. The man smiled at Ross and asked him if he had any spare change.

Ross came out of the park a couple of blocks further down Cambie. He crossed Twenty-fifth Avenue and kept walking. It had been years since he had walked such a long way, in a straight line.

He came upon a jewellery store, made blinders of his hands and peered through the plate-glass window. The store was a treasure chest of wealth. The glass display cases shimmered. An elderly Chinese woman stood behind a counter, polishing the face-sized face of an antique clock. Another, much-younger woman stood idly by the cash register. Ross stepped away from the window. He studied the reflected streetscape in the glass. A transparent taxicab cruised slowly past, transparent driver hunched over the wheel. A transparent bus disgorged two or three transparent passengers. A transparent police car drove by, travelling in the opposite direction.

Ross turned away from the window. He lit a cigarette and watched the police car as it dwindled down the street. The car was more than three blocks away when he finally lost sight of it.

He walked into the jewellery store. Both women looked up. Neither of them smiled. Crossing the threshold, he noticed a security camera mounted high up on the wall behind the older woman. He glanced around, as if getting his bearings. There was another camera over the door and a third camera in a distant corner. Everybody was a film star, nowadays.

The younger woman said, "May I help you?"

Improvising, Ross said, "I'm interested in buying a watch."

She smiled. "For yourself?"

"No, my girlfriend." Ross leaned against the counter. The glass was flawlessly clean, except for his fingerprints. He said, "Something in the range of about fifty dollars." Surreptitiously, he wiped his prints away with his elbows.

The girl offered up a sweet, apologetic smile. "I'm afraid we don't have anything in that price range. You might try Eaton's, in the Oakridge mall."

"Yeah, okay. I'll do that. Thanks." Ross turned and walked away, pushed open the big glass door. Now, what was that all about? If he hadn't spotted the cameras, would he have done something really bad?

He told himself the answer was no.

A woman with a body shaped like an inflatable hand grenade approached him from dead ahead. He veered towards the curb, but she had him in his sights and wasn't about to let him go. The hem of her coat dragged on the sidewalk. The lenses of her glasses were as thick as the glass in the jewellery store's plate-glass door. He experienced a moment of bewildered panic as she thrust something at him. A religious tract. He bolted down the street, turned into a coffee shop, bought a cup of coffee and sat down at a lonely table. The window was misted. The outside world might have been a gigantic aquarium. He added milk to his coffee. Small plastic bins by the cash register held plastic knives and forks, plastic spoons. He pulled the tract from his pocket and began to read.

The end was nigh. Surprise, surprise. Was this supposed to be a news item? The end had always been nigh. *Nigh* was just around the corner from the day you were born. It was nigh-well inescapable, was nigh.

He drank some more coffee. It was okay, but not quite as good as the coffee they served in the slammer. Hotter, though. His hand shook a little, as he thought about how close he'd come to walking straight over to the antique clock, picking it up and hurling it at a display case. Smash and grab. By now, they'd have had his stupid face on every television in town. Or, more likely, have him in cuffs. Or he'd have moved to the *post-nigh* phase of his life. He pictured, from the height of a stepladder, his bullet-riddled body lying on the sidewalk in a pool of his stupid blood. To die a natural death, shouldn't that be every man's holy grail?

No matter how long it lasted, nothing was shorter than a life.

Ross took his time with his coffee. He lit a cigarette and smoked it down. Shannon's twenty lay at the bottom of his pocket. He was a man of property. He had no need to rob and steal.

A thin black man wearing baggy red corduroy pants and a sleeveless T-shirt and an improbably thick gold chain had been sitting at the window table. When Ross had lit his cigarette, the man had glared at him. Now he got up, gave Ross another hard look, and swaggered out of the restaurant. Ross wiped away an arc of condensation from the window. The skinny black guy was standing by the curb, waiting for a break in the traffic.

Ross went over to the cash register and inquired as to the restaurant's refill policy. No refills. Outside, brakes screeched but no metal crumpled. The guy at the cash register didn't even bother to look up. What was another near-miss? Ross paid for his fresh cup of coffee and went back to his seat. The black man lay on his belly in the middle of the street, about fifty feet from a black Honda with a frosted windshield that had stopped at an angle to the natural flow of traffic. The black wasn't much thicker than a shadow. His arms and legs pointed in four different directions. Ross sat there, watching the drama unfold. A police car, an ambulance and a fire-engine-red hook-and-ladder chased their sirens down the street. The black was eased onto a gurney and driven away to be repaired or autopsied. A tow truck scooped up the battered Honda. Another ambulance carried away the Honda's driver, who had not been wearing his seatbelt and as a consequence had suffered a grievous head wound. A fireman with a push broom made small talk with a traffic cop as he swept up bits of debris. A second fireman washed down the asphalt with a hose. A small, glittery object tumbled into the gutter. A shard of glass, probably.

The firetruck left. The cop sorted out the backed-up traffic, climbed into his vehicle and drove away. Ross bought another cup of coffee, his third. He wasn't sure why, but he was enjoying himself. He had no ambition but to sit there, drinking coffee and watching the world stumble by, until it was time for him to meet Shannon.

Half an hour or so later he used the washroom, and when he came out two women were sitting at his table. His mug had been cleared away, his religious tract expropriated.

He went back outside and walked slowly through the rain until he came to a small bookstore. He went inside. A man with pale blue eyes looked him over, nodded in a way that was neither here nor there. The man was tall, well over six feet. He wore a cream-coloured cardigan. Now he was looking at Ross as if he thought he'd met him somewhere before, but couldn't recall the circumstances. Ross looked at magazines for a while and then moved down the ranks of shelves towards the back of the store. Finally he came to the section where the Westerns were shelved. *Dusters*, Garret used to call them. Or *Oaters*. They were the only books Garret ever read. He liked them because those were the days when men were men.

Ross picked up a slim paperback called *Tumbleweed*. The art on the cover depicted a cowboy half-falling off a horse as he scooped up a redheaded beauty. There were Indians in the background. They were tiny and featureless but there were plenty of them, and in their own way they were so real he could almost hear them whooping. Ross had never read a Western, despite all the pressure Garret had put on him. He was more into trade paperbacks, what they called contemporary American fiction. Not that he read a lot of books. It was individual words that interested him, more than the art of stringing words together. He carried *Tumbleweed* back up the narrow aisle to the front of the store, and handed the blue-eyed man a ten-dollar bill. The man rang up the sale, slipped the receipt and a bookmark between the pages, and put the book in a brown paper bag with the store's name and logo printed on it. He sealed the bag with half an inch of Scotch tape and handed the bag to Ross.

The blue-eyed man said, "Enjoy."

Ross nodded. He walked out of the store carrying the book in his right hand. It had cost almost seven dollars, considerably more than he'd expected. But he knew almost nothing about the price of books. Although he had used the prison library from time to time, he was fairly certain this was the first book he'd ever actually bought, unless you counted comics and the odd magazine. As he walked down the street, he slipped the book out of the bag. It was two hundred and twenty-three pages long, but didn't start until page nine. He worked out how much the book had cost, per page, and then stopped in the shelter of an awning and counted the words on a page and, after a few false starts, calculated to his satisfaction the fraction of a penny each word had cost him.

He stuck the book in his jacket's inside pocket, crumpled the bag into a ball and tossed it away.

When he came even with the spot where the black pedestrian had come to grief, he crossed the sidewalk to the gutter and looked down. The glittery thing was the black's gold chain. Ross knelt and scooped it up, gave it a shake. The boxy links were an eighth of an inch thick and half an inch wide. The metal, cold and heavy, weighed three or maybe four ounces.

Ross stood up, glanced around. Nobody paid any attention to him. He found shelter in a doorway. The chain's clasp had bent but was not broken. He fiddled with it for a few moments and then gave up and dropped the chain into his pocket. Man, but it was heavy.

He walked a little further down the street, until he came to a hotel with a bar. Inside, a couple of guys, an older man and someone who could've been his son, but wasn't, sat on stools at the bar. Ross sat down in a padded chair, at a small table made out of a thick sheet of glass perched on a round wooden stem. He lit a cigarette, blew smoke at the ceiling. He had put his hand in his pants pocket and was fondling his gold chain when a heavy-set woman wearing a short red skirt and black jacket came at him from the area of the bar. She stopped at his table, smiled tiredly down at him and then noticed his hand moving in his pocket, and looked away. Ross yanked the gold chain out of his pocket, laid it noisily on the table but kept playing with it, turning the links over and over in his hand. The chain was as supple as a snake. The woman eyed the fat gold links as she asked him what he wanted to drink.

He put the chain back in his pocket. Flicked his cigarette at the ashtray, ordered a pint of draft beer.

Pretty soon he felt as comfortable in the bar as he had at the coffee shop. He finished his pint, started another. The bar slowly filled up. Four elderly women sat down a few tables away, ordered glasses of white wine and chatted animatedly in a foreign language.

An attractive woman wearing a dark blue suit and fluffy pink blouse thumped her fat leather briefcase down on a table, ordered a double vodka martini. She opened her briefcase, scrutinized the contents of a file folder. Her cellphone rang as her drink arrived. Her face suddenly had a pinched and angry look. She plucked the olive from the glass and tossed it in the ashtray, snatched up the phone. She listened for a moment and then spat out a few words and slammed the phone down on the table.

Ross fumbled in his jacket pocket, cracked open *Tumbleweed*. The light was kind of dim, but manageable. He began to read.

The sky was a vast bowl of burnished gold. Nothing moved. As far as the eye could see, in any direction it fancied him to look, the land was featureless and still. But he knew he must not rely upon his senses, for this was Indian country, and he had heard much talk of . . .

Sixty-odd pages later, Ross finished his third pint of beer, and thumped the empty glass down on the table. He was out of cigarettes. The pints had left him feeling bloated and gassy.

Outside, it was dark, and raining, and the sidewalks were crowded. A taxi crawled past. Ross raised his arm, shouted. A woman hurrying past nicked him with her umbrella. He peered up at the orange clock on top of City Hall. He was ten minutes late for his appointment with Shannon. Ten minutes and counting. The hotel was at Twelfth and Cambie. Zellers was twenty-nine blocks away.

He folded his umbrella and began to run.

10

The bedroom walk-in closet was crammed with Mooney's uniforms, civilian clothing, a neoprene wetsuit. Parker searched methodically through the pockets. She turned up a dry-cleaning receipt, several dollars in loose change, a folder of paper matches from a downtown nightclub, contraceptives, a variety of types of lint.

"Jack?"

Willows sat on the bed, Mooney's Sharp electronic data directory in hand. Mooney had a lot of friends, for a cop. Willows had been pushing buttons for several minutes and was only a third of the way through the alphabet.

Parker said, "You know a place called L'affair?"

Willows studied the logo. "Yeah, it's a gay club on East Broadway. Why?"

She tossed him the packet of matches.

Willows smiled. A classic clue. But what did it mean – other than that Mooney was gay?

There are eleven hundred police officers in the VPD. Cops are always quitting or retiring, being replaced. It isn't possible to know everyone on a force that size. Not that Willows *wanted* to know everyone. All police departments are essentially paramilitary organizations, extremely conservative in nature. Willows liked to think of himself as a liberal and a bit of a free-thinker. There were plenty of guys in the department that he didn't get along with. He said, "Mooney was active in the union. I've seen him around. But I didn't know him."

He was learning, though, thanks to the notebook. Mooney had known an awful lot of men, but hardly any women. If he had been gay, he wouldn't have flaunted his sexuality. Willows worked his way through the "J" and "K" listings. Not many surnames started with "K." There was no listing for Killer. He slipped the notebook into an evidence envelope and tossed the envelope in a cardboard box containing several other envelopes.

Coat hangers rattled. Parker was having a good time in there. Willows unscrewed the cap from a plastic bottle of water. He sipped, screwed the cap back on, put the bottle in his jacket pocket. The uniforms had gone back to patrol, the CSU techs had left with their fingerprints and other booty. Bradley had returned to his office, and Eddy Orwell and Bobby Dundas were conducting a door-to-door of the nearby apartments.

Parker backed out of the closet carrying a red-painted metal box about the size of a large lunch-bucket. A combination lock rattled. Willows retrieved the electronic notebook. He hit the recall button, tried "lock" and then the letters "comb."

The word *combination* came up on the screen, above three sequences of two-digit numbers.

11-14-36.

Parker sat down on the bed. Willows read out the numbers and she dialled them and pulled on the lock's hasp. The lock popped open. She lifted the hinged lid.

The box contained a small-frame five-shot revolver and a cheap red plastic photo album with the words *My Holidays* stamped on the cover in gold. It was clear neither the gun nor the album had anything to do with the crime scene, but Willows put on a pair of latex gloves just to be on the safe side. The revolver had been made in Italy. He didn't recognize the brand. There was rust on the barrel and one of the plastic grips was cracked. He flipped open the cylinder. The gun was loaded with 158-grain roundnose bullets.

Parker said, "I'd guess he found that somewhere, decided to keep it in case he needed a throwaway . . ."

She flipped open the album, and then slammed it shut. Her skin glowed.

Willows said, "Now we know how Donald spent his holidays. And that he was definitely gay. We're going to have to go through the whole thing, from cover to cover."

Parker gave him a look. He was right, and she knew it. Lust, and love, were wonderfully dependable motives. What she'd have to do, the investigative trick she'd have to perform, was concentrate on the faces. But the faces weren't always where you wanted them to be . . .

They went through the rest of the apartment, room by room. Mooney's sole indulgence in life seemed to have been his sex life. He had a large-screen television, two expensive video recorders and a cabinet with smoked-glass doors that contained a substantial library of pornography in both VHS and Beta format.

"The classics," said Willows, as he ran a thumb over a dust-free plastic box.

"We'd better go through his receipts," said Parker. "He's even got a foreign-language section. Some of this stuff probably came through the mails but I bet most of it is local. The dealer might be able to give us something."

"As long as it isn't contagious."

Parker smiled. The photo album had been a real gut-wrencher, but her sense of humour was slowly coming back. She heard the apartment door swing open, and then Eddy Orwell's booming voice.

"Anybody home?"

Orwell had his meaty arm casually draped across the shoulder of a skinny kid in his early twenties. The boy wore baggy orange shorts and a teal-blue Grizzlies T-shirt. He needed a shave. His shoulder-length hair was dirty and matted. He was barefoot. His toenails needed trimming.

Willows said, "Who's your new friend, Eddy?"

"This's Graham Aubert. He lives in the apartment right across the hall." Orwell introduced Parker and Willows. He said, "Tell them what you told me, Graham."

"I was up late." Graham offered a lopsided, slightly apologetic grin. "I'm unemployed, so I stay up late lots of times. More often than not, probably."

Willows nodded, but the boy had focused on Parker.

Parker said, "Okay, you were up late . . ."

"Yeah. Watching a tape of *Reservoir Dogs*. Have you seen it?"

Parker shook her head.

"I bought a copy as soon as it hit the shelves. I must've seen it twenty times. More than *Pulp Fiction*." He scratched his belly. "You saw that one, I bet."

"Once," said Parker.

Graham nodded. "There's probably only about fifty people in all of North America who didn't see it. What a great movie." He smiled, showing yellow teeth. "Did you like it? Did you think it was true to life?"

"Uh . . ." Parker glanced at Willows. "It seemed very convincing."

Orwell said, "Anyway, Graham was watching the movie, and it was right at the part where there's a big shootout . . ."

"Everybody's *blasting* away, but I got the sound turned down pretty low because it's late, and the Leggatts have already made a lot of complaints, so I'm kind of on probation with the apartment manager, I gotta watch it or I'm gonna get evicted."

"The Leggatts' apartment is directly above Graham's," explained Orwell.

"They're retired," said Graham. "From life. You can't come right out and ask people about stuff like that, so it took me about a year to figure out their routine, but they go to bed at ten o'clock on weeknights, sometimes stay up as late as eleven during the weekend."

Parker said, "Okay, we've established that you were watching a video and that you had the sound turned down. Then what?"

"There was a bunch of shooting. In the movie. And then I heard a shot that was louder than the other shots. I mean, it wasn't really loud. But it was a little louder than the others. And another thing, I got that movie memorized, not just the dialogue, but the music and sound effects, everything right down to the smallest detail. So not only was this particular shot louder than all the others, but it was out of place. I mean, it wasn't supposed to be there."

"When you heard the shot, what time was it?"

"In the movie?"

"No, Graham. In the real world."

"I don't know." The boy sat down gingerly on the arm of a black leather chair from Ikea. "But I can figure it out."

"How can you do that?" said Parker sceptically.

Graham smiled. "Well, see, I watched David Letterman, and Letterman's show ends at twelve-thirty-five. I'd already put the tape – I'm talking about the *Reservoir Dogs* movie – in my VCR during a commercial break. I hit the *play* button as the Letterman credits rolled, just as his Worldwide Pants logo came on the screen. While the tape was running and the movie was cuing up, I went into the kitchen, tossed my sandwich in the microwave and got a beer out of the fridge."

"What sandwich?" said Orwell.

"A take-out meatball sub I bought at Mr. Sub. I eat there a couple of times a week. It's quick and easy. No muss, no fuss. Usually wherever I have dinner I take something home with me in case I get hungry for a midnight snack. Which I almost always do."

"How often do you eat out?" said Orwell.

"Every night of the week."

"The single life," said Orwell, who had reconciled with his wife. For now. He said, "Man, it's a whole different world."

"So the movie started at twenty-five minutes to one," said Parker. "And when was it you heard the shot?"

"That'd be just after the diamond-store robbery. Mister Pink's on the run, he hauls this woman out of a car, the cops start shooting and he returns fire. There's about thirty shots fired. The scene takes about eight seconds and ends at the twenty-one-minute mark."

"That'd be at four minutes to one."

"Yeah, right. But add another minute and a half for the sandwich, because that's how long it was in the microwave." Graham frowned. "No, wait. Everything's running independently. The TV's on, the tapes unwinding, the microwave's heating my sub. So the extra time doesn't matter, doesn't get added on. Yeah, four minutes to one, give or take a few seconds."

Willows said, "Did you *see* anything, Graham?"

"No, why should I?"

"You heard a shot. Or what sounded like a shot. You know what a gunshot sounds like. Weren't you curious? Most people would get up, go to the window and take a look outside."

"Would they? Is that smart? I'm enjoying a movie, my third-favourite movie of all time, and you're telling me it makes sense to jump up, run over to the window and catch a bullet in the eye? I'm sitting there, my sandwich is nice and hot, I'm working on a beer, comfortable, all settled in . . . Besides, what's to look at? All I heard was one shot and it's already been fired. Or maybe it was a tire blew out. You expect me to pull my curtains, in the dark, see if some guy needs help fixing his car? That's not me, it just ain't me." Graham jerked his thumb at Orwell. "Like I told the detective, I go outside for meals and movies, but that's about it."

"Did you know any of Donald's friends?"

"No, none of them. I never even *met* any of them, except maybe once or twice in the hall, something along those lines. But if that happened, I bumped into somebody, it was just a nod of the head and it's over. Hello and goodbye. There was never any attempt at introductions or anything along those lines. The guy kept to himself. Well, I guess that isn't quite true. He had friends. In fact there was a new guy, came around a couple of times during the past week. But Don and his pals valued their privacy, just like me."

Parker said, "What did Donald's new friend look like?"

"Tall, a little over six feet. Beefy. Muscular. The broad-shouldered type, with a thick neck, like a weightlifter. Short blond hair, spiky. No sideburns, a snub nose."

"Was he good-looking?"

"Yeah, I guess so. He was no movie star."

"Did you notice his eyes?"

"Kind of close-set. A piercing blue. He had a real small nose, almost a cartoon nose. A button nose. It hardly stuck out from his face at all, except right at the bottom, and it was pushed over to one side. Like it'd been broken."

"Complexion?"

"Very pale. Smooth skin."

"The shape of his face, was it oval, or . . ."

"Brick-shaped. Flat on top, square chin. I remember his ears. They were tiny." Graham's hand came up. He touched his ear. "He had a gold earring, in the shape of a pistol."

Willows wrote it all down.

"How much would you say the guy weighed, Graham?"

"I dunno. Couple of hundred pounds, maybe a little less."

"Age?"

"Late twenties? I'm not too good at ages. People always look older to me than they really are . . ."

"Did he ever speak to you?"

"Nope."

"Did you ever hear him speaking?"

"Not that I know of. I mean, sometimes I could hear voices coming from Don's apartment. Maybe it was Don talking, maybe it wasn't."

Willows said, "Did Don's new friend have any scars or other identifying marks?"

"No, definitely not."

"Walk with a limp . . . ?"

"No, nothing like that."

Willows smiled. "For someone who minds his own business, Graham, you sure noticed an awful lot about Donald's pals."

"Not really. But this guy, he kind of stood out. A few days ago, I happened to run into him twice during the same day. The first time was in the lobby, and then outside the building, on the sidewalk. Both times, he averted his head, turned away as if he didn't want me to recognize him. Suspicious behaviour, right? Oh yeah, something else. He was wearing a uniform."

"He was a cop?" said Parker.

"No way. Security guard."

"Who did he work for? Did you notice his flashers?"

"Excuse me, his what?"

"Shoulder patches."

"No, I never noticed. But he had one of those wide leather belts, goes around your waist, over your shoulder and across your chest. And heavy black boots, and a hat with a shiny brim."

"Did he wear a badge?"

"Yeah, a big one, about the size of the palm of my hand. Silver-coloured, in the shape of a shield. It had a number on it, but I can't remember what it was. I mean, it's not like he tried to arrest me."

"Mooney never mentioned him to you, referred to him by name . . ."

"No, never." Graham spread his arms in a gesture intended to encompass the highrise. "A big building like this, you don't watch yourself, pretty soon everybody's your friend, you got no privacy at all. Guys want to go out for a beer. Women start hitting on you . . ." Graham ducked his head. From under his brows, he gave Parker a weirdly coquettish look.

Parker said, "How long have you been unemployed, Graham?"

"Since I quit school. Five, going on six years."

"How do you support yourself?"

"My parents help me. Or I should say, my dad. He pays the rent, deposits six hundred a month into my bank account for food and clothing, what he calls discretionary purchases. Don't misunderstand me, I don't mean to make him sound like he doles it out, is a nickel-and-dimer. For my birthday last year he gave me a real expensive mountain bike. If I'd asked for a car, no problem. Not that he'd run out and buy me a Porsche. More like a Hyundai. But anything I need, all I have to do is ask."

"Nice life," said Orwell, apparently sincere.

"There's only one condition," said Graham. "I have to stay away from my mother. I call her on the phone, go anywhere near her, the deal's off. One false move and I'm on my own."

Nobody knew quite what to say about that. Parker made a small sound that might have been sympathetic. Willows managed to nod sagely.

Graham said, "I'd probably starve to death in about two weeks."

Willows said, "I'd like you to come downtown, Graham . . ."

"What for?"

"We're going to arrange for a police artist, with your help, to make a sketch of the security guard."

"He's a suspect?"

"At this point," said Willows, "*everybody's* a suspect."

"Even me?"

Willows smiled. "Yeah, even you. Will you help us with the sketch?"

"What, now?"

"No, but soon. Probably later this afternoon. We'll send a car around to pick you up, okay?"

"Yeah, sure. I guess so."

Parker asked Aubert a few more questions regarding Mooney's lifestyle, but got no satisfactory answers. Orwell patted him on the back and thanked him for his help.

"Can I go back to my apartment now?"

Orwell nodded. "Yeah, sure."

"I'm gonna relax with a beer, watch a movie."

"Sounds good."

"*Speed*, with Keanu Reeves." Graham squinted at Parker from the open doorway. "Seen it?"

"Yeah, I saw it," said Orwell. "Starring the bus, right?" He led Aubert to the door, let him out and shut it behind him.

Willows said, "Mooney had a throwaway piece, but it hadn't been fired in years. His service weapon was locked away in a drawer. There's no evidence of a shooting in the apartment. So who fired the shot?"

"Maybe whoever killed him had a gun," said Parker. "Maybe there was a struggle. The killer was wounded but cleaned up after himself."

"Sounds pretty unlikely to me," said Orwell.

Bobby Dundas had been outside, prowling the alley with a four-battery MagLite. He held the flashlight loosely in his hand as he entered the apartment. He gave Parker a long up-and-down look. "You're having a real good hair day, Claire."

Parker gave Bobby a glacier-cold look.

Orwell said, "What's with the flashlight, Bobby? You schedule an eclipse?"

"Nooks and crannies." Dundas unbuttoned his raincoat. He held up a bulky envelope, gave it a shake.

Orwell said, "What've you got?"

"A pair of elbow-length, heavy-duty rubber gloves."

"Yeah? Where'd you get 'em?"

"Out of a dumpster. Interestingly enough, the tip of the little finger's missing, left-hand glove."

Willows said, "Why is that significant, Bobby?"

Bobby dipped into his pants pocket, came up with a bright yellow rubber fingertip.

Parker said, "Where'd you find that?"

"In Mooney's bathroom, on the floor beside the toilet. Mel took some pictures. I marked it on my sketch." Bobby gave the bag another shake. "We get a print off these babies, we're off to a pretty good start."

Willows said, "Bobby, can I talk to you a minute?" His face was set as he brushed past Orwell, pushed open the glass slider and stepped outside, onto the scalloped concrete patio. Bobby hesitated, and then came after him. Willows shut the door.

"What's up, Jack?"

"I'm the primary detective on this case. Next time you stumble across a piece of evidence, the first and last thing you do is tell me about it. *Don't* go sticking it in your pocket and wandering off on your own."

"All for one and one for all, right? Hey, I got an idea – maybe we should get joined at the hip. Or is that a move you reserve strictly for Claire?"

Willows gave him a hard look. "Keep mouthing off, Bobby, I'm going to beat you to your knees."

"Yeah?"

Willows dropped his right shoulder, pivoted, and delivered a short left hook that caught Dundas just beneath the ribs. The blow wiped the smile off Bobby's face. Sucking air, his eyes watering, he slumped sideways against the highrise's concrete wall. Willows went back inside the apartment. He shut the door and locked it.

Orwell peered myopically through the glass, as if he couldn't quite trust his eyes. "Something wrong with Bobby?"

"I don't think so, Eddy."

Orwell thought it over for a moment, but not for long. "If you say so, Jack, then I guess he looks just fine to me."

Willows nodded. He appreciated Eddy coming down on his side of the fence, but it was Parker he was worried about. As soon as they were alone, she was going to give him absolute hell for decking Bobby. He knew exactly what she was going to tell him. Cops didn't hit cops. But if the situation *did* require brute force, she could take care of herself.

And he'd better not forget it.

11

Shannon finished her shift, exchanged her ugly Zellers smock and no-style dark blue pants for a bright red mid-thigh skirt and her hip-length fake-leopardskin jacket. In the parking lot, everything was as it should be, except Ross was missing. A pickup truck cruised past. She checked her watch in the glare of the headlights. Eight minutes past seven. Where was he? She rested a hip against the Saab. Kelly rolled down the backseat window, gave her a look. His famous raised-eyebrow look. He said, "Where's Loverboy?"

"Somewhere else," said Shannon. She held up her watch to the red glare of the Zellers sign. Still eight minutes past seven.

Kelly got out of the car, lit a cigarette. The Zellers sign turned his hair candy-floss pink. He hitched up his jeans, scratched his button nose.

Shannon watched people going in and out of Zellers. You couldn't make out anyone's features. All you saw, staring into the wash of light, were black cutouts. Stick figures on the move. She willed herself not to look at her watch again.

Kelly said, "Maybe he was hanging around, saw me get into the car. What's he gonna think, he's supposed to meet some babe, sees a guy crawl into the backseat of her car?"

"He'd think something was up."

"Damn right, unless he's the world's biggest idiot. Could Loverboy be the world's biggest idiot, Shan?"

"Let's hope so. Do us both a favour, okay? If he does show up, keep a low profile."

Kelly made a sound like cloth ripping. He was laughing, but you wouldn't know it by the look on his face. The tip of his cigarette glowed as he sucked smoke deep into his lungs. He sighed with pleasure, hummed softly to himself and began to sing. "When I dream, I dream and dream of nicotine, sweet nicotine . . ."

Ten minutes later, Shannon said, "There he is. I think that's him . . ."

Ross considered himself to be in fairly good shape for a guy his age, but he was exhausted by the time he finally arrived at the mall. Welcome to the real world. It was the exact opposite of the slammer. Here, on the outside, people were in a hurry, and actually had somewhere to go. Had she given up on him?

The Saab's engine was running, the exhaust spewing a snaky coil of pollutants. The car's emergency flashers pulsed red.

She was sitting behind the wheel, waiting. She saw him and pointed at the passenger's-side door, then leaned across and pushed the door open for him. He climbed in, apologized for being late and thanked her for waiting. She told him to shut the door, killed the flashers and put the car in reverse gear. The tires chirped as she aggressively reversed out of the parking slot. Ross leaned back in his seat. The Saab's instrument panel glowed orange. The thump of the radio was borderline subliminal. The wipers flapped back and forth across the rain-pocked windshield. He lit a cigarette.

"Put that *out*, please! This is a nonsmoking vehicle." Shannon punched a button, and Ross's window powered down. They were still in the mall parking lot, but moving along at a pretty good clip. The wind snatched at his jacket. His lapels battered his face. A barrage of fat raindrops stung his face. He filled his lungs with smoke, flicked the cigarette out the window. "How's that?"

"Fasten your seatbelt."

"Yeah, okay."

"How long have you been smoking, Ross?"

"Ever since I started."

"Well, it's time you quit. Only stupid people smoke."

They were on Forty-first, accelerating towards a red light. Shannon braked hard. Nose down, the car slid into the crosswalk, scattering a troupe of Chinese pedestrians. Shannon was clearly undismayed by the near-miss. The Saab's engine throbbed softly. Ross said, "One thing I noticed is that I often feel the urge to act stupidly after sex."

Had she smiled? Fleetingly. She said, "There can't have been too many opportunities for a post-coital smoke in the slammer, Ross. At least, I hope not." Now she was definitely smiling, teeth gleaming in the light. "How long were you in jail? Five years? A cigarette every five years probably won't kill you. That level of abstinence might . . ."

He said, "I'm not going back to jail."

"No?"

"Never."

"You'll never take me alive, Copper?" Her voice was low, throaty, openly taunting.

The light changed. The Saab fishtailed as she hit the gas. Maybe she wasn't as much in control of herself as she wanted him to think. She eased off the gas, and the car straightened out and she punched it again. Leader of the pack. Ross stared out the rain-streaked window at the passing houses. A dog lay on a porch, sleeping. Four lanes of traffic. Who in his right mind would live on such a busy street?

A red light was coming up fast. The Saab's speedometer needle hovered at eighty. Ross told himself she made the trip five times a week and had her timing down to the last second. His right foot pressed against the floorboards. They zipped past a cluster of three or four cars that were travelling in the same direction, but at the legal limit.

The light turned green as they entered the intersection. Ross had a death grip on his seatbelt. He gritted his teeth. A horn blared. Oncoming headlights lit up the Saab's interior. But no damage had been done, other than he'd suffered an overdose of adrenalin. He looked around, his vision blurred by the streaks of rain on the glass. To his left the city's glittery downtown core lifted itself up and pierced the cowering sky. Beams of light leaked from the highrises, expensive hotels, the lightbulb-studded sphere of the Science Centre, a million neon signs, countless office towers, Ford Centre and GM Place – the new sports palace that was home to the NHL Canucks and NBA Grizzles. The dome, AKA B.C. Place Stadium, squatted on the face of the city like a monstrous, low-wattage tumour. The lights of tens of thousands of cars and the hissing lanterns of a handful of street vendors added minutely to the glare. Vancouver was on the march, growing fast. Trapped between the mountains and the sea, the city had no choice but to claw its way into the sky.

Shannon hit another green, made a sharp left past an elevated SkyTrain station. The Chinese restaurant on the corner reminded Ross how hungry he was. They sped down a busy street, weaving in and out of traffic, a blur of two- and three-storey buildings on either side, pressing right up against the sidewalk. There was every kind of store you could think of, lots of East Indian businesses and then, as they kept moving, Italian. The sidewalks were crowded despite the rain. A neighbourhood of restaurants. Ross's mouth watered. His stomach growled.

They drove past a park that lacked trees. Shannon made a right, and then a left and another right and another left. She parked on the wrong side of the street in front of a white clapboard house, under the stark, twisted branches of a some kind of deciduous tree. Ross unbuckled, opened his door and got out, shut the door. Shannon's house was the largest house on the block. The tree was the only tree on the block. He stood there on the wet, unmowed boulevard, trapped in a spiderweb of shadows, listening to the rain bounce off his skull, while she got herself organized, gathered up her purse and keys, a bottle of wine she must've had hidden down there under her seat. Finally she pushed her door open and got out of the car.

Ross's jaw dropped. There was a guy in the backseat, leaning back as if he owned the world. An unlit cigarette dangled from his mouth. He caught Ross's eye, waved sardonically.

Shannon said, "That's my big brother. Kelly. I'd ignore him, if I were you, unless he asks you for a loan."

Kelly eased out of the car, slow but graceful. There sure as hell was a lot of him. More than six feet, and he was no beanpole. He lit his cigarette and then put the heel of his big black boot up against the Saab's open door and gave it a firm push. The door thudded shut. He gave Ross a hard-eyed look mixed in with a sardonic smile, then turned his back on him.

Ross followed Shannon across the sidewalk and up the broad front-porch steps. He held the wine while she segregated her front-door key from many others on the ring.

She unlocked the door, said, "Take off your shoes," in the same tone of voice she might use on a neighbour's unwelcome wayward dog.

Ross kicked off his shoes. With the toe of his stockinged foot he lined the shoes up neatly to one side of the door.

He followed her inside. She told him in a sweet voice to shut the door. When he hesitated, she advised him not to wait for Kelly; her lamebrain brother wasn't quite stupid enough to come inside before he'd finished his smoke. Ross shut the door. He suddenly craved a cigarette.

The house was cold and damp, as if the furnace hadn't been on for a long time – two or three days, a week. The living room was to his right. Narrow stairs trudged into second-storey gloom. Shannon shucked her coat and hung it on a metal hook. He trailed after her, keeping a certain distance, as she wandered into the living room. She said, "Turn the thermostat up to seventy, would you mind?"

Ross did as he'd been told. She switched on the gas fireplace. For atmosphere? He glanced around. A rose-coloured patterned carpet with a tidy fringe floated on a sea of gleaming hardwood. A plump chocolate-coloured leather sofa had its back to the curtained window. A matching love seat squatted at a friendly angle. An antique cast-iron lamp in the shape of a leaping dolphin stood on an oak end table. A pine trunk that had been ruthlessly battered into premature antiquity now served duty as a coffee table. A standing lamp with a fringed, pumpkin-coloured shade cast a pool of light on a small glass-fronted bookcase.

Ross said, "Nice place you've got here."

"It's a rental. I share with two other women, but they're both out of town for the next couple of weeks. Plus there's a two-bedroom suite in the basement. Kelly's staying there now, but he pays the same rent as anyone else. Even so, with the heat and light and everything, it's a stretch. But I get by. Want a glass of wine?"

"Yeah, sure. Thanks."

"There's a corkscrew in the kitchen, top drawer to the left of the sink. Glasses in the cupboard. I'm going upstairs to change. I'll be back in a few minutes."

Ross nodded. "Yeah, okay."

She pointed. "The kitchen's right through there. You'll find it." She gave him a reassuring smile, started up the stairs. He admired the delicacy of her ankles, flex of her calf muscles. She was no calendar girl, but there was a special word Garret had used to describe her that was dead accurate: *vitality*.

He imagined Garret standing where he was standing, thinking the exact same thought, the *vitality* word taking up space in his brain. But Garret would be thinking other things, wouldn't he? He'd be thinking about what he was going to do to Shannon when she came back downstairs. He'd be expecting to drink a glass or two of wine and then make love to her, stretch her out on the leather sofa in front of the gas fire, and do it.

Ross tried to imagine doing it on the sofa with Shannon. His imagination failed him. Man, his imagination didn't even get out of the starting blocks. He went over to the front window and looked out. Kelly sat on a falling-apart wicker chair, his feet up on the porch railing, smoking and looking out at the rain.

The kitchen had dull yellow linoleum on the floor, cream-coloured paint on the walls, track lighting. The refrigerator was fairly new, but the stove had seen better days.

The double sink was stainless steel. There was no dishwasher. A bottle of red wine stood bolt upright on the counter in the shadow of the microwave. Ross opened white-enamelled cupboard doors until he found the glasses, four of them. He put two glasses down on the counter next to the bottle and shut the cupboard door. Then he swung open the door again and got a third glass, in case Kelly thought to join them. He opened a drawer. Stainless-steel cutlery rattled in a pale blue plastic bin. The furnace had kicked in, and the house was starting to heat up. He slung his jacket over a chair, used his shirtsleeve to wipe sweat from his forehead. Where in hell was the damn corkscrew?

"What are you doing, *robbing* me?"

Startled, he jerked upright and cracked his head against a cupboard door that he had failed to shut. The blow staggered him. He clutched at nothing, lost his balance and fell heavily against the counter. The kitchen turned red and then black and then nuclear-bright. The overhead neon flickered like sheet lightning. His head pounded. A clock ticked far too loudly, and far too swift. He took a deep, shuddery breath.

Shannon cried, "Oh my God!" She was right there beside him. She took a single faltering step away from him and stood motionless, clearly aghast.

Ross saw that the ticking sound was caused by fat drops of blood falling upon the yellow linoleum. He brought a hand to his head. His gently probing fingers touched something sticky and warm. Blood, blood, blood. He'd split his skull wide open.

He was . . . *leaking*.

"Don't move." Shannon gripped his arm. She thrust a fat roll of paper towels into his hand. Her bare feet spanked the linoleum.

Ross stood there with the paper towels pressed against the wound. He knew from several minor skirmishes in the prison showers that even superficial head wounds tended to bleed a lot.

The dizziness would soon pass. No way was he going to die. Killed by a cupboard door. It was an unimaginably bland fate. He looked down at the floor, at quarts and quarts of blood. Lightheaded and disoriented, he shut his eyes, and felt much worse.

Shannon had returned. She knelt beside him, wiped blood from his face with a damp washcloth. "You're pale as a ghost. Are you okay?"

He shook his head, no. Big mistake. The kitchen wobbled on its axis.

She said, "You're not going to throw up, are you?"

"I hope not."

"Stand up." She swung a wooden chair around. "Sit down."

Ross sat.

"Tilt your head back. More to the left. *My* left." She was no Florence Nightingale. The washcloth scraped like coarse-grit sandpaper across his head, the lightness of her touch about what you'd expect from a heavy-duty mechanic. She said, "Too bad your hair isn't a little shorter, you'd be easier to clean up. Is that a prison thing, long hair?"

Ross shook his head. Ouch. He was going to have to learn, fast, to be more verbal. He said, "No, that's just the way I happen to like it."

"Me, too. It suits you. But I'd be able to see what I was doing a lot better if I cut it back a little. Would you mind? I always cut Kelly's hair. Or I could drive you to emergency . . ."

Ross sat quietly, a dishtowel draped over his shoulders, as she snipped away at him. She was very fast. When she'd finished she found a mirror and let him have a look at what she'd done – given him a kind of a go-to-hell look that suited him, in a way. But suited Kelly more. She said, "Did you see *The Unforgiven*?"

"Three times a day. Breakfast, lunch, and dinner. For almost five years."

Her laughter was relaxed, feminine. "No, I'm talking about the movie, the Clint Eastwood movie." She patted his head with the washcloth, went over to the sink and held it under the running tap, squeezed out the blood. "Clint was on television, one of those late-night talk shows. He went on and on about how he'd had his hair cut with a pair of sheep shears, or something like that. For authenticity." She resumed washing him. "So he'd look like guys looked back in those days."

"Makes sense to me."

She said, "You've almost stopped bleeding."

"I'm probably running low."

"D'you want to go to the hospital?"

"Not particularly." He tilted the mirror so he could make eye contact. "Do I need stitches?"

"How should I know? Do I *look* like a nurse?"

That was a tough one. What did the prototypical nurse look like? His brain dredged up a faintly remembered watercolour from his schoolboy days.

Shannon said, "You could use a stitch or two, I guess." She moved so she was standing directly in front of him, held up her left hand with her thumb and index finger separated by about a quarter-inch. "That's how long the cut is."

"You're kidding."

"Okay, *that* long." She spread her arms wide as any fisherman.

Ross smiled. She smiled back. He said, "They'd shave me, wouldn't they? I'd look like a monk."

"You? Don't count on it." She went over to the counter and yanked open the bottom drawer, rummaged around in there and soon came up with a plastic container. "These're Melinda's. Prescription drugs. For her migraine but she stopped taking them, because of the side effects. They're pretty strong, so I'd only take one or two, if I were you." She uncorked the wine, carried the bottle and two glasses and the drugs into the living room. She put everything on the pine trunk and made herself comfy at the far end of the sofa.

Leather creaked as Ross sat down. He said, "Want me to pour?"

"Please."

The light from the gas fire warmed her face and lent it a healthy glow. Her eyes sparkled. Her hair gleamed healthily.

Ross poured without spilling. He handed her a glass. No touching of fingers. He drank some wine.

Shannon had traded her skirt in on a pair of faded jeans and a mostly unbuttoned black silk blouse that looked pretty good against her pale skin. She wriggled a little higher on the sofa, crossed her legs yoga-style. "So, tell me about Garret."

"Well, uh . . ."

"He was *so* smart."

Ross was smart enough to agree. He helped himself to the drugs, got lucky with the childproof cap. His head throbbed unpleasantly. He shook five small pills into his hand. The pills were black, banded with yellow stripes. They looked like denuded wasps. He tossed all five pills into his mouth and drained his glass. He glanced at Shannon as he reached for the bottle.

She said, "I stopped visiting him, after a while. It wasn't that it was too far to go, or that I couldn't be bothered, or didn't care." Her look was moderately defiant. "Or had a new boyfriend, because I didn't."

Ross filled his glass. There was one wasp left. He ate it.

"I stopped visiting him because I couldn't stand to see him like that, so miserable and helpless."

Ross had never thought of Garret as miserable and helpless. More like happy as a clam, though there were times, as with most cons, when something inside would snap and he'd suddenly turn short-tempered and violent. Garret had hardly ever talked about what he was going to do when he got out. The way he acted, the man might have been institutionalized. There was nothing he seemed to lack in prison except Shannon, and he spoke of her in the past tense, as if she were something that had been real important to him once upon a time, but not now. Ross didn't blame him. It was hard, to wake up every morning and find yourself face to face with a life sentence. Among the inmates, a popular antidote for creeping insanity was to host an emotional garage sale, clear out all that stuff you cared about but that was forevermore beyond your grasp.

She said, "I sent him magazines almost every month."

"I know you did. I read some of 'em."

"You did?"

"Yeah, sure."

Shannon said, "I didn't think about him all the time, but I thought about him a lot. I could be doing almost anything, suddenly he'd be right there beside me."

Ross nodded, drank some more wine. He noticed that somewhere along the line he had lost his sense of taste. He didn't want to appear unsympathetic, but he hoped she wasn't going to start wading around in the sordid details of life without Garret. His glass was empty. How long had that been going on? What a sorry state of affairs. He offered Shannon the bottle, but she waved him away. He poured himself a refill. No point in standing on ceremony. He realized, with a vaguely witnessed sense of alarm, that he was considerably more relaxed than the situation merited. Had the medication begun to toy with him? He suspected it was so. His suspicions were confirmed a moment or so later, by the sudden blossoming of fireworks somewhere deep in his gut.

"Don't you understand what I'm talking about?" said Shannon.

Ross nodded. He said, "Yeah, of course I do." His voice sounded as if it were coming out of Dr. Reynolds' speakerphone. Shannon's black silk shirt clung to her body. If he squinted, and tilted his head until his neck threatened to break, he could almost see her nipple. What a slug. But should he stop peeking, or was he expected to peek? He drank all the wine in his glass. A few drops trickled down his chin. He said, "I completely agree."

Shannon reached out and took his glass. His head lolled forward. He said, "I'm tired."

"Alcohol and pills on an empty stomach aren't such a hot idea, are they?"

Ross yawned hugely.

She said, "Bedtime, Ross."

"Uh . . ."

She brought him his shoes, helped him to his feet, and led him through the house, turned on the back-porch light and helped him out the door and down the alarmingly steep stairway. She told him that he'd be sleeping in the garage. Ross hadn't the slightest idea what she was talking about. A chilly wind nibbled at him as they hurried, hand-in-hand, down the narrow sidewalk that bisected the backyard.

Shannon unlocked a door, flicked a lightswitch.

Inside, the garage was like a tiny one-room house. No, there was a door over there against the far wall, so there were *two* rooms. But this one must be the largest. Black-and-white photographs covered the walls. Shannon told him the sofa unfolded into a bed. She wished him a good night's sleep, and turned to leave.

Ross said, "Hey, wait a minute." He dug deep in his pocket, handed the skinny black guy's fat gold chain to Shannon.

"What's this?"

"Garret wanted you to have it."

"This was Garret's?" She held the chain, warm from the warmth of his body, against the swell of her breast. Crystalline tears poured down her pretty cheeks. He moved towards her, intending a friendly hug. She yanked open the door and bolted towards the house. Ross stood there under the overhang of the garage roof. He watched her hurry up the back-porch stairs, saw her in a shaft of light as Kelly opened the door to greet her. He saw Kelly put his muscular arm around her. Then the door slammed shut and the light was extinguished.

Was there something wrong with a brother giving his sister a hug? Nope. Not a damn thing. Rain gurgled down a nearby gutter. Ross was still a little dizzy, but the fresh air had revived him somewhat. He lit a cigarette. No matter how you looked at it, there was absolutely nothing wrong with a brother putting his arm around his grieving sister.

Another question: why had he told her the gold chain was Garret's?

An hour or so later, as he lay on the narrow sofa bed listening to the rain batter the roof, the answer came to him as in a vision. He had lied for one reason, and one reason only.

To keep in shape.

12

Willows started the car. The headlights illuminated the flank of a dark blue dumpster. He turned on the heater. The windshield slowly began to clear. Parker yawned. She was tired, and a little bit tense.

The bright yellow rubber gloves had provided them with a solid, but inanimate, lead. It seemed to Willows – and Parker agreed – that Donald E. Mooney's security-guard boyfriend was their best bet.

Parker pictured a would-be storm trooper in a sub-compact equipped with a spotlight and a radio, cruising expensive neighbourhoods in the dark and clammy hours of the night. Or maybe he was a mall cop, one of those tight-jawed, steely-eyed, buzz-cut guys who strutted around with all the panache of a free-range chicken. Or maybe, badass Doberman at his side, the boyfriend spent his nights guarding construction sites.

It had been a long day but now it had fallen into night. Willows and Parker, working separately, had canvassed the ground floor of Mooney's complex, as well as the apartments on the opposite side of the alley that had a line of sight on the dumpster. Parker hadn't been too happy about going over the same ground Orwell and Bobby Dundas had so recently trampled, but Willows easily persuaded her the work had to be done. As far as he was concerned, the murder of Donald E. Mooney was their sole responsibility, whether Orwell and Dundas were working the case or not.

Parker couldn't help wondering why there weren't any pictures of Mooney's boyfriend on the walls of Mooney's apartment. Another question: Why didn't Mooney have a snapshot of his boyfriend in his wallet? Had the boyfriend insisted on anonymity because he was a cop? It was a possibility that couldn't be ruled out. She said, "D'you know any gay cops, Jack?"

"Probably."

"What's that supposed to mean?"

"It means, not that I know of." Willows was bone-weary, chilled to the marrow. He put the car in reverse gear, and held his free hand up to the hot air gushing forcefully from a dashboard vent as he backed away from the looming shadow of the dumpster. He braked, and shifted into drive. They accelerated down the alley, the car chasing its headlights into the gloom.

Parker fastened her seatbelt. Willows had phoned Popeye Rowland and called in his markers. The M.E. had promised to do his best, but even so, it was unlikely that Donald E. Mooney would be autopsied for another twenty-four hours. They had a reasonably solid description of the boyfriend, but no name. The rubber gloves were promising, but they had a nubbly outer surface and a coarse fabric liner that Willows doubted would hold a fingerprint. He checked his watch, and groaned.

Parker said, "What?"

"I should've phoned, to say we wouldn't be home for dinner."

"Don't worry about it, Jack. I talked to Annie at a few minutes past five. She was going to try her hand at a Denver omelette. Sean was out. I should've told you I called. I just forgot, that's all."

"No problem." Willows braked hard, shifted into reverse and gunned it back up the alley to the dumpster.

"Now what?" said Parker

"I just thought of something." Willows got out of the car. He climbed up the rungs welded to the flank of the dumpster, lifted the hinged steel lid and let it drop. The clang of steel on steel echoed up and down the alley. He jumped lightly to the ground. As he got back into the car Parker said, "What was that all about?"

"Noise."

Parker nodded, getting it. "That's what Graham heard, when he thought he heard a shot."

"Maybe. We don't have any evidence that a shot was fired." Willows sat there for a moment, thinking. "Back in a minute." He got out of the car, shut the door against the chill and trotted across the scraggly spring grass towards the front of the apartment building.

Parker rested her head against the side window. She shut her eyes and was immediately confronted by a vision of Donald E. Mooney in his duct-tape suit. What had gone through his mind, as the plastic tube was shoved down his throat, as he gagged on the constant trickle of water, was filled to bursting drop by drop. Drowned, drop by drop.

Willows knuckled the windshield. Parker jerked upright, startled. He'd locked his door. She reached across and opened it for him. He said, "Taking a little nap, were we?"

"Not a chance."

Willows buckled up, got rolling. "Hungry?"

"I should be, but I'm not. Want to stop somewhere, grab a bite?"

"Maybe later." Willows yawned broadly. He covered his mouth with a fist. "Excuse me."

"We're both ready for a little sack time," said Parker. Willows smiled, but kept his eyes on the traffic as he braked at the mouth of the alley. She said, "I wonder how many private security companies there are in the city?"

"It's a growth industry. Something I might get involved in, when I retire."

"Really?" Parker couldn't imagine Willows quitting. Two blocks away, the lights of an ambulance strobed brightly. Willows cut into the curb lane across the blunt nose of a Volvo, made a sharp right. Twenty minutes later he pulled into an empty slot in the police garage around the corner from 312 Main, and ten minutes after that Parker was sitting at her third-floor desk, while he made coffee down at the far end of the squadroom.

Parker hauled a tattered copy of the Yellow Pages out of a bottom drawer. She thumped the book down on her desk.

"If you're looking up security-guard and patrol services, there's thirty-nine of 'em," said Bobby Dundas as he let himself into the squadroom. He strolled towards Parker with his hands in his pockets and a cocky smile on his freshly shaved face. "Plus there's a couple of government-approved training facilities. I wrote it all down, names and addresses, phone numbers. Made a copy just for you." He placed a folded sheet of paper squarely on Parker's desk. "Can you make out my handwriting, Claire?"

"Just barely."

"I'll take the top fifteen and you take the bottom fourteen, okay?" He smiled. "You don't mind if I'm on top, do you?"

Parker gave him an icy look. Bobby kept smiling. He glanced up, as Willows started towards them carrying two thick mugs of steaming coffee. He gave Parker a conspiratorial wink. "Okay, fine. *You* can be on top."

Willows' phone rang as he reached his desk. He handed Parker a mug, picked up.

"Jack, it's Ray Waddington. You're working the Mooney case, right?"

"Yeah, that's right. I've got a witness, guy gave us a solid description of a possible suspect. He's willing to come down, sit in a chair. I told him it could happen sometime tonight, if that's okay with you."

"Make it an hour, maybe a little less."

"Looking forward to it, Ray."

Willows disconnected. He dialled Graham Aubert's number. His witness answered on the eleventh ring. A television blared in the background. Willows heard a siren, shouting, a flurry of shots. He identified himself. "You okay, Graham?"

"Huh? Oh yeah, sure. I was watching *Dirty Harry*. The Eastwood film? It's a classic, absolutely timeless. One of my all-time favourites. Nobody squints like Clint."

"If I send a car over to pick you up, say in about half an hour, would that be okay?"

"To do the sketch?"

Willows said, "That's right, Graham. To do the sketch."

"You and your partner going to be there?"

"Claire and I will definitely be there," said Willows. He rolled his eyes at Parker. "What d'you say, Graham? Can you make it?"

"I said I'd do it, didn't I? Half an hour. You want me to wait outside, on the sidewalk in front of the apartment?"

"No, that's okay. The officer will come to your door. We appreciate this, Graham. See you when you get here." Willows disconnected, lifted his blotter and consulted a list of telephone numbers, dialled. "This's Jack Willows. Third floor, three-twelve Main. Yeah, that's me. Steamed rice, broccoli with beef, something with chicken . . ."

Ray Waddington arrived as Willows chased down the last slippery piece of boneless pork. Waddington was exactly six feet tall, but he was so thin, and stood so erect, that he looked a good deal taller. His thick, longish black hair was combed straight back from a high forehead. His prescription glasses had a pale orange tint. A thin moustache lay like a dark shadow on his upper lip. Ray was a cop. He was also an artist. Willows had never seen him wear any colour other than black when he was out of uniform.

"Jack, how've you been?"

"Not bad. Hungry?"

"Just ate, thanks." Waddington smiled at Parker. "Hey, Claire. Haven't seen you for quite some time. How's the shoulder?"

"Fine, Ray."

Waddington glanced around the empty squadroom. "Everybody else went home, did they?"

"Fired for reasons of gross incompetence," said Willows.

"About time, from what I've heard."

Parker said, "How're the kids?"

"Shirley's flunking French. Again. Toby's got a bad case of chicken pox. He's at the itchy stage. My mother-in-law suggested an oatmeal bath. It didn't work worth a damn, and now the upstairs drain's plugged."

Willows' phone warbled. Graham Aubert had arrived. Willows told the duty sergeant to send him up. He cradled the phone and pushed away from his desk. "Our witness is a guy named Graham Aubert. He's a little weird, Ray, so watch your step."

"A *little* weird? That'll make a nice change. Okay if I use Eddy's desk?"

"Better use mine," said Willows.

The elevator was located opposite the squadroom door. It hummed softly as it ascended. Parker said, "I better grab him before he wanders off and gets lost."

Willows shuffled a stack of canvass reports together and shoved them into the top drawer of his desk. He heard the elevator doors slide open. Parker led their witness into the squadroom. She introduced Aubert to Ray Waddington.

Waddington shook hands enthusiastically. He told Aubert that he was an upstanding citizen and that it was an honour to meet him, offered him a chair and advised him to relax, take his time, enjoy the experience. He dragged Orwell's chair over and sat down, fired up his portable computer. "Ever do any drawing, Graham?"

"Not really."

"I bet I've made a thousand sketches. Mostly perps, the odd victim. I graduated in criminology at Simon Fraser a few years back, but before that I was an art-school student. Man, those were the days. Live models. Totally naked babes." He shrugged. "The stuff I do now, half the time even the faces are fully clothed – beards and masks . . ." He smiled. "Heard the one about the Greek bank robber? Still can't figure out how the teller identified him, since he was wearing a baklava when he did the crime . . ."

It had taken the computer a few minutes to boot, but as

Waddington finished his little spiel, a row of icons blossomed on the screen.

"Okay, let's start with the shape of the face. By that I mean, is it oval, or heart-shaped, or . . ."

"Almost rectangular," said Aubert. "Like I told Detective Parker, he had a face shaped like a brick."

Waddington moved an electronic arrow to one of the icons. He clicked on the icon and five sub-icons appeared on the screen. He clicked on one of these and a rectangle appeared in the centre of the screen. Smiling, he said, "We don't actually have a brick shape, but how's that?"

"Pretty close."

"I can fiddle with it. Like this." He positioned the arrow on a vertical line, clicked a button on the mouse and "dragged" the line, altering its shape.

"No, more like it was. For now, anyway. Can we change it later?"

"Any time you want, Graham." Waddington used the mouse to return the rectangle to its original shape.

"Hair?"

"Blond. Very short."

"We're talkin' crewcut?"

"Sort of, but longer. Spiky. Kind of punk."

"Yeah, okay. Punk it is." Waddington clicked on another icon, and then a sub-icon. He laid the hair on the bald scalp as if it were an expensive wig. "How's the hairline look to you? Too high, too low? Just right?"

"Too high. He's showing too much forehead."

Waddington used the mouse to slowly lower the hairline. According to Aubert, the suspect had a slight widow's peak. He thickened the hair and made it stand on end, then cut and shaped it with the mouse. Finished, he examined his work with a critical eye. "How's that?"

"Pretty good."

"Stand aside, Rembrandt." Waddington glanced at Willows and Parker. In Ray's professional opinion, the suspect's haircut made him look an awful lot like Bart Simpson. But, maybe the guy *did* look like Bart Simpson. Hell, maybe his name *was* Bart Simpson, and he'd had his hair specially dyed and cut so he'd look a little bit like the cartoon character. He had no idea why anyone in his right mind would do anything like that. But then, he was an artist, not a shrink.

"Okay, let's move on to the eyebrows. Here, let me show you a few . . ."

Aubert pointed. "Those ones, the arched ones." He hesitated, and then said, "But they were black."

"Black?"

"Yeah, black."

"You're sure?" Waddington changed the colour of the eyebrows to jet black. "How's that?"

"The shape's right, but they weren't as heavy."

"Thinner?"

Aubert nodded. He looked like he was enjoying himself. Waddington shaved the eyebrows.

"That better?"

"Perfect. It's perfect."

"Good. But something's missing. Did the guy have a nose, Graham?"

Aubert nodded, half-smiled.

"Let's give him a nose." Waddington glanced at his watch. They'd been going at it almost twenty minutes. Aubert was sweating, starting to show the strain. Waddington clicked on an icon and then on a sub-icon that stood slightly apart from the others. The cruelly hooked beak of a bald eagle materialized on the suspect's face.

Aubert's mouth fell open. "What's that supposed to be?"

"My sense of humour," said Waddington.

Aubert frowned. "I don't get it."

Waddington gave Aubert a pained look. "I was just trying to lighten things up, that's all." His face was red. He cleared his throat. "So, how're you doing? Want to take a break?"

"No, let's get this over with."

Slowly, line by line, the face took shape. Waddington added the final touch, a Robert Mitchum-type cleft to the chin. "Okay, that's it. What d'you think?"

Graham Aubert said, "That's him, all right."

"Nothing you want to add?"

"Not really."

Waddington hit the *save* key. He said, "Okay, I'm going to plug this beast into a printer and run off a copy for you to take home. I'm also going to give you a small gift, a VPD fridge magnet, so you can stick the drawing on your Moffat."

"Westinghouse."

"Okay, fine. Westinghouse. Take a look at the sketch every time you grab a beer. It doesn't look quite right, something starts to bother you, some detail, I don't care how small, pick up the phone and give me a call. Okay?" Waddington fished out his wallet, withdrew a card. "That's got my name and work number on it. I'm going to give you my home number too, so you can get in touch with me if I'm off-duty." He borrowed a Bic pen from Parker and jotted down his number, handed the card to Aubert.

Aubert stuck the card in his shirt pocket.

"Don't throw it away."

"I won't."

"Because anybody could find it, call me at home in the middle of the night, talk dirty to my wife . . ."

"I wouldn't do anything like that!"

Ray Waddington rolled his eyes towards the ceiling.

Aubert said, "You're kidding me again, aren't you?"

Waddington nodded. He said, "I was kidding about the fridge magnet, too, Graham."

"You were?"

"I could give you a lapel pin, or a tie clip . . ."

"What about a hat?"

"A baseball cap, is that what you want, a VPD baseball cap?" Ray ran his fingers through his hair, tugged at an earlobe. He said,

"I don't know, those hats are pretty hard to come by. How about a slightly crashed motorcycle, or maybe an old revolver or a surplus Kevlar vest?"

"Let's get him a cap," said Parker.

"Yeah? Really? A cap?"

Parker nodded. She tilted her head for a better look at the computer's colour screen. The hair was kind of weird. Straw yellow, bolt upright, spiky. Cartoonish. Like a grown-up Bart Simpson . . .

13

He'd been dreaming. His parole officer, George Hoffman, had been chasing him through a field. Hoffman had been riding a horse, wielding a sword, whooping maniacally. He'd flushed Ross from his hidey-hole in a blackberry thicket, thundered down on him and was just about to slice off his head when Ross had been awakened by some small, unfamiliar sound.

He lay there, his heart thumping. The room was cold, and the blankets had slipped off him, or he'd pushed the bedding away in his nocturnal struggles. He sat up. There was someone else in the room, breathing harshly. He sat up a little straighter. "Who is it? Who's there?"

A beam of light dazzled him, and then swung sharply towards the ceiling. Shannon's face was illuminated from below. She bared her teeth, making of her face a mask of horror. The beam of light wandered over him, head to toe. He scrambled to cover himself. She said, "Is that a prison thing, to sleep naked?"

"I forgot to pack my pyjamas." Ross bent a leg. He struggled with the blankets. "What time is it?"

"Late. I couldn't sleep. Kelly woke me up, singing in the shower. He works nights, different shifts." She adjusted the beam of the flashlight, widening the focus so the room was lit by concentric rings of suffused light. "Aren't you going to ask me what I'm doing here, standing at the foot of your bed in the middle of the night?"

Ross mulled it over. Finally he said, "It's your place. I guess you can be wherever you want to."

"Damn right," said Shannon mildly. She added. "You were dreaming. Or maybe I should call it a nightmare." As she spoke, she drifted languorously around to the side of the bed, and sat down. She tossed the flashlight on the bed. "Garret used to sleep in this room, when he first started coming around, but before we started sleeping together."

Ross ached for a cigarette.

She said, "I fell in love with him just like that, the moment I first saw him. I don't know what it was. Chemistry . . . I was bouncing off the walls, could hardly keep my hands off him. But I was terrified that I might frighten him away, if I was too aggressive."

"How did you meet him?" Ross had heard Garret tell the story so many times that he'd lost count. The lovebirds had stumbled across each other at one of the clubs on Richards Street. Garret had stolen and strip-mined her purse, showed up on her doorstep that same night claiming he'd found it in the men's washroom.

She said, "I was at a club on Richards, with a couple of friends from work. It was a Saturday night. We were going to go to a movie, but . . ."

Ross yawned. His jaw creaked.

"We were sitting at a table by the dance floor. It was early, and the band hadn't showed up, but there was recorded music . . . We'd been there for an hour or so, drinking. I noticed him standing at the bar. He was wearing a jacket and tie. I thought he was really good-looking, clean-cut and everything. He saw me looking at him, and smiled. I smiled back, and he came over and introduced himself, asked me if I'd like to dance. So we danced and then he came back to the table with me, and sat down.

"We'd been drinking white wine. He ordered a bottle of Chardonnay, and he talked to me, and my friends. I was attracted to him, physically attracted to him. And I could tell he liked me. But there are plenty of good-looking guys around, aren't there, Ross?"

"If you say so."

"What I really liked about Garret was he was obviously hitting on me, but he didn't exclude my friends, tune them out. That was important to me, because it showed that he was considerate."

Ross nodded. There was a draft from the window, cold and damp. He pulled the blankets up a little higher.

"He stayed for a long time, drinking and dancing. Most of the time with me, but every so often he'd take one or both of my friends out on the floor. About one o'clock in the morning, I noticed my purse was missing. Garret spoke to the bartender, who called the manager. He was really upset. We were all upset. The manager told me he'd make sure the janitorial staff kept an eye out for it. He offered to lend me cab fare home, but I had my car, and my keys were in my coat pocket."

"You'd been drinking all night, and you drove home?"

"Losing my purse sobered me up. And I'd been dancing a lot. But you're right, I probably should've taken a taxi. But when you've had a few too many, sometimes it's hard to think clearly, isn't it?"

Ross agreed that it was. He pushed the flashlight around with his feet until the beam was pointing away from him.

"Anyway, I gave my girlfriends a ride back to their apartment, and then I drove home."

Ross knew exactly what was coming.

"I parked out in front, where I parked tonight. I was halfway up the walk before I saw Garret."

Sitting on the porch, top step. Smoking a cigarette and looking down at her, smiling.

Shannon put a hand to her breast. "He scared the hell out of me!"

"I bet he did," said Ross. He could, no problem, picture the expression on her face.

She'd screamed loud enough to wake the neighbourhood for blocks around.

"I screamed, really screamed. And he started laughing. He held up my purse, so I'd understand what he was doing there, and he told me he'd found it in the men's washroom." Her voice softened. "At the time, I knew there was a chance that he was lying. But I didn't care. All that mattered was his cute little butt plunked down on my porch, his wonderful smile that was all for me." She turned a little so she was more directly facing Ross. "Did he ever talk about that night, mention my purse?"

"Yeah, he talked about it. Bent my ear so bad I thought it'd fall right off. You got everything back, didn't you, in the end?"

"Except my credit cards and about eighty dollars in cash."

"Still, I bet he was worth every penny."

She snatched up the flashlight and for a wild and crazy moment he feared she was going to bounce it off his skull. Teach him to mind his tongue, or some other equally valuable lesson. But all she did was stroll out of the room, shut the door behind her without even bothering to say goodnight.

Ross waited a moment, and then he eased out of bed and tiptoed to the window. In the glow of a neighbour's security light, he saw a dark shape detach itself from the house, move towards Shannon. Big brother seemed to have skipped work. Kelly's clothes were dark. If he hadn't been smoking, and had been wearing a hat, Ross might not have seen him at all. Kelly put his arm around his sister's shoulder. They disappeared around the side of the house. Ross thought about wrapping himself in blankets and going outside for a smoke, but it was too late, and too cold. He crawled back into the icy bed and lay there shivering. As he drifted uneasily into sleep, someone shouted his name . . . Or was he already dreaming?

He awakened to an unexpected view of bright blue sky. Directly above him was a large rectangular skylight. The glass had safety wire embedded in it, so the rectangle was a grid composed of thousands of tiny squares. He glanced around, getting his bearings. The studio was sparsely furnished. A gas fireplace stood in one corner. There was the sofa bed, and an overstuffed chair in a shiny, dark green fabric, an ornate oak rocking chair that might've been an antique but was probably a reproduction, if only because it looked so new. The nubby wall-to-wall carpet was cream-coloured, with hints of pale green. And of course there were all those photographs, hundreds of them, on the white-painted plasterboard walls. His bladder was full. He banged a shin on the sofa's iron frame as he climbed out of bed. Ouch!

Man, oh man, but it was strange, being all alone. Privacy. It was an alien concept. He crossed the room and opened a door with a red light bulb screwed into a socket above it. He flicked the light switch just inside the door, and the room was bathed in blood-red light. A low counter and three shallow stainless-steel sinks ran along the back wall. A complicated machine stood on a small, thick-legged table. A few small photographs were fastened by clothespegs to a length of butcher's cord strung from wall to wall. Shannon apparently worked exclusively in black and white. Maybe it was cheaper. Ross took a closer look.

Self-portraits.

Totally shameless nudes.

The photos had been taken in her kitchen, from several perspectives. Ross considered the possibilities. Her camera had a timing device, or she had an accomplice. No, that wasn't the right word. Apprentice. His bladder nagged him. He urinated in the end sink, let the water run and then washed his hands, and shook them dry as he spent a little more time studying the pictures, decided the one of Shannon clothed in Saran Wrap, curled up in a refrigerator, was his favourite.

He left the darkroom, dressed in yesterday's clothes, folded the sofa bed back into itself, replaced the cushions and went outside. He'd expected nothing but blue from horizon to horizon, but the sky was full of churning black cloud, the patches of blue coming and going in those high winds. He lit a cigarette. The backyard lawn was patchy and needing mowing. On the far side of the yard a small patio had been made of ugly concrete slabs. The fence, side and back, was a sturdy six-footer. He moved away from the garage, into a transient patch of sunlight. A moment or two later the basement door swung open and Kelly stepped outside. He wore black jeans, a black leather jacket, black boots. His black baseball cap was on backwards. His sunglasses had perfectly round, anti-glare lenses. He shut the door and locked it, turned and glanced towards the garage, the black glasses zeroing in on Ross like shotgun barrels. Ross felt himself go perfectly still. Cloud raced across the face of the sun and the air suddenly grew chill. Nothing moved but the smoke from Ross's cigarette, which dangled from a corner of his mouth.

After a long moment, Kelly turned his back on him and shoul-dered his way towards the front of the house.

Slugs of sweat crawled all over Ross's body. He exhaled with a whoosh, leaned against the wall of the garage and took a long pull on his cigarette, swamping his lungs with four thousand chemi-cals, including a healthy dose of cyanide. A complex blend, but perfectly realized. Now all he needed was a cup of coffee, a hot shower and change of clothes. His Jockeys, anyway.

He smoked the cigarette down to his fingers, flicked the butt over the fence and into the alley. It had started to rain, again. He went back inside.

Some of the photographs on the wall of the large room were of Shannon, but none of them were nudes. Most of the pictures were of normal, everyday scenes. People waiting for a bus. People getting onto a bus. The bus pulling away, leaving some of the people behind, looking resigned but not angry. He supposed it was the *way* the pictures were taken that was important, rather than the subject matter.

He realized, as his eye was sliding on to the next picture, that one of the people left behind at the bus stop happened to be his old buddy, Garret.

He studied the pictures more closely. There was Garret loiter-ing outside a McDonald's, a Big Mac in both hands, a sloppy Happy Meal smile all over his face. And there he was standing in line at the Cineplex, grinning amiably. The camera's auto-timer, or the assistant or collaborator or whatever, had taken a snapshot of Garret and Shannon down by the Stanley Park seawall, the loving couple oblivious to the blurred, wall-to-wall mass of week-end athletes trotting past in the background.

Here was a completely hysterical shot of Garret grinning wickedly as he mock-sneaked up on an armoured car, his fist shaped into a gun.

And another of Garret and Shannon curled up, naked but unrevealing, the clever intertwining of their sleek bodies giving away nothing at all, in the backseat of the Saab. Looking post-coital and smug.

Ross heard a sound behind him, turned as Shannon hurried in. She had a rolled-up newspaper in hand, and his first thought was that she was going to give him a whack. But no, she was cheerful and smiling.

"What d'you think?"

"Of the pictures?"

"Photographs. No, the weather, stupid."

"Nice to see blue sky, for a change." He smiled. "They're great."

"Really?" She was pleased, he could tell.

She leaned against the open doorway, the rain slanting down behind her, a drip from the eaves, bushes swirling in the fitful wind.

"What do you like best about them, Ross?"

"Uh . . ."

"The composition, contrast, lighting? Cropping? What?"

"Uh, I'm no expert . . ."

"I guess not." Abruptly, her mood changed. "Hungry? Come on back to the house. Let's eat."

Breakfast wasn't quite ready, and wouldn't be, until Ross had showered and shaved. She showed him the bathroom. A razor and other gear had been laid out for him. From a hook on the bathroom door hung a freshly ironed maroon shirt on a metal hanger, faded jeans complete with a brown leather belt. She'd also laid out a pair of beige socks and some nifty bikini underpants, in white silk with fire-engine-red hearts. Were these Garret's clothes, in storage for all these years? Had to be. Not that he had the heart to ask.

She showed him how to work the shower, told him to make sure the sliding glass door was completely closed, to wipe up any spills when he'd finished. He waited until she'd left, then shut the door and shot the bolt and turned to look at himself in the mirror over the sink. His hair was a mess. The stubble on his face softened his features, giving him kind of a wimpy, indecisive look. His skin felt gritty. He turned on the shower, adjusted the temperature of the water blasting from the shower head. He stripped naked. A bar of white soap squatted in a built-in tile dish. No doubt Shannon had used that selfsame bar, run it all over her body . . .

Ross shouldered that licentious thought aside. He washed his hair with shampoo that smelled of flowers. He fumbled a fresh cartridge into the razor, and cautiously shaved. He squeezed out a fat green worm of toothpaste onto his brand-new toothbrush and vigorously cleaned his teeth.

He towelled himself dry, used a white plastic rat-tail comb on his hair. He wriggled into the silk undies, socks, shirt and pants. Not bad, considering.

A pair of almost-new white leather Nikes stood on the floor just outside the bathroom door. Just for the hell of it, he tried them on. The shoes fit like a glove.

He found Shannon sitting at the kitchen table, reading the *Province*. She told him to sit down, poured him a cup of coffee and then busied herself at the stove. She'd scrambled some eggs, fried sausages, heated up some pre-cooked hash browns. The toaster popped. She carried the food to the table, got him a glass of fresh-squeezed orange juice from the fridge. There was a big round wall clock over the stove. The second hand jogged steadily around the dial. He began to eat. Shannon went back to reading her paper.

Eventually she said, "How's your breakfast?"

"Good."

"Why didn't you say so? One of the many things I liked about Garret was that he was so polite."

"Really good," said Garret. "Delicious. Superb."

"Thank you. More coffee?"

He nodded, and then caught himself and said, "*Please.*" She fetched the pot, filled his cup and then her own. He added some milk from a clear glass jug, stirred in the milk with the handle of his fork. When he looked up, she was watching him. He cocked an eyebrow. "Something on your mind?"

"I was just thinking that with your hair cut short you look a lot like him, in a way . . ." She trailed off, as if she'd lost track of her thoughts. She looked down at the paper, and then out the window. It had stopped raining, for now.

"Like who?"

"Garret." She seemed genuinely surprised that he hadn't known who she was talking about. As if there was only one *him* in the world. She said, "You're both about the same height. Garret might've been five pounds lighter. The shape of your eyes is remarkably similar. And you've got the same nose, nice and straight. The overall shape of your face is almost identical, but Garret's cheekbones were more prominent, and he had such nice dimples, when he smiled."

Which was almost never, by the way.

She was looking at him, he suspected, as she might look at something she intended to photograph. Intent, but dispassionate. He picked at his eggs. She said, "Your ears are similar, too. On the small side, set close to your head . . ."

Ross said, "I never thought of myself as having small ears."

"Well, you do. In my opinion."

He stared at her, and she stared back at him. After a moment he shrugged, as if it didn't matter to him one way or the other. "If you say so."

"I do," she shot right back.

She had a temper. He'd forgotten about it, but that didn't mean it wasn't there. A wildcat, Garret had called her, admiringly. As if his ability to deal with her violent temperament somehow enhanced his vision of himself. But why was she upset with him?

Because he looked a lot like Garret, but wasn't Garret. He leaned back in his chair. "In the slammer, me 'n' Garret took care of each other. I watched his back and he watched mine. There were guys in there, met us for the first time, thought we were brothers."

"Did they?" Her eyes softened, lost their flash and thunder. She said, "I can see why." She hunkered forward in her chair, reached across the table and touched his sleeve, traced her fingers across the back of his hand. "You could be him, you really could."

"But I'm not."

"No," she said, "but you *could* be."

14

Ray Waddington exited his portable computer, unplugged the power cord and rolled the cord into a tight coil. The computer after he'd snapped it shut resembled a very slim briefcase. "How many copies you want, Jack?"

"I don't know." Willows thought about it for a moment. "Let's start with fifty."

"That's all?"

"The guy isn't a lost cat, Ray. We aren't going to be stapling his picture to every telephone pole in the city."

Parker said, "But don't take it personally. You're an *artiste*, for sure."

"See you later, detectives." Waddington waggled his fingers at Parker, who waggled back. As he left the squadroom, Waddington agilely stepped aside in deference to Inspector Homer Bradley. Bradley broke stride. "You finished here?"

"Just leaving, Inspector."

Bradley nodded tersely. Waddington kept moving. Bradley focused on Graham Aubert. "This our witness?"

Parker made the introductions. Bradley congratulated Aubert on his sense of civic responsibility. "You need a ride home?"

Willows said, "I lined up a car. I was just going to take him downstairs."

"Do it, Jack." Bradley pumped Aubert's hand again, and complimented him for being an upstanding citizen.

Willows escorted Aubert down to the main floor, and passed him over to a uniform. By the time he made it back upstairs, Orwell and Bobby Dundas had joined the crowd around Parker's desk.

Bradley said, "Jack, Bobby's suggested we film a 'Crimestoppers' spot. What's your opinion?"

"It's too early for that, Inspector." Willows studied the printed copy of Ray Waddington's sketch, as he collected his thoughts. "All we know about this guy is that he visited Mooney fairly frequently during the past couple of weeks. We can't place him at the apartment at the time or even on the night of the murder. At this point, all we can say about him with any degree of confidence is that he was an acquaintance of Mooney's. If he looks good right now, it's only because he's all we've got."

Parker said, "I agree with Jack."

Bobby gave her a look. He smiled faintly.

Bradley said, "Bob?"

"The security guard's all we've got. I say we should use it. How long does it take to slap a 'Crimestoppers' together? Three or four weeks? Let's at least get started on it. If the guy shows up, or is eliminated as a possible suspect, or the case takes a sharp turn in some other direction, fine. We'll drop it. But if that doesn't happen, we'll be ready to roll that much sooner."

Bradley glanced inquiringly at Orwell. Eddy held his peace. Bradley said, "Eddy, are you and Bobby on the same page?"

"We're on the same fucking paragraph," said Bobby Dundas. He smiled. "In fact we're on the same *line*. Right, Eddy?"

"Right," said Orwell.

Parker said, "Another thing. 'Crimestoppers' has a limited budget. We spend a few thousand dollars trying to catch a cop-killer, aren't we leaving ourselves open to criticism?"

"No matter what we do," said Bobby Dundas.

Bradley held up a warning hand. "What *have* we got going for us?"

"Eddy and I've been over the interview reports from the door-to-door canvass," said Bobby. "They don't look promising." He shrugged. "It's a busy neighbourhood, Inspector. People coming and going at all hours of the night. Unless you're wandering around with your head tucked under your arm, you're not gonna get noticed. But we'll do follow-up interviews with the artwork, and there are a few people we weren't able to contact the first time around, that we'll be talking to."

Bradley nodded. "You going to need help with that?"

"If Jack's willing," said Bobby sweetly.

Jack," said Bradley, "what are you and Claire up to?"

"We're waiting on the autopsy and the lab reports. I'll give Kirkpatrick a call first thing in the morning, see if I can light a fire under him."

"That's it?"

"Claire's made a list of stores in the area that might sell duct-tape. We'll do a canvass first thing in the morning. Maybe we'll get lucky, and someone will recognize our suspect."

"The security guard."

Willows nodded, "Yeah, the security guard. If that's what he was. Aubert wasn't too clear on that. He'd made an assumption, that's all. The guy could be a mall cop, or work for one of the armoured-car companies. Or maybe he's a pilot or a mailman . . ."

"Or just a guy who likes to dress up," said Bradley. He rubbed his chin. "I've got Dan and Farley working the Richard Beinhart killing, getting nowhere. Farley wants to talk to the house's owner, Chris Bowers. But his secretary says Bowers decided to spend an extra week in Costa Rica. I'm going to tell them to bag it, assign them to your case."

Willows said, "I don't know what good that would do, Inspector. We're short on leads, not manpower."

Bradley waved away Willows' protestations. "I'll talk to you later, Jack. Keep me up to the minute on this one, understand? Anything breaks, I want to know about it right away." Bradley plucked a cigar from his pocket. He pointed at Bobby Dundas. "You too, Bobby."

Bobby nodded, but Bradley was already striding purposefully towards his pebbled-glass box of an office. When he'd shut the door, Eddy Orwell said, "The man is *agitated*."

"We're all agitated," said Bobby. He winked at Parker, turned away before she could respond.

Willows sat at his desk, picked up the phone and speed-dialled his home number. Annie answered on the third ring. She'd already cooked and eaten her supper, and rinsed the dishes and put them away in the dishwasher. Yes, she'd done her homework, and had her evening all planned, thank you. She was going to watch "The Simpsons" on television, and then go to bed and read for half an hour or so. Sean? He was out. She had no idea where he was. But there was no need to worry. She didn't mind being alone.

Willows said, "I've got some paperwork to catch up on, Annie, but it shouldn't take more than half an hour or so."

"If my light's still on, you can come up and tuck me in."

"Okay, honey."

"Or if my light's out, you could still check on me, if you want."

"I'll do that."

"Promise?"

"It's a promise," said Willows. He told his daughter he loved her, and hung up. Orwell was watching him, a peculiar expression on his face.

"What's on your mind, Eddy?"

Orwell shrugged, and looked away.

Willows was at his desk, trying to make sense of his written notes, when his phone rang. He picked up, identified himself.

"Detective Willows, this is Constable Pat Timmins. Can I meet you and your partner somewhere quiet?" Timmins' voice was barely audible. Willows strained to hear him. He said, "It's about Don Mooney."

Willows reached for his jacket.

Twenty minutes later, he pulled into the mini-parking lot of a Japantown restaurant. It was one of those restaurants that seemed to be springing up all over the city – lacking in potential or ambition, with a too-cute, meaningless name, a little neon scrawled across the window. Inside, everything would be shiny and clean, lacking in soul. The lighting would be too bright, the food palatable but uninspiring.

Pat Timmins was out of uniform, but Willows knew a cop when he saw one. Timmins was sitting in a booth at the rear of the restaurant. Willows and Parker slid into the booth. A waitress drifted over. Willows ordered coffee; Parker a glass of milk. Timmins wanted more hot water for his tea.

Parker guessed Timmins' age at about twenty-seven. His broad forehead was unlined. His close-cropped hair was sandy-brown, his sparse moustache almost blond. His eyes were dark brown. He had a prominent chin. Freckles danced across the bridge of his prominent nose. He looked like a man on the edge of exhaustion.

Willows introduced himself and Parker. Timmins didn't offer his hand. He said, "Thanks for doing it this way. I appreciate it."

"No problem."

Timmins rotated his cup in the saucer. Manipulating his tea leaves, perhaps. He said, "Don and I were friends."

The waitress arrived with the coffee and milk. She'd forgotten Timmins' hot water. But so, apparently, had he.

Willows added cream, stirred.

"Close friends?" said Parker.

Timmins nodded. "Yeah, you could put it that way."

Willows said, "How close were you, Pat?" He drank some coffee, and was pleased to discover it wasn't absolutely the worst coffee he'd ever had. Timmins sat there, eyes downcast. Willows said, "Close enough to touch?"

Timmins nodded. He lifted the lid of his stainless-steel teapot and peeked inside, let the lid drop. "We were lovers," he said

quietly. Willows drank some more coffee. Maybe he'd been wrong
– maybe it was the worst coffee he'd ever tasted.

"Don was a great guy. I loved him." Timmins looked Willows
in the eye. "Really loved him," he said.

Willows waited patiently.

Timmins was fading. The waitress arrived with his hot water.
He drank some more tea.

Willows glanced at Parker, but it was clear that she, too, was
uncertain as to how to respond to Timmins' declaration of love.
Willows waited a moment or two longer and then said, "Pat, would
you like me to remind you of your rights?"

Timmins violently shook his head. "I didn't *kill* him! Is that
what you think, that I want to *confess*?"

"What do you want to talk about?" said Parker.

Timmins slumped against the wall. "Don and I went to Hawaii
last year, over the Easter holidays. He took some raunchy
Polaroids, gave me a few but kept most of them. They're in his
apartment. I knew you'd find them sooner or later, thought I'd
better call you before you got around to calling me . . ."

"Were you and Don living together, Pat?"

"No, we weren't. We did for a while, for just under a year. But I
moved out soon after we graduated from the Academy."

"How long ago was that?"

"Coming up six years. Six years in June. Don didn't think it was
a good idea for us to stay together. He was worried that people
would find out about us."

"That you were gay?"

"It was other cops that he was worried about," said Timmins.
"Straight cops," he amended.

Willows nodded his understanding. The force had recently
instituted a policy of actively recruiting gays, but he didn't know
any straight cops who were convinced that it was a good idea.
Willows believed he was without prejudice. He also firmly believed
that most cops were homophobic, and so he understood Timmins'
hesitation in stepping forward.

Parker said, "What was the exact nature of your relationship, Pat? You and Don weren't living together. Did you have a monogamous relationship, or were there other men in your life?"

Timmins hesitated. Finally he said, "Don had begun to see someone else, recently."

"Who?"

"I wish I knew."

"He didn't mention a name?"

"No, he didn't."

"Have you got any ideas? Is it likely someone who was a mutual friend, for example?"

"I just don't know. Believe me, if I had any idea who he was seeing, I'd tell you. But . . . I don't." His hand trembled as he added hot water to his tea. A bell tinkled as the restaurant's door swung open. A trio of skateboarders, all baggy-ass and swagger, clattered into the restaurant.

Parker reached across the table. She laid her hand on Timmins' wrist. He didn't look up. She said, "Pat?"

"Yeah, what?"

"We've phoned repeatedly but haven't been able to get in touch with Don's father or mother. Do you have any idea where they are?"

"On a cruise ship. They took a cruise ship up the coast to Alaska. One of those 'love boat'–type ships, big as a mountain. They left the same day Don was killed."

"Have you tried to get in touch with them?"

Timmins moved his arm, disengaging from Parker.

"Did you get along with them?"

"Yeah, we got along okay."

"They were comfortable with Don's sexuality?"

"Don got along okay with his mother. She accepted him for what he was."

"But his father didn't?"

"His father refused to talk to him, or even acknowledge the fact that he existed. He's one of those guys, believes all the lies and bullshit; that gays are wildly promiscuous, love to seduce little boys . . ."

Timmins had raised his voice. The skateboarders were staring at him, whispering amongst themselves, snickering.

Willows shifted in his seat, and glanced behind him. Suddenly he was the focus of the skateboarders' attention. Now they were staring at him, whispering about him, openly sneering at him. He turned away. The look in Timmins' brown eyes told Willows what he already knew. That he'd just had the tiniest, most insignificant little taste of what it could be like, day in and day out, from the day you strolled out of the closet.

Parker said, "Pat, don't bullshit us."

Timmins' head came up. He nervously stroked his moustache. "Excuse me?"

"You know damn well what I'm talking about. You and Don were together, in a monogamous and loving relationship, for six years. Then he started playing the field. Seeing other men. Do you really expect us to believe that you weren't upset? That you didn't get angry, lose your temper, say or do something you wish you hadn't? Do you really expect us to believe that all you did was drift off into the distance, quiet and placid as a fleecy little cloud?" Parker drank some milk.

Timmins was sweating, looking more gaunt by the minute. He fumbled in his jacket, pulled out a pack of cigarettes and lit up. He sucked the smoke deep into his lungs and then burst into a fit of coughing. When he had himself under control, he said, "You didn't hear this from me, okay?"

"You know better than that, Pat."

Timmins took another pull on his cigarette. Smoke leaked from his nostrils. He said, "Don was seeing another cop."

"VPD?" said Parker.

Timmins nodded. "Yeah, one of us. An old guy. With plenty of seniority, and pips."

Willows felt a slow churning in the pit of his stomach. Timmins was about to name a high-ranking police officer. A closet homo-sexual who was intimately involved with the victim. The poor bastard had failed to step forward, and now there was a chance he was about to be dragged kicking and screaming into a high-profile murder investigation.

Willows could hardly wait to meet him.

15

Shannon called in sick. She crossed her fingers and told her boss in a low, throaty voice that she had a headache, sore throat, terrible cough, a fever and runny nose, congestion, a sharp pain in her chest. So many lies, but how easily she told them. In truth, she was taking the day off just for Ross. She wanted to show him around. Take him by the hand and lead him to all the places around town that she and Garret had visited, during those hot, stormy days prior to the launch of his spectacularly unsuccessful career as an armed robber, his sudden incarceration for what turned out to be the rest of his natural-born days.

As they approached the Saab, Ross asked if he could drive.

Shannon smiled sweetly, told him no. She deactivated the car's alarm, unlocked the door and eased in behind the wheel, unlocked his door. Ross thought about taking a walk. But he was broke, and it was raining again, and where would he go? Home to mother? No way. By way of compromise, he turned his back on her and lit a cigarette, sucked smoke deep inside his body. Shannon started the car. The Saab had a manual choke. Ross stood there in the scant shelter of the soon-to-bud-but-not-yet-budding branches of the cherry tree, as the car's engine warmed up. Fat drops of cold water splattered on his head and hunched shoulders. The air stank of exhaust fumes; he moved a little distance away.

Shannon leaned on the horn, summoned him with a peremptory wave of her hand. Getting even, he ruthlessly stamped his cigarette butt into the grassy boulevard. Only then did he stroll over to the car. She told him to buckle up, offered him a mint. When he declined, she took his chin in hand and pushed the mint forcefully into his mouth. "Eat it, tobacco-breath."

Ross spat the mint into his cupped hand. It was nothing but a mint. He popped it back into his mouth.

"What'd you think I was trying to do, poison you?" Shannon hit the gas. The Saab lurched into the middle of the road. She said, "You spend ten minutes brushing your teeth and then turn around and light a cigarette. I don't get it. What's the point?"

"I'm an addict," said Ross. He crunched the mint between his molars. "It's as simple as that."

Instantly contrite, she patted his thigh, and then let her hand lie where it had happened to fall. "I'm sorry," she said demurely. "I'm a little tense. Can you blame me?"

"I don't see why not."

She smiled, and gave his thigh a quick squeeze, went back to steering the car. She sure had a wide variety of smiles. A real arsenal. Warm, sisterly smiles. Vague, dreamy smiles. Sexy smiles and every other kind of smile you could think of. Maybe you had to be an accomplished smiler to work the Zellers cash registers. Nah, there had to be more to it than that. More likely, women who had a naturally nice smile worked at improving it, broadening their range. Those who didn't, didn't. He shifted towards her as much as the Saab's bucket seat allowed. "How did you end up at Zellers?" he asked.

"I applied for a job."

"How much they pay you?"

"As little as possible. But it's a living, I suppose."

Ross nodded. "Yeah, I guess it must be. Because you're alive, right? But then, so am I, and I don't make a living, do I?"

"You could if you wanted to."

"Doing what? Washing dishes?"

"I was thinking more along the lines of your natural talents," said Shannon.

What was *that* supposed to mean? A tendency to sleep in late?

They were driving south on Commercial. The sidewalks were crowded despite the weather. But then, if you stayed inside every day it rained, you'd starve to death pretty quick. There was a prosperous-looking ethnic population, mostly Chinese and East Indian. The streetscape was vibrant, colourful, jumping with energy. Prison seemed a million miles away; a drab, alien life on another planet.

Shannon drove him to a block-square, nondescript park. She killed the engine and got out of the car, and shut the door and locked it. More because of the opportunity for a cigarette than anything else, Ross followed her lead. The sky was stuffed with clouds the colour of dishwater. A chill wind toyed with his new haircut. He turned up his collar. The park wasn't much to look at. There were a few bedraggled trees scattered around the perimeter, a three-court tennis enclosure. Off to his left stood the miniature forts, monkey bars, and gaudy plastic piping of a tot's activity centre. A tight group of mothers chatted animatedly. Their socially inept pre-schooler offspring stood quietly by. What else could they do? The children had been so thoroughly bundled up against the weather that they had been rendered virtually immobile.

In the middle distance a large black dog trotted at a fixed pace across the scraggly grass. Ross couldn't pin it down, but there was something about the mutt's posture that suggested vitally important unfinished business. He felt a dagger-sharp stab of envy. He tried to think of what the animal might be up to. Maybe it was looking for a beloved lost puppy. Or a vanished Frisbee, or any mission worthy of its talents. The dog left the park, crossed the street and was lost from sight. Ross lit a cigarette, and saw he'd better buy another pack soon, or decide to quit.

Shannon said, "The night I first met Garret, I told him I was playing tennis the next day. He asked me where, and I told him. Even so, it was kind of a surprise when he showed up."

"I just bet it was," said Ross. She gave him a look. As if accusing him of toying with her emotions.

"A friend of mine, Kathy, and I were batting the ball around, getting some fresh air and exercise. It was right at the end of the summer. September twenty-third. A Saturday, one of those beautiful days that you really appreciate, because you know it'll soon be fall . . ."

Ross inhaled, counted to ten, exhaled a cloud of carcinogens. Shannon's eyes had gone all soft and out of focus. Somewhere high above them in the murky clouds a propeller-driven airplane droned monotonously.

"Kathy served. The ball hit the top of the net and dropped over on my side, and just lay there. I ran over and picked it up, my legs straight, bending from the waist. I looked between my legs and there you were. Upside down, sitting on the bench between the courts."

"Garret was sitting there," said Ross. "Not me."

"That's what I said. I'm talking about Garret, not you." She gave him an irritated look, and began to walk towards the wire-mesh-enclosed tennis courts. Ross trailed along behind. The nets were down. Debris littered the asphalt. A picked-over apple core had been thrust into the chain-link fence. She pushed open the gate, strolled over to a low, green-painted wooden bench. Ross stayed with her. He felt very uncomfortable, walking into this box of wire.

She said, "Sit down, Ross."

"I'd rather not."

"You don't want to sit down? Why?"

He shrugged. "I don't know. I just don't."

"Sit down, *please*," she said. She moved in close, so close that he could measure the span of her pupils, admire the tiny flecks of darker blue caught in her pale blue eyes. She grasped his hand. "There, now I've asked politely. So be nice, okay?"

Ross gingerly sat down on the rain-speckled bench. The cold jumped into him. He shoved his hands into his pockets.

Shannon said, "I felt like I was in a trance. I forgot all about Kathy, and where I was and everything. I walked right over and sat down next to you, like this, so close that we were touching."

Ross held himself very still.

"You were wearing white shorts," said Shannon. "I sat so close that our bare legs were touching. My leg was smooth, and your leg was hairy. I like to flirt, but I don't usually think of myself as *pushy* . . . But I pressed my leg against your leg as if . . ." Her eyes cleared, sudden as a gust of wind blowing a cloud from the face of the sun. She said, "It's cold."

Ross nodded. He took one last pull on his smoke, dropped the butt on the asphalt and kicked it away. He said, "I'm freezing my ass off."

"Me too." She laughed. "And you know something else?"

Yeah, thought Ross, fascinated. You're hungry, and you're about to suggest that we go get something to eat.

"I'm hungry," said Shannon. "Tell you what, let's go get something to eat." She surprised him by tossing him the keys.

Ross followed her back to the car. He unlocked, climbed in behind the wheel, reached across and unlocked her door. He started the engine. Shannon buckled up, gave him an expectant and mildly disappointed look. Telling him silently that he'd know what to do next, if only he could be bothered to think about it. And the strange thing was, she was right. He *did* know what came next, because Garret had told him.

But, though he knew where he was supposed to go, he had no idea how to get there. In many ways this was not an unusual situation. Even so, he felt a little uncomfortable as he followed Shannon's terse directions to turn left or right, or not at all, until finally he turned the Saab's downsloping nose into the parking lot of a chain restaurant.

"Not there!" she said. "Over there!" He parked next to a silver Honda. Was this the exact same slot Garret had chosen when it was his turn to drive? Doubtless. Ross got out of the car. He locked the door and slipped the keys into his pocket. It had been a long time since he'd driven a car. Things had changed in the meantime. Evolved, you might say. Most noticeably, life in the fast lane was considerably faster, though the speed limit had remained constant.

Shannon took his hand, led him around to the front of the restaurant. He held the door open for her when it finally became obvious that she expected him to do so. He followed her inside. The wild lunch bunch had come and gone, and the restaurant was fairly quiet. He guessed that the place was a little pricier than the modest exterior suggested. The tablecloths were crisp and white. A long-stemmed red rose stood in a slim green glass vase on each table. The cherubic fellow who smilingly approached them wore a shiny black three-piece suit, no tie. Smoking, or nonsmoking? Shannon, pointing, told him she wanted the end booth, by the window. The cherub accepted their coats, guided them to the desired table, assured them a waitress would materialize promptly.

Ross wondered what the hell that was supposed to mean.

Shannon said, "Isn't this nice?"

"Very nice," said Ross agreeably.

She reached across the table and playfully slapped his hand. "Would you rather go somewhere else?"

"No, this is fine. Really nice."

She hit him with one of her extra-nice smiles, warm and friendly, good-natured, cheerful, with just a hint of the bedroom. He leaned back, remembered Garret going on and on about what a great smile she had, so spontaneous, such nice white teeth.

Their waitress arrived with a jug of ice-water, menus and a smile of her own, warm but efficient. She wore tight black pants and a low-cut blouse in a semi-translucent, tangerine-coloured fabric that clung to her with no sense of decency. Her long, fiery-red hair was coiled into a painfully tight bun. A twisting curl of hair graced each of her shell-like ears. She had big brown eyes, mauve eyeliner, a plump mouth painted spontaneous-combustion red. As she leaned over the table, explaining the daily specials, Ross could not stop himself from discreetly studying her plunging neckline, the sweetly rising swell of her totally swell breasts.

Shannon decided on the chicken and pasta salad, said she was starving and could they please have a basket of French bread in the meantime? She was about to order on Ross's behalf – grilled chicken breast and French fries – when he broke in and said, "I'd like the grilled chicken breast and French fries."

Shannon smiled a little purse-lipped smile.

Ross recalled that she and Garret had washed down their meal with a bottle of red wine. Italian. Or was it Chilean? No, that was about a week later, at that place downtown, with the waiter who liked to sing. He struggled to remember the name of the wine. Something with a lot of vowels. What *was* it?

The waitress said, "Will you be having something to drink . . ."

Shannon hit him between the eyes with another smile.

He said, "Uh, I think I'd like a beer."

"No, we had wine," said Shannon in a no-nonsense voice. A don't-mess-with-me-or-I'll-mess-you-up voice. Her vehemence startled the waitress. Ross, too.

He said, "Right, a bottle of red wine. Italian." He studied the menu. Where was it. *Valpolicella Classico Superiore*. Whew. The waitress headed for the kitchen.

Ross said, "The first time around . . ." He tailed off. What was he trying to say, exactly? Or even approximately. Shannon was staring at him, big-eyed and apparently adoring. He said, "Garret liked to get into the chicken, huh? Did he eat his fries with his fingers, or use a knife and fork?" And something else was bothering him. Ketchup, or vinegar? Shannon's eyes were cold. He could see she was plenty pissed off at him, but holding herself in.

She said, "I never think of him that way. In the past tense. As someone that's gone from my life. So *please* don't talk about him like that."

"Okay," said Ross.

The redhead was back, with the bread and the wine. She did a little face-acting as she uncorked the bottle. Her nail polish was a dead-perfect match for her lipstick. She offered Ross the cork.

He glanced at Shannon. Was that a tear in her eye? She nodded faintly. He accepted the cork. Now what? She made a rolling motion with her fingers. He turned the cork slowly between his thumb and index finger. Shannon mimed returning the cork to the redhead, and that's what he did. A splash of wine was poured into his glass. He tasted, and approved. Shannon's glass and then his own was filled. The redhead went away.

He said, "Do I like bread?"

"Help yourself."

He separated a slice from the mass, smeared on a generous helping of butter and took a great big bite. The bread was soft and chewy; the crust nice and crisp. In prison, he'd worked at the in-house bakery for a couple of years. Guys did all sorts of disgusting things to the bread. Spat in it, and worse. Much worse. He drank some wine, chewed on his bread. The rose's scent perfumed the air. He could learn to live like this, given a chance. He drank some more wine and then convulsively drained the glass and helped himself to the bottle.

Shannon told him to slow down. It was unwelcome but solid advice, and so he took it. He helped himself to another slice of bread, more butter. She was watching him. Scrutinizing him. He looked out the window. Her reflection didn't blink. He reached for his wine glass and then thought better of it and drank some ice-water instead. The waitress arrived with more bread, assurances that their meals would be along shortly.

By accident or design, she did not lie.

Garret tore into his chicken. He added ketchup to half his fries and sprinkled vinegar on the rest, ate some with his fork, others with his fingers. Shannon didn't seem to object to his foolishness. Her demeanour was demure, as she nibbled her way into a mound of pasta. Only rarely did her fork clang against her knife. She patted her mouth frequently with her napkin. Her eyes were downcast. When she'd eaten her fill, she laid her cutlery neatly down. The waitress pounced, swept away the dirty dishes. Ross felt marginally safer, now that his date had been disarmed.

He poured the last of the wine into his glass. The waitress wondered aloud as to whether they might care for dessert. Shannon already knew what she wanted – fresh local strawberries with whipped cream. The waitress was visibly stricken. California strawberries were available, but it was months too early for the local variety. Shannon flinched, but was quick to recover. Imported would do nicely. Much to Ross's surprise, she ordered another bottle of wine.

But then, thinking about it, he remembered Garret telling him that's what she'd been like. Careful, at first. Cautious. But then, getting a little buzz on, snatching at the controls. Riding him like a bumper car, before he knew it.

Ross sat up a little straighter. How could he have forgotten? Shannon had hardly touched her dessert. She'd paid for the lunch with cash, hadn't let Garret anywhere near the cheque.

Afterwards, she'd driven at high speed to a cheap downtown motor-hotel, paid for a room with her Visa card, grabbed the key and . . .

Room 317.

All the sordid details came flooding back. The toilet dripped. The shower curtain was mildewed. The towels were so thin they might've been cut from worn-out sheets. So were the walls. The air-conditioner sounded as if its throat had just been cut. The queen-size bed worked just fine, though. No problems there. Ross remembered that the carpet was a solid dark blue, and that it had recently been shampooed. You could still smell the soap, if you got down on your knees for a sniff.

The second bottle of wine arrived, and Ross filled their glasses to the brim. Some time later, the strawberries were served. Shannon stuck a finger deep into her whipped cream.

Garret had told him about these next few moments over and over again. Ross could hardly bear to look. But he had to. And he did. Because it was part of the deal.

16

Willows was up at seven. He pushed aside the curtain and looked out the bedroom window. Rain. By seven-thirty he'd showered and shaved and was down in the kitchen, making breakfast. The coffee pot had finished dripping by quarter to eight and the toaster popped about thirty seconds later. He buttered the toast, sprinkled on a mix of cinnamon and sugar, filled the Starbucks mug Sean had given him and sat down at the dining-room table with a copy of the *Sun*. It was his habit to start with the sports section, work his way backwards through the paper until he was finally ready for the doom and gloom of the front pages. The Canucks continued to flirt with the possibility of missing the playoffs. The Grizzlies were doing about as well as could be expected. He was reading a lengthy piece about a golfer who'd earned just under half a million dollars for playing fifty-four holes, in the sunshine, in Hawaii, when Annie came into the kitchen.

"Morning, Dad."

"Good morning, honey." He tilted his cheek for a kiss. The hug was an unexpected bonus.

She said, "You're up kind of early, for someone who was up so late."

"Time and tide . . ." Willows went back to the article on the golfer. His dad had played the game with considerable skill. In his mid-twenties he'd turned down an offer to work as assistant club

151

pro. Willows had swung the driver pretty well when he was in his late teens. What had turned him away from the sport? He couldn't remember. A healthy disdain for money? He hoped not.

Annie carried the kettle over to the sink, poured in some water and put the kettle on a back burner. She turned on the gas and then came over and sat down at the table. She poured cereal into a bowl, milk over the cereal. She began to eat.

Willows ate a piece of toast, drank some coffee. "How's school?"

"Okay."

"How'd the math exam go?"

She shrugged. "Okay, I guess."

Willows went back to the article on the golfer. He tried to imagine himself being paid five hundred grand in bloated U.S. currency simply because he was skilled at pounding a dimpled white ball. No matter how great the stress, it was still easy money, if you had the talent to earn it. He heard Claire's footsteps on the stairs. Annie glanced up as Parker entered the kitchen. Her smile was as wide as her face.

"Hi, Claire."

"Morning, everybody." Parker bent and kissed Annie fleetingly on the cheek.

Willows thought Parker looked almost as tired as he felt. Small wonder. They'd worked until a little past three in the morning, toured the most popular of the city's gay clubs with photographs of Donald E. Mooney and the high-ranking cop Pat Timmins had fingered – a senior inspector named Mark Rimmer. It was thirsty work but Willows hadn't touched so much as a beer. The cigarette smoke and strobe lights had given him a headache. As far as he knew, they'd learned nothing of value.

The kettle was boiling. Parker said, "Is this for me?" Annie nodded. Parker said, "Thank you, honey." She turned off the gas, poured a little water into the teapot, swirled it around. "How was your math exam?"

"Pretty easy. I got ninety-four percent, forty-seven out of fifty."

"Not bad."

"I tied with Greg Foster for best mark in the class."

"Greg Foster . . ." Parker frowned. "You've mentioned his name before, haven't you?"

"We're working on a science project."

"How's that going?"

"Really well. We're trying to make an artificial crystal. There's a prize for the biggest one. I'm going over to his house after school."

"Have we got his address and phone number?" said Willows from behind his paper.

"I gave it to Claire a few days ago, Daddy."

Parker rinsed the teapot, tossed in a teabag and poured the pot full of water. She said, "Do you need some lunch money, Annie?"

"It's okay, I'm brown-bagging it." She smiled. "I made myself a sandwich last night. Greg and I are going to spend the lunch hour in the library."

"Have I met Greg?" said Willows, frowning.

"The blond with the crewcut," said Parker. She lifted the teapot's lid, filled her cup and walked over to the table and sat down. She leaned against Willows and kissed him lightly on the mouth.

Willows glanced at his daughter over the top of his newspaper. Parker had been living in his house and sharing his bed for almost six months. He'd talked the situation over with Annie and Sean before Claire had moved in, but even so, he was still a little self-conscious when she was openly affectionate. But was it better for them to try to conceal the way they felt about each other? Not really. He returned Parker's kiss with enough enthusiasm to raise a smile.

He was bent over the dishwasher when Sean rattled his knuckles on the shatterproof glass panel in the back door. Willows went over to the door and unlocked it. "Just getting in?"

"Yeah." Sean's tone didn't invite further questions. He brushed past Willows, got a Coke from the fridge and walked out of the kitchen.

"Hey, where're you going?"

"To bed." Sean strolled down the hall and turned into his bedroom. The door slammed shut.

Willows shot the back-door deadbolt. One of these days, hopefully in a decade or less, Sean would find a job that paid him enough to become self-sufficient, and abandon the family nest in search of a life of his own. It was something to look forward to, but at the moment it seemed about as remote as a golfing weekend in Hawaii. Willows turned on the dishwasher. The nice thing about machines was that, within their limits, they could usually be relied upon to do what they were told.

A few minutes later, Annie's new friend arrived. Greg knocked on the front door, pushed his nose against a bevelled-glass panel. Annie yelled that she'd be with him in a minute. She collected her lunch from the fridge, hugged Parker, gave Willows a peck on the cheek, ran down the hall, grabbed her coat and schoolbooks.

"Watch the traffic!" yelled Willows.

The door slammed shut. For a moment or two the house was strangely silent, and then the thud of Sean's stereo asserted itself.

Parker rinsed out the teapot.

Willows said, "How can he sleep with that racket?"

Parker shrugged. She took him by the arm and led him down the hall. "Let's get out of here, Jack. We've got work to do."

The night janitor had switched Willows' desk photos with Eddy Orwell's shots of his beaming, dysfunctional family. Willows put Eddy's pictures back on his desk where they belonged, and retrieved his own small collection of snapshots. Annie beamed up at him. Sean was smiling too – the photo had been taken several years earlier, before he'd had time to fine-tune his attitude.

Willows phoned Christy Kirkpatrick. The coroner was overloaded, but promised Willows he'd fit Mooney in if he had a cancellation.

"A cancellation? What the hell does that mean?"

"It means I won't get around to him today unless I put in some overtime."

"So put in some overtime. The guy's a cop."

"*Was* a cop."

"*Is* a cop," said Willows.

Kirkpatrick sighed heavily into his ear, then disconnected. Willows cradled the phone. The late Donald E. Mooney was a high-priority item for two solid and irrefutable reasons: he'd been murdered, and he'd been a fellow officer. But on the other hand, in this particular case, it seemed unlikely that the autopsy results would help further the investigation. Mooney had almost certainly been drowned in his bathtub. There was no bullet to be retrieved, no knife wound that could be matched to a suspect's weapon.

Willows sat there, steaming. The first twenty-four hours were crucial; he was running out of time and could think of only one line of investigation he might reasonably pursue.

Parker's phone rang. She picked up. "Parker. Homicide." She tensed, reached for a pencil and scratchpad. "We're still interested. Yes, I remember you. Could I have your name, sir?" Her pencil moved slowly across the paper. Willows walked around to stand behind her. She'd drawn a question mark. She said, "Sure, I can be there. But I can't make it in half an hour. I'll need more time than that." Another pause. "Perfect." She drew another question mark. "I'll bring him if you want me to. You sure you want me to?"

Smiling, she cradled her phone.

"What was that all about?"

"Remember the guy at L'affair? The tall guy with the bandit moustache, shaved head, black leather vest?"

"C'mon, Claire, you're going to have to do better than that. There must've been a hundred bald guys with moustaches."

"No shirt, lots of chest hair, black leather shorts. I'm surprised you don't remember him, because he liked you a lot, Jack."

"Oh, *him*."

"That's right. Him."

"What'd he want?"

Parker said, "He just identified Mooney from our photo. Remembered his first name, that he was in law enforcement . . ."

"Yeah?"

Parker glanced around. The squadroom was empty except for the civilian staff, who were down at the far end of the squadroom, out of earshot. Even so, she lowered her voice to a whisper. "He identified Rimmer, too."

"By name?"

"He knew his first name, but that's all. I got the impression he doesn't know Rimmer's a cop."

Willows said, "That's okay with me."

Parker signed a sludge-coloured Ford out of the police garage, rattled the keys as she walked across the oil-stained concrete towards the vehicle. She waited until Willows had fastened his seatbelt and then pulled out of the slot and drove slowly towards the exit. The first drops of rain pebbled the windshield as they left the building. She switched on the wipers, braked for a jaywalking cop who was bowed under the weight of a cardboard box overflowing with file folders.

Parker made a right and then another right, came to a full stop and then gunned it, taking advantage of a break in the traffic. She made a left on Main and drove south across the breadth of the city, all the way to South East Marine Drive. She made another left, drove a little less than a mile and made a right. They drove past several blocks of light industry and warehouses. Parker slowed as the asphalt ran out and the road narrowed to a single lane of loose gravel generously studded with potholes.

Willows braced himself against the dashboard. The Ford bottomed out as they hit a particularly deep hole. Muddy water obliterated the view. Parker adjusted the wiper speed. They drove past a fire-blackened mattress, a broken jigsaw puzzle of jagged concrete chunks. A length of seine net hung between two small trees. Caught in the net were the black feathers and white bones and dull yellow beak of a small bird. Parker hit the brakes. The Ford shuddered to a stop with the front bumper overhanging a greasy clay slope that led down to the slow-moving river.

The Fraser was much narrower here, split in two arms by Mitchell Island, named after Alex Mitchell, the first man to farm the island's lush soil. Times had changed. A hundred years ago the island had been covered with small cedar and spruce trees. Now the chief geographical feature was a mountain of junked automobiles.

The airport was on the far side of the river, miles away.

Parker turned off the engine. They got out of the car. A narrow path wound down to the river. More slabs of concrete had been dumped along the bank to slow erosion caused by marine traffic.

The tide was on the ebb. The silt-brown waters moved swiftly towards the sea. Twenty feet offshore, a fourteen-foot aluminum boat powered by an outboard motor idled against the current. The leather-boy from L'affair was at the tiller. He'd changed into his day clothes – cuffed jeans and a red-and-black lumberman's jacket, a well-used Mr. Lube baseball cap. But that was him, all right. Thick neck, chipmunk cheeks, pug nose. He was in his late twenties, too far away to see the colour of his eyes. Parker made her way gingerly down the path towards the water's edge. Willows followed close behind.

The prop kicked up a little water as their informant cut in towards the shore. Despite the vagaries of the current, he managed to manoeuvre the little boat until it was almost, but not quite, close enough to touch. Smiling, his teeth white against the black moustache, he said, "This is as close as we're going to get, my friends."

The chunks of concrete were damp, slippery with a layer of green mould. Willows crouched low. The boat's motor burbled throatily. A flagpole-sized log drifted by. The river was swollen with rain and snowmelt; the water was moving along at a pretty good clip.

"What's your name?" Parker had to raise her voice almost to a shout in order to be heard above the sound of the river and the motor.

"Milt. They call me Milt." He grinned mischievously. "Please don't call me Milton. No last names, okay? Not that I'm wanted for anything serious . . ."

Parker smiled, "Okay, Milt. What d'you know that you want to tell us?"

"Donald was a friend of mine." A minor change in the speed or direction of the current caused the nose of the boat to veer suddenly closer. Milt shifted into reverse gear and twisted the throttle. The prop churned up a froth of dirty water, and the boat's stern dipped dangerously low. Milt throttled down, shifted gears. The boat eased back into position. He said, "Was Don a friend of yours?"

Willows shook his head. "I didn't know him."

"I thought all you cops knew each other."

"All eleven hundred of us? I couldn't stand having that many friends, Milt."

"Yeah, well. Don kept pretty much to himself, I guess. Who can blame him?" Milt's face was tight. He said, "The department isn't exactly at the cutting edge of political correctness, is it?"

Parker said, "Milt? We're all here for the same reason. Because a man's life was taken and we want to bring his killer to justice."

"Yeah, right." The boat moved away and then back. A deep-sea tugboat pushed upstream against the current and tide. A hundred yards behind the tug, an empty barge kept pace. Willows hunted for the towrope but couldn't find it. But he knew it was there.

"The other picture you showed me back at the bar," said Milt to Parker, "the picture of the old guy, the guy wearing the glasses. Mark." He paused. "I kept thinking about trying to remember where I'd seen him."

Parker waited.

"There's a place out in the Fraser Valley that hosts parties. Usually there's only four a year, one every three months. It's a couple of hundred bucks to get in, there's a cash bar . . ."

Willows said, "What's the attraction, Milt?"

"Well, it's kind of exclusive. You've got to be a member or the guest of a member. No pun intended. Once you're in, anything goes. There's films, live entertainment. You can do whatever you want, wherever you want to do it, with whoever you want to do it to. Or you can just watch, if that's what makes your heart turn over . . . The guy in the picture, Mark, is a watcher."

"Is he a regular, at these parties?"

"I wouldn't know. I only went just that one time, about six weeks ago. I was a guest, a friend of mine invited me."

"So the next party's in about another six weeks?"

"Somewhere in there."

"Out in the valley?"

"Yeah, that's right. And that's all I'm gonna tell you."

"Tell us who hosted the party," said Willows. "Nobody'll ever know you spoke to us."

"Tell you what – I'll think about it." Milt threw them a mock-salute, pushed the tiller towards Willows. The prow swung around, towards deeper water.

Willows reasoned that if Milt was so eager to end the conversation, he must know something worth talking about. Impetuously, he lunged forward. His hands clasped the gunwale as the length of his body hit the water. The boat heeled over, and then surged forward. Parker shouted words only she understood. Willows' hip thumped against the side of the boat. He felt himself being pulled forward through the water. He caught a quick glimpse of the metal-studded leather sole of Milt's heavy boot. A jolt of pain ran up his arm. He fell into the churning water, heard the thrashing of the propeller and felt the swirling water slap his cheek as the boat accelerated past him. He spat a mouthful of river, lifted his head to get his bearings. The boat was already a silvery-white dot in the distance. He was facing downstream, drifting along at a good pace. He flexed his fingers. All present and accounted for. He kicked out, and realized that he had lost a brogue.

17

Ross knew the drill. Back there in the slammer, Garret had told him how it went over and over again, so many times that Ross had inadvertently memorized just about every last word. But sometimes Garret had given him a slightly different version of the same story, changed some small, insignificant detail. For example, he often exaggerated his sexual skills and appetites and then felt bad a day or two later, for talking that way, and contritely insisted that none of it was true.

Ross would look up from his hardcover Roget's. "So, what're you sayin', that she's a virgin?"

"Yeah. I guess so."

"A twenty-three-year-old virgin."

"Right."

Ross elbowed Garret in the ribs. "As far as you know, she's a virgin. Which, if it's the truth, would be entirely your fault."

Then Garret's fists would come up, and Ross would back off, keep himself looking serious as he apologized, admitted he'd stepped over the line . . .

The way it was supposed to go today, on their first date, Shannon would splash back most of the second bottle of wine, pay the bill with her Visa card and then grab his hand and tell him she wanted to take him downtown, show him something, if that was okay with him. Getting him to co-operate, involving him,

160

turning him from a slack-assed bystander into an active participant. It was the same technique they'd used in prison, during
group counselling sessions.

So, Ross sat there in his chair, relaxed, his legs splayed out in
front of him under the table, enjoying himself quite a bit as he
watched her down glass after glass until finally both the bottle and
glass were empty. She waved the waitress over, requested the bill.

Ross asked – a hypothetical question – if he could help out with
that, maybe take care of the tip.

Shannon waved him away, hauled out her well-used Visa card.
As they were going out the door, she touched his arm and told
him there was something downtown that she wanted to show him.

Teasing her a little, Ross said, "Oh yeah? Like what?"

"You'll see!" Shannon was not one of those rare, unfortunate
women who are impervious to the effects of alcohol. She was
clearly feeling a little loose at the knee. Her tongue was not quite
in sync with her brain. She mumbled a few words Ross wasn't able
to stitch into a comprehensible sentence, as she charted an
unlikely course across the parking lot. Ross still had the keys. He
unlocked the passenger's-side door and helped her into the car. A
guy in a blood-smeared apron leaned against the restaurant's open
kitchen door, smoking a cigarette. He smiled indolently at Ross.
Was this the fellow who'd cooked his chicken? He hoped not.
Shannon leaned across the seat to unlock the door for him. Her
skirt rode high.

Ross was fast becoming a fan of time travel. He believed himself
more than ready for their next destination.

Following Shannon's slurred and frequently contradictory
instructions, Ross drove deep into the heart of the downtown core
and right out the other side. Cruising north on Burrard, he
couldn't help noticing that the street had lost an awful lot of its
down-home charm. Still following Shannon's directions, he hung
a left. Immediately he was caught up in an artful web of one-way
streets, roundabouts and cul-de-sacs. Against all odds, he eventually found himself on the right street. He pulled up in front of a

tall, bulky building that was thickly covered in ivy. Big ivy. Some
of the vines were thicker than his wrist. Could this be the love-
nest Garret spoke of in such glowing terms?

He killed the Saab's engine and followed Shannon inside the
building. Three or four steps had to be climbed to reach the lobby.
The lobby was small, plenty of dark wood and subdued lighting.
This was definitely the hotel Garret had told him about. But to his
surprise Shannon veered away from the front desk.

He followed her down a long corridor, into the bar. She made a
beeline for a window table, and he couldn't really blame her –
despite the inclement weather, the view of the harbour was not
much short of spectacular. But the table, like all the other window
tables, was occupied. By Kelly. Shannon sat down, shrugged out of
her coat. They smiled at each other. She said a few words, he
turned and squinted across the smoky room, peered through a
pair of binoculars fashioned from his hands. He waved casually at
Ross. Meanwhile a waiter in black pants and a white shirt moved
in on Shannon. The guy was already in third gear, accelerating
fast. Ross loitered. But when Shannon waved him over, he was
there in a jiffy, quick as a well-trained yo-yo on a very tight string.

Shannon ordered coffee, cream and sugar. Ross said he'd have a
glass of beer, something domestic, whatever was on tap. She cancelled the coffee, ordered a dry white wine.

"Ross, I think you've already met my brother, Kelly."

Ross nodded. Kelly slouched low in his chair, arms bulging dra-
matically, his purple golf shirt rippled by washboard stomach
muscles. A tick too much time went by before he offered his hand.
All that beef. Ross expected the handshake to shatter a random
selection of his smaller bones, and it was true that Kelly's hand
had all the flex of a chunk of kiln-dried maple. But the man had a
grip like a Prozac jellyfish that belied his carved-from-granite
appearance. And he had a nice warm smile, too. Ross had met the
guy's identical twin brother in the joint, plenty of times. The
whisper-quiet, kill-you-in-a-minute crowd. But why should Kelly
find him objectionable? Merely because his sister was drunk, in

broad daylight, in a hotel, with a parolee she hardly knew? Ross had first-hand knowledge of where that kind of thinking could lead a careless person. Straight to emergency, so the trauma unit could get busy extracting pieces of chair from his brain.

It was a small table, but Ross did what he could to distance himself from Kelly. He shifted his chair so he could more easily soak up the view, and not quite so easily be kicked between the legs.

Shannon said, "You guys do recognize each other, I hope?"

Chuckling inanely, blue eyes sparkling with amusement, Kelly reluctantly shook his unnaturally blond, buzz-cut head. A mostly full longneck bottle of Budweiser stood on the table by his right elbow. He'd been picking at the label, but not getting anywhere, possibly because his fingernails were chewed to the quick. "Yeah, I remember him. Your new house guest, right? Garret's buddy. The ex-con." Ross lit a cigarette.

"You two've got an awful lot in common," said Shannon.

"We do?" Kelly sounded a tad doubtful. He held the longneck between his thumb and index finger. He lifted the bottle to his mouth. The waiter was back. Shannon picked up her wine glass and dunked her nose into it, like one of those goofy mechanical birds that don't know when to stop. Ross sipped at his beer. He smoked his cigarette. Down by the beach, a loving couple strolled hand in hand, oblivious to the rain. So sweet. He drank a little more beer, just a sip. He counted nine freighters in the harbour, great big go-anywhere deep-sea monsters.

Kelly had resumed destroying his Budweiser label. The man was on a mission. Tiny pieces of silvery paper littered the table.

Shannon said, "What you've got in common is, you're both my tenants."

Kelly rotated his bottle a quarter-inch.

Ross said, "How d'you mean?"

"I'm living in the basement suite," said Kelly. He gave Ross a look that measured him to the tenth of an inch.

Ross went back to admiring the view. On the far side of the

street there was a strip of anemic-looking grass, a few spindly trees, an unoccupied park bench. A blue-and-white cruised slowly past, the cop's face a pale blur behind the rain-swept glass. The cop was sitting bolt upright, as if he'd just come on shift.

Ross thought about the Saab. The gas tank was three-quarters full. The keys were in his jacket pocket. What if he drained his beer, asked Shannon to order another for him, mentioned that he had to take a leak and would be back in a minute, jumped in the Saab and blew town?

He drained his beer. Said, "I gotta take a leak." The waiter was right behind him, within easy reach. Ross touched his arm. "Bring me another beer. Make it a pint this time."

The waiter nodded, scooped up Ross's empty glass. Ross said, "Where's the john?" The waiter directed him towards the lobby. Ultra perfecto. Except, he really did have to go to the washroom. But that was okay. He could make a side trip on his way out.

But as he stood at the urinal, he realized he'd left his jacket on the chair back there in the bar. Lordy. He zipped up, washed and dried his hands and ran his fingers through his hair.

As he left the washroom, he saw that Kelly was leaning far out over the table so he could keep an eye on the washroom door. Kelly waved coquettishly, gave Ross an ironic smile. Even at that distance, his teeth looked big as sugar cubes.

Ross walked back to his chair, sat down. Kelly was still smiling, but there was something weird about his smile. As Ross stared at him, his front teeth fell apart, dissolved into a gooey white mess. Kelly reached out, grabbed a few more sugar cubes from the bowl and popped them into his mouth.

Now what? Ross sipped at his new beer.

Kelly used the edge of his hand to bulldoze the pieces of label off the table. Ross expected him to scoop them up in his other hand, but Kelly was content to let his litter drift to the carpet. He said, "You and Garret were pals. Did he ever talk about the armoured-car robbery he and that other kid, Billy, tried to pull off?"

"From time to time."

"He tell you about the two hundred grand that went missing?"

Ross nodded. "Yeah, he might've mentioned it, once or twice." Once or twice every hour or so, that is.

"He tell you what happened to it?"

"Yeah, he did. He even told me where it is. But I spent it already, on lottery tickets. So don't get your hopes up."

Kelly gave him an iceberg look. Shannon playfully slapped her brother's arm. "Leave him alone, quit bothering him."

"Am I *bothering* you, Ross?"

"Bet your ass. But since you probably irritate just about everybody you meet, I'm not gonna worry about it."

"Tough guy, huh?" Kelly went back to picking at his Budweiser label. It seemed like antisocial behaviour, but Ross couldn't fault him for his obsession. After all, he was so close to finishing, and had already invested so much time.

Shannon stood up. The force of her personality pulled Ross to his feet. He helped her into her fake-leopardskin coat. She said, "We happened to be in the neighbourhood and I thought it might be nice if you two had a drink together, got to know each other, a little. But we really have to be going . . ." She dipped into her purse, dropped a crumpled bill on the table.

Kelly went back to industriously picking at his Budweiser label. Somehow the task seemed absolutely suited to his talents.

Outside, Ross said, "What was that all about?"

"Nothing. I wanted you to meet him, that's all."

"Sure, but why?" He unlocked the passenger's-side door, but it seemed that more was required of him. He opened the door for her, waited until she'd made herself comfortable and tucked in her skirt, then shut the door and walked around to the far side of the car and got in. He buckled up, started the engine.

Shannon said, "I thought he might be able to help you."

"Do what?"

"Recover the money."

"Garret's money?" Ross turned on the heater. He rolled down his window a few inches, shook a cigarette out of his pack and lit up. Shannon didn't look very happy about it, but didn't complain. He inhaled, averted his head and blew a stream of smoke out the window.

"What's so funny?" said Shannon.

Ross shrugged. "Ask somebody with a sense of humour."

Following her directions, he drove over the Burrard Street Bridge and then south on Burrard, past the eternal – so far – flame set in the middle of the grassy span outside what had been a Coca-Cola factory but was now just another office building. They drove past the barred windows of one of the few retail firearms dealers that remained in the city, the glossy showroom of a Ferrari dealership.

Shannon told him to make a right on Broadway. Now, at last, finally, he knew where he was going.

She treated him to a cup of coffee at the 7-Eleven. They sat in the car, drinking coffee and looking at the liquor store and the big grocery store, which was now an IGA. What did the letters IGA stand for? Inferior Goods Available? Or how about Intensely Gluttonous Atmosphere? Or maybe . . .

"Cut it out!"

He jerked his head around, startled.

She said, "What the hell's so funny, Ross?"

"Intensely Gluttonous Atmosphere," said Ross, deadpan. Shannon looked confused, and it did not suit her. He pointed at the glowing red letters of the grocery chain's enormous sign.

Shannon drank some coffee, made a face. She balanced her paper cup on top of the dashboard. The windshield began to fog up. Now it was her turn to point. "That's where the armoured car was when the shooting started. And right over there – see that black Volvo?" Ross nodded, but he was looking at the wrong car. She got him straightened out, made him follow the line of her finger. "Right there, that's where the first guard went down. And the other one was just over there. See the woman with the grocery cart? Just to her left is where the fat man stopped singing."

"Fat man?" said Ross, bewildered. Who was she talking about? The gamut of human emotions whizzed across the contours of Shannon's face like time-lapse clouds. Shadow and light, shadow and light. She was going to fly apart, if she didn't get herself under control. She said, "The fat man. He wasn't anybody important, just a guy who happened to walk out of the liquor store at the wrong time. Carrying a case of beer. Billy shot him, don't ask me why. Garret shot the other two, the guards. He killed them both, and then he was shot. In the shoulder. The driver of the armoured car shot him." She reached up, adjusted the rearview mirror so it reflected the cinderblock flank of the 7-Eleven. "That's the wall they drove into. In a stolen Cadillac. In fact, they drove right through the wall, knocked a bunch of display cases flying, made a real mess of things."

"A Cadillac," said Ross. "Excellent choice. Bet you couldn't pull a stunt like that with a Honda." But what did he know about cars? Still, it was a good question for the salesman, next time he found himself in a showroom. I love the independent suspension and the side-impact panels, and air bags. But tell me this, Jake. How's that baby handle a brick wall?

Shannon said, "I wish you'd quit doing that."

"Doing what?"

"Smiling, and staring vacantly off into space."

He rested his hand lightly on her knee. "I was thinking about you."

"Well, that's different." She patted his hand, and then grabbed his little finger and bent it sharply back. The pain would have brought him to his knees, had the Saab's cramped architecture allowed it. "Stare vacantly off into space all you want," she said. "You can even drool a little, if it makes you feel better. But don't tell me about it. Do us both a favour and leave the manhole cover on the sewer of your mind."

They drove down Maple to Tenth Avenue, following the path of Billy's flight from the botched robbery. He'd run to where he'd parked his number-two getaway vehicle, the Ford Pinto, on Tenth Avenue, west of Arbutus. The Saab straddled a set of railway tracks as they waited for the light to change. On the far side of the street there was a strip of shops; a drugstore, grocery store, a theatre with a tall glass front, lots of lights. Hardware store, restaurant, bowling alley. A fifteen-foot bowling pin stood on the roof. Ross looked in vain for the ball. Maybe it had rolled away.

The light changed. Shannon showed him exactly – to the inch – where the Pinto had been parked. Following her instructions, Ross circled the block and turned left on Arbutus. They followed the hill down Arbutus to Point Grey Road. Ross made a left. Now they were heading west again, past low-slung apartment blocks, a waterfront mini-park hardly bigger than a blink, expensive houses.

One of the newspaper articles on the armoured-car robbery had included a map of the getaway route. Ross knew they were getting close. He eased up on the gas. Shannon said, "Park right there. See the garage?"

Who wouldn't? The garage had a green-tinted glass roof. A glass-roofed garage – what a great idea! Above the peak of the roof the address, 3682, was written in hot-pink neon. The house itself was set well back from the street, behind a six-foot-tall boxwood hedge growing tight against a wall of textured concrete blocks. But for a gate made of wrought iron, the house wouldn't have been visible from the street.

Ross gave it a little gas, and the Saab crept forward a foot or so. Now he had a much better view. The house was low, flat-roofed, modern-looking, the wood siding stained an understated silvery grey. The windows facing the street were a lot smaller than he'd have expected them to be, had he bothered to think about it. But then, although Point Grey Road was only two lanes wide, it offered a scenic route to the beaches and the university, so there was a lot of traffic cruising by. The house fronted on the ocean, and there'd be a view of the city and mountains as well, so that's where the windows would tend to congregate. In fact, he wouldn't be surprised if the far end of the house were nothing but glass.

He said, "This is Billy's girlfriend's place, right?"

"Nancy Crown," said Shannon. "She wasn't exactly his girlfriend. I mean, she was a married woman, she had a husband, all of that. Billy met her before the robbery, hijacked her car, took her for a ride, and then stole her purse and let her go. That's how he knew where she lived. But they weren't *dating*, or anything."

"Billy died here, didn't he?"

She nodded. "He sure did."

Ross lit a cigarette. This time he didn't roll his window down quite so far. He said, "They're still living here, the Crowns?"

"The place was up for sale, it was on the market quite a while, until a few weeks ago. Nobody wanted to buy it. Who'd buy a house where someone had died violently?"

"I would, if the price was right."

"Well, I guess they weren't so anxious to sell that they were ready to *give* the place away."

"It's Nancy and Tyler, right?"

She looked at him, mildly surprised. "Yes, that was his name, Tyler. When the house didn't sell, I guess they decided to hell with it, they'd stay put. Time heals all wounds, isn't that what they say?"

They sure do. But no amount of time healed those who, for example, had been shot dead, or left to drown in a backyard swimming pool. Ross eased the Saab forward a few more feet. A narrow concrete sidewalk ran down the side of the house. There were security lights high up, under the eaves, and that would be the least of it. Somebody like Billy turned up unexpectedly, with a crush on your wife, if you had any sense at all you didn't stint on security.

He thought about Shannon's Budweiser-drinking bro, Kelly. Or whoever he was, whatever his name was. He expected that, any time now, Shannon was going to tell him how helpful Kelly would be, if he decided to break into Tyler and Nancy's house, in search of the missing two hundred and twenty grand.

Kelly had the look of a helpful person, all right. The kind of helpful person who would cheerfully tip you into an early grave.

18

Parker felt a twinge in her shoulder as she extended her arm. Her gunshot wound acting up again. Willows ignored her offer of help. He crawled awkwardly up the sloping wall of shattered concrete. It was slippery going, and he had already taken a bad fall. His pants were ripped. There was blood on his knee, and she saw he'd lost a shoe. Well, if he didn't want any help, there was no point in loitering. She made her way back to the car, radioed in a request for a patch through to the coast guard. The department was on a tight budget; probably couldn't have afforded to get a helicopter aloft even if they'd owned one. The marine patrol rarely strayed beyond the confines of False Creek, English Bay and the perimeter of Stanley Park. Parker got through to the coast guard. No chopper was available. The nearest vessel was twenty minutes away. Bad news, but predictable. She cradled the mike.

Willows sloshed towards her through the weeds. He was limping, had the look of a man who'd seriously overestimated his ability, and knew it all too well. Parker reached across to unlock the door. She started the engine. Willows opened the door but made no move to get into the car. He drew his Smith & Wesson, ejected the magazine, tilted the pistol at an angle and racked the slide. Muddy water dribbled out of the mechanism, collected in the palm of his hand. He thumbed copper-jacketed 180-grain hollowpoints out of the magazine until it was empty, then gave it a shake. The Smith was still leaking unhealthy-looking fluids.

Parker said, "You shoot anybody with that, they're likely to die of rust."

Willows didn't see any point in soaking the front seat. He reached in and unlocked the back door and got into the car, shut the door. He was shivering violently, and he couldn't stop.

Parker turned on the heater. "Where to, Aquaman? Home for a shower and a change of clothes?" She found him in the rearview mirror. "Or maybe you'd prefer to hop straight into the old Maytag?"

Willows said, "I almost had him." His teeth were chattering, and it wasn't just the cold. He'd come *that* close to nabbing their informant. But he'd come equally close to getting caught by the boat's propeller. Looking on the bright side, there were no fish flopping around in his pockets. He said, "I've got spare clothes in my locker, but no shoes. We'd better go home."

Parker nodded. She alerted the dispatcher that they were out of service, backed the car away from the river, made a U-turn and stomped on it.

A little more than an hour later, Willows shut Bradley's pebbled-glass door behind him, and he and Parker took turns bringing the inspector up to speed on the latest nasty twist in the Donald E. Mooney investigation.

After they'd briefed him, Bradley took a moment to gather himself. With the tips of his fingers, he delicately prodded the Haida-carved cedar cigar box his wife had given him as a farewell gift, following the divorce. When he had the cigar box squared away to his satisfaction, he focused his bloodhound eyes on Willows and said, "Let me make sure I've got this straight, Jack. You're telling me Mark Rimmer is a *suspect*?"

Willows nodded.

Bradley turned to Parker, seeking confirmation.

Parker said, "We've had two independent witnesses corroborate the fact that Inspector Rimmer was a frequent patron of a downtown club that's a known hangout for gays. One of those witnesses claims the inspector has attended exclusive gay parties, sexual free-for-alls, somewhere in the Fraser Valley."

"How reliable are your witnesses?"

Willows said, "One of them is a patron of L'affair, a downtown club. He claims he was a casual acquaintance of Mooney's."

Bradley snorted derisively. "Not nearly good enough, Jack."

"Our other witness is a cop," said Willows bluntly. "He and Mooney lived together for a while. They'd had a relationship for the past five years, until Mooney bumped him for Rimmer."

"Jesus Christ." Bradley opened the lid of the box, and let it drop. He slumped low in his chair. "What've you got on Rimmer?"

"Not a thing. So far."

"You haven't queried records, or surveilled him?"

Willows shook his head.

Bradley glanced at Parker. "Mooney's ex. Who is he?"

"Constable Pat Timmins."

"What d'you know about him?"

"Not much, yet," said Parker. "He's got a motive."

"What about an alibi, has he got one of those, too?"

Willows said, "He worked the four to twelve, traffic."

"Alone?"

Willows nodded.

"Kirkpatrick fine-tune the time of death yet?"

"As far as we know, it's still somewhere between eleven and two. I doubt Christy'll do much better than that."

"Jack, you're telling me Mooney hasn't been autopsied yet, aren't you?"

"This afternoon, Inspector."

Bradley rubbed his jaw. "Mooney's ex-boyfriend, Timmins. What was he up to between end of shift and two in the morning? That's a pretty big window. Was he able to account for his time?"

Parker said, "His story is, he took a cab to the Bino's on Denman, had dinner and then walked to the Blue Horizon where he drank 'three or four' beers. He then took another cab back to his apartment. He'd rented a movie – *Bad Boys* – from Blockbuster. He watched the movie, rewound, went to bed."

"*Bad Boys*. What is that, a porno film?"

Parker suppressed a smile. "Strictly mainstream. Cops-and-robbers stuff, Inspector. Los Angeles, drugs and guns."

"An action film." Bradley looked out the window. Rain fell steadily, the way it does in Vancouver when it's going to rain for days or even weeks on end. He rubbed a smidgen of dust from the sill. "Doesn't sound like much of an alibi to me." Turning away from the window, he said, "Lean on him. Lean hard. Let's see which way he tilts."

"What about Rimmer?" said Willows.

"You planning to question him?"

"Not unless I have to."

Bradley nodded. "Very wise, Jack. Pull Timmins' file. Let's see what he's been up to. Meanwhile, I'll do a little discreet snooping, see what I can dig up on Inspector Rimmer. Wouldn't it be nice if somebody in vice had a nice fat file on him? But I'd never know, would I?" Bradley checked his watch. The Timex his son had given him almost eight years ago had finally died, and he'd treated himself to an entry-level Rolex. His jeweller had sold him the watch at 20 per cent off list, and suggested he pay it off over a period of twelve months, interest-free. Would he have gotten such a great deal if he wasn't a cop, and didn't happen to live right around the corner from the guy's store? He said, "What time have you got?"

"Quarter after," replied Parker.

"No, I mean exactly."

"Exactly quarter after."

"You're two minutes slow. Jack?"

"Quarter after," said Willows without bothering to consult his watch.

Bradley sat up a little straighter in his chair. The Rolex glittered in the light as he waved a casual goodbye. "Keep in touch, kids."

Willows dialled Kirkpatrick from his desk. The pathologist was out. He called records. He named half a dozen uniforms he disliked, and then Timmins, and politely asked the clerk to send up the files. The other names would provide a smoke screen, if Timmins turned out to be innocent. And if he wasn't, no harm done. Willows thanked the records clerk for her help, and gently disconnected. If the files beat the union rep to his desk, he'd be a lucky man indeed. He tried Kirkpatrick again. The phone rang three times, and then the pathologist picked up. "He's right here in front of me, Jack. If he was alive, you'd have called in the nick of time, so to speak. Try me again in an hour, okay?"

Willows disconnected. Parker's head was bent over her desk. She was reading, again, the rambling witness statement Graham Aubert had made to Orwell. He glanced up as Eddy Orwell pushed open the squadroom door so hard that it banged against the little rubber-tipped stopper that was designed to prevent the door from banging into the wall. Orwell looked smug as a thug who's stolen a rug.

From his desk, Dan Oikawa said, "What's up, Eddy?"

"Plenty," said Orwell. "Where's Bobby?"

"Who?" said Farley Spears from his desk.

"My partner, dipstick."

"Oh, *that* Bobby," said Oikawa. "Beats me, Eddy. But if I were looking for him, first thing I'd do is check the biggest mirror in the building."

When the laughter had subsided, Willows said, "What've you got, Eddy?"

"Bobby and me agreed that if I came up with something, I'd tell him before I talked to anybody else. Especially you, Jack. No offence."

"Eddy, I'm the primary on this case. Not Bobby. So whatever you've got, spit it out."

"We have no secrets here," said Spears.

"Amen to that," said Oikawa. "So tell me, Farley, still got that problem with your bowels?"

Spears gave Oikawa the finger.

"I take it that's a yes?"

Under Willows' unrelenting glare, Orwell eased down into his chair. He fumbled in his pocket for his spiral-bound notebook, flipped it open and wet his thumb, found the page he was looking for. "Graham Aubert, the kid who lived across the hall from Mooney?"

"We know who he is, Eddy."

"Yeah? Don't be too sure, Jack. See, it turns out Aubert isn't anywhere near the homebody he pretended to be. Bobby said we should check, see if the kid's got a sheet. Turns out he's got a king-size sheet. Stole his first car at the tender age of eleven, a Toyota, and he's been keeping busy ever since. Lots more cars, a couple of counts of theft under fifty . . . In June of 'eighty-nine he sledge-hammered a jewellery-store window, grabbed a handful of gold rings and watches and glass, severed a vein and started bleeding all over himself, turned around and ran into a steel light-pole. Knocked himself cold and was captured, caught eighteen months and did six." Orwell angled his notebook to the light, frowned as he attempted to decipher his scrawl. "A little over three years ago he was busted for break-and-enter, pleaded guilty and did a year less a day. In January he was charged with sexual assault. The charges were dropped when the victim – who happens to be his mother – turned turtle, swore to God she'd deny everything if we went to court."

"Who can blame her?" said Spears. "The kid made a mistake. So what? Sounds like your average disenchanted youth to me."

Oikawa said, "A model citizen, by today's standards."

"Damn right," said Spears. "All he did was steal a few cars and bust a few windows, and rape his mother." He pointed an accusing finger at Orwell. "Who the hell are you to relentlessly harass the poor kid, treat him as if he were some kind of criminal?"

"It's not as if he *murdered* somebody," said Oikawa.

"Even if he did," said Spears, "he probably had a good reason."

"Like what?"

"Like he had a problem with his bowels, and somebody with bad taste made the fatal mistake of poking fun at him," said Spears darkly.

Oikawa smiled. "Now hold on a minute, you're going too far."

"Where's Bobby?" said Willows to Orwell.

"I wish I knew."

Oikawa said, "I understand he's hustling that new civilian at Traffic and Firearms."

Orwell shrugged. "Could be."

Spears said, "What's her name? Ruby?"

"Ruth."

"Perfect," said Oikawa. "Ruth, meet Ruthless."

"What's so funny?" said Bobby Dundas as he entered the squad-room. He smiled at Parker. "Did I miss a punch line?"

"It was one of those 'spontaneous humour' situations," said Spears. "You had to be there, but you weren't."

Dundas frowned. "You get what we were after, Eddy?"

"Yeah, I got it."

Willows said, "You're going after Graham Aubert?"

The lines in Bobby's forehead deepened. He glanced angrily at Orwell. "We're thinking about bringing him in, asking him a few questions."

"Well, fine."

Bobby's forehead smoothed out. He glanced suspiciously at Parker, back to Willows. Blinking rapidly, he said, "You don't have any objections?"

"Not at all. Sounds like a good idea to me." Willows smiled. "Grill him till he spills 'em, Bobby."

Dundas leaned a hip against Orwell's desk. "Mind telling me what you and Claire are up to?"

"Not much," said Willows. "We're looking at the possibility that Mooney recently broke up with his boyfriend."

"Got a name?"

Willows nodded. Bobby Dundas thought it over. He decided, for reasons that weren't quite clear to him, not to ask.

"Who is it?" said Orwell. "Anybody we know?" Pleased with his witticism, he winked at Bobby Dundas.

"Probably," said Willows.

Bobby straightened. He said, "Eddy, we've got work to do. Let's get the hell out of here." His tone was sharp, and Orwell let it be known by the spark in his eye and the expression of surly disdain that seeped across his beefy face that he didn't like it one little bit. But he said nothing, and was quick to follow his partner out of the squadroom. The door hissed shut. The automatic lock clicked softly.

Spears said, "Your suspect's a cop?"

"Could be, Farley. Do you really want to know?"

"Man, I thought you were yanking his chain. A *cop*?"

A few minutes later, a clerk from records arrived with Willows' files. He emptied the brown manila envelope onto his desk. Timmins' file was third from the top. He flipped it open.

A colour head-and-shoulders photo of Timmins was stapled to the folder's inside front jacket. At the time the picture was taken, Timmins' hair had been a little darker and a little shorter. His upper lip was bare. He looked considerably younger, probably younger than his age. He wasn't a wanderer; his address and phone had been the same for the past four years. Willows tried his home number. The phone rang four times and then the answering machine kicked in. Willows disconnected as Timmins asked him to wait for the beep.

Parker raised an inquiring eyebrow.

"Nobody home," said Willows. "Or maybe it's that he isn't in the mood to answer the phone. Want to take a drive over there, peek in the window?"

Parker reached for her coat.

Timmins lived in a house built on a seventeen-foot-wide lot, one of only a handful of such lots allowed in the city. From the street, the building looked pretty much like an ordinary – but severely emaciated – house. The pink clapboard siding was overly cute, and the architect had slapped on a bit too much finicky detail for Willows' taste. But the house was only about twelve feet wide. Anything that small was doomed to look cosy. Willows wondered what it would be like to live in such an unusual dwelling. It must be similar in many respects to living in a landlocked boat. There weren't many windows on the side of the house, and those that did exist weren't much bigger than a porthole. Fire regulations. Willows opened a cedar gate with a rounded top. He held the gate open for Parker. A strip of lawn not much wider than a man's tie separated the house and double garage. He turned right, walked past a curtained window and knocked on the enamelled surface of a metal-clad door.

A black cat with a white ear ambled around the side of the house. It crouched low when it saw them, then turned and ran.

Willows thumbed the doorbell, waited a few moments and then bruised his knuckles on the door. No response. He stepped away from the door and pressed his face against the window's cold glass, peered through a narrow gap in the curtains. On the far side of the room a man lay on his back on the beige carpet, a leg hooked awkwardly across the floral-patterned sofa. He wasn't moving. A pool of red had collected on his chest.

Willows pulled on a pair of latex gloves. He tried the door. It was unlocked, but there was a safety chain. He stepped back and kicked hard. The heel of his shoe struck just below the shiny brass doorknob. The door crashed open and knocked over a spindly wooden table. A clear glass milk bottle that had been converted into a vase bounced off the hall carpet. Water seeped eagerly into the dense fabric. A dozen red roses lay on the floor like widely splayed, scarlet-tipped fingers.

Willows slid open the pocket door that led to the living room. The corpse had disappeared.

19

Ross drove another half-block down Point Grey Road. Shannon told him to make a left and park. Where? Anywhere you want. Parallel to the curb. He pulled up behind a white Lexus. She told him to kill the engine, and got out of the car and locked her door. Ross followed her lead. What else was there for him to do? She took his hand and led him across the street, down a public right-of-way between two expensive waterfront houses. A flight of concrete stairs descended steeply to the beach. She insisted that Ross go first. He held tight to the metal handrail. A seagull gave him the eye as it sailed gracefully past. The tide was out. He could smell the sea, things that had died and begun to rot.

During their time in prison, Garret had told Ross over and over again that Shannon was a totally hot babe, couldn't get enough of it. Et cetera. Et cetera. Blah, blah, blah.

Ross had believed every last steamy word of it. At the time, it had seemed like the sensible thing to do. But now he was wondering if his idea of what Shannon should be was getting in the way of who she really was. At the hotel he'd wrongly assumed that she intended to rent a room and seduce his socks off. Instead, they'd strolled into the bar for drinks with muscle-boy. He'd been caught off balance by this unexpected turn of events. His defences at half-mast, he'd been vulnerable to whatever games they had in mind.

Fragments of shell crunched underfoot as Shannon jumped

lightly down from the last step to the sandy beach. Ross paused to light a cigarette. She gave him a mildly disapproving look, then grasped his hand and led him along the beach towards Nancy and Tyler Crown's opulent waterfront home. Below the strip of sand upon which they walked, the beach all the way to the waterline was gooey-looking mud speckled with rocks. It was a landscape that was drab and inhospitable, appallingly unclean. If any life forms prospered here, they would reside at the lowest end of the food chain, and were not in the slightest danger of ending up on a plate.

To his right, walls of concrete rose thirty feet into the air. At high tide the footings would be under several feet of water. His fingers and Shannon's were still interlocked. She pointed almost straight up. Had some dreadful omen suddenly appeared in that grim and drooling sky? No, she was pointing towards the summit of the massive concrete breakwater.

"That's where they live – right up there. And that's probably where they've got the money stashed. There's a wall safe in the basement, inside the wine cellar."

Wine cellar? Ross stood there, smoking his cigarette. He said, "How'd you find out about the safe?"

"The real-estate agent told Kelly, and Kelly told me. And I told you, and that's how *you* found out."

Ross nodded. A glass-panelled fence ran along the top of the wall. The filled-in swimming pool where Billy had drowned would be just beyond.

"Could you climb that wall if you had to, Ross?"

"No way."

She smiled. "I bet you could fall off it, though."

It wasn't a question, but a statement of fact. Or maybe it was a warning.

Shannon relinquished her grip on his hand. She turned and started back the way they'd come. Ross walked down the gently sloping beach towards the water, until the sand was overcome by an evil-smelling, sticky muck. He bent and picked up a shiny black stone about the size of a deformed golf ball, turned and faced the house and reared back and threw as hard as he could. The stone lifted up into the sky and sailed over the top of the glass-panelled fence and was lost from view. He waited for the sound of breaking glass, but heard only the faint murmur of small waves upon the shore, the low hum of traffic.

Shannon waited for him at the top of the steps, where she sat huddled with her back to the wind and her hands in her pockets. She was sitting square in the middle of the step, blocking the way. Ross paused with his hand on the steel-pipe rail. He could have looked up her skirt if he'd wanted to. And he did want to. Her panties were black, the fabric sleek and shiny. He looked his fill, and looked away. Lit a cigarette. The way she'd been sitting, *posing*, he was fairly certain he'd been expected to take a peek. But even so, what a creepy thing to do. Shannon stood up. She looked down at him, a twisted smile on her pretty face.

He said, "Is there a plan?"

She laughed. "Of course there's a plan."

"Let me guess. I break into the house, tell Tyler Crown I'll beat his wife to a pulp unless he opens the safe. He opens the safe. I grab the cash and run back home to your welcoming arms. Is that it?"

Shannon laughed. "Not really. We don't expect you to handle Tyler all by yourself. Kelly will be there, helping out."

A black BMW with smoked windows cruised slowly past. Shannon moved in on him. She'd topped up her perfume. She moved in so close he could see nothing but her, smell nothing but her. She grabbed his lapels. The leather squeaked – or was it him? She leaned into him, kissed him chastely on the mouth. Her lipstick jumped all over his taste buds. She gave him a playful shove, pushed him, as in a foreign film, right to the edge of frame. He was dizzy from the taste of her lipstick and the sweet, musky scent of her. She relinquished her hold on his – on Garret's – leather jacket. He swayed backwards, and the first of all those swiftly descending concrete steps rose up to meet him. He clutched at the rail, saved himself.

A large dog, black with a golden-brown saddle, trotted partway up the stairs and then, for reasons which would never become clear, turned around and hustled back down again, and disappeared from view.

There was a kid in the slammer, a twenty-year-old kid, who'd missed his dog so much he'd tried to hang himself, because he couldn't stand the pain.

Ross didn't want to go back to that dark place again, for sure. That dark place that was all walls and no sky. He pulled hard on his cigarette. Another glossy black BMW with smoked windows crawled down Point Grey Road, but in the opposite direction.

He had a strong feeling that something important, or at least significant, was about to happen. He took another pull on his cigarette, hugged the smoke into his lungs for a slow count of five, exhaled.

A gull drifted past, leaving no shadow upon the asphalt.

Shannon said, "Do you find me attractive?"

"Huh?" Ross yanked the cigarette out of his mouth. He nodded. "Yeah, sure. You bet I do."

"What is it that you like about me?"

They were back on familiar ground, but Ross needed a moment to adjust, turn to the right page and find his line.

She nibbled at her lower lip. Impatient, and letting it show.

"Your eyes," he said not a moment too soon. What had Garret said about her eyes? That they were the windows of his soul. He said, "I'm just crazy about your eyes."

Really? Those sly eyes sparkled. "What else? Come *on*, don't be a tease, *tell* me!"

The wind was picking up. It raced up the steps, mussing his hair and blowing invisible-but-irritating scraps of the world into his face.

She said, "Don't give *me* a hard time! You know what you know!"

He thrust his hands deep into his jacket pockets. Shannon slipped her arm through his and pressed against him. They moved in lock-step towards the Saab.

"I love the way you smile," said Ross. "And the way your eyes crinkle up, the sound of your laughter, and the way you just kissed me, as if you've never kissed anyone before."

She said, "Now you're talking."

But she couldn't have been more wrong. It was Garret who was doing the talking – Ross was nothing but a complicated, no-strings puppet from the grave. He said, "I'm crazy about your legs, too."

"You are?"

"You know I am. You've got great legs."

"I do?"

"You know you do." Ross was rolling now. He'd had a thousand front-row seats to this particular performance, had listened in on the conversation so many times he knew every word by heart. What had briefly confused him was the unscheduled change of location. He was positive, absolutely sure, that they were supposed to be down by the beach in front of the vine-choked hotel. This was supposed to be a post-coital chat. Everything had gotten all messed up when they'd gone to the bar instead of renting a room. Events were occurring completely out of sequence. Kelly was the problem. Where had *he* come from? Garret had never mentioned his name.

"What else?" said Shannon. "Tell me more . . ."

Ross kept talking as they crossed the street. He searched for the white Lexus but couldn't find it. The Saab was where they'd left it. A white cat stared complacently at him from somebody's front porch.

Shannon said, "I'll drive."

He gave her the keys, dropped his cigarette butt on the sidewalk and squashed it underfoot. She was already behind the wheel, turning the key. He got in beside her, fastened his seatbelt.

"The way you walk," he said, "so confident and sexy. It just drives me crazy with desire."

She gave him a tired look, put the car in gear and gunned it
away from the curb.

Ross said, "Where are we going now?"

She made a U-turn and ran the stop sign. They barrelled at high
speed towards the city. "I want to show you something," she said.

"Yeah? Like what?"

"Me," she said. "I want to show you me."

This time, they parked the Saab in the hotel lot. This time,
Shannon climbed the steps to the lobby and turned right, instead
of left. She was in the lead by several strides as they marched
briskly, in single file, past the dozy clerk at the reservations desk.
She punched the elevator's *up* button right on the nose. The door
slid open without delay. He followed her into the elevator. She
said, "Fifth floor." He hit the button. The doors slid shut. The
overhead lights picked out highlights and gave each strand of
Shannon's hair a radiant, healthy glow. Ross was standing to the
side and slightly behind her, so he was looking at her in profile.
He shook a cigarette out of the pack, stuck it in his mouth and let
it dangle. He was still admiring her when the elevator doors slid
open. He followed her out of the elevator and down a wide corridor with white-painted walls and a dark carpet. Shannon
seemed to know exactly where she was going; she had not consulted her key and there'd been no hesitation as they'd exited the
elevator. She stopped in front of a door numbered 517. She turned
the knob, pushed open the door, took him by the arm and led
him inside.

The deadbolt shot home. Ross glanced around. She'd rented a
suite. The hotel was old, and the owners had wisely resisted the
urge to renovate the place to death. There was a modest entrance
hall, a short corridor that led towards an open doorway and
another room. Shannon slipped out of her coat, tossed the coat
on a straight-back chair. She slipped her arms around Ross's neck,
got up on her tippy-toes and kissed him on the mouth.

He groped for her, but she was gone.

He followed her through the open doorway and into the suite's living room. Ivy clawed at the window. Beyond the panes of glass, the ocean lay flat and listless.

The room was furnished with a colour television, a writing table and a comfortable-looking chair. To the left of the television stood an overstuffed, plum-coloured chair. A matching sofa had its back to the window.

Kelly lay prone on the sofa, watching the television. To Ross's eye, he did not seem surprised in the slightest by their sudden appearance. Kelly pointed the set's remote control. He tapped a button and the television shifted channels. He hit the button again, returning to the original channel. He hit the button rapidly, tapped it so quickly that the television was unable to keep pace with his demands. Except for the bright blue channel numbers jumping in the top right corner, the screen was black. Kelly hit the *off* button. The TV made a faint crackling noise, and all the life went out of the screen. He lifted a weary arm. "How was the beach?"

Shannon rolled her eyes. She said, "How'd you get in – pick the lock?"

"No, a maid. You two lovebirds case the joint?"

"Excuse me? Did we what?"

"Check out Nancy and Tyler's opulent waterfront home, sniff around, get a feel for the place. You know, case the joint."

"Sort of." Shannon glanced at Ross. "We did what we could, to the best of our abilities." She smiled enigmatically at her brother.

What did that smile mean? Ross had no idea. Were Shannon and Kelly, related or not, really stupid enough to believe they could waltz into somebody's house five years after an armed robbery the occupants were only peripherally involved with, kick some ass and just like that be two hundred thousand dollars' wiser? Lemon-meringue pie in a cotton-candy sky.

But let's say Billy *had* dropped off a bag of armoured-car cash at the Crown house. Wouldn't Nancy and Tyler have spent every penny of it, by now? Were they so unimaginative and parsimonious that they couldn't think of anything to buy? Shannon had told Ross that shortly after Billy had been bear-hugged by fate, the Crowns had flown to Europe, where they had frittered away six long months. Six months in Italy, Germany, France. Paris, France. Expensive restaurants. Fine wines. Five-star hotels. Fat tips. Ross couldn't even begin to imagine how swiftly the money would disappear. Man, you couldn't *burn* it that fast.

The sofa creaked as Kelly effortlessly unfolded himself, swung his legs around and stood upright, his physical presence taking up an awful lot of room, requiring a disproportionate amount of space. He yawned hugely, and checked his watch – a bulky, gold-coloured machine that nested deep in the fine, curly blond hair that covered his wrist. "Whoa, it's late!" He winked at Ross. "Gotta run!"

Shannon said, "Talk to me tomorrow, okay?"

"At work?"

"Probably not." Shannon glanced at Ross, back to Kelly. "I think I'll take a couple more days off."

"You deserve it, sweetheart. Or, at least, you soon will." He snatched up his jacket and sauntered towards the door. "Have fun."

Shannon waited until the door had closed behind him and then went over and shot the deadbolt. She told Ross she was going to take a shower.

Ross said, "Okay."

She mock-flirtatiously batted her eyes. "Care to join me?"

What kind of question was that. They hardly knew each other. But then, in a way that somehow mattered, that wasn't exactly true. They'd corresponded. Exchanged deep thoughts. There had been a meeting of minds. She'd assured him repeatedly that she wanted to see him the minute he was released. She'd even sent him a picture – a shot of her spread out in the sunshine on the lip of somebody's backyard pool. She'd worn a skimpy black one-piece suit, her hair had been a little shorter . . .

Shannon said, "Go ahead, think it over." She cocked a hip. "Take your time, Ross. We've got the room until eleven tomorrow morning, so there's no big rush."

Ross moved slowly towards her. He fumbled with the top button of his shirt. Or, come to think of it, *Garret's* shirt.

In the shower, Shannon was all business. Ross braced himself against the white-tiled wall as she washed him from top to bottom, and all points in between. Her hands moving briskly, she lathered every square inch of him. The pressure she applied was constant, and relentless. She had no favourite nooks, no favourite crannies. The way she treated him, he might have been the family station wagon.

She slapped him on the rump. "All done. Rinse."

He turned and turned beneath the shower. Water drummed off his ribs, the top of his skull. Frothy clouds of soap raced down the drain. His skin was red from the heat. His genitals seemed to weigh a ton. Finally, when he was as clean as he would ever get, he said, "Your turn."

"That's okay, I'll do myself." She jerked a thumb. "Out, hand-some."

Ross pushed aside the blank white shower curtain, and stepped carefully out of the tub. Standing on the hotel's plump white bathmat, he towelled himself dry. Management had provided disposable toothbrushes, a small tube of Crest toothpaste. He brushed his teeth and spat, rinsed and spat again. On the other side of the shower curtain, Shannon hummed a tune he did not recognize.

The bedroom window was open an inch or two; gauzy curtains fluttered in the tarnished light. The queen-size bed looked huge. He turned aside the duvet and slipped beneath the sheets. It had been more than five years since he'd made love to anybody but himself. More than five years was a long time. He reached behind him and plumped up the pillow.

The breeze from the open window was chilly, and damp. He climbed out of bed and went over to the window and slid it shut. Way over there on the far side of the harbour, lights vanished into the late-afternoon haze. He counted the freighters in the harbour. Thirteen. He turned back to the bed.

Shannon lay on her side, facing him, her body from her shoulder down covered by the sheets. She'd arrived so recently that the duvet was still settling around her, adapting to the shape of her body.

He stared at her, all those delectable hills and valleys. Shannon's attention was no less intense but considerably more focused. Just at that moment, there was no chance of eye contact.

20

A crumpled red cotton handkerchief lay on the carpet by the sofa, next to a pair of stereo headphones. The headphones leaked a shrill whining sound. A Chieftains CD jewel box stood upright on a Pioneer player.

Parker said, "Pat, it's Claire Parker . . ."

Timmins appeared in the open doorway, wild-eyed, his service pistol clenched in his fist. He wore faded jeans and a white shirt. His hair was tousled and his feet were bare. Parker stood absolutely motionless in the middle of the room, as the tinny music raged, and her heart thumped percussively.

Willows said, "I knocked, and you didn't answer. I looked in through the window and saw you lying on the floor." He pointed. "The handkerchief was on your chest. Through the window it looked like a pool of blood. I thought you'd been killed."

Timmins hesitantly lowered his pistol.

Parker said, "Sorry about the door, Pat."

Timmins braced himself against the doorframe and leaned backwards, so he had a clear view down the hallway to the door. He absorbed the fact of the broken chain, ran his fingers through his close-cropped hair. "You scared the hell out of me. I was half-asleep, believe it or not." He ejected the magazine and tossed the gun on the sofa, tucked in his shirt. "There's coffee, if you're interested."

Willows accepted the offer. Parker declined. The detectives
followed Timmins into the kitchen. Timmins poured from a
Mr. Coffee into two floral-patterned mugs. "Milk or sugar?"

"Milk," said Willows. "I'll get it." He opened the refrigerator
door on a glass jug of cranberry juice, a few individual-size bottles
of Perrier and a one-litre waxed-cardboard container of homoge-
nized milk. The milk's expiry date had long since passed. He
stepped back. The refrigerator door swung shut of its own accord.
He said, "I've changed my mind – I'll take it black."

Timmins handed him a white mug decorated with taxi-yellow
trim and a splash of pale blue forget-me-nots. Willows had been
hoping for the mauve mug with orange trim and mock-daisies,
but let it pass. Timmins fished in his shirt pocket for cigarettes.
He lit up, averted his head and exhaled a roiling cloud of carcinogens towards the ceiling.

"Interesting house," said Parker. "What is it, two bedrooms?"

"Two and a den, but all the rooms are pretty small."

"You own the place?"

"Rent. It belongs to my parents. They bought it as an invest-
ment, about ten years ago. I've been here since Don and I split
up." Timmins drank some coffee. He flicked ash in the sink.
Outside, the cat meowed plaintively.

A lightweight pine table and two pine chairs stood in the corner
by the window. Parker sat down, making herself at home.
Timmins' eyes flickered, but he said nothing.

Willows said, "Pat, we'd like you to tell us what you know about
Inspector Mark Rimmer."

"Not a damn thing. Why would I?"

"Those parties out in the valley – you've heard of them, haven't
you?"

Timmins nodded warily.

"Ever go to one?"

"No, never."

"Turn down an invitation?"

"No."

"You're sure about that?"

Timmins pulled on his cigarette. He looked Willows straight in the eye, as he said, "I'll answer your questions, Detective. But don't try to interrogate me, because I'm not going to put up with that kind of bullshit."

Willows smiled. He said, "Pat, did you ever meet Don's neighbour, a kid named Graham Aubert?"

"Yeah, once or twice, in passing."

"What'd you think of him?"

"Not much." Timmins reached behind him and turned on the tap. He held the butt of his cigarette under the water and then opened the cupboard door beneath the sink and tossed the cigarette into a plastic garbage can with a throwaway plastic liner. He turned off the tap, dried his hands on a paper towel. "Graham's kind of weird. A weird kid. I'd drop by Don's apartment, knock on the door and bingo, there was Graham. Always shovelling the same load of bullshit – he'd heard a noise and thought it was somebody knocking on *his* door. Fat fucking chance. The guy hasn't got any friends. You're asking me what I *thought* of him? Not a fucking thing." Timmins lit another cigarette. His hands were trembling. He glared into the sink.

Willows said, "Did Don attend any of the valley parties?"

"Not that I know of."

"Think he might've?"

"No, I don't. Don wasn't a promiscuous person. He wasn't like that, not at all."

Willows let that pass. He said, "What about Rimmer?"

"Ask him."

"I will, when I get around to it. In the meantime, I'm asking you. Rimmer's a lot older than Don. Old enough to be his dear old dad. Did Don ever speak to you about the nature of his relationship with Inspector Rimmer?"

"No, of course not."

"You were still friends, though. Weren't you?"

Timmins shrugged. "I don't know what I meant to him. All I

know is what I wanted. How he felt . . ." Timmins looked as if he might burst into tears.

Willows said, "We got in touch with Don's parents, by the way. They're doing what they can to get back as quickly as possible." He put his mug down on the kitchen counter.

Timmins glanced at the untouched coffee. It was all the reason he needed to give Willows a sardonic look. But Willows liked his coffee with milk, and no other way. And that's just the way it was.

It was Parker's turn to drive. She started the engine, put the car in gear. "Where to, Jack?"

Willows reached for the Motorola. He got the dispatcher to patch him through to the third floor. There were no messages from Christy Kirkpatrick, but Peter Singer had called twice. Had the lawyer located Sheila? Willows realized with a shock of guilt that he'd hardly given his wife a thought since he'd last spoken with Singer. Had his feelings for Sheila deteriorated to the point where he no longer cared about where she was or what had happened to her?

No, he refused to believe that of himself. He had blocked her out because he was overloaded, stressed out, worried.

The city morgue, with its pale orange brick façade and mullioned windows with white-painted trim, was located on Cordova Street, just around the corner from 312 Main. The cutting was done on the top floor. There was an elevator, but it was unheated, the walls and floor and even the ceiling were sheathed with panels of stainless steel. Willows had taken to using the stairs, and Parker fully approved. A trip in the elevator never failed to leave her feeling like a newly minted member of the undead.

They reached the top-floor landing. A fan rattled overhead. They walked side by side, close enough to touch, down the long, unusually wide corridor. Willows pushed through double swinging doors that led directly to the operating theatre. He held the door for Parker. She followed him inside.

The room was about twenty by twenty, perfectly square. The overhead fluorescents were bright enough to light a stadium. The floor and two walls were clad in bright blue tiles. The other walls were lined with lockable, refrigerated stainless-steel drawers that at first glance resembled enormous filing cabinets. A matched pair of zinc tables dominated the room. The tables stood directly beneath a massive cast-iron and frosted-glass skylight. Many years ago, Parker had come into the room when the lights were out and the moon was full. The moonlight had fallen upon the tables and made them gleam unnaturally, as if they had a cold and eerie life of their own. It was a moment she recalled vividly each time she entered the room, a moment she doubted she would ever forget.

The zinc tables were each three feet wide and seven feet long. Now that the city had an NBA franchise and an in-season population of basketball players, was seven feet long enough?

The tables stood exactly forty-two inches above the tiled floor at the head, with a one-inch decline to the foot. A never-ending stream of cold water flowed the length of the table, gathered itself into a shallow trough and then swirled down a three-quarter-inch copper pipe that vanished into the floor.

Both tables held a body. The corpse on the closest table was covered in a lime-green sheet. Christy Kirkpatrick was at work on the second table. He wore a pale green smock, a green cap, disposable surgical mask and safety glasses. The small rotary saw he held in his rubber-gloved hands emitted a shrill whine that dribbled away into silence as he switched it off. He put the saw down on the table between the corpse's legs, and used a small pry-bar to pop off the top of the skull. Willows caught a glimpse of long, dirty-blond hair. Wrong body.

He lifted the sheet on the other table. Donald E. Mooney stared dully up at the ceiling. A tiny fragment of silver – a speck of duct tape – gleamed in the curve of his nostril.

Willows said, "Christy!"

Kirkpatrick twitched. He glanced over his shoulder. The mask shifted slightly as he smiled. He raised a hand.

Willows pointed. "How much longer are you going to keep Mr. Mooney waiting?"

"As long as it takes, Jack. An hour, maybe. Why? Are his appointments starting to back up?" Kirkpatrick's voice was muffled by his mask. He waved Willows over. "C'mere, take a look at this."

But Willows had seen a human brain before, and firmly believed that if you've seen one, you've seen 'em all. He said, "I'll be at my desk, Christy. Call me when you're ready to go."

Kirkpatrick nodded, his back to Willows. The sweet perfume of bone dust drifted across the room.

Except for the two civilian staff, the squadroom was empty. Willows checked his message slips. Peter Singer had called again. The word *urgent* was underlined just beneath his phone number.

Parker said, "Want a coffee?"

Willows nodded, picked up his phone, dialled the lawyer's number. Singer's secretary put him through without delay.

"Jack, thanks for calling back."

"What's up, Peter?"

Singer said, "It's about the guy your wife's been going out with, Jack. Robert King."

"What about him?"

"When you mentioned his name, it rang a very small bell. I made a few calls, checked the guy out. He was back here a few years ago, got involved in a stock scam, was fined and lost his trading privileges. That's not an easy thing to do in Vancouver, Jack. Anyway, he bounced right back. Talked an elderly widow out of her life savings, and left town. Moved to Toronto, where he pulled the same stunt. The victim pressed charges, but dropped them after her dog was killed, her Volvo torched. The police couldn't prove a thing. Did Sheila have any money, other than the cheques you sent her?"

Willows took a deep breath. The squadroom shimmered. He clenched the telephone and was only vaguely aware of Parker hovering at his side. He said, "Not that I know of. Her parents have some money. She may have asked them for a loan." Willows' mind raced. What the hell was going on?

Parker said, "Jack . . ."

"I've got a name for you, Jack. Detective Jeff Culver."

"He's with Missing Persons?"

"Fraud," said Singer. He gave Willows Culver's number, tried to reassure him that it was too early to assume the worst. Willows cut him short, thanked him for his help, and gently cradled the phone. He couldn't believe how quickly Singer had turned up evidence that Sheila might be in trouble. He felt guilty, depressed, incompetent.

"What was that all about?" said Parker. She'd put Willows' coffee mug down on his desk by his elbow, and was sipping from a bottle of iced tea. He told her about Singer's phone call. He picked up the phone, dialled the Toronto number Singer had given him. The phone at the other end rang eight times before it was picked up. Willows identified himself, and asked to speak to Detective Culver. He was told that Culver was out of the building, and invited to leave a message. He gave the disembodied female voice at the other end of the line his office and home numbers, briefly explained the nature of his call. He was about to hang up when Eddy Orwell and Bobby Dundas led Graham Aubert into the squadroom.

Bobby waved. "Hey, Claire." Aubert was in cuffs. He was jerked off balance as Bobby veered suddenly towards Parker's desk. "Get anything out of Timmins?"

"He confessed," said Willows. "Didn't anybody bother to tell you?"

Bobby's jaw dropped. His mouth gaped open. Three golds crowns, too many amalgam fillings to count. Parker had always assumed that "jaw drop" was a cartoon expression meant to convey surprise. But look at Bobby! His mouth continued to hang open. Willows' little joke had resulted in a sudden loss of muscle control, due to overwhelming astonishment, and shock. Bobby's teeth clicked together as he finally shut his mouth. He managed a synthetic laugh, pointed at Willows with a finger that was rigid and trembling. "Think you're pretty funny, huh?"

Willows said, "Put the finger away, Bobby, before you sit down on it, and hurt yourself."

Bobby's glare was full of vinegar and venom. He renewed his grip on Aubert's arm, pushed him towards the interrogation room.

Parker's phone warbled. She picked up, listened a moment. "Okay, we're on our way over." She cradled the phone and drank the last of her tea. "That was Christy. He's sharpening his axe, says he'll be ready to start on our boy in a few minutes."

Willows picked up a stray pencil. He made a note to ask Culver to fax him King's rap sheet and photograph. What was he going to tell Sheila's mother and father? What in hell was he going to tell the kids?

Parker touched his shoulder. She let her hand lie there. "Why don't I take care of the autopsy. There's no point in both of us attending."

"Yeah? You sure?"

"I'm sure."

Willows had second thoughts. Toronto operated out of a time zone three hours ahead of Vancouver – or twenty-one hours behind. He checked his watch. It was entirely possible Culver had already left for the day. Or he could be working a fresh case, be gone for hours. There was no point in spending the rest of the day in a holding pattern, waiting for a call that might not come. He checked his desk to make sure the drawers were locked, gave Parker a crooked, apologetic smile. "I think I'll tag along with you."

Parker glanced behind her, towards the front of the squadroom. The two civilian secretaries were hard at work. Orwell and Bobby Dundas had shut the interrogation-room door. She said, "It's a date," and bent over Willows and kissed him firmly on the mouth.

21

Shannon smelled of hotel soap, Crest toothpaste, the perfume she'd dabbed here and there in carefully positioned pheromone ambushes. Her skin was warm, smooth as anything this world has to offer. She and Ross lay beneath the sheets on opposite sides of the bed, holding hands, and chastely kissed each other for what seemed to Ross like forever and a day.

Eventually he made a move on her, disengaged a hand and did a little preliminary exploring, groped the terrain. She reacted by bending his fingers backwards, almost deafened him with her outraged shouts. He scooted back to his own side of the bed, apologized.

Where had he gone wrong? His memory of Garret and Shannon's first full day together, tangled and complex as it had been, was clear as a bell. He had been confused by the unscheduled stop at the bar and then the trip out to the beach. But now that he was back on track, right where he belonged, he'd thought everything was going to be okay. Predictable.

He rolled over on his side, reached for his shirt. He shook a cigarette out of the pack, and lit up.

Shannon said, "This is a no-smoking room."

"Yeah?" He rolled over again, so he was facing her. She lay on her back with the sheets tucked under her chin. Her eyes glittered. Her hair had that tousled look favoured by the kind of girls who posed for automotive-parts calendars. The bedding blurred the shape of her body, but he'd taken a good long look at her in the shower, and for a fleeting, exquisite moment, he'd had a handful of her. The memory seared his brain like a steak on a grill. He said, "I always enjoy a cigarette after sex. Most men do."

"Men who smoke."

"Yeah, right. Men who smoke. I'd stand corrected, but I'm too tired to get up."

Shannon inched a little closer. She cupped her chin in her hand. "Are you telling me that we just had sex, Ross?"

"Sort of."

She smiled. "What's that supposed to mean?"

He worked on his cigarette, flicked a half-inch column of ash neatly into a curved depression in the base of the bedside lamp.

Garret had told him everything. Every tiny, intimate detail. With the aid of Ross's thesaurus, he'd recalled the soft, yielding weight of Shannon's breasts as he had held her in his arms. The nubbly texture of her nipple, as he'd suckled. The hard grinding of their bones as she moved beneath him, how the lamplight had pierced her eyes . . .

Shannon said, "Five years, that's a lot of Saturday nights without a date."

Ross shrugged. "Seemed like it at the time. Now I'm not so sure." He took a final pull on his cigarette, mashed the butt into the lamp's metal base. He put his hands behind his head and locked his fingers, rocked his shoulders back and forth until he was nice and comfortable. He shut his eyes.

The first time Garret told him about going to the hotel with Shannon, they'd been walking aimlessly around the middle of the yard, taking care not to walk in a straight line that would carry them into a wall, remind them of who they were and where they were. It was late October, sunny and not too cold, the sky clear, nothing above them but endless blue. Looking back, the way Garret had acted at the time, it was likely that the tumour already had a good hold on him, that he was already dying . . .

Garret said, "Remember that picture I showed you, my girl-friend?"

"Sharon?" As if he didn't remember.

"*Shannon*, dipshit." Garret cuffed him playfully on the side of the head. "I ever tell you about the first time we did it?"

"Did what? Grabbed a couple of straws and shared a milkshake?"

Garret wasn't smiling. At that moment, he looked as serious as anybody in the yard. "What I'm talking about, the first time we made love."

"No, you never told me about that." Ross slowed, drifted a couple of steps off the line they'd taken, shook out a cigarette and lit it.

Garret stopped walking. He turned around and came back. "Gimme a smoke."

Ross shook a cigarette out of the pack, handed it over. He sparked his lighter. Garret took the lighter out of his hands. He lit his cigarette and slipped Ross's lighter into his pocket, blew smoke into the yard, glanced idly around and then back to Ross. "Want me to tell you about it, how it went?"

"Not if you're gonna wake up in the middle of the night and wish you hadn't."

Garret thought that over for as long as it took him to haul in another double lungful of smoke. Exhaling, he said, "I see your point." His upper body tilted left as he fished deep in his pockets for Ross's lighter. He handed the lighter back to Ross. They wandered around the yard for another ten minutes or so and then Garret said, "She had this park she wanted me to see, where she played tennis. Then we went to a restaurant and had lunch, a really nice lunch, with wine. Italian wine." Garret tried on his accent. "*Valpolicella Classico Superiore*. And then we went straight to the hotel. What I mean is, she *dragged* me to the hotel."

"What hotel?"

"A downtown hotel, across from the water. The Sylvia. Real nice place. Very clean, nice and quiet, reasonably priced. Ever stay there?"

Ross shook his head.

"They got ivy growing all over the walls, all the way to the top of the building. Open your window and look around, there's vines everywhere, some of 'em thick as your arm, twisty and green. You can hear birds chirping away in there, squirrels and what have you . . ."

"Chimps?"

"No chimps, Ross." Garret's mouth twisted around a grin. "Plenty of monkey business, though."

In the slammer, two things that were never in short supply were time and bullshit. Garret was an experienced convict, an expert at verbal foreplay, who knew how to grab that big clock by the hands and turn it to his advantage. Eight long days had come and gone before he finally got around to telling Ross about what Shannon was like in bed.

"Hot," Garret said as they lounged in a patch of watery sunlight. Low-altitude clouds scudded overhead. A bitter wind swooped the length of the yard, snatched up whatever particles of debris it could find, and flung them in the faces of those convicts stupid or desperate enough to brave the elements.

Ross said, "Yeah?" He shoved his hands into his pockets and turned his back to the gale. The fitful wind tore at him, snapped at his loose-fitting denim jacket and made his hair ripple like a wheatfield.

"Hotter than a Thanksgiving turkey," said Garret. Then, finally, he told Ross what Shannon liked to do, in between the sheets.

Garret had a way with words. His description of those hours spent in bed with Shannon were minutely detailed, incredibly graphic.

But was he speaking the gospel or had he told a hundred lies?

Ross sat up, adjusted his pillow behind him and leaned back against the headboard. He lit another cigarette.

"Shannon?"

A long silence. Then, "What do you want now?"

"Just to tell you that I'm sorry if I've pissed you off." Ross paused. He was acutely aware that he'd better choose his words carefully. A misstep at this crucial point in the proceedings could be fatal to their romance, such as it was. He said, "Garret told me about certain things you and he did, stuff that happened between you, important experiences you'd shared." Ross's cigarette glowed bright. He exhaled with a rush, flicked ash in the general direction of the floor. "Then, this morning, those same things started to happen to me."

"Like what?" Shannon's tone was harsh as a raven's.

The light in the room had never been strong. Now that they were well and truly into the hindquarter of the day, it was fading away at a gallop. Ross was grateful for whatever gloom was available; he had no desire to make eye contact.

He said, "Well, like going to the park, the tennis courts. And that real nice restaurant you took me to, and now here we are at the Sylvia Hotel."

Ross waited a moment, giving her a window of opportunity, should she wish to jump through it. But if she saw the chance, she gave no indication that she cared to take it. A minute or two passed in congealing silence and then Ross said, "I guess I thought things were going to keep on going the way they'd been going . . ."

"What's that supposed to mean?"

"Well, when you invited me up to your room, just like you invited Garret, I guess I made the mistake of thinking we'd end up passing the time in the same way that you and he had done."

"Keep talking."

But her tone was so icy that Ross fell silent.

She said, "What kind of things do you think you're talking about? No, wait. Let me guess. *Sex* things?"

Ross nodded, his head jerking. But by now the light was so far gone that it was impossible for her to see him. He said, "Yeah, that."

"Garret told you we came up here, to this very room, and had *sex*?"

"Well, no. He never said what room it was."

"But he told you we had *sex*?"

"Made love," said Ross miserably.

The bed squeaked as he reached for the lamp. He warned Shannon that he was going to turn the light on, so she'd better shield her eyes. He switched on the light, turned towards her.

She said, "Well, he lied. Or maybe he didn't. Maybe I'm a little confused about how I feel right now. Is there something wrong with that?"

Ross said, "No, of course not."

They lay there, facing each other, looking into each other's eyes. They were no more than a handspan apart. Breathing the same air. Sharing a bed, both of them alive in that same tiny sliver of time in the endless history of the world. What were the odds? A sentimental fool could drown in his own tears, just thinking about it.

Ross wondered what she saw when she looked at him. He itched to know *who* she saw. Was it him, or was it a dead man, a handful of dust?

The sheets moved. Shannon's hand touched him. She inched a little closer. Her breath warmed him. He could feel the heat of her body, coming at him in waves. She said, "What are you thinking?"

He shrugged. That slight movement brought him into fleeting contact with the swell of her breast. She gave no indication that she'd noticed. He said, "I'm just wondering where your friend Kelly fits in."

"I told you, he's my brother."

Ross smiled wearily. "C'mon, there's got to be more to it than that. For example, why did you meet him in the bar? And what was he doing up here, in the room?"

"When we arrived at the hotel, I noticed his car parked on the street. The old orange Datsun? With the rust? That's Kelly's car. So I knew he was here, and that he was probably in the bar, having a beer."

"Wait a sec. Are you telling me his presence was a wild coincidence?"

"Well, no. Not exactly. He knew I planned to bring you here. But please don't ask me why he showed up."

"Intrusive personality," said Ross.

"Excuse me?"

"He's pushy."

"What was I supposed to do, ignore him? The reason we only stayed for one drink was because I assumed that, if we left, and he didn't think we were coming back, he'd eventually go home."

"But he didn't go home, did he?"

"Well, I can't help that."

Ross lit a cigarette. He felt like he'd been parachuted into a maze with no exits. He said, "But *why* was he waiting for us?"

"I don't know! He's my big brother. Naturally he thinks he knows what's best for me, even though he doesn't."

Ross worked hard to make sense of this piece of intelligence, or perhaps a far better word was bullshit. Shannon was in her mid-twenties. A woman a quarter of a century old was nobody's child. She'd have the same basic needs as anybody else, any other woman. If she wanted to take him to a hotel, what was wrong with that? Nothing. So, bullshit aside, what had *motivated* Kelly to get mixed up in business that was none of his concern?

He asked her.

She said, "Kelly was a friend of Garret's."

"Oh yeah? He never mentioned him."

"Not a close friend," said Shannon. "But they had certain things in common, mutual friends . . ."

Ross pulled on his cigarette. He'd been studying her closely as she spoke, and he was fairly sure that, so far, most of what she'd been telling him was either the truth or a lie. He said, "Was Garret involved in criminal activities, at the time?"

"Not that I know of. In fact, after he did those terrible things and they put him in jail, I often wondered if it was my fault that he'd turned to a life of crime."

"How d'you mean?"

Shannon said, "Before he met me, Garret was . . . I remember he described himself as kind of idling through life. Not doing much, but getting by. But then he met me, and he felt differently about things." She gave Ross a dazzling smile. "But where could he take me that didn't cost money?"

"Beats me," said Ross.

"That was when he teamed up with Billy. At first all they did was break into cars, stuff like that."

"Small potatoes," said Ross. "But then they got ambitious." Or, another word, *greedy*. "Decided to take on the armoured car, get rich all at once, in one big chunk."

She nodded. A tear welled up in the corner of her eye. It hung there for a moment, glistening, and then tumbled slowly down her cheek, into the corner of her mouth. She licked it away.

Ross said, "When you come right down to it, the only reason people do what they do is because of who they are, deep inside themselves. Think about it, Shannon. How a person behaves has got nothing to do with anything outside himself. Not really. It's what's coiled *inside* a man's heart that counts for everything."

His cigarette had burned down to the filter. He lit another. "Garret could've won the lottery, it wouldn't have made the slightest difference to the way he acted, the path he chose."

Shannon had drawn away to the far side of the bed. Ross didn't pursue her but neither did he put a stop to his chatter. "You really think it mattered to Garret whether or not he was going out with you? He tried to rob an armoured car but it wasn't money he was after, even if he didn't know it at the time. See, we talked about this kind of stuff all the time, when we were in prison. 'Exploring the Inner Self,' they called it. Group therapy sessions. What Garret wanted, above anything else, was to feel like he was alive. He was so far gone, so royally fucked up, that the only way he could do that was to make other people die."

Shannon was crying now, in full flood. Her pretty face twisted by grief, the sounds she made tortured and animal-like, not at all musical.

Ross felt much worse than awful. He said, "Look, I'm sorry . . ." Man, if she didn't stop crying, they were going to need a canoe. He said, "What in hell are we *doing* here, anyway?"

In a strangled voice Shannon replied, "It was Kelly's idea." She leapt out of bed, disappeared into the bathroom. She blew her nose violently. The toilet flushed. She climbed back into bed. "He told me it would be a good idea if I seduced you."

Ross was dumfounded. Finally he collected himself. "Why?"

"So you'd help us get back Garret's two hundred thousand dollars."

Us?

Was Shannon being manipulated by her money-grubbing brother? If so, what a totally rotten fate. Man, she'd be better off having no brother at all. Ross wanted to take her in his arms and hold her close, comfort her and make her feel better. Sooth her with words. Remind her that every cloud had a silver lining. Assure her in honeyed tones that everything was going to work out just fine, in the end. Remind her that whatever happened, it was always for the best. You only went around once, right?

Ross's problem was that almost everything he'd learned that was of any real value had been taught to him in the slammer. But how pertinent were those hard-earned truths on this side of the wall? He could think of nothing to say to her that wouldn't have looked right at home on a bumper sticker.

He eased out of bed, scrambled into his – Garret's – underpants. He buttoned up Garret's shirt, pulled on Garret's jeans. He zipped up. He shoved his feet into his socks. He tucked in Garret's shirt. Where were his borrowed Nikes? He found the left shoe lying on its side beneath the bed, laces trailing wantonly across the carpet.

But where was the other shoe? On hands and knees, he patrolled the carpet from wall to wall. Shannon was crying again, had really cranked up the volume. He felt like a whipped dog, though he was the one who'd doled out the anguish. All he lacked was a tail to tuck between his legs.

He found the missing shoe, put it on. His cigarettes were on the table by the bed. He crawled over there, keeping a low profile. His groping hand closed on the package. Shannon grabbed his wrist. She held on tight and wouldn't let go.

She was snuffling, but the wailing had stopped. He raised his head an inch or two. There she was, watching him.

"Why did you tell me all those horrible things about Garret?"

Ross refused to tell her. She pleaded with him. When that tactic gained no ground, she swore feistily at him, and beat him about the head with her small fists hard as walnuts. He wouldn't budge. Not a word. In his mind, she had to figure out for herself why he'd told her the ugly truth about the convict she had loved.

It wasn't a complicated situation. If she wasn't able to figure it out for herself, it was because, at heart, she didn't really want to know.

He snatched up Garret's nifty black leather jacket and headed for the door. Stood quietly with his hand on the knob, ears twitching, as he waited in vain for her to cry, "Don't leave me!"

After a moment he turned and walked slowly down the hall towards the elevator. The hotel was silent. He reached the elevator, pushed a button. The doors immediately slid open. A portly gentleman in a baggy brown tweed suit peered disapprovingly out at him. The doors began to slide shut. The gentleman stabbed at the elevator's control panel with the tip of his loosely furled umbrella. Ross lurched forward. The doors slid shut, and the box with its cargo of human misery began its slow descent. Ross imagined he could still hear her crying.

His bruised heart plunged giddily downward at such tremendous speed that the elevator soon lagged far behind.

22

Christy Kirkpatrick was impressed. But for the fact that he'd been wrapped from head to toe in duct-tape, and then drowned via an ersatz intravenous, Donald E. Mooney was in damn fine shape.

"He must've spent a lot of time in the gym," said the pathologist. "You don't get definition like that without working at it." He glanced at Willows. "D'you pump the iron, Jack?"

"Pancakes," said Willows. "I pump the pancakes."

"The blood came back this morning," said Kirkpatrick. "Pure as the driven snow." He leaned against the autopsy table, hip on steel. Willows wondered how much weight he'd lost during the past few months. The pathologist's skin clung to his bones. He was verging on gaunt, and it seemed to Willows that his lustrous eyes were a little too bright. Kirkpatrick noticed that he was being scrutinized. He nodded very slightly, as if acknowledging that his situation merited attention.

The pathologist jerked a thumb at the corpse. "His kidneys, heart, liver, everything was in tiptop shape. His lungs, though full to the brim with water we have not yet analysed, but very much doubt was Perrier, were a lovely shade of pink. He didn't smoke, or take drugs. If he drank alcohol, it was in moderation."

"He hadn't been drinking when he was killed?"

"Not a drop – except for the tap water that drowned him, of course. I wish I could be more helpful, Jack." Kirkpatrick tugged at his ear. He cast a sidelong glance at Parker. "I hear you've got a suspect," he said in mock-conspiratorial tones.

"We do?" said Parker.

"I understand that it was an inside job," said Kirkpatrick. "Scuttlebutt has it your suspect's got *pips*." Taking note of the expression of dismay on Willows' face, Kirkpatrick hastily added, "But of course, it's only a rumour."

There was no point in grilling Kirkpatrick. He was a slippery fish, and even if he did give up a name, they'd never trace the rumour back to its source.

Parker's beeper vibrated against her hip. She checked the readout. Jerry Goldstein had called from the RCMP crime lab. She used Kirkpatrick's telephone to call him back. Goldstein picked up on the first ring.

Parker identified herself. She said, "What've you got for us, Jerry?"

"Not much. But probably more than you expected. The rubber gloves are manufactured in China. One thousand gross were shipped to the Vancouver distributor a little over six months ago. Prior to the date of the murder, six hundred and twelve gross had been sold to a total of three hundred and eighty-seven restaurants. The majority of the restaurants, more than two hundred of them, are located in the city or suburbs. I've got a complete list, if you're interested."

"I'm *very* interested," said Parker. "Send it right over, Jerry."

"Consider it done. Now just bear with me for a minute . . ." Parker heard the rustle of paper. Goldstein said, "We found a partial thumbprint inside the left glove. Nothing you could use in court. But there were traces of soap, which, sparing no expense, we've been able to identify."

There was a small silence. Parker said, "If you're waiting for a round of applause, forget it."

"Soma Soaps," said Goldstein. "Available in bulk only, no retail sales. It's a highly abrasive product, used by restaurants to clean pots and pans. You'd just love to get your hands on a box, wouldn't you?"

"Sounds to me like you're standing on one right now," said Parker.

"You can buy the stuff at almost any kitchen-supply whole-saler's. It's a very popular item. But nowhere near as popular as the gloves, lucky for you."

Parker said, "Have you got a list of Vancouver-area restaurants that bought both gloves and soap?"

"Would you buy me lunch if I did?"

"Eventually."

"Next week? Tuesday at noon?"

"C'mon, Jerry. Cough it up."

"You're going to be knocking on forty-one doors," said Goldstein. "Want me to send over the list, too?"

"Please."

Goldstein chuckled into the phone. "Forty-one restaurants. Chinese, Greek, Italian, Spanish, Vietnamese, you name it. I hope you don't have a weight problem, Claire."

Neither Willows nor Parker had expected much from the autopsy. Even so, the results had been disappointing. Both detectives had clutched a tiny splinter of hope that Kirkpatrick, working hand in hand with Donald E. Mooney's corpse, would provide them with a lead, no matter how tenuous or slender.

On the other hand, Jerry Goldstein had worked hard and done well; there was a decent chance that the rubber gloves found at the crime scene had come from his list of forty-one restaurants, and forty-one was a manageable number, given that there were now three teams of detectives working the case.

The faxed list of restaurants was on Parker's desk by the time she and Willows made it back to 312 Main. Parker made half a dozen copies. Bradley was in his office, his ghostly shape drifting behind the pebbled glass of his door. Willows knocked, and Bradley bade them enter. The inspector sat at his desk, in his burgundy leather chair. His uniform jacket hung from the oak coat rack he'd recently picked up at an auction. Bradley had rolled up his sleeves. His regulation tie was loose. His new bifocals lay on his desk blotter, next to a dismantled fountain pen. The tips of his fingers were stained dark blue. The man was all cop, thought Willows, repressing a smile. Parker briefly explained the significance of Goldstein's list.

"Forty-one restaurants," said Bradley. "When're you going to start your canvass?"

"At the first sign of hunger pangs," said Willows.

"Chuckle, chuckle." Bradley wiped his inky fingers on a tissue. "They'd never admit it, but Eddy and Bobby have been spinning their wheels, getting nowhere. Ditto Spears and Oikawa." Bradley glanced out his window. The sky that moved across the glass was every shade of grey. The forecast was for rain, and plenty of it. Sometime yesterday he'd lost his umbrella. He said, "Shut the door, Claire."

Parker shut the door.

Bradley said, "I've made a few discreet inquiries about my fellow officer, Inspector Mark Rimmer." He smiled ruefully. "At least, I sure as hell hope they were discreet inquiries. I wouldn't want him to know I was interested in him. He might get the wrong idea, and we wouldn't want that, would we?"

"What'd you find out?" said Willows.

"Internal Investigations has got a file on him that's thicker than a telephone book. Vice has been watching him for years."

Parker said, "What's he been up to?"

"Nothing it would benefit the department to hang out on the line. But he hasn't done anything illegal, either. Rimmer's deep into group sex, but he's stayed clear of the downtown clubs, any-where local where he might be recognized. Once or twice a month, he wriggles into a hairpiece, glues on a false moustache and prowls the glitter-domes as far afield as New Westminster. He's a charter

member of a group-grope club out in the valley. Doesn't mess with
the kiddies or corner boys, thank Christ. He spends a disproportionate amount of his salary on the sex-chat lines. Runs a "help
wanted" ad in the local magazines. Aside from a healthy aversion
to juvies and hookers, he's about as discriminating as a great white
shark."

Willows said, "Bobby worked vice for more than three years,
before he was rotated into narcotics. He must've known all about
Rimmer."

"Yeah, sure. But would it jump-start his career to say so?"
Bradley picked up his glasses. He peered at Willows through the
split-screen lenses. "I don't want to involve Internal Investigations
in this little caper. Not yet, anyway. You up for putting in a little
unauthorized overtime, Jack?"

"Are you asking me to surveille him?"

"Covertly, of course."

"If you yanked his file, he'll find out about it sooner or later.
Probably he already knows. He'd spot me in a minute."

"Could be."

Parker said, "Is that what you want?"

"Absolutely not. We know that Rimmer and Mooney had a
thaing going on, so I don't see that we've got any choice but to
treat Rimmer as a suspect."

Willows said, "Do me a favour, Homer. Put Bobby on Rimmer.
Skulking in doorways, slouching in cars. It's what he does best,
and he loves to do it."

"You don't much care for Bobby, do you, Jack?"

"Does anybody?"

Bradley leaned back in his chair. He put his feet up on his desk,
folded his arms across his chest.

Parker said, "What about Timmins?"

"He's still in the running. But I'll tell you something: Aubert's
my favourite suspect."

"Why is that?"

"He isn't a cop."

"True, but he isn't a dishwasher, either. Where did the gloves come from?"

"How should I know? None of them are dishwashers. Maybe the gloves were used as a sexual accessory."

"How does the soap residue fit in?"

"Why ask *me*?" Exasperated, Bradley ran the palm of his hand across his thinning, close-cropped hair. "Beat it, detectives. Hit those mean streets." He smiled, putting the department's dental plan on display. "Ever watch 'The X-Files'? 'The Truth Is Out There,' if you can believe Scully and Mulder. And believe me, I do."

Parker pointed at the window. "Out there?"

"Out *there*," corrected Bradley, indicating his door.

Willows slumped into his chair. There were three pink message slips by his telephone. Peter Singer had called twice. Inspector Mark Rimmer had called once, not ten minutes earlier.

Willows phoned his lawyer. Singer was in court. His secretary didn't expect him back at the office until the following morning. In response to Willows' query, she primly informed him that she had no idea why Singer wanted to talk to him.

Willows cradled the phone. Parker was watching him, openly curious. He told her that Rimmer had left a message.

"You going to call him back?"

"Sure. Why not?"

Willows dialled Rimmer's extension. The inspector picked up on the second ring.

"Inspector, this is Detective Jack Willows. You called me?"

There was a slight pause. Rimmer said, "No I didn't, Jack. Why would I want to talk to you?"

Willows said, "My mistake, Inspector." If Rimmer said he hadn't called, then he hadn't called. Simple, wasn't it? "Sorry to have bothered you."

Rimmer hung up. Just before the line went dead, Willows was

fairly certain he heard Rimmer softly mutter the word *asshole*. But perhaps he'd been mistaken . . . Willows hung up.

Parker said, "That was a short conversation. But was it sweet?"

"Rimmer just wanted me to know he's aware of our interest in him. He's giving me a chance to back off."

Willows checked Farley Spears' desk, and then Orwell's and then Oikawa's and finally Bobby Dundas'. Rimmer had left messages for all four detectives. Willows went from desk to desk, snatching and crumpling.

Parker said, "What are you doing, Jack?"

"Homer's going to ask Bobby to keep an eye on Rimmer. Bobby'll risk it, too. He's an ambitious guy, willing to take a chance. But he's nobody's fool. If he knew Rimmer was already watching his back, he wouldn't go anywhere near him."

"But now he won't know, will he?"

Willows rolled the message slips into a tight little ball and tossed them into his wastebasket. "Not unless you tell him." He smiled. It was his first smile of the day, and Parker was warmed by it. He said, "All this treachery has given me an appetite. Want to get something to eat?"

"Sure," said Parker.

Willows was in the mood for a cheeseburger. Like many Vancouverites, he believed the White Spot made the best burgers in town. He drove south on Main, past the imposing sandstone façade of the Carnegie Library and the pale, blank faces of the local street-level dealers and their clientele, through the fading heart of Chinatown and on towards the elevated SkyTrain monorail, a cluster of new highrises.

At Twelfth and Main, Willows made a sharp right on the green. He drove west on Twelfth to Cambie, eased into the left-turn lane. The light was red. City Hall loomed behind them, the four clocks with their orange dials that faced east, west, north and south all clamouring to tell a slightly different time.

The light changed. Willows let the car crawl forward half its length. There was a break in the flow of traffic, but he didn't take advantage of it because there were pedestrians in the crosswalk. A horn blared. He glanced in his rearview mirror. The driver behind him gave him the finger. There was another break in the traffic, but Willows didn't take advantage. He waited until the light turned red, and then gunned it through the intersection, leaving the other driver stranded in his wake.

Parker said, "Nice move, Jack."

"Sometimes it's mature to act immaturely," said Willows. He turned off Cambie at Thirteenth. It was well past the lunch hour and the parking lot was more empty than full.

Inside, they were shown to a booth with room for four. Their waitress arrived with a bright smile and two glasses of cloudy ice-water. The detectives politely declined an opportunity to examine the menu. Parker ordered tea and a shrimp sandwich on toasted whole-wheat bread, Willows a cheeseburger with French fries and coffee. When the waitress had gone, he held his water glass up against the light, then put the glass down on the table and pushed it away.

Parker said, "Forty-one restaurants use both our crime-scene gloves and the same brand of soap that was found in the gloves. If we're really unlucky, we'll have to canvass all forty-one of them. So what are we doing *here* – at a restaurant that isn't on the list?"

"Warming up," said Willows. He leaned across the table, and took her hand. "Getting in the mood," he added with a comically demented wink.

23

Ross stood on the sidewalk outside the hotel, feeling the damp seep up through the soles of his inherited shoes. Now what?

A yellow taxi cruised past. The driver eyeballed Ross, as if willing him to raise his arm and flag him down.

But what use was a ride when there was nowhere that he wanted to go? He stepped away from the shelter of the hotel, trotted across the street and looked up, counted windows until he reached the fifth floor. Which room was Shannon's? Probably that one – but maybe not. Small creatures bobbed and weaved in the tangle of ivy, disturbing dead twigs and desiccated leaves, random bits of debris. A brown bird about the size of a sparrow nibbled industriously at some invisible-but-no-doubt-delectable source of nourishment. It stepped off the vine and plummeted abrupt as a stone down to the second-storey level, drifted over the sidewalk and then curled back towards the building at suicidal speed. At the last possible second it flared its wings and braked hard, alighted gracefully on a vine thick as Ross's forearm. The bird glared at him with a glossy black eye the size of a pinhead, ducked its head and began to preen.

Ross was distracted by a trio of young women who happened to jog past. Above the slap of their sneakers on the sidewalk, and the hiss of their skimpy garments and the sibilance of their chatter, he heard a sudden, heart-rending squawk. Where the small brown bird had been, a halo of startled feathers hung for a moment, and then slowly and silently drifted down. In the undergrowth, something scuttled furtively.

Was that a speck of blood that glistened upon that spinning twig? Despite the lack of sirens or flashing lights, Ross was inexplicably drawn to the disaster. He was crossing the street when some small, abruptly detached thing tumbled to the sidewalk. A clue? He bent and picked up a petite leg that held no residual warmth. The black and curling claws were sharp as tacks. The knee joint moved smooth as silk in its minuscule socket as he repeatedly bent and straightened the leg. It was no puzzle as to why the limb had been discarded. Not a scrap of flesh clung to those diminutive and feeble bones.

He stood there, the weightless fragment of corpse cupped in the palm of his hand. After a few moments he put the leg in his jacket pocket. By now the three joggers were mere specks of fluorescence in the distance. Ross's mind was a blank. What should he do now?

He lit a cigarette and smoked it halfway down, then turned his back on the hotel and began walking along the street. There was a weird-looking, kind of Jetsons-style futuristic apartment block on his left. The building stood on a pair of sturdy concrete legs, for a better view of the water. The façade was mostly glass. The balconies flared in and out; there were no straight lines, other than the verticals. Further on, there was a take-out Greek restaurant. Ross turned left, putting his back to the ocean. He walked past a dry cleaner's, a grocery store, a small branch of a large bank and then the hard white lights of a chain fast-food restaurant. Across the street there was a Starbucks coffee shop, a barber's. The barber's red-and-white pole tried unsuccessfully to screw itself into the sidewalk.

A rusty orange Datsun pulled into the Starbucks parking lot across the street. The Datsun was burning oil, and then it wasn't. Kelly had killed the engine. The driver's-side door swung open. Kelly got out of the car, tossed his keyring high in the air and caught it neatly behind his back. He turned and looked directly at Ross and then strolled across the parking lot and disappeared inside the coffee shop.

Ross waited for a break in the traffic. He trotted across the street and into the Starbucks. Kelly was sitting at a table near the back, facing the door. Two large paper cups stood on the table. As Ross drew near he said, "I bought you a *latte*, is that okay?"

Ross sat down, angled his chair so he had his back to the wall and was facing both Kelly *and* the door. He pried the lid off his coffee cup, sniffed.

"I sprinkled some cinnamon on top," said Kelly. "Most people I know like chocolate, but I figured you for a cinnamon kind of guy."

Ross sipped at his coffee. Good. He stirred in the cinnamon with a slim wooden stick.

Kelly said, "Shannon likes chocolate. Can't get enough of the stuff, piles it on, she might as well drink a melted candy bar . . ."

Ross told himself to do what he'd done in the joint, when he had no idea what to do. Which was, keep his face blank and his mouth shut tight, his ears wide open.

"She's a lady who likes her sweets," said Kelly. He smiled, and lifted his paper cup in a casual toast, pointed at Ross with the pinkie finger of his free hand. "She likes her sweeties, too."

Ross didn't know quite how to respond to the remark, or if he should try. Out on the sidewalk, an old man shuffled past. He stopped by a table, picked up a cardboard cup and looked deep inside, carried the cup over to the gutter and spilled out a mouthful of coffee, gave the cup a shake and resumed his journey. Ross said, "What'd he do that for?"

"What?"

"An old guy just walked past, he grabbed a paper cup off a table, poured out the last of the coffee and stuck the cup in his pocket. What's he want with an empty cup?"

"He's a beggar." Kelly sized Ross up. "You been away for a few years. People don't like to touch hands anymore. It's AIDS, maybe.

You wanna make a few bucks, you gotta have a paper cup, something people can stick the money in without risking contact."

"Makes sense," said Ross, with more conviction than he felt.

"Disease," said Kelly. "That's what people are afraid of, disease. Lethal diseases. Who can blame them? Not me, I'll tell you that much."

The jaunty topping of foam on Ross's *latte* had collapsed in upon itself and assumed a somewhat bedraggled look. Ross sipped delicately. His upper lip was freckled with cinnamon.

"Nice haircut."

"Yeah – you like it?"

"Spooky, how much you look like Garret. Even the way you walk, that roll of the shoulders, kind of a bold swagger."

Ross said, "You notice things like that, do you?"

"Shannon mentioned it, pointed it out to me." Kelly showed his teeth, but the display of enamel had nothing to do with a smile. "You calling me a queer?"

"Hell no," said Ross.

"'Cause gay is one thing I'm definitely not." Kelly thumped Ross on the shoulder with a lightning punch that would have hurt even more, had it not been so friendly. "I'm cheerful," he said, "but you better not call me gay."

"Got it," said Ross.

"Think we could get along, you and me?"

Ross shrugged, buying time. He contemplated his choice of lies.

"I don't mean you have to fall in *love* with me," said Kelly. "I'm asking, could you stand me long enough so we could do a job together?"

"Bust the Crown house?"

"You're way ahead of me, aren't you?" Kelly shook his head in admiration. "Man, you're so far up the road all I can see is dust." He drained his *latte* and crumpled the cardboard container in his fist. "Yeah, I'm talking about the Crown house. *Home invasion*, they call it. A standard break-and-enter, but you stick around for a few hours, get to know the victims." His smile was grim. "It's a friendlier kind of crime, in a way . . ."

"The two hundred grand, whatever's left of it by now, what makes you think it'd be in the house?"

"That's where I'd keep that kind of money, cash that didn't belong to me, big bucks that some innocent person had died for. But what difference does it make where they've got it? See, that's why there has to be two of us, in case the cash is in a safety-deposit box or somewhere else off the premises. So if hubby has to go somewhere to get it, one of us can stay with him while the other holds hands with Nancy, the intention being to give him a reason to hurry back home."

"How do we divvy up the cash?" said Ross.

"Three-way split. Shannon gets the same as us because without her we'd have nothing."

Kelly kept working on the paper cup, his big hands compressing it into a smaller and smaller ball. "I figure, if the money ain't in the house, that you should stay with Nancy. Shannon wouldn't trust me to be nice, but she'd figure you'd be a dependable baby-sitter because you're already getting as much hot sex as you can handle . . ."

"Makes sense to me," said Ross.

Kelly studied him closely, seemed satisfied with what he saw. "I got a plan, a real good plan." Kelly's pale eyes glittered. "See, I rented a bunch of movies with the same kind of plot, about people who want valuable things other people have got but maybe don't deserve to keep. In these movies, the people who do the stealing are the good guys, so their plans always work out pretty much as expected. I watched some of those movies five or six times, Ross. I took notes, written notes about the things these people had to do to get what they were after. And also, how things sometimes went wrong. In other words, I'm working both sides of the street, the sunny side and the dark side. You ever notice how, in movies, things *always* go wrong for the bad guys?"

Ross said, "It's been a long time since I've watched a movie about bad guys."

"What I did, I went to a drugstore and I bought a special note-book and three different colour ballpoint pens, red, green, and black. Whenever the movie bad guys, the criminals, whenever they did something that was smart, I wrote it down on the page in green ink. They made a mistake, or did something stupid that came back to haunt them, I used the red pen. C'mon back to Shannon's, I'll show what I figured out, see what you think."

Ross said, "Wait a minute. What about the black pen, when did you use the black pen?"

"Well, what I meant to do, I was going to use it to write down stuff that happened differently than was expected, because of unforeseeable events."

"Like what?"

"Well, for example, a sudden change in the weather. Like a thunderstorm, where a bolt of lightning knocks down a tree that falls across the road. Or an unexpected downpour causes a flood that takes out a bridge. Stuff like that."

"Acts of God," said Ross.

"Or a little girl walks into the path of an onrushing getaway car, or some guy's coming to the house to repair the furnace, but nobody knows about it, and it turns out the guy is a martial-arts expert . . ." By now the paper cup had been crushed into a ball about the size of a marble. Kelly began to pluck at it, as if he hoped to reconstruct it, bring it back to life.

Watching him, Ross was reminded of the Budweiser label.

Kelly said, "Almost all the movies had stuff that happened that you could never in a million years guess would happen. Weird coincidences. Or like you said, acts of God. So I never did use the black pen. I figured, what was the point? There's always the element of chance and you can't do nothing about it." He put the coffee cup down on the table. He'd done the best he could to repair the damage he'd caused, but the cup was so battered and wrinkled that it looked as if it had aged a thousand years. Ross sympathized.

Summing up, Kelly said, "Nobody can predict the future."

"Or if somebody could, he'd be down at the track, making bets."

Kelly stood up, stuck his hands in his jacket pockets. Ross hoped like hell that nothing showed in his face as he considered the absolute predictability of Kelly's future. Maximum security, or a bullet.

Kelly pushed his chair away from the table, legs squeaking across the floor like a quartet of tortured mice. Ross gritted his teeth. Kelly said, "I'm going back to Shannon's. Want a ride?"

"Why not?" said Ross, acting casual, though he felt as tangled up inside as the ivy clinging to the Sylvia Hotel. He'd been on standby, a bystander alertly waiting for something to happen, an opportunity to react. Now, finally, the pace had begun to accelerate, they were closing in on the narrow end of the funnel.

As Ross trailed along in the wake of Kelly's broad shoulders, he thought again that it might be wise to formulate a plan all of his own. But what was the point? Hadn't Kelly said that things *always* went wrong for the bad guys? But that was in movies. Ross crouched and looked at himself in the Datsun's side mirror. That was him, all right. But who was he?

Depending on your perspective, you could muster a pretty solid argument that he, too, was one of the bad guys.

Maybe, just maybe, he'd turn out to be the baddest of them all.

24

Jerry Goldstein's list of forty-one restaurants had been split, according to the city's geography, among the three teams of detectives. Orwell had whined so loudly about the workload that he and Bobby had been made responsible for only thirteen restaurants, all of them concentrated in the downtown core, whereas the other two teams each had to check out fourteen restaurants spread over a wider area.

Willows and Parker were working the southeast side of the city. They'd decided to start with the most distant restaurant in their sector, an Italian *ristorante* called Romeo's, that was so far out on Kingsway it was within an accurate pistol shot of the city boundary. Parker's thinking was that the least convenient locations were most likely to yield positive results. Willows found her logic well-nigh infallible.

Kingsway is a six-lane strip of asphalt flanked by car lots and motels, malls ranging in size from modest to gargantuan. Willows kept pace with the traffic. He slowed and signalled a left turn as he spotted the restaurant's neon sign, the off-street parking lot. He waited for a break in the oncoming traffic, then lost patience and hit the lights. He burned a little of the taxpayer's rubber as he aggressively made his turn. Parker was already unbuckling her seatbelt as he pulled into the lot and killed the engine.

The restaurant had looked small from the front, but Willows

saw that the building, though narrow, was deep. They walked around to the front entrance. Music stolen from an elevator leaked fuzzily from a pair of exterior speakers. The plate-glass door was smeared with fingerprints. They pushed on through.

A small-scale Luciano Pavarotti bore cheerfully down on them, his ruddy, bearded face barely able to contain his smile. He took Parker gently by the arm, then seized her again and more forcibly with his dark and glittery eyes, and told her in a voice soft as a brand-new feather pillow that she was an extremely lovely woman, as desirable a dish as he had ever seen. His name was Leone, the lion. His great desire was to put her in a window table, that she might draw a crowd, and make him rich beyond his wildest dreams.

Parker showed the lion her tin.

Leone stepped back. His lustrous eyes lost their court and spark. It was as if a glass of champagne had suddenly gone flat. He clapped his beefy hands together with great energy, as if meeting himself for the first time.

"This *can't* be about the *kitchen*! Not again! *Dio mios*! Is it *my fault* that these *tiny scuttling creatures* love me so much? I beg of you, what *more* can a man do, for God's sake!"

Willows tweaked a colour photograph, a no-nonsense head-and-shoulders shot of Donald E. Mooney, out of a buff envelope. "Do you know this man?"

"He's with the health department?"

"You tell me."

The restaurateur tilted his glossy head towards the photograph, studied it as carefully as any reasonable person might expect him to. Regretfully, he said, "No, I don't think so."

"You don't know him?"

Leone shook his head. "No, I don't believe I do." He moved his bulky upper body in such a way as to shake off any hint of culpability. "Should I know him, do you think?"

Willows slid the photograph back into the envelope. He withdrew a copy of Ray Waddington's sketch.

"How about him?"

"Do I know him?"

"That's what we want to know," said Parker.

"No, never. Did he make a complaint? Was there something he found in his food?"

Willows, offended by the proprietary way that Leone had taken Parker by the arm, said, "Yes, it was something truly horrible that he found in his food."

Trident Steak & Seafood was on Forty-ninth Avenue, just east of Knight. From the street, the restaurant looked closed. If there were lights on inside, they were dim bulbs indeed. Willows tried the door. It was unlocked. He stepped inside, glanced around.

Parker said, "Hello? Anybody home?"

The door creaked shut behind them, the click of the latch small as an afterthought. The cash register was dead ahead; to the left there were a dozen tables and a small bar. The tables had been set. Glass and cutlery gleamed in the dim light from the windows. Dozens of glasses hanging from wooden racks above the bar reflected spots of green and red from the ship's lights on either side of the bar. Dehydrated starfish, clamshells, glass floats, sand dollars and bits of driftwood had been caught in coarse green netting. Fleets of ships that had unwisely sailed into glass bottles hung from near-invisible lengths of fishing line. Willows reached up and touched a bottle with the tips of his fingers, made it sway gently, so the vessel within seemed to rise and fall upon a shifting sea.

A door behind the bar swung open, admitting a stub of a man spotlighted by a beam of watery grey light. The man wore a bright yellow rain-slicker and matching sou'wester. He kicked the door shut behind him, grunted as he lifted a heavy cardboard box up on the bar. He was in his mid-sixties. His full beard was silver shot through with parallel streaks of black. His ruby lips clutched a smoking corncob pipe. His eyes were bright blue. From the knee down, his left leg was a sturdy wooden peg with a shiny brass-bound tip. He sliced open the top of the box with a clasp knife, tossed the knife on the bar and reached inside. He grunted again as he pulled out a six-pack of Heineken beer. He began to stow the bottles in the bar cooler.

Parker said, "Excuse me . . ."

"Christ! Repel all boarders!" A trio of bottles rattled on the bar. The clasp knife's blade flashed green and red.

Willows said, "Police!" He flipped open his badge-case, identified himself and then Parker.

The blue eyes sized them up. Willows first, then Parker.

Parker said, "Are you the owner?"

"Moniker's Ahab O'Brien. And yes, I am the owner. Lock, stock and octopus, she all belongs to me." Sparks bubbled in the bowl of his pipe. He exhaled a fogbank. "What can I do for ye, mateys?"

"Ahab?" said Parker with a trace of disbelief.

"I had it legally changed, after I lost my pin. Leg, to the likes of you. I was a landlubber back at the time. A longshoreman, and a good one, until a damn cable slipped and a pallet-load of cin-derblock fell on my leg and sheared it off clean as a cleaver, just below the knee. I'd always talked about owning a restaurant. I was halfway through my rehab when I saw that the chance to live my dream had fallen right out of the sky. By the time I got out of the hospital, rehab had evolved into Ahab. My lawyer, God bless his soul if he's got one, negotiated a fat lump-sum payment from Workers' Comp. I've been in business coming up eight years. I used to open at eleven for lunch, but now it's just dinner, five to midnight, no reservations. In a few more hours, they'll be lined up at the door, just you wait and see."

Willows sat down on a padded barstool. He reflected that he had never met a barstool he didn't like. Feeling quite at home, he showed Ahab the photo of Donald E. Mooney.

"Yeah, I know who that is."

"You do?" said Willows, startled.

"The dead cop, right? His picture was in the paper. Front page, the *Province*."

Parker said, "That's it? You saw his picture in the paper?"

"Well, I never *met* the fella, if that's what you mean."

"You're sure?"

"Of course I'm sure." Ahab was indignant. His blue eyes blazed. He lifted up his wooden leg and thumped the floor vigorously enough to make the bottles of beer dance a jig.

Willows told himself he wasn't thirsty, but merely suggestible. He slid a copy of Ray Waddington's artwork onto the counter.

"How about him?"

"Nope."

"Take your time," said Willows. "We're in no hurry."

"Yes, I can see that for myself, and I only wish I were in the same boat." Ahab went back to shifting bottles from the box to the cooler.

Parker propped her card against the bar's portside light. The light stained the card green, turned the raised gold lettering shiny black. She said, "If you should think of anything . . ."

"I'll drop everything, including a dime."

Willows eased off the stool. He deepened his voice to a harsh rasp and said, "Avast, me hearty!"

"Same to you," said Ahab. He flipped the cardboard box belly-up, slashed at it with his knife until it collapsed of its own weight upon the bar.

An hour later, they had crossed two more restaurants off their list. Parker had taken a turn behind the wheel. She was pulling into the parking lot of a Chinese restaurant on Broadway, in the heavy shadow of the elevated SkyTrain monorail, when the Motorola crackled, and the dispatcher told them Inspector Bradley wanted them to proceed, with all due haste but circumspectly, to Brillo's, a restaurant in Yaletown.

Willows had never before heard a dispatcher use that particular phrase, "all due haste but circumspectly." It sounded weird. Maybe it was a direct quote. Bradley's speech could get pretty flowery, in season. He verified the address and signed off.

Brillo's was relentlessly modern, hard-edged and glittery. The tables were six-inch-thick slabs of clear acrylic on a twisted frame-work of sandblasted steel. Buried in the acrylic were the corpses of small, fluffy animals – mostly white lab rats, but there was a sprinkling of gerbils and guinea pigs. A family of field mice, Mom and Dad and the kids, close to a dozen of them, caused Parker to break stride.

She passed another table, another block of ice-clear acrylic; a school of voracious rainbow trout pursued a hatch of pale-green winged insects.

Was any of it real? It certainly *looked* real.

The restaurant was empty. She'd noted the hours of business as she entered; the place was open for lunch from eleven-thirty to two o'clock, and then open again from six p.m. until two o'clock in the morning. She and Willows reached the bar, walked up three steps to a second level. The restaurant was much larger than it had appeared; tucked away around a corner from the bar were another twenty or more tables. Bobby Dundas, Inspector Bradley, Orwell and a balding, bullet-headed man in shirtsleeves were sitting at a table against the far wall, near a double swing door that flew open and expelled a waiter, allowing Parker a brief view of the kitchen.

Bradley swivelled in his chair, acknowledged Willows with a nod of his head, smiled at Parker. Bobby pulled an empty chair towards the table, patted the seat and gave Parker a wink. Parker got her own chair, gave Orwell a look and then sat down be-tween him and Bradley. A glossy print of Donald E. Mooney's morgue photo lay on the table, slightly overlapping a copy of Ray Waddington's suspect sketch. A heavy glass ashtray held a smok-ing cigar. Bradley's thin mouth held another. Willows leaned casu-ally against the wall, his hands in his overcoat pockets.

Bradley said, "What took you so long?"

"He was driving," said Parker.

The bullet-headed man was the restaurant's owner, Lonnie Papas.

Bradley said, "Mr. Papas recognized Ray's sketch, Claire."

Parker glanced admiringly at Mr. Papas.

Bobby said, "We still don't know who the guy is. He was seen hanging around the restaurant, loitering."

Mr. Papas retrieved his cigar from the ashtray, stuck it in his mouth at a jaunty angle. Parker recognized the design on the cigar's band. It was one of Homer's.

The inspector's index finger poked the sketched suspect in the eye. "Whoever the guy is, he was willing to pay serious money to have Mr. Papas' new employee, a short-sheet ex-con named Ross Larson, punched out. We don't know a whole lot about Ross yet. He assaulted a guy in a bar, caught five, finished his bit the day before Mooney was killed."

Mr. Papas said, "The busboy, Jerry, he told me everything about the fight."

"Mooney have anything to do with putting him away?" said Willows.

Bradley said, "We're checking. Not that we know of." He pointed the hot end of his cigar at Lonnie Papas. "Mr. Papas is a solid citizen, a good-hearted man. He hired Larson sight unseen, on the advice of Larson's parole officer."

"My good friend George Hoffman!" volunteered Mr. Papas. Pleased with himself, he beamed at Parker. Cigar smoke seeped from the double-wide gaps between his teeth. His dark eyes watered.

"Mr. Papas and Mr. Hoffman have an agreement," said Bradley. "Mr. Papas is constantly looking for opportunities to repay this great country for allowing him and his family to become full-fledged citizens."

"How nice," said Parker.

Willows' smile was faint. Orwell studied his fingernails. Bobby Dundas rearranged his features merely by passing a slow hand across his face.

Parker said, "Mr. Papas, did Ross Larson give you a home address when he started working for you?"

"Yes, of course!" Papas rotated his hands energetically. Cigar ash tumbled to his lap and he impatiently brushed it onto the floor. "But I threw it away, all the information, when he quit!"

"After the fight with Ted and Robert?" said Orwell. "A couple of car jockeys, worked nights."

"Yes, of course!" said Mr. Papas.

"Anybody talk to these guys?" said Willows.

"Mr. Papas fired them," said Bobby. "They were part-timers, working for tips."

"I give you their phone number, but . . . ," said Mr. Papas. He shrugged theatrically.

"Disconnected," said Bradley.

"We got a witness, though," said Bobby, "a guy *does* still work here . . ."

"Jerry!" said Mr. Papas.

"Yeah, Jerry, that's him. The busboy." Bobby leaned back in his chair. He gave Parker a crooked smile. "Ever stand around, waiting for a bus? What we're doing here right now, all of us, we're waiting for a *busboy*."

Orwell slapped his thigh. He cackled unconvincingly, like a half-bright rooster confused by an eclipse.

"When's Jerry due," said Willows to Bradley.

Bradley checked his watch. Twelve minutes, and Mr. Papas tells me that he's never late."

Parker stood up. Bradley gave her an inquiring glance, but said nothing when she offered no explanation. She helped herself to a menu from a stack on the bar, flipped it open. The evening's specials had been paper-clipped to the main menu. Harried Hare with Various Vicious Veggies. Yummy. Lambasted Lamb Accompanied by Persecuted Peas and Pummelled Potatoes. Delicious. Who could possibly resist the lure of Savagely Slammed Salmon with Ruthlessly Rumpled Rice and Cruelly Crushed Carrots? The appetizers and desserts had been treated similarly. What kind of people ate here? Parker wondered. Young people, obviously. Young people with money, and a taste for the tasteless.

She wandered aimlessly about the tables, the low chatter of her fellow detectives in the background. The theme had been repeated a number of times, but with different species of fish, some of them wildly exotic. Frozen in the depths of a window table, eleven gerbils and a miniature football faced off against eleven small brown animals Parker believed to be moles . . .

The busboy, Jerry, pulled in right on schedule. He was about thirty years old, of average size and weight. He wore heavy black workboots, faded jeans and a clean white sleeveless T-shirt. His thick black hair was about an eighth of an inch long. His coarse black eyebrows had been pruned into segments. He wore three tiny diamond studs in his left ear. His eyes were the colour of rust.

Bradley pointed at a chair, told him to sit. He asked him for his full name, age, and address. Orwell wrote it all down.

Bobby Dundas said, "Ever do any time, Jerry?"

"A long way back, when I was a juvie."

"What'd we wrongly accuse you of?"

"Uh, aggravated assault. Extortion." Jerry smiled. "I did my time, got myself rehabilitated."

"How long you been working here?"

Jerry twisted an earlobe as he thought about it.

"Almost one year!" said Mr. Papas.

Jerry lit a cigarette, offered the pack. No takers. He said, "Yeah, that's right, about a year. It's March, right, and I remember I started around the middle of June. So we're talkin' eight or nine months, somewhere in there."

"George Hoffman get you the job?"

Jerry hesitated, shrugged. "Yeah, I guess so. What d'you guys want, anyway?"

"To solve a murder," said Bradley. *Murder.* How he loved that word.

"Hey, wait a minute!" Jerry leapt to his feet, but Orwell was quick to push him back into his chair. Orwell stood beside him, his sledge-hammer fist resting lightly on the ex-con's shoulder. The busboy said, "Swear to God, I never killed nobody!"

Bradley showed him Mooney's morgue photo. "Not even him?"

Willows said, "Talk, Jerry. Tell us what you know."

Jerry said, "I'm riding the bus, on my way to work. That guy right there, the drawing, he gets on, sits beside me even though there's lots of empty seats. Says he'll pay five if I lay a pounding on the new dishwasher. I got no idea what he's talking about. He grabs my arm, tight enough so I know he's got me. Drops a bundle of twenties in my lap, tells me it's two down and the balance when I get off shift. Promises he'll lay a pounding on *me*, I don't do what I'm told."

Bradley said, "So what did you do?"

"Told him I didn't want any part of something like that, but that I know a guy who might be interested."

"Who?" said Bradley.

"Orville."

"Who's he?"

"Works in the kitchen," said Mr. Papas.

"He cooks?"

"No, nothing like that. Collects dirty pots, takes them to the dishwasher. Also, some prep work. No meat, vegetables only. Wherever he's needed, that's where he goes."

To Jerry, Bradley said, "So, Orville beat up the dishwasher?"

"No, not Orville. He took the deuce and sold the job to Ted and Robert, the car jockeys, guys out front do the valet work."

Bradley said, "You're telling us, Jerry, that this guy gave the two hundred to Orville, and he paid Ted and Robert to punch out the dishwasher."

"Right. What Orville kept in his own pocket, I wouldn't know. All I can tell you, I never profited a single dime."

Bradley rattled Ray Waddington's sketch, gave it a good shake. "And there is no doubt in your mind that this definitely isn't the dishwasher, Ross Larson."

Jerry lit another cigarette. Half a ton of confused cops. A thousand pounds. More than four hundred and fifty kilograms. It was quite a sight. He said, "Yeah, you got it." He ejected a ring of smoke. "Finally."

25

He knew the city fairly well, but Kelly was driving, and it was his car and he'd paid for the gas. So Ross kept his mouth shut for a long time, until finally Kelly made a wrong right, turned into an alley, cut his lights and reversed the Datsun into a battered dumpster. The big metal container boomed hollowly as the Datsun's rear bumper made contact. Ross's head snapped back. He said, "What's going on?"

Kelly laughed through his teeth. The sound he made was so abrasive and lacking in humour it would've made a deaf man tremble. His chest pushed up against the Datsun's steering wheel as he reached under the collapsed, threadbare seat. Metal glinted dully.

Kelly hefted the pistol in his hand. "Know how to handle a gun?"

"Store it unloaded, under lock and key."

This time, Kelly's laughter had a little less of an edge to it. He pushed a small button that projected high up on the handle of the gun. The magazine slid out, fell into his lap. Gleam of brass.

Kelly said, "You got ten shots. That's the law, ten-round magazines. So you can pull the trigger and the gun'll go *bang* how many times? . . ." An elbow thumped Ross in the ribcage.

"Ten?"

"Right, ten. So, you got to start shooting, make 'em count." He handed Ross the gun, butt-first.

Ross had never held a pistol before. He had no idea what to do with it, other than point it away from him and keep his finger off the trigger. "Is there a safety?"

"No safety."

There had to be something else . . .

Ross said, "What am I going to need a gun for?"

Kelly gave him a look. "To shoot people, what d'you think? Or you might need it to take care of a guard dog. But people, mostly." Kelly's grin was extra-sly. "If any shooting needs to be done, the odds are pretty good it's people that you'll be shooting at. In the meanwhile, you better stick that weapon under your jacket, where it don't show."

Ross sucked in his stomach and thrust the pistol down the front of his pants, adjusted the gun so, if he accidentally shot himself, it would be in the leg rather than the genitals. Far better to bleed to death than suffer an unscheduled castration. He zipped his jacket.

Kelly told him to get out of the car, not to lock the door. He flashed his own weapon, an ugly, snub-barrelled revolver. Ross climbed out of the car. His door and Kelly's slammed shut one right after the other. Ross followed Kelly towards the mouth of the alley.

"I don't know if you noticed, but there's a grocery store right around the corner. Next to the store there's a place sells computers, but it's closed. Next to the computers there's a Chinese restaurant. Your choice, Ross. What's it gonna be – the grocery store or the restaurant?"

"How about none of the above."

Kelly tilted his head, gave him a snaky, sideways look. "How you expect to amount to anything, you got no pride or enthusiasm in your work?"

At the mouth of the alley, Kelly turned left and walked casually along the sidewalk. Traffic sped by. Ross held his hand to his face, shielding his eyes from the glare of lights, wind-borne grit. They reached the corner and made another left. Stepped wooden shelves in front of the grocery store provided a display area for dozens of large white plastic buckets filled with bunches of purple and red and white tulips, roses in red and white and yellow, hothouse daffodils, long-stemmed mauve flowers Ross couldn't identify. He noticed there were more *kinds* of flowers than colours.

"What the hell you looking at?" said Kelly.

Ross trotted after him, catching up. Side by side, they walked briskly past the computer store. The store was all lit up, the windows protected by a grid of white-enamelled steel. Not too long ago, one of the many differences between jail and the world was that jails had bars. Now they were everywhere. Driving Shannon's Saab, he'd noticed shop after shop that had protected itself against break-and-enter or smash-and-grab. Soon the whole city would look like a prison, cells all over the damn place.

Kelly had his face pressed up against the Chinese restaurant's window. Ross waited. The place was crowded. Lots of families, kids with chopsticks. At the rear, mottled orange-and-white fish drifted in a brightly illuminated glass tank. After a few moments Kelly backed away, leaving a smeared noseprint on the glass.

"Too many people in there," he said. "Probably not much cash in the till anyway. Chinese like to use plastic."

Ross said, "As opposed to honest white folks like you and me?"

All business, Kelly said, "Follow me."

Ross followed him back down the narrow sidewalk in front of the stores, past Computer Village and into the grocery store. As they entered, Kelly cannily dragged his left foot, knocking loose a wooden wedge that had held the door open. "Oops!" he said, as the door swung shut behind them. The cash register was on the right. An elderly Chinese man stood behind the counter. A born lightweight, he wore plaid pants and a white dress shirt. His eyes were dark, soft and moist. Ross got the impression nothing much would surprise him.

Kelly bellied up to the counter. He unzipped his jacket almost all the way down. "Gimme a pack of cigarettes."

"Sure, what kind you want?"

Kelly said, "What brand you smoke, Ross?"

"Player's Light"

Kelly gave Ross a long, steady look and then pulled a crumpled ten-dollar bill out of his jeans pocket. He tossed the bill on the counter, picked up the pack of cigarettes and tossed it over his shoulder to Ross. "Enjoy yourself to death, partner."

The sale was rung up, and the cash register clanged open.

Kelly drew his revolver. He held the gun close to his body, told the man to empty the cash register, put the money on the counter. In silence, the man did as he was told. But he was a pretty cagey fella. He had the wit to start with the drawer holding the smallest-denomination bills, and he was taking his own sweet time, wasn't he?

Kelly whacked the cash register with the barrel of his gun. "Get crackin', dimwit!" Grinning, he turned to Ross. "He had any brains, he'd want us out of here quick as possible!" He snatched the wad of cash out of the grocer's hand, reached past him and yanked the cash drawer out of the register. A couple of twenties lay on the tray. Kelly scooped them up, stuffed the money in his pocket. Then he pointed his gun at the man and fired three measured shots, hitting him high on the chest with the first two, catching him in the shoulder with the third, as he dropped. Ross was stunned. He stood there, barely able to hold himself erect. Kelly leaned over the counter. He poked Ross in the ribs with the revolver's smoking muzzle. "Your turn."

"Uh . . ." Ross's mind was a pinwheel, firing off sparks and smoke, making plenty of noise, spinning in circles, going nowhere.

"C'mon, it's your turn." Kelly's eyes bulged, spittle flew. He yanked Ross's pistol out of his pants and thrust it into his hand. "Like they say, *Just do it!*"

Ross leaned over the counter. The grocer's chest was a mass of blood. His white shirt had been scorched and peppered by the muzzle blasts. His eyes were wide open. A little disappointed. The bleeding had stopped. He didn't appear to be breathing, and no wonder.

His hair needed combing. He was quiet as a watercolour.

Dead, for sure.

The revolver made a double click as Kelly drew back the hammer. He screwed the gun's hot muzzle into Ross's ear. "Him or you, partner."

Ross leaned over the counter. He pointed the gun straight down, shut his eyes and pulled the trigger. Click. He pulled the trigger again. Another click. Kelly said, "You gotta rack the slide, you wanna get noisy." He snatched the pistol out of Ross's hand. Ross turned his head and opened his eyes, observed how Kelly drew back the slide and let it snap forward, stripping a round from the magazine and pushing it into the breech. The pistol's hammer was back. "Try it now, junior gunsmith."

Ross took the pistol, aimed, and pulled the trigger. The gun jerked in his hand. The shot deafened him. Kelly held up two fingers. Ross stared at him, bewildered, and then realized Kelly wanted him to shoot again. He squeezed off several more rounds.

Kelly grabbed his arm, relieved him of the pistol. "Take it easy, killer. Them nine mils cost seventeen-ninety-five a box, plus tax." He slapped Ross on the back. "Get his wallet."

Ross gave him a look that said no.

"Hurry up, asshole!" Kelly poked Ross in the belly with the revolver, poked him hard. Ross went around behind the counter. He tried not to step in the blood, but there was too much of it, and it seemed to be everywhere he put his feet. The grocer had a roll of cash in his back pocket thick enough to choke a giraffe. Kelly had wandered over to a display rack and was stuffing his pockets with Mars bars.

"Get you something?"

Ross shook his head.

"You ain't hungry?" Kelly signalled mild disapproval by making a soft clucking sound. He grabbed a handful of breath mints.

On the way out, Kelly helped himself to a big tin bucket full of bunches of white roses at $6.99 per half-dozen. He unwittingly left a trail of candy bars all the way to the getaway car. Ross, following along behind, scooped up most of them. They climbed into the Datsun. Kelly dumped the candy and bucket of roses on the backseat. He shoved the key in the ignition, started the engine, put it in reverse and stomped on the gas. The Datsun was no muscle car, but it had horses enough to shift the dumpster. The big steel box moved slowly at first, but quickly picked up speed. As they reached the mouth of the alley, Kelly slammed on the brakes. The dumpster shot into traffic, with predictable results. Kelly shifted into first gear and punched it. The Datsun's tires slithered and then grabbed hold. At high speed, they fled the scene of their crimes.

Some few minutes later, Kelly glanced in the rearview mirror. What he saw caused him to spew the kind of language Ross hadn't heard since prison. He turned and looked back. The bucket had overturned, flooding the backseat. There were roses everywhere.

"Clean that up! Get *rid* of it!"

Ross rolled down the back window. He tossed the bucket onto the road, threw out handfuls of flowers. Most of the candy bars seemed okay. Several bunches of roses had escaped with their stems intact, so he kept them. There was nothing he could do about the drenched backseat.

They were, by Ross's calculation, about halfway home when Kelly pulled the semiauto. He handed the pistol and several loose cartridges to Ross and told him to reload the thing. It wasn't a difficult task. Ross had a feeling that most if not all guns must be fairly easy to operate – if only because the simple-minded criminals who used them would be helpless if faced with even a reasonably complicated mechanism. Not that Ross was inclined at that moment to underestimate Kelly's intelligence. The man might not be overly bright, but he was ruthless as a tick.

He tried to insert another round into the magazine, but it wouldn't fit. He replaced the loaded magazine in the handle of the gun, felt a tiny spasm run through the weapon as the magazine clicked home.

Kelly held out his hand, palm up. Ross gave him back his gun.

Shannon ignored the roses. You'd think she was allergic. Glaring hard at the blood-spattered sleeve of Kelly's jacket, she said, "What the hell have you two idiots been up to?"

"Zellers' customer-relations folks teach you to talk like that?" Kelly smiled crookedly. He said, "I took my partner for a test-drive, see how he'd work out." He studied the splash pattern on his jacket as if noticing it for the first time. "Resistance was offered. Things got a little loud, a little messy . . ."

"You shot somebody, didn't you."

"Well, yeah. But he asked for it."

Shannon's eyes were small and bright. "You are such a *fucking idiot.*"

"Ain't she the sweetest?" Kelly sauntered over to the fridge and yanked open the door, peered inside, grunted in triumph as he located the beer.

"Ross, did he really shoot somebody?"

Ross shrank before the heat of Shannon's anger, the fierceness of her gaze.

"We *both* shot somebody." Kelly wiped his mouth with the back of his hand. "How it went – I shot first and then it was Ross's turn. Slippery seconds, and he just wouldn't stop, kept pulling the trigger. Because he liked it, I guess. Or maybe believed he needed the practice. Which is true." He tilted his head, made a gurgling sound as he drank some more beer. "Wisdom in mayhem. Ask any cop – dead men make unreliable witnesses." He slapped Ross heavily on the shoulder. "Right, partner?"

"You betcha," said Ross amiably. His head ached and his throat was dry. He went over to the sink and drank from the cold-water tap.

Shannon said, "We talked about this, Kelly. And we agreed we could do this without killing anybody."

"*You* agreed that's what we could do. I didn't say nothin' about it either way, if you check your notes. You expect me to trust somebody I don't know for sure is gonna stand fast under pressure, hold his ground and not fuck up or screw me around? Or spill his guts in a minute, if the cops get their hands on him? I had to test the man's mettle, Shannon. Get him involved. Think about it. Think about it for just one minute, you'll see how right I am."

Shannon stood there in the middle of the kitchen floor beneath the overly bright fluorescent ceiling lights, not looking at anything in particular. Hardly showing any signs of life at all, really, as if the situation were so repugnant to her that she had withdrawn deep inside herself, shut down all her systems. Denial. But then, as quick as that, her eyes cleared and she focused on Ross, gave him a weary look, a you-let-me-down-and-I'm-tired-of-you look, resigned but flinty-hard, cold as a snowball's heart. In a voice so devoid of emotion it might have been computer-generated, she said she needed a drink.

There was a bottle of red on the counter. Ross found the corkscrew in the top drawer, next to the Ikea stainless-steel knives and forks. He opened the wine, opened cupboards until he found the glasses. He poured two glasses full, handed one to Shannon and kept the other himself.

"Toast," said Kelly. He stepped forward and hoisted his can of beer. Ross lifted his glass. Kelly banged the can against the glass. He put his arm around Shannon's waist and touched his beer to her glass. "To success," he said. "To happy endings!"

Ross drank some wine. It tasted pretty good. He drained his glass and went over to the counter and poured himself a refill. As he stood there, bottle in hand, he happened to glance up. Kelly was staring at his sister, and she was staring right back at him.

Ross witnessed a swift exchange of data. An iris-to-iris exchange between brother and sister of line after line of intense, silent-movie dialogue.

Kelly told Shannon that, like it or not, she was going to do exactly what they'd agreed she was going to do.

Shannon replied that she didn't like it one goddamn bit.

He told her it was almost over, that they were *this* close. There was no backing out now. They were committed. The die was cast. She caved in, let him dominate her. Acquiesced.

Then they were smiling at each other, eyes full of mirth and conspiracy, dark secrets.

Ross thumped the bottle down on the counter, breaking the spell. She asked him to fill her empty glass. As he poured he said, "So, when're we going to visit Nancy and Tyler?"

"Soon," said Kelly. He smiled. "That quick enough for you, killer?" He glanced at his watch, manufactured a yawn. "It's late, and I'm tired. I'm gonna hit the sack." He grabbed another beer from the fridge, sauntered over to the basement door and opened it wide. He tossed Shannon a wink that, to Ross's eye, was licentious and perverted. "Sweet dreams, kids."

The door squeaked as he pulled it shut behind him. His boots thumped down the stairs, fading into silence as he slowly descended. Soon enough, the only sound Ross could hear was the quick rasp of Shannon's breathing.

She gave Ross a brittle grin, and slipped her arm through his and leaned against him. He was acutely aware of the weight and warmth of her breast, soft but firm as any breast could be. She looked up at him and whispered that Kelly was right. It was getting kind of late.

"Time for bed?" said Ross, hating himself.

She wriggled a little closer. "Time for a shower, *then* bed."

Ross nodded. No argument there. In the kitchen's bright light he had noticed tiny teardrop-shaped speckles of dried blood on his fingernails, the backs of his hands, his wrists. There must be near-invisible splashes of blood all over him. He was a walking abattoir.

Ross thought that they must need him an awful lot. But not for long. He could hear Kelly moving around down there in the dark basement almost directly below him, making loud unidentifiable sounds. Raw fear sucked every last drop of moisture from his mouth.

Shannon showered first, and then it was his turn. He dawdled beneath the spray as if it might be the last shower of his life. By the time he walked into the bedroom, she was sleeping soundly. He eased into bed and turned out the light.

Downstairs, the basement door creaked. A few moments later Ross heard the refrigerator door slam shut, and a few moments after that the hiss of Kelly's beer as he cracked it open. Ross listened, tracking the sounds as Kelly made his way down the hall from the kitchen to the main-floor landing at the bottom of the stairs.

Ross lay there, listening hard, hearing nothing but the hum and crackle of his own blood twitching along his veins.

Minutes slipped by, until an hour and more had passed. He drifted off, snapped awake. Eased out of bed and went over to the window. It was about a twenty-foot drop straight down, to the sidewalk. He tried the sash. Nailed shut. He slipped back into his nice warm bed.

Downstairs, Kelly shifted his weight and a floorboard creaked. A faint hiss signalled that he had cracked open another can of beer.

Or maybe that snaky sound had leaked out of *him*.

Shannon rolled over on her side so she was facing him.

In the yellowish near-darkness, Ross crept towards her inch by inch. Downstairs, Kelly had turned on the stereo and was singing along, off-key and out of tune. Ross needed to be loved. His mouth grazed upon Shannon's warm flesh. She sighed contentedly. He moved a fraction closer, until there was a gentle collision that reverberated through his soul. He settled himself clumsily upon her.

Carpe Tart Diem.

26

Alicia told him every time he got it cut, had been telling him ever since they'd been married, that it was time to lose the afro, it was a stale joke, made him look old – she told him whatever she could think of that might motivate him to get a proper haircut. But there was no way in this big old world that George "The Man" Hoffman was going to lose the 'fro. The way he saw it – and he knew damn well he was right no matter what insults Alicia hurled at him – the way he saw it, that beehive-shaped thatch of greying hair up there on his roof served notice that black people, Afro-Canadians, had a history, a recent history, of standing up to be counted.

The afro was a statement of intent, a warning. Hoffman sneered at his fellow blacks – professional basketball players and the like – who wilfully shaved their heads bald. He believed his aggressively unstylish haircut conveyed a message that said, "Mess with me, you *know* you gonna be hurt."

Well, maybe. But more likely it was Hoffman's enormous size – he loosely resembled a hirsute Shaquille O'Neal – that intimidated the never-ending stream of paroled convicts and lifetime losers whose very presence soiled the sacred turf of his office.

When his door swung open, Hoffman glanced up from his fried chicken with the baleful countenance of a disturbed grizzly. He was on his lunch hour, goddammit all to hell. When he saw that his unscheduled visitors were cops, his scowl deepened. He tore the last shred of meat from a wing, noisily sucked the marrow from the bone.

Willows flashed his tin.

Hoffman dismissed the need for official identification by casually stirring the air with a plump chicken leg. Crumbs of deep-fried fat sprinkled his desk, but this was a matter that could best be attended to in privacy. "What can I do for you? And please don't look at me like that. I could've been eating ribs." He guzzled half a can of Coke as Parker unfolded Ray Waddington's much-travelled sketch and laid it on his desk.

Willows thought for a moment that Hoffman's sharp inhalation signified the shock of recognition; but no, he was merely attempting to extract a fragment of meat caught in the wide gap between his teeth.

"Nice work. Who's the cartoonist?"

"Know him?" said Parker, tapping the sketch lightly on the nose.

"Nope."

"You're sure about that?"

"Yeah, positive." Hoffman glanced longingly at the leg he held in his left hand. Though he was tempted, he did not fold. "I never laid eyes on the guy – not in this life, anyway."

"Maybe with a moustache? Or five years younger? Different haircut? Take your time, George."

"Hey, I'm on my lunch break. Like it or not, the answer is no. Sorry, folks, but there it is."

Parker said, "One of your cons started work at Brillo's a few days ago. We talked to his boss last night."

"Yeah, Ross. Started and finished, what I hear."

"What can you tell us about him, George?"

Hoffman tossed the chicken leg back in it's red-and-white striped take-out container. "I can tell you what I know. His full name, date of birth, what he did. But, you ask me about the bile roiling around deep down inside him that defines who he *really* is, what he's capable of, well, I got no idea about that. My gut instinct, I don't believe he's one of them *baaad* boys. Why, what's he done?"

"Something to attract our attention," said Willows.

"Ross Andrew Larson, that's the joker's name in full." George drank some Coke. "He seemed okay, really. I cut him some slack, let him stay with his mama, 'stead of a halfway house. He made parole about a week ago."

"You got him the job at Brillo's?"

"Yeah, that's right." Hoffman smiled. "Scrubbing pots."

Parker said. "That was a nice thing for you to do, George."

"Well, I'm a nice person." Hoffman's long black fingers vanished into his hair as he scratched industriously at his scalp. "You got a problem with that?"

"Not at the moment, George."

"What the hell's that supposed to mean? You come waltzing in here, I'm eating lunch. Look at my chicken. It's getting cold. How d'you think Colonel Sanders would feel about that?" Hoffman leaned back in his chair. "You folks accusing me of something?"

"No way, George. It's Ross were interested in, not you."

Hoffman leaned back in his chair, assumed a thoughtful pose. "It's one of those short, unhappy stories. Larson beat some guy half to death, claimed the dude propositioned his sister in what you might call excessively graphic terms. Sis denied it. The victim was hurt bad. Larson's defence cut no gravy with the jury. He caught eight to ten, despite the fact that until then he'd kept his sheets nice and clean."

"No previous offences?" said Parker.

"What I'm saying, ma'am."

"Detective Parker."

Hoffman nodded, drained his Coke, tossed the empty in his wastebasket, slid open the bottom drawer of his desk, came up with a fresh can. He popped the tab. "A couple of weeks into his sentence, some guy, a biker, came at him with a shank. Why was never established. Anyway, Larson turned the guy's own knife on him, wounded him mortally. All the investigation did was wipe his ass. Self-defence. Except for that one incident, he was a model prisoner during the entire five years he spent in the joint."

"Prime material for a dishwasher's job."

"Yeah, that's the way I saw it. Want his mother's address?"

Willows nodded.

Hoffman pushed away from his desk, the wheels of his chair squeaking as he crab-walked across the cramped office to a black metal file cabinet with magazine pictures of Abbie Hoffman and Bette Midler taped to the side. He yanked open a drawer, pulled a buff file folder. He crab-walked back to his desk, opened the folder and wrote Mrs. Larson's address and telephone number down on a sheet of yellow paper. He tore the paper from the pad, handed it to Willows. "Don't get your hopes up, Detective. The old lady's been calling me five, six times a day, wondering what in hell happened to her wayward son. He spent his first night of freedom at home, then skipped. Never said a word of goodbye."

"You violate him?"

"I sure did. He's on the hot sheet. You see him, you go right ahead and bust him, give him a special kick in the ass just for me."

Parker said, "Got any leads for us, George?"

"Like what?"

Parker smiled. "How should I know? So far, all we've established is that he isn't at his mother's. But he has to be somewhere, doesn't he?"

"Alternate destinations, that what we're talking about?"

"Could be," said Parker.

Hoffman snatched a chunk of fried chicken from the bucket and attacked it voraciously. His cheeks bulged. He chewed and swallowed, rinsed away the debris with a mouthful of Coke, wiped himself clean with a paper napkin. "Okay, let's say I came up with something. I hand it over, you promise to go away and not bother me any more?"

"Promise," said Willows.

Hoffman pointed a drumstick at Parker. "What about you?"

"Cross my heart," said Parker.

Hoffman spent the better part of a long minute perusing the contents of the file folder, and then, seemingly with great reluctance, told them Ross had a pal in the slammer, a guy named Garret Mosby . . .

Willows' head came up. He was assaulted by a sudden vivid flashback of the crime scenes on Broadway, spiralling flames outside the gas station and blood on the snow, the red pulse of the armoured car's alarm light, the screams of the wounded. He remembered the dull, faraway look in Garret's eyes as he'd taken the shotgun away from him . . .

He remembered that two hundred and twenty thousand dollars had gone astray, never been recovered.

It was all coming back now, a blur of details rushing towards him at high speed down that narrow, twisty piece of blacktop called memory lane.

A constable named Donald E. Mooney had been on patrol that night, alone in a blue-and-white. He'd engaged in a hot pursuit of Garret's partner, Billy.

Willows remembered the Pinto smoking on the snowy boulevard, tires blown, the car shot to pieces. Billy gone . . .

Hoffman said, "Garret had a girlfriend, Shannon Brown. Way I hear it, she stuck with him right through to the end. When he died, she got into a pen-pal thing with Larson. A few months before he was paroled, she gave the office a call, said she had a regular job, an income, that if Larson needed someone to sponsor him, she'd do what she could." Hoffman bent over his notes. "Said she had a basement suite, and that there was a room in the garage. He could stay with her if he had nowhere else to go."

"What'd you say?"

"Well, I got confidentiality problems. You know that. But anyway, off the record . . . I asked her if she knew him at all, other than the letters. Surprised me by admitting she knew all about the broker and the biker."

"You give Ross her number?"

"Hell no, of course not! He never asked for it and I wouldn't have given it to him if he did. But there'd be no need – they were writing each other nearly every week. He's got her address, or he wouldn't have known where to mail his letters."

Willows said, "Write it down, George."

Hoffman tore another sheet of paper from his pad, scribbled energetically.

Parker said, "If he calls, call us."

"He won't."

"But if he does, call."

Hoffman said, "I will. But he won't." He dipped into the bucket, fished out another chunk of chicken. A back, this time. Hadn't he told the counter boy he didn't want any damn backs? How could anyone call this a piece of meat, and look him in the eye as they took his hard-earned money? Man, this was nothing but little bitty bones and deep-fried fat. It had nothing to *do* with food.

Sure was tasty, though.

Willows started the Ford, turned the heater up full. He switched on the wipers. Parker said, "Forget it, Jack."

"Forget what?"

"Driving over to Shannon Brown's house, kicking in a few doors just to see what's on the other side."

Willows smiled.

Parker said, "We can't place Ross at the Mooney crime scene, and what little evidence we have tying him to the scene is tenuous and circumstantial."

"True, but he's all we've got, and it seems reasonable to assume he's involved in Mooney's murder. Ross and the guy Graham Aubert described, the blond with the buzz-cut, obviously know each other. We can get a warrant based on Ross's parole violation."

The windshield was starting to fog up. Willows adjusted the flow of air from the heater.

Parker said, "We get our hands on the right magistrate, we should be able to convince him that we have sufficient reason to believe that Ross is hiding out at his girlfriend's."

"Has sought refuge," said Willows.

"Even better," said Parker, getting to the nub. She glanced around. "Where are we going?"

"Main Street. The vortex. While you're getting the warrant, I'll sit tight on Napier, covertly observing the premises."

Parker said, "Why don't *you* apply for the warrant, and *I'll* drive over to Shannon's."

"You type faster." Willows glanced at Parker.

"Don't do anything precipitous, Jack."

"Who, me?"

It was a quick run up Terminal and over the viaduct and along First Avenue, down Victoria Drive to Napier. Willows waited for a break in the traffic, made a left and drove slowly down the narrow, steeply cambered road. He slowed to negotiate the concrete roundabout squatting malevolently in the intersection. Shannon Brown lived in a two-storey clapboard a little more than halfway down the block. The house was easy to identify because of the large, polished brass numbers prominently displayed over the front door.

There were two cars parked in front of the house: a black Saab and a decaying orange Datsun.

The windows were opaque. Willows noted the Datsun and the Saab's plates as he drove past the house. At the end of the block he made a left. He drove as far as the lane and turned left again. The rear third of the backyard was flooded with rainwater. The house's back door opened on a small sundeck. He'd caught a quick glimpse of a basement door at the side of the house, before the neighbour's fence had obscured his view. The garage seemed to have been converted into an illegal self-contained apartment.

He navigated the roundabout again, parked where he had a clear view of the Saab and Datsun. He called in the tags and requested a search.

This was for the most part a blue-collar, working-class neighbourhood. The weren't many cars parked on the street, and none of the cars were new. The majority of the houses were on the small side, mostly drab, pre-war single-storey stucco dwellings. Willows had rolled his window down a crack to keep the glass from fogging up. Now and then the sound of hammering or the raucous whine of a power saw drifted downwind from a church in the next block that was undergoing repairs.

Several hours crawled past. Dusk was settling upon the land when a prototypically nondescript brown Econoline van pulled over to the curb at the far end of the block. Willows sat up a little straighter. He reached for the binoculars. The van's side door slid open, and a man climbed out. He reached inside the van, slung a canvas bag across his shoulder and slid the door shut. The van pulled away. The man walked rapidly up the street to the first house, reached into the bag and pulled out a newspaper or flyer. He tossed the paper onto the front porch.

Willows watched the man work his way up the street, cutting across the unfenced front yards, flinging the papers onto the porches.

The radio crackled. The Saab was registered to Shannon Lucy Brown, of 2229 Napier. The Datsun was registered to Kelly James McConnell, also of 2229 Napier. Willows wondered what Kelly looked like, up close and personal. Did he have close-set, piercing blue eyes, spiky blond hair, and a button nose? Was he by any chance the beefy, broad-shouldered type?

The man reached the white clapboard house. But this time, instead of tossing the newspaper onto the porch, he slowly climbed the steps. When he reached the porch, he lingered near the front window, took his time lighting a cigarette. When he finally made his way down the steps, he seemed to tread lightly, as if to avoid alerting the occupants of his presence.

Willows glanced in his rearview mirror. The brown van squatted twenty feet behind him. The windshield was pebbled with rain, and it was impossible to see inside. The driver's-side door swung open. In the mirror, Bobby Dundas looked as if he were about three inches tall.

Willows let Bobby claw at the door for a moment, then reached over and unlocked. Bobby climbed inside, carefully arranged his rust-coloured cashmere topcoat beneath him so as to minimize wrinkling.

"Glad to see me, Jack?"

"I always like to know where you are," admitted Willows.

Eddy Orwell had tired, was starting to lose his stuff. His last pitch bounced off a porch railing and vanished in a cluster of decorative shrubbery. Taking himself out of the game, he skipped the next house, trotted across the street. Willows reached back to unlock the rear door. Orwell's cheeks were bright red. His breath smelled of mint. He shook rainwater from his hat and rubbed his hands briskly together. "Man, it's wet out there."

Bobby didn't try to hide his impatience. "Talk, Eddy."

"There's glass panels in the door, but you can't see much. I took a quick peek in the living-room window. You can see right through to the back of the house. The living room's at the front, then the dining room. There was a guy sitting at the table, working on a beer."

"In the dining room?" said Bobby.

"Yeah, the dining room."

"What'd the guy look like, Eddy?"

"I couldn't tell you. There was a light on inside, but all I saw, really, was his silhouette."

"Young guy, old guy . . ."

Orwell shrugged.

"He was just sitting there?"

"Yeah, just sitting there. In a chair. I didn't see him at first, because the light was so bad, and because he was just sitting there, not moving. Soon's I saw him, I pulled back."

Willows said, "Could he have been Ross Larson?"

"I don't know. Maybe. But like I said, it's dark in there. Sorry, Jack, but it could've been anybody."

The car smelled of damp clothes, cinnamon-flavoured breath mints, cheap aftershave. Willows rolled down his window a few more inches.

Bobby said, "You're telling us you saw him?"

"Who?"

"Larson. Ross Larson."

Orwell said, "What I'm telling you, I didn't see him."

"Wait a minute, Eddy. Back up. You're told us the guy you saw could've been anybody, right?"

Orwell had to think about it. He said, "Yeah, right."

"If the guy you saw could've been anybody, obviously that includes Ross Larson. So what you're saying is, it might've been him."

Orwell said, "Or maybe he was in the kitchen with Shannon. How should I know?"

Bobby rolled his eyes. He shot his cuff and made a show of checking his solid-gold, diamond-studded Rolex.

Willows said, "Nice watch, Bobby. Must've cost you, what, about thirty grand?"

Bobby chuckled. "More like thirty bucks. It's a knockoff, Jack. Made in China. I bought it off a guy was selling them outside my hotel, when I was in Honolulu last Christmas. He had two whole armsful of 'em, every brand you can think of, and more."

Bobby gave his arm a shake. The cashmere slid down over his wrist. He said, "Where in hell is Claire?"

A woman came out of the white clapboard house. She was young, in her early twenties, and wore black jeans and a fake-leopardskin jacket. She shut the door and locked it, then crossed the porch to the top step, paused and looked up and down the block. Willows rotated the binoculars' focus knob. The woman swam sharply into focus, well-lit by a nearby streetlight. Her shoulder-length hair was thick, auburn, waffle-iron wavy. Her skin was very pale, her features delicate, feminine. Her mouth was a small, bright fire. She turned and looked directly at him.

Orwell said, "Looking for me, sweetheart? Here I am. Mr. Wrong, who's totally right for you." He leaned over the seat and reached for the horn. Willows batted his hand away.

The woman hurried down the steps and across the boulevard, unlocked the Saab and got in. Willows heard the door slam shut.

Bobby said, "You call in the plates?"

"Both cars are registered to Shannon Lucy Brown, of 2229 Napier," said Willows. The lie went down smooth as an oyster.

Orwell said, "That's gotta be Ross's girlfriend. Shannon Brown. Where's *she* going?"

"Maybe you ought to tag along behind," said Willows.

"She's all yours, Jack. No way me 'n' Eddy are wasting our talents on the dame." Bobby winked at Orwell. "Not on company time, anyway." He drew his semiauto from his Bianchi shoulder rig, ejected the slide into the palm of his hand. He pressed the ball of his thumb down hard on the topmost cartridge. Satisfied that the magazine was fully loaded, he slid it back into the pistol.

The Saab's engine caught. A dense cloud of black smoke exploded from the exhaust.

"Diesel," said Bobby. The gun lay in his lap.

Orwell said, "Nah, the engine's falling apart. What you deserve, you buy anything French."

"What're you talking about? Saabs are made in Sweden."

"France," said Orwell. "Nuclear tests. Man, the way those people behave, they're worse than the Iraqis."

The Saab started towards them. Willows ducked low, found himself nose to nose with Bobby. The Saab drove slowly past. They sat up.

To Orwell, Bobby said, "Worse than the Iraqis? What d'you know about French people?"

"What I read in the headlines," said Orwell. He leaned forward, rested a meaty hand on his partner's shoulder. "There's something else, Bobby."

"Yeah? What?"

Orwell was about to answer when the front door swung open again, and two men came out of the house. Bobby snatched up the binoculars. Willows turned the windshield wipers to max speed. Bobby said, "How d'you adjust the focus on these damn things? . . ." The men trotted down the steps and climbed into the orange Datsun. Bobby said, "Damn!" He tossed the binoculars down on the seat.

Willows took a look. Glare from the Datsun's windshield made it impossible to see inside the car.

Orwell said, "Why'd the woman lock up, if those guys were still inside the house?"

"Maybe she didn't want them getting out," said Bobby.

Orwell grunted softly, a small sound of disbelief. He said, "Good thinking, Bobby."

"Hey, I've known plenty of women like that, women who like their men to stay put, want to be able to go shopping or whatever, know that when she gets home the guy's gonna be right where he was when she left him."

"Out in the garden," said Willows. "Or buried under a slab of concrete in the basement."

Laughing, Orwell said, "I bet Bobby's known plenty of women *just* like that."

The Datsun pulled away from the curb, tires slithering on the wet asphalt as the driver made a tight U-turn. Willows glimpsed a bulky shape behind the wheel, a bright shock of improbably yellow hair.

Bobby said, "You going after them?"

The Datsun rounded the corner at the far end of the block. Give them five minutes, they'd have caught up with the Saab.

Willows said, "I told Parker I'd wait here until she showed up with a search warrant."

"Like hell!" Bobby holstered his pistol, pushed open his door and ran back towards the Econoline. Orwell hesitated, cursed, and went after him. Bobby hadn't bothered to shut his door. Willows left it open.

A patrol car hovered at the corner, caught in Willows' side mirror but out of sight of the house. The Econoline's engine roared into life and then the van raced past, Bobby at the wheel. Willows rolled down his window, stuck his arm into the falling rain. The patrol car surged forward, braked to a stop alongside Willows' car. Parker said something to the uniformed cop behind the wheel that made him smile happily. She got out of the patrol car, hurried around to the passenger's-side door of Willows' car and got in, shut the door behind her. The uniform put the patrol car in reverse, and gunned it.

Parker said, "Where'd Bobby go?"

"He has no idea," said Willows, as he rolled his window back up. "He's engaged in the pursuit of a suspect vehicle. The fact that he hasn't got a hope in hell of catching up doesn't really matter. Get the warrant?"

"No," said Parker, "I didn't."

"I don't think that matters either," said Willows. "Buckle up." He powered into a U-turn, hit the lights and siren.

"Where are we going, Jack?"

"Nowhere we haven't been before."

"Don't mess with me, Jack"

"Hoffman told us Ross Larson and Garret Mosby were best buddies at William Head. Mosby's dead. Ross had a standing invitation to come and stay with Shannon, Garret's ex-girlfriend. She left the house not ten minutes ago. I'd bet my pension that Ross and our suspect in the Mooney killing – the behemoth with the dyed-blond buzz-cut – left a few minutes later."

"You saw them?"

"Yeah. At least, I think I did. It was just a quick look, but one of them answered to Ross's general description, and the other guy was big, really big, with short blond hair."

A portly, middle-aged man wearing a black suit and reversed white collar clapped his hands to his ears as they rocketed past the church. *Hear no evil*, thought Parker.

She said, "Mooney was on duty the night of the armoured-car robbery on Broadway, wasn't he?"

Willows nodded, kept his eyes on the road.

Parker thought about it, but not for long. Garret's pal Ross gets out of prison, Mooney dies. Ross shows up at Garret's ex's house.

A mutual friend fits the description of the suspect in the Mooney murder. What tied the whole thing together was the two hundred thousand dollars that had never been recovered from the armoured-car robbery. This was all about cash – the second-best motive. If they'd killed Mooney and come up dry, where would they go next?

Willows said, "They're hunting for the money. They thought Mooney had it, and now they're headed for the Crown residence."

Parker nodded. The waterfront home on Point Grey Road. The house with the garage made of green-tinted glass where Billy, spurned by Nancy and chased down by Tyler, had come to grief in the backyard pool.

3682 Point Grey Road.

Willows killed the Ford's flashers and siren as they sped across the viaduct towards the city's glistening downtown core. He had no idea where the brown van had gone, no desire to suffer the pleasure of Bobby's company. The viaduct was elevated and highly visible. Bobby, realizing he'd lost the Datsun, might decide to circle back in the hope of picking him up. The far end of the viaduct was coming up fast. Willows eased off the gas. GM Place, the new home of the Canucks and Grizzlies, was on his left, the building's yellow tiles reminding him as always of a gigantic urinal. He activated the flashers and sirens again, bulled his way through a red light and hit the gas. The Ford fishtailed the length of the block. He slammed on the brakes. The car made a shuddering nosedive lefthand turn onto Cambie, the Goodyear *a cappella* quartet screaming at full volume, streaks of rubber smearing the pavement as they shot past Queen Elizabeth Theatre.

Willows made a right on Pacific. He drove west at high speed over the Burrard Street Bridge, kept to the right as they headed into the home stretch, a straight run down Point Grey Road.

He remembered the layout of the grounds and somewhat quirky design of that big house as clearly as if he'd been there only yesterday. And now he was only three or four minutes away, rushing backwards in time.

The light at the T-intersection of Point Grey Road and Arbutus Street was green, a cluster of pedestrians at the curb; Willows slowed, glanced left. There was a grocery store halfway up the block; it was the best place in town to buy fresh flowers.

He tried to remember the last time he'd given Parker flowers...

27

Kelly made a right on Burrard, a left on Second. They drove past the steamy windows of an upper-floor health club. Not far off, the green maple leaf of a Canadian Tire sign shone brightly. Kelly came to a full stop at a stop sign, signalled and made a right turn. They drove circumspectly past a red brick secondary school enclosed by a rusty wire-mesh fence. The light at Cornwall was green. Kelly made a left, swung past a Chinese restaurant and then a pizza joint, flashes of neon.

They were almost there. It was a straight run, just a few minutes' scenic drive, to the clifftop waterfront house at 3682 Point Grey Road. A silver Jaguar flashed its lights behind them, and squawked pitifully. Kelly was cruising along at the speed limit, and what could be worse? The Jag nosed into a gap in the traffic, shot past at speed and gained at least two car lengths on them, before its progress was blocked by another vehicle.

"Life in the fast lane," said Kelly.

Ross lit a cigarette, his third of the ride. He inhaled, sucked that sweet and wonderfully potent mix of chemicals deep into the twin pits of his lungs, held his breath for a slow count, and then let go.

They drove past a park that featured lots of mowed lawn but only a few trees. Beyond the stretch of grass Ross caught a glimpse of the city's biggest outdoor swimming pool. A curving cement wall and walkway separated the pool from the harbour. He saw that the tide was out. Wet sand glistened darkly. They cruised past a few apartment blocks and then a cluster of older houses, a mini-park with another view of the harbour. The road curved sharply to the right, past large, modern houses that offered few windows to the street but would be all glass on the side that faced the water. Kelly tapped the brakes, shifted down into second gear. The speed limit, posted on white signs attached high up on metal lampposts, was a staggeringly slow thirty kilometres – or eighteen miles – per hour.

He said, "Must be nice."

"What's that?" said Ross.

"Owning a house worth a couple of million bucks, having the kind of clout, you want a special speed limit on your block, all you got to do is pick up your phone with the direct line to City Hall, tell the mayor what you want."

Ross said, "Yeah, must be nice."

Traffic was piling up behind them. Horns blared. Kelly glanced down at the speedometer. The needle held steady at a shade under thirty k.p.h. He braked at a crosswalk for a woman wearing a yellow rain-slicker plastered with reflective tape. The woman was flanked by a brace of standard-bred poodles that had been dyed black and white, like dalmatians. She gave Kelly a terse nod as she passed by the Datsun's front bumper.

Kelly said, "You're a very sick person, but you're welcome." He waited until she'd reached the far curb, then hit the gas. "School zones, that's twenty kilometres. But everywhere else in the city, it's fifty. Fifty and people do sixty, minimum, more likely its closer to seventy. Eighty and faster on the main streets and bridges. But look at this. Thirty kilometres an hour. You didn't smoke, weren't caught in the clutches of that filthy habit, you could probably get out and jog alongside, not lose any ground."

"I bet I could do it anyway," said Ross.

"Yeah, really?" Kelly seemed to think about it. "You're telling me, if I pulled over, let you out, went back to driving at thirty clicks, that you could keep up with me?"

"If you started off slow, didn't accelerate too fast."

Kelly dropped a hand from the wheel to his lap. "How'd I know you wouldn't take off in the wrong direction? Make like a banana, and split."

"Why would I do something like that?"

"Because you're just slightly dumber than you look." Kelly reached out and grabbed Ross's thigh, squeezed hard.

"*Christ!*" Ross jerked free, banged his knee against the lightly padded underside of the dashboard.

"That hurt? Sorry."

The road had straightened. There was oncoming traffic but it was a block or more away. The lead car in their parade pulled sharply out and roared past, horn blaring. Another horn passed them, and then another. A blank white face shouted a curse.

Kelly's teeth glinted in the light from the dashboard. "Some people sure are brave, they get themselves tucked into a big steel box." He made a left turn, drove past a half-block-wide strip of grass and parked in black shadow cast by a towering evergreen, killed the engine and lights. He tossed the ignition key in the ashtray, told Ross to grab the plastic Zellers bag containing his fish knife and Maglite and duct-tape and other odds and ends. Ross noted that the guns weren't in there – the bag wasn't heavy enough. Kelly told him to get out of the car and not to lock the door.

Kelly unlocked the Datsun's trunk, reached inside. He shrugged into a puffy, dark blue nylon jacket that was almost the same colour as his pants. The jacket had a big silver badge appended to the breast, epaulettes with silver stars. His shiny-brimmed hat sported another outsized badge. He put on the hat and slammed the trunk shut, straightened his spine.

They walked the half-block to Point Grey Road. It was close enough to full dark for a gimme. As they crossed the puddly street, there was a faint buzzing sound. The neon address crackled hesitantly into life, a softly glowing worm of pink, slightly out of focus in the rain.

The cast-iron gate was unlocked. Kelly didn't seem surprised.

He pushed it open and they passed through. He swung the gate shut behind them, took Ross's arm in a gentle-but-firm grip and led him down a broad pathway of interlocking brick.

Ross noticed that there was room enough in the garage for two cars, but it held only one – an older-model Camry.

The house squatted there, oyster-grey plank siding, no windows that he could see. Indirect lighting illuminated several large clay pots containing small trees that stood on either side of the front door, which appeared to be made of a solid sheet of a reddish-gold metal. Bronze. Or maybe copper.

There was no doorbell or knocker.

Back there in the library, hunched over the microfiche machine, Ross had peered at harsh black-and-white newspaper photographs of this same yard. He rocked back and forth a degree or two off vertical as he vividly remembered the swimming pool, Billy's corpse floating face down in the placid water. Cold water slid down his throat, seeped into his lungs. He felt the weight of it, a black fluttering at the corners of his eyes, his body growing cold . . .

He shuddered. The image fragmented and dissolved. He said, "How're we supposed to get in?"

Kelly gave him a pixie grin. "Don't worry about it. Everything's been taken care of." He turned the knob and pushed. The door swung slowly open. He reached under his jacket and drew his pistols, tossed the semiauto to Ross, who caught it with both hands.

The house was lit up like a film set, every light blazing. The entrance hall was huge; six-metre ceiling, pale oak floor, gold wallpaper. Kelly motioned Ross forward. He walked down a thickly carpeted hall to the kitchen.

The refrigerator hummed softly. A wall clock marked off the seconds. On the granite counter stood most of a bottle of Dewar's, a white plastic ice-cube tray, an open pack of Lucky Strike cigarettes, and a heavy crystal ashtray with a lit cigarette balanced on the rim.

Ross helped himself to the cigarette. It was stronger than it looked. He coughed, and thumped his chest.

At the far end of the kitchen there was a wall of glass, sliding glass doors that opened on a low wooden deck, steps down to the backyard. His heels clicked on Mexican tiles as he walked over to the door, slid it open. He stepped outside. The air smelled of salt. The lights of a dozen freighters moored in the harbour glowed a rancid orange. Miles away on the far side of the water, West Vancouver sparkled dully in the mist. Off to his right, the city's west end was all lit up, boxy towers of light climbing ponderously towards the yellow underbelly of the sky.

The drowned body was long gone, naturally. But why was he surprised that the pool had been bulldozed, filled in, buried? The patio of interlocking bricks might have been an outsized headstone.

A gas barbecue huddled beneath a bulky black shroud.

Beyond the barbecue there was a kind of half-assed garden, spindly dead plants, pots of crumbling red clay, a straggly rose-bush and a handful of larger plants Ross couldn't have identified if his life depended on it. At the far end of the yard, a wall of clear glass or Plexiglas panels reflected the lights from the house. The waist-high panels allowed all but the terminally stupid to enjoy the view with little risk of plummeting fifty feet to the beach.

Kelly lifted a black-gloved finger, crooked it and summoned Ross back inside. Ross slid the door shut. Guns in hand, they toured the ground floor. Other than the entrance hall and kitchen, there was a den, family room, a guest bedroom with en-suite bathroom, two free-standing bathrooms and a cramped-but-functional laundry room.

Ross detoured back into the kitchen. He snuck a second Lucky and lit it from the stump of the first.

They made not the slightest sound as they climbed the carpeted stairs to the second level. Kelly told Ross to lead the way. He followed along behind, never quite close enough for a kick in the teeth.

At the front of the house there was an exercise room, a very large room filled with weights, various complicated machines, a stationary bicycle with only a few miles on the odometer. There was a big Sony television, a Toshiba VCR, plenty of mirrors. Kelly found the remote, turned on the television. "Cheers." The volume was turned high, but Kelly didn't seem at all concerned about the noise. Ross wondered what the hell was going on. Did Kelly know, somehow, that there wasn't anybody home?

Kelly switched on a treadmill, fine-tuned it until it was running at top speed. But still going nowhere, Ross couldn't help notice.

Next to the exercise room there was a sauna, and adjoining the sauna a bathroom with three identical pink marble sinks and a big jetted tub made out of something that looked like marble, but wasn't. Kelly hit the tub's rim with the barrel of his revolver. It gave off a hollow, unconvincing ring. Some kind of plastic.

Next to the bathroom was the sewing room. A machine sat on a polished mahogany table. There was an ironing board with a steam iron on it, lots of open shelves containing everything from scraps to entire bolts of cloth.

The last door on that floor led to a storage room containing a variety of sports equipment. Golf clubs, fishing rods and tackle, hockey pads and sticks, a rack of baseball bats. No firearms or edged weapons, though.

On the water side the house was stepped, to accommodate the sundeck on each level. The second floor was smaller than the ground floor and the third floor was the smallest of them all. As they climbed the thickly carpeted steps Ross guessed there'd be the master bedroom, a smaller bedroom, one or two bathrooms, and that'd be it.

The first door led to a bathroom. Kelly used the muzzle of his gun to push aside another. This door led to a cramped bedroom containing two single beds, a matching bureau. A glass vase of dusty, time-wilted paper flowers stood on the bureau. A magazine lay on the nearest bed. Cleavage. Big hair. Ross checked it out. *Cosmo*.

The only door remaining was the last untouched door in the house. Kelly said, "Your turn." He stepped aside, and waved Ross forward with his gun hand.

Ross put his hand on the knob. He turned and pushed.

The door swung open on the master bedroom.

The far wall was all glass, with a view of the harbour. Ross's eye was drawn to the king-size bed, a monster with an ornate metal frame, silver tubing with chunks of gold hanging off it. The bed was angled to the wall of glass. Shannon lay beneath the sheets, curled up in a defensive posture. A bruise the size of a fist ripened beneath her eye. She looked as if she were having a truly miserable time.

Kelly brought up his revolver. He sighted in on George Hoffman. "Don't make any false moves, George." He glanced at Shannon. "Or is it already too late?"

Shannon gave him the finger. Ross was the recipient of a bitter look.

Kelly said, "Learn anything?"

Shannon said, "Nothing I wanted to know."

Hoffman, speaking to Ross, said, "What the hell's going on?"

"Never mind him," said Kelly. Two quick strides took him to Hoffman's side. He pointed and pulled. A gout of flame spewed from the revolver's barrel. The blast was so loud it hurt. The concussion made the glass wall shimmer. Shannon screamed, clapped her hands to her ears and curled into a shapely ball.

Hoffman's afro had taken a direct hit.

The air reeked of scorched hair. Hoffman's lashes fluttered. His fingers twitched at the sheet that covered him.

The revolver's cylinder rotated through sixty degrees as Kelly pulled back the hammer. He said, "What'd you do it for?"

"She *seduced* me!"

"No, not that, stupid."

Hoffman had backed up against the metal headboard. The tight-curled hairs on his chest looked like peppercorns. He kept glancing nervously towards Ross, as if hoping for a signal, guidance.

Kelly said, "Have you got any idea what this is all about, George?"

"No, sir. I certainly don't."

"Don't lie to me, George."

Ross lit a cigarette, one of his own, a Player's Light. He glanced around, looking for an ashtray. Behind him and to his left, a partly open door led to an en-suite bathroom. He started towards the door.

"Hold it right there!" yelled Kelly.

Ross pinched the match and dropped it in his shirt pocket.

Kelly sat down on the edge of the bed. He crossed a leg and rested the weight of the revolver on his thigh. "George?"

"Yes, sir."

"Call me Kelly."

Hoffman nodded. His chest glistened with sweat. He lay still, contemplating the ceiling.

Kelly said, "You and Donald were pals, right?"

"Not really."

"Donald who?" said Ross.

"Are you calling him a liar?" said Kelly.

"Who?" said Ross.

"Donald E. Mooney," said Kelly. He brought up the pistol, blew another hole through Hoffman's afro. Shannon curled into a slightly smaller ball. The sheet clung to her hip. Ross told himself it was no time to stare. Kelly said, "You calling Don a liar, George?"

"He seemed like a nice enough guy to me."

Kelly drew back the revolver's hammer. "Okay, are you calling me a liar?"

The parole officer's chest heaved. Sweat bubbled on his face. "No way! Me and Don bowled a couple of times a month, that's all. An inter-league thing. The teams'd have a beer afterwards, shoot the shit, conversation going back and forth. But there was nothing special between us. We sure as hell weren't *friends*."

"Your hair stinks, George."

Hoffman gave Kelly a hard, back-to-the-wall look. "So would yours, if somebody shot it."

Kelly mulled it over for a moment or two. Finally he nodded. "Good point. Now make another one. Why would Don lie to me? Why would he tell me you and him were the very best of pals?"

"To save his ass? Or maybe because you were killing him too slowly, and he was desperate to get it over with."

Kelly's shoulders slumped. He said, "You disappoint me, George. I was hoping you'd come up with just about any reason but that one."

Hoffman rose up from the sheets, arms extended, like a bad actor rising from the dead. If Kelly's intention had been to fire another warning shot through Hoffman's afro, he should have aimed two inches higher. Hoffman grimaced as the bullet smacked into him, nipping a half-circle out of his right eyebrow. His cheeks ballooned. His sad eyes bulged. A handful of blood spattered the wall behind him. Chunks of bullet and chips of bone clanged off the metal bedframe. Hoffman fell soundlessly back, collapsed against the ruined, shot-up pillow. A few small feathers spiralled up into the smoky air.

Shannon raced for the bathroom, slammed the door. She'd run right past Ross, but he had no idea if she was stark naked or wearing a tuxedo and patent-leather shoes. Well, if she was wearing shoes she was right this minute throwing up all over them. He pressed the small button halfway up the grip of his pistol. The magazine fell to the carpet. Empty. What do you know. Imagine that.

Kelly said, "You think you're so darn smart."

It was going to sound terminally dumb, but Ross felt he had to say it anyway. "You didn't have to shoot him."

"Yeah, I did so. He was coming at me. Besides, that's partly why I invited him over. If he couldn't help me with the money, at least I could shoot him. Make an object lesson of him, so you'd know I was *serious.*"

"What about the grocer? You must think I'm a pretty slow learner, Kelly."

"The grocer was an accident. One of those spontaneous-combustion type things. I could've cancelled Hoffman, but it would've seemed like such a waste, because of all the time me 'n' Shannon spent setting him up."

Serious. Was that a synonym for stark raving mad? Ross didn't think so. If he made it out of here, managed to extricate himself from this situation, he'd have to look it up. He jerked a thumb at the bathroom. "Who is that, in there?"

"Shannon Lucy Brown."

"No, I mean, who *is* she?"

"A person who has a very strong ambition to take early retirement from Zellers." Kelly studied Ross closely as he said, "Also, she's my fiancée. Plus, she's gonna be my next victim, you don't tell me what happened to the two hundred grand." He smiled. "A triple threat, but you don't care what happens to her, do you? Okay, fine. Then *you* can be my next victim." He flipped open the revolver's cylinder, worked the extractor and ejected the three spent and three live rounds into the palm of his hand. He dug into his pocket for fresh cartridges, reloaded, snapped shut the cylinder. Indicating Hoffman, he said, "He sure is dead, isn't he?"

"I'm no doctor."

"Don't fucking quibble with me. Anybody can see that's one dead parole officer. You're in any doubt, go ahead and resuscitate him. Take a shot at it, Ross. Give him a great big kiss, let's see what happens."

Blood had dribbled out of the entrance wound and down into the corner of Hoffman's eye. Ross willed him to raise his hand and wipe the blood away. Hoffman wasn't having any of it.

Kelly went over to the bathroom door. "You okay, honey?" He flinched at the response, moved away from the door.

Ross said, "Where are the Crowns, Nancy and her husband? What's his name?"

"Tyler. Divorced. He's in Bermuda, taking a breather. She's living with her sister, somewhere in the interior. The house has been vacant three months. It's listed at one-point-eight million, but open to offers. Sharon Lewis has the listing. She's with Re/max. Or is it Sutton? A very persuasive young lady. But not too observant. I left the main-floor bathroom window unlocked. All she cared about was that I'd remembered to flush."

"One-point-eight's a little out of my range."

"How about two hundred and twenty thousand?"

Ross said, "I don't have the money. Is that what you think? You might as well shoot me now, and get it over with."

"Yeah, okay." Kelly lifted the revolver, fully extended his arm. He squinted down the barrel, shut his left eye and then thought better of it and opened the eye wide and shut his right eye. Perplexed, he wiped his brow with the back of his hand and squeezed both eyes shut. But only for a moment.

Shannon had stopped being sick. The two men stood there, listening to her cries of sorrow.

Kelly said, "I think she really liked him. Jealous?"

"Not yet. Give me a little time to let it sink in."

"Hand me that bag," said Kelly. "I got some stuff in there I'm gonna have to put to a use it was never designed for."

Ross offered the plastic Zellers bag. Kelly took it. He told Ross to strip to his shorts and lie belly-down on the carpet with his hands clasped behind his back. He fished around in the bag, pulled out a fat roll of duct-tape and bound Ross's hands and then his ankles, yanked off a foot of tape and sealed Ross's mouth. He began to bury him in tight coils of tape, starting with his feet and working his way slowly up his body. From time to time he rolled Ross over, this way and that. He grunted as he worked, the force of his concentration gleaming in his eyes. Ross raised his head, glanced down the length of his silver body. The tape couldn't have been any tighter. The coils were almost perfect, overlapping a half-inch or so, hardly any wrinkles.

Kelly caught him looking. He paused, straightened his back. "So I take pride in my work. So what. Is there something wrong with that?"

Ross said, "Mrrph!"

Kelly lost interest in him. He was busy, busy, busy. A demented spider, trussing up his prey.

28

Willows gave it a little more gas as the road steepened. They topped the rise just in time to see the car in front of them, a dark blue Pontiac Sunfire, rear-end a silver mini-van. Sheet metal crumpled. Sparks flew. Bits of orange plastic and a shower of safety glass sprayed the road. Willows hit the brake pedal with both feet. The Ford slewed sideways. He corrected, saw that he was going to hit the fool in front of him. He fought the steering wheel as the car drifted across the solid yellow onto the wrong side of the road. He was pleased to see there was no oncoming traffic. He managed to get the car under control. Parker was rigid in her seat, her eyes wide.

Half a block distant, a vehicle had ploughed into the blunt stern of a bus as the bus had started its turn off Point Grey Road on to MacDonald. Flares littered the roadway. The stricken vehicles were burning briskly despite the rain, thick coils of acrid black smoke spiralling into the sky. There had been several other minor accidents, as the traffic had backed up. Willows heard the growly foghorn whoop of a firetruck. He glanced in his rearview mirror. A hook-and-ladder was coming up fast, and he was blocking the road. The Ford's shocks bottomed out as he gunned it up over the curb and onto the sidewalk. He killed his siren. The firetruck blew past, and the Ford rocked in the slipstream.

More cars were piling up behind them, jamming the road. Willows heard another screech of brakes, the impact of another collision. He backed the Ford onto the road and drove slowly forward. The sidewalks were already filling up; the Ford's whirling fireball stained white faces red.

Willows had hoped to extricate himself from the jam by driving south on MacDonald, but as he approached the corner he saw that the traffic was already backed up the better part of a block. A trapped ambulance was trying to work its way free. A uniformed cop waved his flashlight. Willows had already slowed the Ford to a crawl. He braked and rolled down his window.

The cop was yelling at him over the blare of horns and sirens, but Willows couldn't hear a word he said. Parker had bailed out and was running hard towards the fiery heart of the accident. Willows unbuckled his seatbelt. He pushed open his door, forcing the startled cop to scramble aside.

There was a whoosh as a fireman levelled a chemical extinguisher on the flames. A cloud of white smoke billowed up around the base of the fire, but in a moment the blaze had reasserted itself. In the lurid orange glow of the flames Willows saw that the bus had been rear-ended by a nondescript brown Econoline van.

Eddy Orwell sat hunched on the curb beyond the fire. There was blood on his face. A paramedic crouched beside him, a latex-gloved hand on Orwell's arm. Willows reached them a stride behind Parker.

The paramedic glanced up. "You know this guy?"

Parker nodded. She knelt down beside Orwell. He'd suffered numerous cuts and scrapes, all of them apparently superficial. His nose was broken and he was bleeding steadily but unspectacularly. She said, "Eddy, are you okay?"

Orwell grunted. Fat drops of blood spattered on the pavement.

The paramedic said, "Hey, buddy, you okay?"

"Eddy?" said Willows, joining them.

This time, Orwell completely failed to respond. The paramedic spoke urgently into his radio. He caught Willows' eye. "There's cops back there trying to clear a lane through the traffic. A gurney should be here in a minute or two."

Orwell said, "Jack?"

"Right here, Eddy."

Orwell said, "Not me." He wiped his nose with the back of his hand, and groaned softly.

With unforced cheerfulness the paramedic said, "Yeah, it's you. But don't worry, you're gonna be just fine."

"Not *me*," said Orwell. He reached out, clutched Parker's sleeve. "Bobby," he said.

Parker glanced at the paramedic, who gave her a look roughly equivalent to twirling his finger around his ear.

Orwell said, "It wasn't me. It was Bobby."

"You're telling me Bobby was driving, is that it?"

"Not me," said Orwell patiently.

The paramedic told Willows that the van's driver had been removed from the vehicle and rushed to St. Paul's. Bobby had been unconscious, his injuries undetermined. A few minutes later, Orwell was eased into an ambulance. By then the fire was under control. Traffic was being rerouted, the jam efficiently cleared. But it was another five minutes before Willows was able to extricate the Ford. He drove south on MacDonald, made a right and drove past Tatlow Park, made another right on Balaclava and then a left on Point Grey Road. They were only a few blocks from the Crown residence, and closing fast.

A block from the house, he killed the siren and fireball. Parker spotted the orange Datsun on a side street. Willows radioed the dispatcher and requested backup. He drove up on the sidewalk in front of the house. A white Camry was parked in the garage. He eased his foot off the brake, let the Ford creep forward a few more feet, until the driveway was effectively blocked. He turned off the engine, unfastened his safety belt and slipped the keys in his pocket, swung open his door.

Parker reached out, clutched at his sleeve. She said, "Jack, let's wait for the backup, just this once."

"Next time," said Willows firmly.

Willows broke free, climbed out of the car. Parker watched him walk around the front of the car, open the gate and pass through. She lost sight of him, and felt a sudden moment of panic, pulse accelerating, her heart beating in her chest as if something had shaken loose. She unbuckled her seatbelt and pushed open her door. Willows was at the front door, then moving away, a dark shape gliding into the shadows. She hurried to catch up as he disappeared around the side of the house.

A security light snapped on, and Parker was blinded by the glare. She averted her face. Shadows jumped out at her as another light blossomed. Rain fell in streaks of white. There was a tall wooden fence on the left, decorative shrubbery. Parker drew her pistol. The backyard opened up in front of her. For a moment she thought they were at the wrong house, and then she realized that the pool had been filled in.

They climbed three low steps to the sundeck. The kitchen was brightly lit, empty. Willows tried the sliding glass door and was only mildly surprised to discover that it was unlocked. He slid the door open and he and Parker entered the house.

Upstairs, a woman was crying. Parker's heels clicked on the tile floor as she crossed the kitchen. She walked down a wide, thickly carpeted hallway, was momentarily dazzled by the foyer's bright lights, gold wallpaper. She unlocked the front door and opened it wide. Willows swiftly checked the main-floor rooms. He and Parker ascended the stairs to the second floor.

The crying had stopped, replaced by a low humming, a soft, insistent drone. They moved in tandem down a central hallway towards the front of the house. Willows drew his pistol. The sound was coming from behind a closed door. He put his hand on the knob. Parker moved to the side, her drawn weapon in a two-handed grip, held at shoulder height.

Willows eased the door open a crack. He glimpsed movement and hit the door with his shoulder.

"Police!"

Farrah Fawcett stared at him, her blue eyes icy cold, full of disdain. Cut to a Jeep Cherokee commercial. But the television was silent; the source of the low hum a treadmill's electric motor. Willows backed out of the room. He shut the door. Parker was already on the stairs, moving cautiously upwards, taking it one step at a time.

No matter how persuasively Kelly begged and pleaded, Shannon would not unlock the bathroom door.

He said, "C'mon babe, open up." Man, he was trying *so hard* to be nice. He rattled the knob. "I gotta go, Shannon. Let me in, willya? C'mon now, don't be a bitch!"

No response. Nothing. Not a word. He rested a foot on Ross's chest. It was going to be a close thing, with the duct-tape. He'd used all of two rolls and most of the third. He said, "You okay in there?"

Ross stared up at him. A six-inch length of tape sealed his mouth shut. The rest of him, except for his eyes, was wrapped up good and tight. He could hardly breathe.

Kelly rattled the door again. "Open that door right this minute, young lady!"

"Go away! Leave me alone!"

The door muffled her voice, but the tone was unmistakable. Venomous. Acidic. Kelly smiled. Shannon was seriously irked, likely to stay that way for hours. Once she got in one of her moods . . .

"I'm gonna kick it in, sweetheart!"

Kelly stepped back. He lifted his foot. Ross squeezed his eyes shut. He was so thoroughly trussed up there wasn't even room to flinch.

"I mean it, babycakes!" Kelly took a half-step backwards, got set and lashed out. Wood splintered. The door crashed against the toilet hard enough to dislodge a chunk of porcelain. Shannon sat on the edge of the tub, hugging herself. Her cheeks were puffy and her eyes were red. She stared at Ross just long enough to identify him, then looked away.

She said, "What're you going to do to him?"

"Whatever it takes."

"Did you have to shoot George?"

"Hoffman? It was self-defence, honeybunch. Him or me. I had no choice, and that's no lie." He tore a handful of toilet paper from the dispenser. "Blow your nose." He stepped out of the bathroom, got a grip on Ross's shoulders and stood him upright. He pogo-sticked him into the bathroom, grunted as he tilted him sideways and bulled him into the tub. He got him upright and let go. Ross fell rigid as a tree. His head hit the white tile surround. His bound feet slid slowly along the bottom of the tub until he was wedged at about a twenty-degree angle.

Shannon said, "If you think about it, he looks kind of like a really skinny Oscar."

"A what?" said Kelly, grunting as he worked Ross into position, rolled him over so he was on his back, his head directly below the shower pipe.

"You know, those prizes they give away for best actress and best movie . . ." Her face was suddenly white, pinched. "The *Oscars!*"

"Yeah, right. Feeling a little better now, baby?"

She glanced at Ross. Reluctantly said, "Maybe just a little bit."

Kelly went back into the bedroom for the clear, flexible plastic tubing and the rest of the duct-tape. What else did he need? His knife. Coming back into the bathroom, he said, "That's my girl." He used the sharp blade of the knife to poke a small hole in the middle of a foot-long piece of tape, inserted one end of a ten-foot length of tubing through the hole. He bent and ripped the tape from Ross's mouth. "Got anything you'd like to say, while you still got the chance?"

Ross's eyes watered. He clenched his teeth.

Kelly chipped away at an incisor with the knife. "Remember how I opened the door? Polite at first, and then not so polite?" The point of the blade skidded off a tooth. Ross cried out, as best he could. Kelly shouted, "*Where's my money!*" He shoved the end of the plastic hose into a nostril, pressed the tape down over Ross's nose. He bound the hose in place with tape until he was certain it was secure, that Ross couldn't breathe except through his mouth.

He put the tape and knife aside, reached up and unscrewed the shower head.

Ross was watching him. Tremors of fear made him twitch and jerk. Kelly said, "Would you hold that for me, babe?" He tossed Shannon the shower head. She snatched at it and missed. It clattered on the floor and rolled behind the toilet, and she began to cry.

Kelly thrust the other end of the plastic tube into the exposed end of the water pipe. He wound tape around the tube and pipe until he was satisfied that he'd made a watertight seal.

Ross was staring up at him, and Kelly didn't like it. He tore another strip from the roll and dangled it over Ross's eyes.

"See, what happens now, I turn on the water. It drips down the tube and into your nose, drives you crazy. But you can breathe through your mouth, so it's okay. Uncomfortable, but survivable.

"But, after a while, I tape your mouth shut. And you can't breathe, and the water keeps sliding down that hose, drop by drop.

"You're dying, Ross. Asphyxiating. Drowning. Bummer, huh?"

Ross had just noticed Kelly's earring. It was gold, in the shape of a pistol.

"But then I use my knife to cut a hole through the tape. I save your bacon, and you're grateful as hell. You tell me where the two hundred and twenty grand is and now it's *my* turn to be grateful. How grateful? Would I let you go? Sure. Why not?"

Kelly turned on the tap, adjusted the flow. A few drops of water slithered down the tube.

He was vaguely aware of Shannon moving behind him, as he followed the progress of the water down the tube. A part of his mind heard the tiny, church-bell ring of the knife as it touched the rim of the tub. The delicate echo of that bell was drowned in a raucous clamouring of much louder bells. Alarm bells. He twisted towards her, his arm coming up.

Shannon had a businesslike, no-nonsense, two-handed grip on

the knife. She lifted the blade up over her head like some kind of goddamn Aztec princess, as Kelly yanked the revolver from his waistband. He swung the barrel around, regretting the damage he was about to do, the thousands of dollars he'd spent on her orthodontist about to go right down the fucking drain . . .

The knife plunged into him, and tore his heart asunder.

He choked on her name. She fell back, drifted away from him. What had she done with his knife? The way she was looking at him, he might've been a million miles' distant. He'd pushed her too hard, asked too much of her. First Mooney, then the grocer. Hoffman. Sex and death. Fine. But not so close together, maybe. Give her time to adjust . . . Or was it that she had a thing for the ex-con . . . *Where was his damn knife?*

Uh-oh.

He staggered out of the bathroom. A tall guy in a dark suit and a very attractive woman with the blackest hair he'd ever seen were shouting at him, pointing guns at him.

Yelling, mouths open.

Kelly could feel the blood rising up in him, a hot tide that kept rising and rising. He felt the blood flooding his lungs, creeping into his throat. His world turned a bright, pulsating red, the way it did sometimes when everything got all fucked up and he had no idea why.

But then – and this had never happened before, so it took him completely by surprise – his world turned black.

29

By the time the cops finally stripped the last of the tape away, Ross was primed to go home to mother and sleep for a week. But, unfortunately, the night had just begun. Downtown, in a room filled with audio and video equipment, the detective with the flinty look in his eye – Jack – asked him if he wanted a lawyer.

Ross said, "What for? I didn't do anything."

The nice-looking woman, a stunner, really, said, "Why don't you start at the beginning, Ross?"

"Yeah, okay. Don't get me wrong, I'm not trying to be a smart-ass, but how far back d'you want me to go?"

"How did you and Kelly get tangled up?"

Ross told them the whole story, from start to finish. How he and Garret had met, back there at William Head. That first time he'd ventured into the yard, and there was Garret, another white boy, of similar age. Looking tough but not homicidal. At first glance, a person he thought he could get along with, especially since he sensed he wouldn't last a week unless he had someone to watch his back.

He explained the history of his involvement with Shannon Brown. How he and Garret had paced the yard in all weather, Garret telling him over and over what a beautiful, passionate and wise woman she was. How he'd come to know her so well, in a weird kind of way, thanks to Garret. He told them about writing a letter of sympathy to Shannon following Garret's untimely death by natural causes. How they had become pen pals.

He tried to explain how he had become obsessed with her, couldn't wait to meet her when he finally got out. He readily admitted he was in violation of his parole, should have stayed at home with his mother instead of moving in with Shannon. But hey, it wasn't like he knew how it was going to turn out in the end. Right?

He couldn't help smiling as he told them all about Kelly's wild ideas regarding the missing loot from the armoured-car heist. That Hoffman and a cop friend of his who was on duty the night of the robbery had the dough. He explained that Hoffman and the cop were buddies, apparently. They bowled in the same league . . . No, he didn't know the cop's name.

He told Willows and Parker that Kelly originally believed that Garret might have somehow made off with the missing loot. How he'd manage to do that was a mystery, since he'd been arrested at the crime scene. But, for years, Garret worked hard at convincing Shannon that he knew what he was talking about. Some of his chatter must have rubbed off on her, and Kelly. So that finally, when he'd run out of alternate possibilities, the crazy bastard decided Ross must know where the cash was stashed.

No, Ross said, straight-faced, Kelly had never even mentioned the name Donald E. Mooney, or any variation thereof.

Yes, Kelly had shot George Hoffman. Shot him as he lay there on the bed. Shot him without warning, and showed no remorse.

No, neither he nor Shannon had any idea that Kelly was going to pull the trigger until he'd actually done it. In fact, Ross doubted if *Kelly* had any idea what he was going to do until at least several minutes after the fact. And Ross had the impression that even then, Kelly was often unaware as to *why* he'd acted in a particular way. In Ross's opinion, Kelly was no deep thinker. More of an action-figure type of guy.

No, he didn't know anything about a grocery-store robbery, or a shooting on Cambie Street, just below King Edward Avenue. But, come to think of it, Kelly had come home last night carrying a bunch of flowers and a pocketful of candy bars ... The guns? Both the pistol and the revolver belonged to Kelly.

Ross was amazed they'd even ask him if he owned a gun. He was an ex-con, he'd done time for a violent crime and he was on parole. Of course he didn't own a gun. What did they think, that he was *nuts*?

All of this came slowly, word by word, over a period of many hours. Ross established the pace right from the start, considering each question the cops put to him from every angle he could think of. When they tried to rush him, he apologized for taking up so much of their valuable time, and slowed down even more. He took his time partly to retain at least partial control of the situation, but also because he sincerely did not want to miss any of the important details. Much of his story they already knew, if they'd bothered to talk to Hoffman. And there were a few things Shannon could tell them, if she was in the mood. All he could do about that was cross his fingers and hope for the best.

Another cop came in, a white-haired old guy with a limp, carrying a tray. He'd brought coffee for the men, tea for Parker, donuts for all. He put the tray down on the table and left the room. Ross never saw him again.

He and the cops sat there, taking a coffee break, acting as if they were the best of friends. He was hungry. No, a better word, famished. The donuts smelled delicious. There were two cinnamon and one jelly.

He waited patiently for the cops to choose. When they saw what he was up to, they told him all they wanted was coffee. Neither of them ate donuts, if you could believe it.

Ross ate all three, the cinnamon first, the jelly for dessert.

He asked them how Shannon was doing and the woman, Claire, said she was doing just fine.

Willows asked him if he thought that he and Shannon would be staying together, when this was over.

Ross said no. He sensed that the cop was trying to lull him into a false sense of security, asking him what he'd do when he was free to do anything. As if that time was only a moment or two away. But the truth was that he didn't want anything to do with Shannon. She was not the girl for him, at least not unless he had to go back to prison, do some more time. If that was the case, it turned out the only way she could touch him was with a letter, well, that would be just about perfect.

Claire asked him point-blank, staring him right in the eye, so close he could hardly focus on her, if he knew what had happened to the missing two hundred and twenty thousand dollars.

Ross said no. He wet his finger and cleaned up the sugar and cinnamon the donuts had shed onto the paper plate. Parker was still eyeing him, making up her mind. He told her no again. Not forcing it, because that would be asking for trouble and trouble was the last thing he wanted.

He asked Willows if they were going to violate him, and Willows told him he believed Hoffman had already set the wheels in motion. Ultimately, the decision as to whether Ross's parole would be revoked would be made by his new parole officer.

Ross pointed out that he was co-operating fully, to the very best of his ability, and that he certainly hoped that was taken into consideration.

Excuse me, what was he doing *where*? At the Crown house? Kelly had told him George Hoffman wanted to meet him there, that Hoffman had phoned and left an urgent message. Yeah, you bet he'd thought it was kind of an odd request. Or order, or however you wanted to put it. No, it hadn't occurred to him that Kelly was lying. Hoffman's Camry was parked there in the garage, so naturally he'd assumed everything was okay.

Parker asked him if he believed Kelly was going to kill him. Ross said he knew in his heart he was going to die.

When Shannon's time came to make the simple choice of spilling the beans or being charged with at least one and maybe two counts of first-degree murder, not to mention kidnapping and unlawful confinement and various and sundry other charges, she thought it over for the blink of an eye. She was innocent. Of course she'd co-operate. What did they want to know?

Everything.

Yes, she had seduced Hoffman. Effortlessly talked him into meeting her at the Crown house, after Kelly had determined that the house was vacant, the owners scattered to the four strong winds. It was Kelly's idea. What did he have in mind? She had no idea. She hadn't asked. Kelly was a mean sonofabitch. He terrified her. Was always watching her, spying on her. Ask Ross. Kelly hit her, sometimes. Look at the eye he'd given her.

Is that why she'd stabbed him, because she was afraid he was going to hurt her again?

Shannon wasn't too sure what had motivated her. She was pretty sure she'd stabbed Kelly to save Ross. Kelly had told Ross he was going to kill him, if Ross didn't give up the money. She knew he'd meant it, because she'd seen him shoot Hoffman, and he'd admitted he'd shot the grocer, and she believed he had murdered that policeman, Donald Mooney . . .

Back up a minute. What money?

From the armoured-car robbery. They listened patiently while she told them about the armoured-car robbery, everything she knew.

Wait a minute. Kelly wouldn't hurt Ross if he told Kelly where the money was. If he believed he was going to die . . .

But Ross doesn't know where the money is.

How can you be so sure?

Shannon said that Kelly had turned on the water, and it was running down that pipe, into Ross's nose. Ross was *drowning*. He was helpless as a kitten. He knew he was going to die and that there wasn't anything he could do about it. Not a damn thing. He'd given up. She said she could see in his eyes that he had no idea where the money was, and that the look of helplessness in his eyes just drove her crazy. George was alive one moment and dead the next, it was all over before she knew what had happened. But

Kelly was planning to kill Ross slowly, drop by drop. She had to do something, to try to save him. The knife was in her hands. Kelly turned and looked at her. He drew his revolver and she knew he was going to shoot her.

How did she know he was going to shoot her?

By the look in *his* eyes. And because he'd just shot George Hoffman, hadn't he? Shot him dead and not cared in the least.

Had Ross mentioned the grocery-store robbery, or recent shooting?

No. Absolutely not.

Did she think he might be involved?

No. Absolutely not . . .

The interview continued. A Möbius strip of questions and answers, until Shannon was too tired to think straight. But by then, the interrogators were equally exhausted, incapable of summoning up a decisive verbal assault. Fresh troops were brought in. Shannon revived. She told her story all over again, from first page to last. There were inconsistencies but they were minimal, and unimportant.

Shannon had turned *chanteuse* at the drop of a fedora. But though she desired to please, she lacked talent. She'd sung like a crow.

Bradley swivelled his chair towards the window. It was dark as dark can be. Late was long, long ago. He was beyond exhausted. His arthritic knee ached. He stifled a yawn.

Willows said, "There's no doubt Kelly James McConnell killed Mooney. The duct-tape, rubber tubing, security-officer's uniform . . . We've got all the physical evidence in the world. And I'd bet every dollar in my wallet that we'll get a match on the two guns that were used in the Cambie Street grocery-store murder, so we'll pin that one on him too. *Plus* Hoffman."

"I met George a couple of times," said Bradley. "In court. He was a nice enough guy, but he had a reputation as a womanizer."

Willows nodded. He'd heard the same thing about George – that he had a fatal weakness for the weaker sex.

Bradley opened his Haida-carved cedar cigar box. He selected a *Tueros* cigar, held it to his nose and sniffed appreciatively.

Willows said, "We've got nothing on Ross Larson. No witnesses to the grocery-store robbery, nothing to tie him to the Mooney killing except the gloves. But Jerry, the busboy at Brillo's, did a pretty good job of describing Kelly James McConnell, when we asked him who paid him to punch out Ross."

Parker said, "The fact that McConnell was in the process of bumping off Larson could also be seen as a point in Larson's favour, depending on how you look at it."

"I suppose." Bradley rolled the cigar in his fingers. He was salivating. Over a cigar. He was getting old. But what a sweet scent! "What about the woman?"

"Shannon Brown."

"Yeah, Shannon." Bradley yawned hugely, apologized.

Willows said, "We believe Shannon was involved in Kelly's search for the missing two hundred and twenty thousand, Inspector. What we don't know and have no way of knowing is the degree of her involvement. Did she set Hoffman up, knowing or even suspecting that he might be injured, or killed? I just don't know. We'd never prove it, without a confession."

"She likely to confess?"

"On her deathbed, maybe."

Bradley yawned again. His jaw creaked. He said, "It'd be awful nice to lock *somebody* up."

"We can nail her for break-and-enter," said Parker. "Or we could give her a medal for saving Ross's life."

"Is that what she did – saved his life?"

"She thought she'd saved his life. She intended to save his life. She had no way of knowing we were in the house."

"She got a sheet?"

"No, she's clean."

Bradley said, "You finished with her?"

"We aren't finished with either of them," said Willows. "Hoffman might've fooled around a little, but he didn't deserve a bullet in the brain."

"Sounds good, Jack. When you and Claire are ready, let's run through the evidence together, see what we've got."

Willows nodded. But he had a gut feeling the case was going absolutely nowhere, that no matter what crimes they had or hadn't committed, Ross Larson and Shannon Lucy Brown were eventually going to walk.

Parker said, "How's Eddy?"

Bradley revived a little. "He's fine. A mild concussion, broken nose, sprained wrist." He waited for Parker to ask him about Bobby Dundas, and then realized that she wasn't interested. He glanced at Willows. He'd seen that look on Jack's face before. He was interested, all right. In a cold beer.

The streetlights were still on, but the sky had brightened to the east, and in another half-hour or so the sun would be up.

Willows parked in front of the house. There was somebody on his porch. He tensed. The sixty-year-old paperboy trotted down the steps towards him, cut across the lawn towards the neighbour's house. Willows unbuckled Parker's seatbelt, got out of the car, and went around to her side and opened her door. Her head came up. She opened her eyes and peered at him, a little disoriented. She smiled.

It was too early for Annie to be awake. She'd left a message taped to the front door. Sheila was in Mexico, staying at Alvarado, a small town on the gulf. She was perfectly all right, and she was having a wonderful time. Parker went upstairs, to take a quick shower. Willows went into the kitchen. He turned on the cold-water tap, rinsed his face and dried himself with a paper towel, then got the bottle of Cutty down out of the cupboard and poured himself a small one. He read Annie's note again, thought vague thoughts about Sheila and what it must be like in Mexico, then crumpled the note into a ball and tossed it in the garbage.

Somewhere in the backyard, a Steller's jay squawked unmusically. Now Tripod and Barney, who'd been sleeping on Sean's empty bed, wanted out. He stood in the open doorway and watched as the two cats engaged in a short-lived hot pursuit of the jay. He shut the door, splashed a quarter-inch more Scotch into his glass, and started upstairs, fumbling with his shirt buttons as he went.

Parker was in bed, snuggled under the duvet and showing only the tip of her nose. He softly called her name, but she had already fallen asleep.

He got his terrycloth robe from the closet, taking care not to let the hangers rattle.

A few minutes later, as he stood in the tub with the hot water beating down on his shoulders, he suddenly realized that he had all but forgotten about the Richard Beinhart case. Who'd stabbed Beinhart? Not his pals, Willows was certain of that. His primary suspect had to be the owner of the house, the dentist, Chris Bowers. Why had Bowers left on an unscheduled holiday the day after the murder, if not to avoid being questioned?

It was easy enough to see how it might have gone down. Richie, given the responsibility of collecting and paying the rent, had fallen prey to temptation and squirrelled away the cash for his own benefit. Bowers had come to the house, let himself in. Everybody had been drinking, all five tenants were drunk. They were always drunk. Possibly, by the time Bowers arrived, they'd drunk themselves insensible. The dentist had shaken Richie awake. Been a little rough with him, maybe. There'd been an argument. Richie, angry or terrified, had snatched at one of the knives on the table. Bowers had grabbed the other knife . . .

Well, maybe. Or maybe not.

One thing for sure, the prospect of a murderous dentist was kind of appealing. It was certainly worth looking into.

Willows sluiced away the last of the soap, turned off the shower. He stepped out of the tub and took a towel from the rack. The more he thought about it, the more he liked the dentist.

He towelled himself dry and put on his bathrobe, went downstairs for one last drink, and a quick peek at the Atlas.

Now then. Where in Mexico, exactly, was the small town of Alvarado?

30

The cops left it up to Crown Counsel – the prosecutor's office. It was a no-brainer, a non-starter.

Ross walked.

Shannon walked too, but in a different direction, which was just fine with him. He lit a cigarette, and watched the traffic roll by, as he waited for a bus to take him home.

His mother was working the afternoon shift, and he'd lost his key to the house, so he sat on the front step under the shelter of the porch roof, looking out at the rain, and smoking. After a little while, half an hour or so, Kiddo joined him. Jumped up on his lap and snuggled in. It was a cosy situation. Ross stroked the cat behind its fuzzy ears. Kiddo made a sound like a six-cylinder diesel engine.

Ross considered the situation. This crossroads at which he found himself, at the end of a high-speed journey that had led him in a more-or-less flawless circle.

Kelly was dead, so that took care of him.

George Hoffman had left a wife and children behind, but the woman was young and attractive, in line to benefit greatly from her husband's generous government-subsidized life-insurance policy. Plus, Hoffman had voluntarily stuck his iron in the fire. He was a full-grown man and should have known better. If the payment he'd made was considerably out of proportion to the offences he'd committed, well, that certainly wasn't Ross's fault.

Ross had given Shannon an awful lot of thought, when the cops weren't spitting in his face. Grilling him. The fact that she'd put a knife in Kelly complicated the issue. But Ross was confident she'd stabbed Kelly for reasons that had nothing to do with him. Besides, she hadn't saved his bacon, since the cops had arrived a few seconds later anyway. No, he'd searched his soul, and the way he saw it, his debt to Shannon amounted to a big fat zero.

Anyway, there was nothing he could do for the Hoffman family or Shannon or anybody else, even if he wanted to. He had his own life to worry about, and it was time he started living it.

Had Shannon's love for Garret been a sun-moon-and-stars kind of thing? Maybe, in the days and nights that followed their first meeting, in the nightclub. But Ross believed that after Garret was incarcerated, Shannon's love had faltered. His impression was that she had become a specialist in long-distance romance, but was a complete flop at hand-to-hand combat.

Had she grieved out loud for Garret's soul? Not that he could remember. Though she'd danced him through a few of the steps she and Garret had taken, she hadn't exactly been inconsolable.

He'd hoped that Shannon had the missing two hundred and twenty grand; that she had been holding it for Garret. He'd hoped she was afraid to tell Kelly about it because he'd take it away from her, hoped she wouldn't dare spend it on herself for fear of retribution from Garret.

Ross chuckled at his stupidity. Cigarette smoke leaked from the gaps between his teeth. He'd hoped that Shannon had fallen for him after Garret had died, that she was the kind of woman who needed somebody, that the letters they'd written to each other had meant something to her. Fat chance. He'd dreamt of great wealth, but the financial highlight of his adventure was pinching fifty dollars from his mother's sugar bowl.

He'd hoped for far too much.

He lit another cigarette. Kiddo stirred lazily in his sleep.

He was facing eighteen months of getting to know his new parole officer. Eighteen months of washing dishes, or cars, or slinging hamburgers. Assuming he kept his nose clean, he'd be a free man one year from next September. But free to do what? *Anything.* Somehow, the concept of limitless choice wasn't as scary as it had been, only a few days ago. He sat there on the porch, Kiddo in his lap, smoking and looking out at the rain, feeling content with the world for the first time in years.

The cops, during the course of their interrogation, had repeatedly asked him to describe his relationship with Garret. It was the armoured-car loot they were chasing. He'd told them again about how he and Garret had first met, out in the prison yard. As he'd repeated his story, time after time, something had kept nagging at him; a half-formed thought had tugged his brain but never pulled free.

But now, at last, it all came racing back. A high-speed rush of memory that took the corner on two wheels and went straight at him, the collision head-on and inevitable.

The first time he'd met Garret. Two white boys of similar age sharing a light out in the yard. The wind carrying the smoke away. Garret sizing him up, grinning crookedly as he told his stupid little joke.

"How many thieves does it take to screw in a lightbulb?"

Ross thought it over. Shrugged.

"What lightbulb?" said Garret from beyond the grave.

Ross sat there on the porch, the cat snuggled into his lap, sound asleep, trusting. He looked out at the rain, listened to the musical sound of it impacting on the skin of the world. Would it ever stop raining?

Much more important, how was he going to come up with the fifty bucks he owed his mother?

Now available in mass-market paperback

HEARTBREAKER

"This is the eighth and best book in the excellent series featuring the Vancouver police team of Claire Parker and Jack Willows. As always, Gough turns in a stellar collection of characters." – *Globe and Mail*

"Mordantly funny ... moves at top speed." – *Sunday Oregonian*

Shelley has it made. He's tall, dark, and handsome, has a great body, and believes, without having thought about it much, that "skin deep is plenty deep enough." Shelley's arranged his life in a way that affords him maximum comfort for minimum effort. He moves from one upscale house-sitting job to another, supporting himself with petty theft and the occasional job as a nightclub bouncer, part-time work that leaves him with lots of free time to work on his tan, develop his pecs, and polish his luxurious leased car.

But a day on the beach turns sour when Shelley makes two crucial mistakes: he breaks into a car belonging to off-duty police detectives Willows and Parker, and he picks up a gorgeous beach-bunny named Bo. Shelley is astonished at how quickly Bo worms her way into the most intimate details of his life – and equally surprised to discover that he's falling in love with her, and falling hard. Bo seems fond of Shelley, too. But Bo's former "business associates" want her back, and are eager and willing to do anything it takes to get her.

Meanwhile Willows and Parker are investigating the murder of a sleazy real-estate agent at a luxury penthouse condo, and, as the events in this fast-paced mystery bring everyone together, the results are – literally – explosive.

M&S Mystery   0-7710-3447-4 $7.99

Other Laurence Gough mysteries available in mass market:
Fall Down Easy   0-7710-3443-1 $6.99
Killers   0-7710-3441-5 $7.99